man or
mouse

man or mouse

MATT WHYMAN

FLAME

Hodder & Stoughton

Grateful acknowledgment is made for permission
to reprint excerpts from the following copyrighted works:

Translation © Christopher Fry 1975, 1996. Reprinted from
Edmond Rostand: **Cyrano de Bergerac** translated by Christopher Fry
(World's Classics 1996) by permission of Oxford University Press.

SOME LIKE IT HOT © 1959 United Artists Corporation All Rights Reserved.

First published in Great Britain in 2000 by Hodder and Stoughton
A division of Hodder Headline

1 3 5 7 9 10 8 6 4 2

A CIP catalogue record for this title is available
from the British Library

ISBN 0 340 76902 5

Typeset by Palimpsest Book Production Limited,
Polmont, Stirlingshire
Printed and bound in Great Britain by
Mackays of Chatham PLC, Chatham, Kent

Hodder and Stoughton
A division of Hodder Headline
338 Euston Road
London NW1 3BH

For Emma, as ever.

behind the screens

Hard Drive: Philippa Pride, David Godwin, Emma Whyman
System Support: the 'Hod Squad', Penny Jones, David Kirkup, Simon Buglione
Start Up: Mike & Rosemary Whyman, Bob Giddings, Rose Tremain
Technical Help: www.thesite.org, Greig@Russo, Peter Cowley
Interface Panel: Kirsty McLachlan, Phil Griffiths, Brian Chapman
'Software' Expertise: Lynsey Conway & Dr Wallace Dinsmore
Crash Recovery: Suzanne Cleminshaw, G & B {{xxx}}
Sound Card: Orbital, Count Basie
Laptop loan: JJ Wilson

My story, the prompter everyone forgets!
The voice in the shadow, another claims the kiss.

Cyrano de Bergerac, Edmond Rostand (1897)

Persuading a friend to ask someone out on your behalf can
cause untold grief and confusion. The bottom line is you
can never be sure how she'll handle it.

'Ask Anita', B magazine (1998)

an apology

Being an online babe has its hazards. A dark side, even. Cruise the Internet in search of some action, you'll tap into it for sure. The chat rooms might appear to be the perfect platform for meeting potential partners, but a girl has got to be careful. Believe me, you could be talking to *anyone*. It's far too easy to be seduced by a sultry screen name, or charmed by the right choice of words, and there's only so much you can give before you're committed to risking it all.

People forget themselves, of course. Let loose in a medium where nobody knows you're true identity, it's only natural that you go places you probably shouldn't. Take me. I lost myself in a virtual middle ground where bisexual women could click with each other before coming together in the real world. It was there I connected with one in a way I never thought possible. Hooking her via my keyboard was one thing. Reeling her in was another. Check out my tackle, and you'll appreciate why. It's a simple truth, but also kind of embarrassing.

I'm a bloke, all right?

An impostor called Reynard, Rennie, or sometimes just Ren. A nice guy at heart, whatever you choose to call me, but an apology of a man.

Don't stop now, or dismiss me as a dick. All I did was follow my heart. Male or female, haven't we all been there? Done something dumb because at the time there seemed no other way? Okay, so I went a bit further than most. I even got good as a girl. But much as I tried it just didn't come naturally. There are things in my genes that won't be suppressed. Stuff like size. What can I say? I'm a boy. It *matters*. Why not step into my space and see for yourself. A top floor converted workhouse in Hoxton Square, East London. Plush pad, but no parents. The pay-off for becoming an orphan many years earlier. Fresh from drama college, it meant I could at least afford a place to pretend I had made it. My folks, they always warned it would be a struggle. Consider accountancy, they said. Architects are never out of work. There'll always be antiques. Anything but acting. I asked them to name me an accountant. They never did get back to me, and looking back I'm almost relieved. For they were right. The breaks have been hard to come by and the right exposure critical to a career. Thanks to my online performance, in fact, I find myself much overlooked in one realm but a soaring star in the other.

I wish I could swing it both ways, but right now that's about the story of my love life.

the explanation

1

I first tapped into the joy of cybersex one month after Christine asked me to close down our relationship. Four weeks after the hottest fox I'd ever dated finally stopped twitching in my presence and said, 'I've not been myself for some time.'

There she stood, with her back to my computer and her eyes dipped from mine. I still remember how she glanced at me then. Her lashes lifting like the wings of a resting butterfly. Any other time, I would have regarded her look as a bedroom summons. On this occasion, I feared that particular invite had just been withdrawn. For ever.

'It's alright,' I assured her. 'I can see what you're trying to say.'

A pause unfurled between us. Under pressure or stress, words never did come easy to Christine. As always, it was her body language that spoke volumes. She hugged herself now. Unaware of how tight she had just pulled her jumper. I would miss our conversations.

'Say something,' she said. 'Anything.'

'OK, well, it looks like rain.' Which wasn't strictly true. But under the circumstances it should have been. Christine didn't even try to smile. If anything, she just looked more uncomfortable. I figured I would have to get real. Soberly, I said, 'Would it help if I put the words in your mouth?'

'I'm sorry, Ren, I just don't know how to tell you—'

'That you want to finish with me.' She looked at her shoes. I was right. 'So do you want to tell me why?'

'I'm not sure I can.'

'You want *me* to tell me why?'

'Would you?' She seemed suddenly relieved. I had only said it to jolt a reason from her. What did I know? Evidently, I would have to give it a shot.

'Is it my work?' She shook her head. It wasn't that. 'My *lack* of work? I know it's been a long time, but I'm between auditions. Honestly, one day soon I'm going to land the role of a lifetime. I know it. Have faith. I'll be someone soon.'

She bit her bottom lip, her eyes searching mine. 'It's not that. Can you try again?'

'Christine, I've no idea. This is a complete surprise and I'm not going to hazard any more guesses. I've just dumped myself, for crying out loud. Kick me when I'm down if you must, but please don't ask me to put the boot in on your behalf.'

'I'm so sorry.'

'For what? Just say. Put me in the picture.'

'The truth?' She braced herself for a beat, then breathed out again. 'The truth is I just don't know. It doesn't feel right. That's all. I don't feel right. About me. About us.'

'That's it?'

'It's over.'

I turned to the window, drawn by the sound of a motor pulling up on the street below, then sensed her presence right beside me. Christine. My soon-to-be-ex-girlfriend, swan-like and serene. Just as she had appeared to me for the first time eighteen months earlier. Floating up beside me at the theatre bar to ask if I had change for the phone. Back then her taxi home had failed to materialise, and she needed the coins to call up another. I told her I would gladly help. Providing she was happy to help break my only note by joining me for a drink. We shared a common bond, having both been blown out that night. One hour earlier, in the auditorium behind us, the curtain had fallen on *Cyrano Sings*. A musical adaptation of the Rostand classic. The show had been a sell-out hit, turning the cast into stars overnight. Which was why Christine had found me. The understudy. Staring into a shot glass, my prosthetic nose sprung back up on my forehead. Having watched my colleagues move on to a bigger party, it was she who persuaded me to persevere with my passions. An outlook on life I carried right up to the moment she finished with me.

'I guess some sex is out of the question,' I murmured, then realised she was closer than I thought.

'You didn't really mean that, did you?'

I thought about this for a second. Recalled how it had worked the first time, when finally we abandoned the theatre bar for a nightcap back at mine.

'That would kind of depend on your answer,' I replied eventually.

Christine tried to hold back a smile, and kissed me lightly on the cheek. Even a farewell fondle would have been fine by me, faced as I was with a famine, but by then she had broken away.

'I've been wanting to say something for weeks,' she said. 'But I was scared you might react badly. Do something desperate.'

I wondered what she meant, at first. Struggled to picture myself hugging her ankle as she attempted to leave my space. Then promptly picked up my thoughts from the floor.

'You thought I might top myself?'

'God, no! I just didn't think you'd handle it so well.' Christine hesitated here, though I wished she had just stopped completely. 'I was worried you might cry, actually.'

'Oh.' This time I couldn't meet her eyes.

'Thank you,' she said. 'I never thought you'd take it like such a man.'

Being a man means taking it on the chin, right? Whatever punches life throws, you can't be seen to hit the ring. You got to stay on your feet. Dancing and weaving. Blocking and jabbing. Being a man about things. Which I did. For at least five minutes after she left me. I was a man when Christine closed the door on my space. I was a man as she appeared downstairs in the square and slipped into the waiting cab. And what a man I was when she turned in the seat and watched me from the rear window. Me responding with a jaunty tip of the head and a brave smile, just like her own. A signal that I would be fine. No problem. That I'd be back on form before her taxi had even delivered her home. Fighting fit for the next bout. Prepared for all comers. Not locked away in my spiritual dressing room for the next four weeks. Staring punch drunk into nothing. My pep talks coming from the pizza delivery boy and whoever I had crooning through my speakers. Willing myself to forget about her. Taking it as only I knew how.

'You took it like a girl,' observed Sweet William, my florist and dealer. 'I can't believe I'm even *hearing* this from a guy.'

It was the first time I had seen him since the split. My reason for steering clear kind of spoke for itself. Willie was a bitch, but I loved him nonetheless. Just like everyone around here who relied on him for a smoke. I hadn't actually planned on telling him about Christine, but my dealer knew more about me than I did. A knack he had with his customers. Always pulling the right bunch out of the racks.

'It wasn't like that,' I told him, warming my hands on my take-out cup of latte. 'Not really.'

'Why didn't you beg her to stay? Plead for a second chance?'

'Willie, I have my pride.'

'But no girlfriend,' he added. 'I know which one would help me sleep easier.'

We broke for a customer. Sweet William in his puffa jacket, rolling up a dozen tulips to order and then twisting the wrap like a giant spliff. His stall was rooted a couple of minutes east from me, at the most verdant end of Columbia Road flower market. The place was humming, and not just because of the honey bees. Anyone looking for a bit of colour in their life came here. Drawn by the blooms and the bawling traders. Truly an urban jungle. Sipping my coffee, I watched a party of floral hunters file by, each with a bunch of long-stemmed lilies slung over their shoulders. I stepped aside to let Willie's latest punter bring up the rear.

'So how you feeling now?'

I should have felt hollow, empty and lost, but I was too hungover to be sure.

'Fine,' I said anyway. 'I'll get over it.'

'No you won't,' he said confidently. 'There's no way you'll just let this lie. Not until you know why she broke up with you.'

I told him Christine hadn't been able to say. That she didn't have a reason as such. My dealer declared that to be horseshit. Privately, I had to agree.

'Everyone has their reasons, Reynard. She's just unwilling to hit you with the truth.'

'You think there's someone else too, don't you?'

'Any other man would've asked that straightaway,' said Willie. 'Why didn't you find out when you had the chance?'

'You know how it is,' I protested. 'You don't think of the right questions until afterwards.'

'Such as how you could let a fox like that slip through your fingers.'

'The way I see it, I'm sure she'll get back to my email.'

'Excuse me?' said Sweet, recoiling from his counter. 'Your *what*?'

Like most men in my position, I had set out to sever all links with my ex. If Christine didn't want me, then I didn't want her either. To begin with, at least. After a defiant few weeks, I contemplated putting in a phone call. Just to check she was doing OK without me. Nothing else. Not really. Unless of course Christine read my mind. Interpreted 'How you doing' for 'What are you doing and who with'. And that risked a response I needed to hear but couldn't be sure how to handle. So, basically, it was out of the question, ringing her. Even if I got through to her answermachine, I'd only stumble on my words. Leave myself wide open for a knockout.

What I needed was a way to get through without actually making a direct connection.

Which is why I'd been drawn to sending an email instead. The night before. Clean out of hash, but stoked up on slammers. That's if tequila minus the salt and the lemon counts as a slammer, and not just an alcoholic death wish. Either way, it fuelled my conviction that I was doing the right thing. Sitting in front of my computer back then, I lifted the bottle to my lips and poured out my heart. The words came naturally. Man and machine united. I told her I was doing fine. Great. No problems. That it would be nice to meet up some time. Hear how she'd been coping without me. That was if

I could squeeze her into my schedule, of course. Then I deleted the lot in a half-drunk fit of self-disgust, and bashed out my one burning question. *Was there another guy?* To be sure she picked it up I dispatched it to her workplace. Some paperless PR company that turned its employees into hopeless online junkies. Quite a first fix for the day, I thought. A reminder that I hadn't finished with her yet.

Even as I told him this, I could see my dealer harboured doubts. The big man checking his nails, unwilling to hear me out straight. Wincing at the tale of my online endeavour.

'You really think she'll reply to something like that?'

'It was me I would.'

Sweet William shook his head. 'You've set yourself up for a fall,' he said. 'You don't have the balls to ask her direct, how you going to cope if she doesn't get back to you?'

'I'll manage.'

Willie slapped a wand of delphiniums onto the counter and began to strip away the excess leaves.

'You'll crack,' he said finally, as if his opinion of me could have fallen either way. 'I swear, without some answers it'll fuck you right up.'

'Thank you, Dr Ruth.' I glowered at him from over the rim of my cup. My latte had cooled fast, but Willie was only just warming.

'Man needs reasons, right? For living and dying. For the purpose of his existence. That's why we make good explorers. Good philosophers. Fine drug-takers. Give us a mystery, we'll seek out the answers. Try to make sense of our shit. So when a fox like Christine takes a walk and you blow your chances of finding out why, it's only natural you look to yourself.'

'It is?'

'Sure.'

'Wow! I had no idea florists could dig so deep.'

He shrugged like I should take it or leave it, and began to wrap the flowers.

'Ren, you're a regulation male. There's only one conclusion a guy like you can reach. One explanation why she left without reason.'

'Is this going to make me feel better?'

'So I'm your doctor all of a sudden?' Willie flaring suddenly. 'Of course it's not going to make you feel better, but at least you'll have your answer.'

I lit a cigarette, one of his, and bid him continue. Sweet William leaned in close, conspiratorial.

'Sex,' he said. 'It has to be she had a problem with the sex.'

'With me?'

'Well, certainly not with whoever's banging her now.'

'*Willie!*'

'All I'm saying is, that's how it looks from this side of the stall. You don't measure up to her needs, she finds someone who can hit the spot. *Every* time.'

'Bollocks,' I said, spitting smoke. 'Christine would've said something first.'

'Sure she would, Reynard. If she wanted to destroy you. Believe me, nothing can ruin a man faster, finding out he doesn't deliver. Far kinder that she leaves you to draw that conclusion on your own terms.'

'You think I should call her?'

'Too late,' my dealer declared. 'You've already made contact once. Thrown the ball into her court. Do it again, you'll start to look desperate. Like no one else'll play with you because you really are a limp dick.'

'I *never* disappointed,' I countered, returning to my senses. 'Sweet, don't even look at me like you're thinking that way.'

I would have had it out on the pavement, the argument that is, had Willie not cut off our conversation by yelling aggressively at a juvenile trader on the stall opposite. The boy hurried across, cutting a swathe through the passing shoppers. It was reassuring to see my dealer had some influence. That or an apprentice.

'I have to go,' Sweet said, and threw me the delphiniums he had just finished wrapping. 'See a man about some bluebell bulbs.'

'Bluebells? You're not smuggling them out of woods or anything, are you? That's illegal.'

'So is that,' said Willie, and jabbed a finger at the bunch in my arms.

I made for my wallet, knowing that when I got home I would find a quarter ounce of Red Lebanon tucked inside with the stems.

'On me,' my dealer insisted. 'This is a charity case.'

'No way,' I said. 'I'm fine. Really.'

But Willie wasn't listening, and marked his departure with a kid punch to my shoulder. I tried not to flinch, despite the force of the blow.

'Look after yourself, Reynard. And treat the flowers with some respect this time, eh? Such a shame to lose a thing of beauty like that.'

2

A fluttering of lights, and my modem launched into its mating call. The shrill trill. The burst of white noise. The silent wait for a reply.

'Go get her,' I muttered. 'Don't crash on me now.'

Behind me, half a dozen deep velvet delphiniums splayed proudly from the neck of an empty tequila bottle. Sweet William's advice about women I had discarded like the wrapping. The man was a florist. He worked with flowers. Simple things. Only time they had a problem was when someone like Willie took a pair of secateurs to their stems. No, if Christine was seeing someone else then what better way for her to come clean than by email. To talk to her screen, not to my face.

My welcome page began to build. I closed my hand over the mouse. Ready to step over the virtual threshold and check my mail. Below my monitor, there on the ledge of my hard-drive, a cling-filmed cube of hash remained unopened. Having got home ready to roll, I found that just being in the presence of technology offered the same soothing influence as a spliff. For here was something I was involved with on an intimate basis, but which unlike Christine wasn't programmed to screw up my life. If anything, a PC was designed to *enhance* my life. Not that I used it for anything more than email, and even then I tended to send far more than I received. My agent being a master in the art of the silent reply. In my book, no news meant no work. Simple as that. Still, my computer didn't just gather dust. My ex made better use of it than I did. Tapping into work at night, so she said. Working through her backlog. It was a shame she didn't share some of its functional aspects, in fact. Like the error code that appeared whenever it froze on me and crashed. That way I could've looked up Christine's problem in a trouble-shooter's guide. Even learned to watch out for it in future models.

'Hey there!'

I had post. An email, as predicted.

Only it wasn't from Christine but from my less-than-powerful agent. The prospect of a casting should have thrilled me, were it not for the fact that a) it was for a cat food commercial; b) the ad was being shot here, but nobody would get to see it. Unless they watched telly in Korea; and c) they were after an actor who could 'play second fiddle to a feline'. I sighed, feeling typecast again. Every gig he had got me I played a submissive role of some sort. On *Crimewatch*, my finest hour, I featured as a petrol station attendant on night shift. The one who did exactly what he was told with a twelve-bore at his temple. Asking me to play the putz was like asking a fat guy to do a fat role. It came naturally. All too easy. I guess I should have been glad for the chance of work, but my agent had to go and finish by revealing I was all they could afford from his roster.

'Thanks,' I muttered. 'Bastard.'

Still, at least I knew what I was doing the next morning at ten.

Summoning a blank email, I tried to picture the woman whose absence had consumed my month. But every time her face appeared to me, Sweet William emerged right behind. Wagging his finger. Telling me to leave it be.

---

email to: LaChrissy
from: Ren125733
subject: apologies

Christine,
Sorry about message from last night. Bit pissed.
Still, would love to hear from you. Check you're ok.

Reynard :o)

Hitting send made me feel so much better. For about a nanosecond. Then all manner of doubts overwhelmed me. Why did I admit I'd been drinking? Did I really have to sound so perky? And what the fuck was I doing finishing with a stupid side-on smiley? I felt like a geek. Wished I had opted for snail mail. At least then I could have waited by the pillar box until the next collection and begged the postie to return it. This, however, was irreversible. Immediate. Embarrassing. In cyberspace, there was no going back. My dealer was a bitch, but I should have listened to him. I logged off, reached for the hash, and vowed never to be seduced into making contact like that again.

Getting stoned was a mistake. I should have got slaughtered once more instead. At the very least, a drink would have reinforced my sense of defiance over the split. You get dumped, you drink, you think, 'Fuck it, her loss', and fall over. With a couple of long, solitary smokes, the only thing reinforced is your sense of utter paranoia.

Six hours later, hunched under the full moon of my desk lamp, I listened to the modem shriek for the twentieth time since darkness fell. It was beginning to sound like it was laughing at me.

No post, sad-boy.

'Where are you?' I wondered to myself, and tried to delete the vision in my head of the bastard who was obviously keeping her busy. Certainly busier than I had ever managed, I thought bitterly. I was about to log off and skin up a mother, when something appeared on the screen. Something which caused my dope-shot eyes to widen right out.

Christine had just logged on. This I knew because her screen name had appeared in my Cyber Circle. An ever-present little window that informed me whether friends and colleagues and Tony Curtis were online at the time. Not that Tony was a close personal acquaintance or anything. More an inspiration. I had never dared to send him an email. Nothing so direct. OK, nothing at all. I simply hoped that one day the old wolf might come across my screen name in a celebrity e-zine and add *me* to *his* Circle. But TC was a dream, and Christine was reality. Right there before me, but as good as a million miles away. In this virtual confessional, perhaps we could finally speak our minds.

'Hi,' I said, addressing the screen as if she could hear me somehow. 'You're working late.'

Still my mail box stayed empty. She must have checked her post,

I reasoned. Wasn't it the first thing everyone did when they went online? I wondered whether she'd stepped away from her desk for a second. Gone to fetch some coffee, not finish off with her boss, though sadly this was the thought that stayed with me. I waited impatiently. Buckled a paper clip. Used it to pick at my keyboard plaque. Flossing at the crap that had fallen through the gaps. The dust. The dirt. The crumbs of digestive biscuit. My ex, always munching at the monitor.

'Talk to me, Christine.'

I double clicked on her screen name, and opened up a Quick-E. If I slipped her a note this way, a little window with my message inside it would override whatever she was doing online at the time. What's more, it would stay there, stuck to the inside of her screen, until she dealt with it.

Quick-E to: LaChrissy

Ren125733:	Hi Christine, get my emails?

I hit send, imagined the very same window popping up on her side of the void. Arriving out of nowhere just to keep her on her toes. I cracked a knuckle, anticipating her response, and proceeded to go through both hands. If she wasn't scrambling into her clothes, I thought, then perhaps there was an explanation I had previously dismissed. That maybe she was in fact trying to call me. Sitting there with the engaged tone, waiting for me to get offline and plug the phone back in.

Quick-E to: LaChrissy

Ren125733:	Would it be better if I logged off so we could speak? Or perhaps we could meet for a quick chat. Just let me know.
	I'm easy. xx

By the time I decided to send a follow-up, I had rolled another joint. The handsome block of hash which earlier had crowned my hard-drive was now about the size of a raisin, and my brain wasn't far behind. Normally, I was used to sharing a smoke. With Christine gone I had pretty much taken to consuming her share.

Quick-E to: LaChrissy

Ren125733:   If this isn't a good time, perhaps we can do it later.

I sat back for a moment, inhaled on the spliff as if it were my last, then worried that I should have been a bit more assertive. Demanded that she quit treating me like I didn't exist. Which was fast how it felt to me.

Quick-E to: LaChrissy

Ren125733:   How about one hour from now? I just want to talk. It won't take long, I swear.

I winced at my words, imagined my numerous messages now littering her screen. Nevertheless, I created a fresh window. A final missive. Just to clarify things. For my sake, at least.

Quick-E to: LaChrissy

Ren125733:   It's nothing heavy, of course. But naturally you're on my mind and I wondered if you've been sleeping with someone else.

I dispatched the note, thought back over my question, and howled at the ceiling.

Quick-E to: LaChrissy

Ren125733:   Sorry. Slightly emotional tonight.

It was too much. My head wasn't connecting fast enough with the action on the screen. I was just the stoner firing blindly, waiting for Game Over. I wasn't even sure I had a life left.

Quick-E to: LaChrissy

Ren125733:	Do I sound like a cyber stalker?

This time I covered my eyes. Hoped my PC would spare me and just shut down on the spot. Instead, into that bleak moment came one rare, life-affirming chime. A reply. I had a *reply*.

Quick-E to: Ren125733

LaChrissy:	Ren, is that really you?

Christine, at last! My fingers machine-gunned the keyboard, firing off a question which I had struggled all evening to dismiss as a blank.

Ren125733:	Was I just a lousy lay?

In the empty seconds that followed, as my message shot across the virtual landscape, it seemed entirely probable that every surfer in cyberspace had turned to look my way. I could almost hear her response, whistling back up the phone wire.

LaChrissy:	Don't make me change my screen name.

Shit. Shit. *Shit.* I knew I couldn't leave things like this, and hit one key as if it were a panic button.

Ren125733	xxxxxxxxxxxxxxxxx
LaChrissy	This has to stop.
Ren125733	XXXXX{sorry}XXXXX

I stopped smothering kisses onto her screen. Overcome by the need to get out quickly. Just turn round and flee. Go some place Christine would never look for me. Start a new life completely. All I had to do was swing my cursor to the toolbar and log off. But then I wondered why she hadn't done the same. It had to be that something demanded her attention more than I did. One minute after our final exchange, in fact, her name was still there in my Cyber Circle. Haunting me. Taunting me. Seducing my hand to pull back on my mouse. I opened up my Circle preferences, and hit the Socialise button. A basic command that combed the chat rooms for her virtual presence and pinpointed her location.

'Where are you?' I asked myself. 'What are you up to?'

It was a click, nothing more. Yet this one had all the impact of a judge's gavel. Hitting me so hard it left a permanent kink in the course of my love life. For better and also for worse. Slack-jawed and stunned, I found myself drawing ever closer to the revelation there on the screen. Coming so near, it almost sucked me right in.

3

Don't talk to me. Don't even *ask* if I'd like coffee. Just shut up and pour. Any man walks into a dressing room with an expression that sour, you'd be sensible to comply. Right?

'You look tired,' said the producer at my casting as I slumped into the chair. 'I trust you didn't have a heavy night? Our clients are keen we hire some fresh-faced talent.'

I glanced up at the mirror, realised I was frowning almost as darkly as the elfin with the attitude behind me. Still, I managed to muster a smile when she handed me the cup I craved.

'Thanks,' I mumbled. 'Just didn't sleep too well, that's all.'

These were the first words to pass between us since she had escorted me up from reception. I hadn't expected her to speak at all, in fact, and that suited me just fine. I was in no mood to chat, let alone peddle cat food. Certainly not after clocking my co-star. While mooching around downstairs, waiting for my call, the revolving doors had gone into a spin and two handlers from the animal agency appeared carrying a cage between them. Inside, nestled on a velvet cushion, was one of those Persian affairs with a shag pile pelt. I groaned, and saw my acting career unravel before me. For it was, without doubt, a girl's pet. The kind of companion Christine had always wanted. Not me.

'Don't worry about it,' the producer said suddenly.

'Pardon me?' I glanced over my shoulder, and wondered then if it wasn't just my mood she could read. Maybe all my anxieties were scheduled on her clipboard. Actor present? Tick. Freshly dumped? Tick. Still reeling from finding his ex-girlfriend getting carried away with her keyboard in chat room Free2Flirt? Double tick. Underscore.

'About the way you look,' she said finally, midway down her list. 'Make-up can work miracles.'

'Oh, right. Thanks.'

'Just relax. She'll be along in a minute.'

Alone in the dressing room, I set about draining my coffee. As the cup emptied out, I clamped the rim with my teeth, rested my feet on the shelf in front of me, and clasped my hands behind my head. It felt like a good recovery position. A caffeine drip in place of an oxygen mask. The patient waiting for his wounds to heal.

Tilting the chair on its back legs, I found I could gaze right up at the dregs packed into the bottom of the cup. It didn't reveal much. Not like my computer screen the previous night. There in that shameless chat room, where anyone could come in with a question or a comment, I had witnessed Christine hold court like a hussy. Engaging in the kind of talk that never once passed between our pillows. In stoned awe, I followed this steadily scrolling dialogue of secrets and desires. My self-confidence shrinking with every line. I learned that she most liked to make love under a power shower (I had a bath with one of those dribbling hose attachments); that a massage was the best way to get her in the mood for sex (I'd always assumed it was pizza); and that whispering in her ear intensified her orgasms (I tended to yell, once, then roll over and die).

Despite my humiliation, I just hadn't been able to bring myself to confront her with a Quick-E. Let alone submit my own question. Instead, I floated at the bottom of the list, hoping she might spot my screen name and scram. Then I rolled another joint and considered the possibility that she *knew* I was watching, which left me feeling so seedy that I quickly logged off. Besides, I'd had better things to do. Like cleansing my space of all Christine memorabilia. From the photographs propped along the windowsills to the box of tampons on the bathroom shelf, every last trace of her got bagged up in a bin liner. Right then, I didn't give a shit that I was still in the dark about how the applicator thing worked. Was it spring-loaded, or what? I just added it to my mental list of things I didn't understand about women but always meant to ask. Another time, I had thought back then. Another chat room.

'What a bitch,' I muttered into the beaker, reflecting on the situation. Slowly, the slurry at the base of the cup began to slide.

I tilted my head another degree, rocking the chair even further. Keen to test my powers of control. At the same time, I became aware of a presence close behind me. The make-up artist. It had to be her. A heart-stopping honey with mile-high cheekbones and a half-skewed smile. Then again, she was upside down in my field of vision. It could have been just a look of pity. 'Talking to myself,' I said sheepishly, upon which the coffee dregs went into free fall.

It was going to be a long session.

In the presence of great natural beauty, it's industry standard for a guy to look at himself and feel like a major-league ugly. The ring of bright bulbs round the mirror didn't do much for my self-confidence. Nor the fact that I'd just found myself at the bum end of a relationship. As the woman entrusted with the impossible began brushing my forehead with foundation, every pore appeared set to spring a pimple. The bags beneath my eyes seemed slung like hammocks. Great cracks rent my lips. Even my ears swung outwards for the occasion. At the same time it was clear that I was looking at an artist who eschewed her own craft. No blusher. No liner. No lippy. No nothing. She didn't need it. This fox *glowed*. Like God Himself had scrubbed her clean. Christine would hate her, I thought. Not least her avalanche of glossy black hair. My ex being the kind of blonde who couldn't step outside without first seeking permission from a mirror.

At intervals this miracle worker would stand back and eye me objectively. I pitied her task. If my head were made of clay, I thought, at least she could have kneaded it in and started afresh. It was one of those close-confine situations that begged a breezy conversation. Anything to discharge the atmosphere. The longer the silence lasted between us, however, the harder it was to think of something to say that wouldn't sound like I was hitting on her. Wasn't it always the way? In the past, I had been forced to give up on several female hairdressers. All because I paused for thought and then stalled. It's all right when a man invades your personal space to measure you up for a suit, peer inside your ears or check out your teeth. In that situation, it's cool to stay quiet for the duration.

It means nothing. You're there for a necessary service. All thoughts are elsewhere. But when a simmering vision like this rubs up against you during the course of her work, you have to keep the dialogue flowing. It's vital. Because if you don't, she'll suspect you're abusing the intimacy. That you can't speak your mind, because there's only one thing on it.

'A brown paper bag might be easier,' I quipped in desperation. 'Just don't put the eye holes too close together.'

She smiled, the make-up artist, but it was more like a reflex response. Standing in front of me now, she began teasing my hair back with her fingers. I was determined to keep talking, no matter how sad I sounded, so long as it kept things clean. But any such thoughts were entirely laid to waste when I chanced to notice some unmistakable nipple action going on beneath her T-shirt. She wasn't wearing a bra. I closed my eyes, yet even there I found nowhere to hide. All I could do was submit to the burn.

This would never happen online, I thought. Last night had shown me that. Hit the chat rooms in the same way Christine had and, wallop, I could be intimate with a stranger in seconds. Who cares what anyone looked like. It's what you can do to each other via the keyboard that counts. When it came to meeting new people, the World Wide Web guaranteed equality for all. Unless, of course, your spelling sucked. Me? I figured I could be word perfect. Touch sensitive, too. Given the right opportunity. But first I had a casting to command, as the producer returned to inform me. I couldn't say for sure exactly how long ago she had slipped back into the dressing room. It made no odds, really. A well-placed cough informed me that I had been caught gawping at something I shouldn't. Just to make things all the more awkward, the make-up artist continued working right in front of me. Closing off my chances to look at anything but her mesmerising breasts.

'Uplifting, isn't it?'

'Huh?'

I had no idea how to answer. I couldn't even be sure that the producer was talking to me, in fact. More so when she circled around and said, 'I wish I got that kind of attention first thing every morning.'

Once again, the fox in front of me stepped away to check her work. Leaning back against the shelf beside the producer now. Outclassing her in every way. Another pair I couldn't handle. Too extreme by half.

'Tell me,' I asked, keen to move on, 'is there a script for this audition?'

'More a framework. It depends how you both get on.' There she was again, everything in twos.

'I don't foresee any problems. Not from my point of view.'

'So you've worked with animals before.'

'If you count some of the meatheads hired for *Crimewatch*.'

The make-up girl pressed her fingertips to her mouth, and I could see she was masking a smile. I thought I'd been funny, and beamed back at her. Then the producer caught my eye and I just knew the joke was on me.

'That's just boys being boys,' she said. 'This is about handling pussy.'

I heard her right, but chose not to react. Instead I pursed my lips and waited for the pair of them to pull themselves together.

'Very good,' I said, finally. 'Had that come from me I would've been frog-marched from the building.'

'Times change,' she said, still smirking. 'Nice young man like you should be able to deal with it.'

It wasn't even mid-morning, and already two women had left me feeling like a loser. I removed the make-up bib, stood up and loosened out my arms. In the face of ridicule, I was ready for the role.

'OK, ladies,' I brought my hands together smartly. 'Show me the camera, then let's see who wears the trousers.'

The bleeding had stopped by the time the cab dropped me off. My left cheek, sporting three livid scratch marks, made me look like Bruce Lee-lite. The little git had raked me just as soon as I set its food down. Only after the audition was abandoned did I learn they had starved the cat for twenty-four hours. To ensure its 'enthusiasm', as they spun it. By rights I should have been the one who flounced from the set. Not my co-star and its entourage. I agreed to try again the next day, however, but only because I was made to feel so responsible. The producer assuring me these things happened, but intimating all the same that it had probably picked up on my negative vibes. I should have been outraged, but I couldn't disagree.

I blamed Christine for all this. One month since the split, and my self-confidence remained as fragile as ever. My poise upstaged by an over-pampered pet. I needed more time, I resolved, on crossing the square back to my space. I was still vulnerable. Not just to ridicule from a sour-faced producer, but to visions like the make-up artist. A woman whose presence made me see what I was missing. Someone with confidence and composure, that's how I wanted to be. One who could strike up a conversation as easily as a match. A man who could make a fox smile for all the right reasons. Inciting passion, not pity. Which frankly was all I could expect unless I found my feet as a free agent. Got myself a life again. In this frame of mind, it didn't help to find a bunch of crimson roses propped against my front door. I ripped off the note from the Cellophane wrap.

Thinking of you – Sweet William

'Jesus,' I sighed to myself. 'Who died?'

OK, I was single again. But with a little readjustment, in my head and in my home, I would be fine. Just dandy. I needed no more sympathies from my dealer. Nevertheless, I was a little pissed off to discover that his gift didn't actually contain any drugs. The flowers, I realised, had been intended as a gesture in their own right. Me and the Puffa needed to speak. But only after I had proven to myself that everything would be alright. That when it came to women I remained in the loop.

The only problem was I couldn't find the spark to make the effort.

Hoxton was littered with bars, all of them fur-lined by foxes, but the prospect of getting *out* there just didn't appeal. After eighteen months in a relationship, it was like I'd been emotionally institutionalised. Familiar with nothing but couple things, which invariably meant staying in. Watching the telly with Christine. Sharing a bath. Feeling lucky, so I thought, and ordering up a Pepperoni Hot.

I considered inviting my dealer to come with me, but Willie went to pieces with women if they took a shine to him. Sure, he could talk about them. He could counsel them. He could supply them with any kind of bouquet or blow. But if a fox became sweet on Sweet the man would get so shy it was embarrassing to watch. A case of a florist who had spent too long practising on his plants. Still, they thrived on Willie's words. Which was why I usually took his advice. Outside, rain really was beginning to drum on the skylights.

'Forget it,' I told myself. 'Why bother getting soaked.'

It was approaching lunchtime, but I had lost my appetite. Normally, Christine would pop out from work and have a bite with me. Maybe dessert in the bedroom. I wondered what she was doing instead. Instinctively, and with a sharp upswing in my spirits, my attention swivelled round to the computer.

If it was good enough for Christine, I thought, waiting for my hard-drive to reach speed, it was *ideal* for me. An Internet relationship. A date without the hassle of actually meeting anyone. Not until you were sure about them, at any rate. First, however, before I made my presence known, it was only courteous to offer up a little about myself.

Screen Name:	Ren125733
Real Name:	Reynard. Ren, for short. Rennie at a push
M/F:	Male
Age:	27
Marital Status:	Single, as if I need reminding
Location:	London
Occupation:	Thesp

Interests:	Women, if they'll have me
Watch Word:	'Still searching . . .'

My Virtual Vitals took under a minute to compose. Personal information that any social surfer should file if they wanted to make a connection of some sort. The Vitals Vault was available to anyone who wanted to search for a match by category, be it by what they did, where they lived or what they liked and with whom. I kept my details brief. Figured I would save my breath for a metropolitan female fan of the theatre who wanted to find out more.

Stabbing decisively at the return button, I sat back and looked forward to regaling Sweet William with tales of my conquests to come.

4

'Ouch, what happened to you?'

I turned the other cheek, waited for Sweet to finish with the customer before me. It looked like a complicated deal. A transaction between my dealer and some towering trustafarian that involved a tray of Busy Lizzies and little change from a fifty note.

'It's not what you think,' I assured him.

'Nor was that,' he winked, as the punter slipped away. 'It's just that I know how to hide my indiscretions.' Beckoning me closer, my dealer promptly clamped my face and held me there for a detailed inspection. 'So tell me she was a tiger.'

'Cut it out,' I complained, pulling free from his grip. 'Although she was no kitten, I have to say.'

'You sure it was a *she*?' My dealer's anvil face flattened into a grin. 'Looks to me like someone tried to scratch out your eyes.'

I took it on the chin, then brought him up to speed on my casting disaster. As I cursed the cat once more, Sweet William surreptitiously worked a small polythene bag from his money belt. It contained a handful of small dark seeds.

'And here's me thinking you were going to pieces,' he said when I had finished. 'Least you're still going nowhere with work. It's a positive sign, keeping business running as usual.'

'I'm just having a bad run of luck, Willie. It'll pass.'

Looking one way then the other, my dealer tipped the contents of the bag onto the counter. I watched him divide the pile into three.

'You get the flowers, by the way?'

It was very thoughtful, I told him, but there had been no need. Really. He shrugged, shredded three strips from a 'commiserations' card and began to fold in the seeds. I started feeling a little paranoid, what with so many people bustling by the stall.

'It was your ex suggested I deliver you a bunch. She said you seemed a little gloomy. Needed your life brightening up a little.'

'You spoke to *Christine?*' I cut in, but Willie hadn't finished.

'Believe me, you can't get much brighter than roses. Even at this time of year, if you know the right supplier. Just keep them away from draughts, Ren. Change the water daily. I guarantee you'll be looking at a two-week bloom.'

'You said you spoke to Christine?' I said again. 'How is she? Did she say anything else about me?'

Sweet William stopped what he was doing for a beat, and showed me his palms. Every whorl and crease had been soiled by his work. Especially his lifelines.

'She just dropped by first thing this morning. Nothing more.'

'First thing? Did she look like she'd just got up, or was she on her way home?'

'Calm down, Reynard.'

I pictured Christine in a shirt. One of those outsized, uncuffed numbers borrowed from a bloke. In my mind's eye, it was all I saw her wearing. That and a shagged-out glaze in her eye.

'She was on her way home, wasn't she? Why else would she be up first thing?'

'To buy flowers, maybe? Best time of day. Get them while they're fresh.' In one sweeping move, Willie pushed a wrap in my direction and seized the other two from view. The deal brought me back to my senses.

'Thanks,' I said, hurriedly pocketing my present.

'She also mentioned you'd spoken online.'

'Oh.'

'Didn't I tell you to steer clear?' he said testily. 'Were you listening when I said that you'd bring bad shit upon yourself if you made contact with Christine like that?'

'I was impossibly stoned at the time, you know how it is.'

'Getting stoned has nothing to do with it. Man, if you're gonna do drugs, at least be disciplined. I gave you that hash so you'd kick back and make peace with your problems. Not start gibbering to your ex about being a big disappointment in the sack.'

I felt my cheeks reddening up. 'She told you?'

'Everything.'

My ex had never been blessed with the gift of discretion. One time I told her that Suzi Quatro had been responsible for my first wet dream. My next birthday, her little sister gave me Suzi's Greatest Hits.

'I bet Christine didn't tell you what she was doing online at the time,' I countered. 'Did she happen to say she was in some sleazy chat room, flirting with anyone who happened to catch her eye. I was shocked, Willie. Truly.'

'That's her affair. Look after your own.'

'Actually,' I said proudly. 'I've done just that.'

'You have?'

'Let's just say Christine's not the only one to make new friends on the web.'

'You pulled?'

I was about to drum up a couple of catches for his benefit, but hesitated just a moment too long.

'You got burned, right?'

I hung my head.

'How bad, Reynard?'

I told him about my social web debut earlier that day. How I had completely misjudged the game. 'There are thousands of women out there on the net, Sweet. But a thousand and one men, with double the number of dodgy chat-up lines.'

'Dodgy in what way?'

'"There's a party going on at the end of my knob. You can be the bouncer."'

'That's dodgy.'

'"Sit on my face, let me guess your weight."'

'Dodgy and depressing,' agreed Sweet.

'Yeah, and as a result I couldn't even introduce myself without women thinking I'm a slimeball.'

'Ain't that always the way?'

'At least in the real world you get the chance to prove you're basi-cally a decent bloke. Online, so many men abuse the anonymity to air their predatory instinct that no female will even risk responding to a basic hello.'

'You think I could deal in cyberspace? Sounds like a market in need of mellowing. Something to bring these people together.'

'Willie, we're dealing with screen names like MassiveWun, JapEye, ShagU24/7, Deano69XXX.'

'Subtle.'

'WristDeep, even. Can you believe it, a name like that?'

My dealer frowned.

'Deep in what?'

'It doesn't matter,' I assured him quickly. 'All I know is it means I can't get a fox to trust me. My gender marks me out as a wanker.'

'No it doesn't.'

'Believe it, Willie. As soon as she clicks on my Vitals, finds out I'm a man, she immediately assumes I'm typing with one hand.'

'Are you?'

'God, *no!*' I protested. 'Give me some credit. I'm hurting here. All I want is a someone who understands what I'm going through.'

'Reynard, you got to stand out from the competition. Don't be the guy who's just fallen through the floor of a relationship, the loser who's waiting to be kissed better. Get out there. Show some spunk!'

'Now you're sounding like the other guys.'

'Check out the demand is what I'm saying. Find out what your market needs, then get off your knees and start supplying it. How do you think I stay afloat as a florist?'

I fingered the packet in my pocket, but didn't like to say.

'You think maybe I should change my Virtual Vitals a bit? Make myself sound more available?'

'No. I'm advising you to shut down that fucking computer and get out some.'

I let his comment ride, for I could understand why my dealer found it so hard to get his head round my efforts. The last time he handled a computer, it had probably been on its way out of an office window under cover of darkness.

'Tomorrow night,' he declared, clapping his hands together, 'I plan to reintroduce you to the real world. Show you how things have changed in the year and a half since you last went out as a free agent.'

'Willie, I'm not so sure I'm ready. I tried it this morning, came home bleeding.'

'That was work. This is pleasure.'

'So what do you have in mind?'

'Man, VIP are my middle initials.'

'Very Important Puffa?'

'I'm serious,' he said, and thumped the cutting table. 'You step out with Sweet, it means you're a winner. Someone going places. I don't want to hear one more word about your virtual insecurities. I want to hear about you, Ren. You're the man. A class player. Back by popular demand. It means I want to see you run with the ball again. I want to see you weave and sprint for the box. I want to see you *score.*'

5

As a rule, I never have been much of a team player. It doesn't help that I suck at sport. Always have. Ever since school. But I guess what really put me off back then were the showers afterwards. All that cod male bonding, forged at someone else's expense. The wet towels whipped into knots. The terror of having your tackle exposed to laughter and ridicule. You wouldn't get that kind of crap in the changing room next door. This I knew for a fact because someone had drilled a hole through the partition wall. Peeking into their world, for the second or so before I got hauled away by the next boy, I was amazed at the lack of any tension. The apparent ease with which girls could chatter in various states of undress. Maybe they were just as self-conscious about their bodies as we were. But unlike us they didn't cover it up by acting the twat.

It wasn't just football I loathed. Other team sports turned me right off too. Still do. Like moving in on a fox en masse. What is it with guys who feel the need to bring along the equivalent of a back four when they hit on a girl they fancy? Whether it's just sheer insecurity, or a throwback to the pack-hunting instinct, having your friends in your face makes it so much harder to get a result. You can't say a damn thing without the risk of someone sniggering or rolling their eyes. And if by chance the girl in question happens to reveal a little too much of herself, you can be sure one of your number will blow the whistle and stop you savouring the moment.

Which was why I gave thanks for being a solo player, the next day in the studio dressing room, when the make-up artist accidentally tipped a carton of cotton buds from the ledge in front of me. Had I brought any mates along to bolster my bid to actually start up a conversation this time, their subsequent wolf whistles would have given the game away. Instead, I was free to just follow with my eyes as she dipped down to retrieve the sticks. Watching her hem line ride up her thighs, and her vest yawn away from her chest. Wondering exactly what it was about this woman that kept making my heartbeat quicken. It was a beautiful sight. Criminal in some ways, too. Not just because she possessed an indecently-formed figure, but because I should have done the right thing. Offered to help instead of helping myself at her expense.

At the same time, I would concede to one advantage in playing with a team, and that's the forewarning you get when trouble looms from behind.

'Eyes up, soldier!'

The producer. There in the mirror. Snapping the door shut behind her. Looking at me with a face like frost. Before I could recover from the shock of seeing her there, she had tipped her clipboard flat and ticked something off her list. Something near the bottom.

'Are they ready for me yet?' I asked weakly.

The make-up girl rose again, mercifully unaware of my little misdemeanour, and returned to the job she had just been finishing. Dabbing the scratches on my cheek with a cotton bud daubed in cover-up. The producer moved to one side, slipping out of my line of sight.

'I'll take you down in a moment,' I heard her say. 'You and I need a talk first.'

'We do?'

'About the way you project yourself,' she said, and there she was again, back where I could see her. No longer in the mirror but right in front of it. I had been caught by her twice now, stealing a peek at a work of art without a ticket to the gallery. Not a major crime, some might say, though my appreciation had extended this time to a lick of my lips. It didn't look good, I admit. Guys like me were above this kind of thing. In public, at least. The producer waited for the artist in question to finish. Set her clipboard on the shelf when finally we were alone.

'If you want to relate to felines, Reynard, you have to respect their sixth sense.'

I didn't follow. That, or I didn't want to. Either way, I nodded cautiously.

'Don't try to outsmart them,' she continued. 'They know what you're doing and what you're thinking.'

'Even when they're not watching, right?' I said this without a trace of humility. Yes, I knew what I had done was wrong, but was it really any of her business to lecture me about it? The way the light left her eyes, I could see she thought it was.

'We're always watching,' she said darkly, and stooped to reach a cotton bud the make-up girl had missed.

'Don't flatter yourself,' I muttered under my breath. 'Who would look at you?'

'What was that?' There she was again, where I least expected her. Back on her feet, scowling. Had she heard me? It just kind of came out when she had bent down, and for a second we eyeballed each other. Then I considered the fact that I was here for a casting, and that she probably had a say in hiring the best man for the job.

'I'm sorry,' I surrendered. 'I'm just a little tense right now. Guess I'm keen to get it right this time around.'

She scanned my face, looking for cracks in my apology, and the tension seemed to leave her.

'The cat's been fed this morning,' she said, resting back against the shelf once more. 'You'll be fine. Just don't try and stare it out like you did yesterday. That's asking for trouble.'

I grinned, despite myself. So did she. I hadn't even realised she had seen me trying.

'I'll do my best,' I assured her.

'Just be yourself. That's all we want from you. Be relaxed. Be natural.'

'Thanks,' I said, and reached round to untie my bib. 'If only the same advice applied to all aspects of my life.'

'It does.'

'Not with the one that matters most,' I said.

'Girl trouble?'

'What else is there?'

I considered pressing her discreetly about her colleague, but I didn't exactly feel I'd earned her trust on that subject. So instead I told her about Christine. About my attempt to meet women online, and the Neanderthals I encountered who fought for their attention. I figured slagging off my own sex would help us bond a bit better.

'Not all chat rooms are that bad,' she reasoned. 'Some can be really enlightening.'

'You think?' I straightened up in the chair, surprised by her disclosure. She hadn't struck me as the interactive kind, certainly not offline at any rate. Still, I was keen to find out more. 'Enlightening in what way?'

'There's one I know could really help you out, in fact.' The producer broke off for a moment, gazing over my head as the intercom summoned our presence on the studio floor. 'Sounds like the cat's getting scratchy,' she quipped, and motioned for me to follow her.

'This website,' I reminded her on our way out into the corridor. 'What's it called?'

Without turning, she said, 'Purradise.'

'*Purradise?*'

'Something like that.'

'Sounds like a cattery.'

'It is,' she called back. I hurried to keep up. 'In a sense.'

Whatever sense she meant, I couldn't fathom it during the casting. Then again, I was more concerned about the extra one belonging to my co-star. The sixth sense it insisted on using against me. I only had to sink the fork into the food and the bugger would flatten both ears. Swishing its tail one way then the other as I hurriedly scooped a hunk of jellied gristle onto the plate.

'Take it easy,' I warned, smiling like a sap for the camera. 'Be cool.'

We wrapped without further incident, though the cat was reluctant to get back inside the cage. Still, I couldn't resist stepping up to the bars as I left and woofing at it when nobody was watching. A domestic pet had probably scuppered my chances of getting the gig, I thought, on spinning out of the doors and into the street, but at least I was free to lead my own life. Even if my own handler had ruled that a party was the place to find some direction.

6

Doesn't every man own a special shirt? One that hangs on his clothes rail looking like it's got no business being there. Looking like an exotic parrot perched among street pigeons. A shirt that should belong to someone else's wardrobe. Someone far more magnetic than him. Someone able to walk into the classiest lounge in town and have a tall one appear on the bar before he's even raised his hand. A shirt that does all the necessary talk without any exchange of words. A shirt that sounds all the right notes. On that guy's back, it looks entirely natural. Nothing out of the ordinary. On ordinary guys like me, rookies who've had no reason to get out there in eighteen happy months, the special shirt looks like a million. A million in old money.

'You're a player,' I kept saying into the mirror. Eventually, I resorted to pointing at myself at the same time. Just in case my reflection thought I was talking about someone else. 'A player, like the man said.'

I wasn't convinced. I really wasn't. I had last worn my special shirt on my first date with Christine. Original fifties button-down. Black with rhinestone detail. It required confidence to pull off. A kind of inner swagger. But no matter how many takes I went through in the mirror, it no longer felt tailor-made for me.

I was due to meet Sweet at ten, but I felt like a berk. A bad cowboy. If my dealer really expected me to saddle up with someone at the club, I would have to talk better than I walked. What I needed was a quick rehearsal, but I only had fifteen minutes spare. Twelve less the time it took for the computer to boot up and connect to the net.

Purradise. That's where I'd been told it was at. A place where I hoped to restore my faith in myself as a man. In my browser's navigation bar I tapped in www.purradise.com, then sat back as the website began to load. If the producer was a switched-on sort of woman, I figured the website would reflect her taste. The virtual equivalent of a lounge bar, maybe. Not one featuring a garish yellow background with blue paw prints all over it. The picture completed, and I was faced with a welcome menu that left me feeling confused, deflated and also a bit depressed about the human race as a whole:

purradise.com
Uniting cat lovers around the world!!

Fancy meeting people with a passion for our furry friends?
Then find your purrfect partner, here! Prowl through our photo purrsonals, chat in the 'cat' room, or get your claws into a whole litter of feline-related features, hints and tips.
Happy huntin', mousers!

Was the producer having a laugh? I couldn't be sure. Though I began to form an opinion when the music kicked in. A simple electronic version of 'What's New Pussycat?' That or the webmaster was so besotted by his pet that he had recorded it prancing across the keys. Either way, sparked by the kind of curiosity that drives someone into a freak show, I clicked into the 'cat' room.

'What am I doing?' I asked myself. 'This can't be right.'

The place was packed. This I knew because the screen names of everyone present were listed alongside the main window: Mouse-Trap1. TomKat. FleaPowda. Mewler. StrayRay. CyberSox. KittyKate. Lives9. And me, Ren125733. Things went kind of quiet when my distinctly un-catty name appeared at the foot of the list. As the digital dialogue slowed to a halt, I wondered what was expected of me. Like perhaps I needed to spray the virtual walls to make my presence known. I gave myself two minutes, tops. Enough time to be sure this wasn't the enlightening experience promised, before I sought out the cat flap and went someplace else. The virtual equivalent of fucking off round to the neighbours after having just been fed.

Ren125733:   Hi, room.

KittyKate: Hey, Ren {Kitty makes space for Ren in front of fire}.

I leaned back in my chair, sighed some. The brackets bit didn't bode well. Role-playing of some kind. Way too Dungeons and Dorks for my liking. Still, it had to be worth cuddling up to this Kitty, just to see how she'd react. With some unease, I bracketed my way beside her.

Ren125733:   Thanks, Kitty. Nice and cosy now.

KittyKate: prrr prrr prrr {Kitty licks Ren}.

'Get a life,' I reasoned out loud. 'Get real.' To be honest I was a little lost for words. I was about to backtrack from the room, when another presence made it clear I was treading on his paws.

Quick-E to: Ren125733

TomKat: Hey, pal, KittyKate doesn't need another mate.

Did these people really believe they were *feline*? I had to find out. Call his bluff, if only so I had good reason to get mad with the producer when I saw her.

Ren125733:   What? You want to discuss this in the alley?

TomKat: {Tom prepares to pounce}.

Ren125733:   How old are you?

TomKat: {hissing} Fifty-two.

Immediately my scorn compressed into something more serious. I'd had him down as a student, or an inmate, and his partner for a fox.

Ren125733:   How about Kitty?

TomKat:	**Not much older.**

In a flash I closed the Quick-E window, to find my ears were being cyber-washed.

'Yuk! No! Cut it out!' I yelled, stabbing at the exit icon. Closing every window until there was nothing on my screen but the navigation bar containing the website address. I sat back again, staring at the dotcom from which I'd just escaped, then realised that perhaps I might have made a wrong assumption. For how could I be sure the producer meant purradise.com? A website address could have a number of different endings, from dot-this to dot-that. Quickly I put my hunch into practice.

purradise.net did not exist.

purradise.org was under construction.

purradise.co.uk was a different story entirely. Closer to home for a start. Closer to my hopes of finding a decent chat room being more to the point. A website built like a lounge bar. Subtle hues and minimalist design. In short, just a pastel pink background with an 'enter' icon at its heart.

'Now we're talking the same language,' I said to myself, and reached for my mouse once more.

Where purradise.com was inhabited by scatty pensioners with personality disorders, its British counterpart was even busier, more vibrant and altogether more promising. Maid4U. StollyPolly. Sappho22. BarbiGyrl. CyberDoll. NoKenDo. The place was *rammed* with women. The list scrolled off the screen. Every name calling out to me for attention. Begging for a Quick-E, though I knew not to be so presumptuous. An unsolicited approach was just too forward. The kind of thing a regular shark would do, not me.

As a newcomer to the room, I was expected to address one and all, then wait for any interested parties to make their own approach. I let my fingers flutter over the keyboard, and then executed the virtual equivalent of a polite cough.

Ren125733:	Hi, room. 27/male/London. Anyone Interested in a Quick-E?

I prepared for the invitations to arrive. At the same time, however, I wondered why nobody was talking around me. Apart from my own opening lines, the chat room was utterly silent. Devoid of conversation, once again. I felt like the teacher in a school canteen. The one who'd just asked to sit with the kids. After about a minute of waiting around, and conscious that I couldn't be late to meet Sweet, I decided to just go for it. Pick off a screen name that took my fancy, and hit on them regardless. If I kept it polite, I thought it couldn't hurt.

Quick-E to: StollyPolly

Ren125733:   Hi, Polly! Free to chat?

I allowed her a second to reply. To stop whatever she was doing, and even check my Virtual Vitals if she wished. It was obscenity free, so there had to be hope. As I waited, however, the email icon blinked on at the foot of my screen. I had post. Not from Christine, I discovered, but my agent. To my amazement, it seemed the commercial people had lapped up my performance at the recall that morning. The animosity between myself and the moggy had bagged it for us both. 'An original take on the old relationship between pet and owner', so they had said. I was required for filming the next day at eleven. Short notice, I know, but still my ten percenter had confirmed that I would be there. He had my diary. Which meant simply that he knew I wasn't doing anything with the rest of my life unless the call came via his office. For someone working so late, which didn't bode well in any business, my agent seemed delighted. So was I. More so when StollyPolly responded to my invitation. But then I read her note. In full.

Quick-E to: Ren125733

StollyPolly: No.

I was in fighting mood. If I was to break down Polly's barriers, I had only a matter of minutes in which to do it.

Ren125733:	I'm not like the others.
StollyPolly:	No shit? Go away. Leave.
Ren125733:	Maybe we can talk later?
StollyPolly:	Read my Vitals.

I did as I was told.

Screen Name:	StollyPolly
Real Name:	Will reveal all if you have what it takes
M/F:	Female, what else?
Age:	25
Marital Status:	Single bisexual
Location:	London
Occupation:	Too boring to mention
Interests:	Meeting bifems online
Watch Word:	'Lads, stick to the real world'

This last instruction I ignored. Not because I was ignorant, but because I didn't regard myself as that kind of man. A *lad*. The kind of man for whom ignorance is an art form in fact. That she was bisexual was kind of cute, I thought. A bold statement, too. But I liked her so much more for it.

Quick-E to: StollyPolly
| Ren125733: | So what does it take, Polly? |

Tact, perhaps? Taste? Temerity?

| StollyPolly: | Tits. |

'What does that mean?' I asked myself, then frowned when she spelled it out.

StollyPolly: (o)(o)

I exhaled, long and hard. My three strikes were way out.

Ren125733:   One final thing?

StollyPolly: Piss off.

Ren125733:   K. Bye then.

StollyPolly: Bi Bi.

I closed the dialogue box. Found myself faced once more with the chat-free chat room. This time, the absence of any dialogue made me feel like everyone was watching me. Like I was the odd one out. The only straight screen name present, I suddenly suspected. It was a fact I confirmed with a start as I scanned the list for clues. Diva32. LadyMuck. In2chyk. GenuFem. This wasn't just a bi thing, this was a *girl* thing. All of them together. No boys allowed, as I realised to my horror. A glance at the name in my browser window and I was out of there as fast as my mouse would carry me. Purradise.co.uk – all-girl Heaven

Clear of the website, racing to switch off and ship out, I chanced to see that Tony Curtis had come online. My Cyber Circle having been hidden by the second cat house that night to leave me feeling like a flop. It was as if I'd found him waiting backstage for me. This vintage valentino, laughing at my plight. An impossibility, seeing that he didn't even know I existed, but the fact that we shared the same gender made me think he'd go easy. Unlike Sweet William, I remembered, who wouldn't be so forgiving if I turned up late. What's more, he would probably go on to pulp me if I tried to explain the reason for my delay. With no time to rethink my outfit, I hurried to get clear of my space. Leaving behind his wrap of strange seeds but taking a question with me. One which I hoped might prove redundant under Willie's guidance. For it was becoming increasingly clear to me that the rules had changed since I last played the dating game. And if I was to connect with a woman again, then first I would have to find out what I was doing so wrong.

7

'Nice shirt,' said Sweet, when I found him at the bar.

This was in the Purgatory Room at the Pandemonium. A gallery overlooking the club itself, but mercifully cut off from the masses by a soundproofed Perspex window. It was a class affair. Low lights pooling each table. Cigarette smoke hanging in veils. Bouncer at the spiral stairs and a dealer in a quilted number that I didn't dare criticise. Still, it had sleeves, and was far less offensive than the living hell I had fought through to find him. Some launch for yet another lad's magazine. *Staple,* I believe it was called. Not my kind of lifestyle, but Willie was well-connected. Which was why my dealer had guaranteed my name would be on the upstairs list.

'You don't like the shirt, just say so.'

'No, I do. Really. It looks good. Special.'

I tried to draw the barmaid's attention, but she was too busy ignoring me to notice.

'Is it that obvious?' I asked, conscious that my rhinestone buttons were sparkling madly.

'This is your first night out in over a year. Making the effort is a triumph in itself.'

'Willie, I appreciate what you're doing, but I'm just not sure what you expect me to achieve.'

My dealer silenced me by lifting a finger. A gesture which also seemed to be responsible for the appearance of two plum-coloured cocktails. I had no idea what was in them and my expression said as much.

'Gin and Daisy.' He raised his glass. 'Don't ask. Just drink.'

I would have preferred a lager, anything without a cherry in it, but Willie always liked to dictate the drinks.

'Thanks,' I said, then pulled a face with my first sip. 'Sweet, I'm really not sure I'm up to this.'

'Relax, it's not like I brought you here to get married.' My dealer raising his voice just a notch too loud for my liking. 'All I expect is that you have some fun.'

'Fun? I should be at home, Willie, mooching over photographs, playing our song.'

'You and Christine had a *song*?'

'No,' I covered quickly.

'Did so. It came too easy.'

'OK, she had a song.'

'Chicks always get to do the choosing.' He paused to drain his drink. 'I long for the day when I deal with a couple brought together by "The Ace of Spades".'

'Well, it meant something to her ...'

'Christine dug Motorhead?'

'Hell, no. Christine was a ballad kind of girl.'

'"The Ace of Spades" is a ballad, Reynard. Best catchy-ass boy's ballad ever.'

'Whatever,' I said crossly. 'But it's that kind of baggage I have to handle on my own right now. At home.'

'At home is for getting ready to go out.' Willie levelling with me now, closing in with his bar stool. 'You gotta wake up to the fact that ladies love you, man. They always did. They always will.'

'Sweet, I can't even score a damn drink.'

'Believe me, they love you. Mind and body.' The way he said it, loading that last word like he did his joints.

'You want me to get *laid*?'

'Call it catharsis. You need to move on.' Willie scanned the room, his eyes lingering on the tables where the prettiest girls were sitting. I sank into my cocktail.

'Behave,' I hissed at him. 'Don't make it so obvious.'

'Why not?' he retorted. 'Don't be so shy about your sexual needs.

Women like a man who's honest about himself. They know what's on your mind. Don't even try to hide it. They're not stupid, and it's insulting if you try to pretend otherwise. As long as you're up front with style and respect, it's OK. Take a leaf from your online brothers, just don't swallow the whole damn bible.'

'They're not my brothers. And I don't know I can play it so confident.'

'You can. You're just a little rusty.' My dealer's eyes fixed on a lone figure who had just floated into the room. A honey-haired fox in a red evening dress. 'Tell me you wouldn't want to sleep with her, we'll go home now. Leave her to the grown-ups.'

'Sweet, cut it out.' I practically had to stop him from waving her over.

'What's wrong with wanting to party?' he argued. 'Isn't she here to party too? This is a party, isn't it?'

Quietly I confirmed that it was.

'Then *entertain* her, bitch.'

'But things have changed, Willie. Eighteen months is a long time.'

'Women don't change. Men just understand less about them.'

'It's still a problem.'

'Not if you let her do the talking. Get her on a roll, all you have to do is look in her eyes and glance at her mouth every minute or so.'

'Her mouth?'

'Shows you're mesmerised by her words. Foxes love a listener. Forget about chat-up lines. Leave that to the wankers. It's not big and it's not clever. You want to impress, go in with a good question.'

'Like what is it with those slider things always knocking round the bathroom, that sort of thing?'

My dealer pulled back smartly. For a beat I thought he might come back and nut me.

'All I'm saying is don't fuck up by talking about *your* troubles. You're here tonight for her, understand me? She won't want to hear about Christine, just like they don't want to hear about it in cyberspace.'

'You think so?'

'Man, I know so. You talk to a plant about your problems, she withers. Can't fucking wait to die. But convince her she's a thing of beauty, refresh her roots at intervals, she's guaranteed to bloom. Maybe even blossom, if you play it right.'

I turned to study the girl in question one more time, and looked right back when I saw she was heading our way.

'Don't look up, Willie. Shit. Just react to me. Laugh or something.'

Willie drew two cigarettes from the pack. 'Smoke?'

'Anything.'

My dealer sparked me up. At the same time, I drew breath to ask him about the seeds, just to keep the conversation moving. But by then she had pulled up at the bar, directly behind Sweet, and I found myself lost for words.

'Your call, Reynard.'

I glanced at her again, and froze when I caught her eye. She smiled. I smiled. We both looked away. Upon which Sweet William made his own move.

'Stone me, look at the state of that!' His attention was locked on something behind me. I looked round, but I still didn't follow. Not immediately. All I could see was an empty booth. Then I saw the parlour palm, jammed into the gap behind, and remembered who I was with.

'It's just a tree; leave it out.'

'Look at her fronds. All curled up and yellowed.'

'This is a nightclub, Sweet. You don't get much sunlight in here.'

'That's no excuse,' he countered, and lurched from his stool to address the whole room. 'Where's the fucking *humanity*?'

I sensed the centre of attention focus right in on us.

'Willie,' I pleaded, still smiling. 'Not now.'

'Bollocks,' he thundered. 'That's criminal abuse. Torture. The management need consulting.'

I looked at my lap as Sweet William muscled his way to the spiral stairs. Wished the surrounding chatter would pick up quicker.

'Nice friend.' She was looking right at me now, the fox with the hair and the dress.

'Mother Nature's finest defender.'

A pause followed. Just for a beat. Not long enough to set into silence. I couldn't handle two in one day.

'Can I get you a drink?'

She ordered a vodka martini, and asked why she hadn't seen me here before.

'It's a long story,' I said, but stopped right there, remembering what Sweet had said about sounding sorry for myself. Then I thought of my forthcoming cat commercial, and figured I could make an impression before I came on strong with the questions. 'I'm in films, basically. Always a reshoot to take up your free time. How about you?'

'Films? *Really*? What kind?'

'Animal films,' I said, wincing inwardly. Realising that I had probably just scotched my chances to be the listener. I focused on her eyes, tried to think of a way to shift the attention across to her. Which was when she said:

'So what are you? A vet?'

'No. More a kind of . . . handler.'

'Wow,' she said, close enough now for me to see my own reflection in her gaze.

'Someone's got to do it, I guess.'

She didn't look much over twenty. Great skin. Great mouth too, in a full-lipped, forbidden kind of way.

'Is that how you got your face all scratched up?'

Watching her lips as Willie had suggested, I said, 'Better I get a few cuts than someone gets their head ripped off.'

'Amazing.'

'I'm Reynard, by the way. But friends call me Ren.'

She held out her hand, said her name was Zoë. I came to my senses, said Zoë was a nice name. Glad to have her back under the spotlight of the conversation again. She said that she was here because her flatmate worked for the magazine being toasted downstairs.

'But it looks as if I've lost her now.' She looked at me, lamb-like, with just a cursory glance over her shoulder.

'You want to sit down?'

'Sure.'

I sensed the mood shift a gear, and directed her to the booth behind me. The chase was on. We talked. About her. My input diminishing to little more than nods and smiles. Just as Sweet had told me. Nurturing her all the way. I freshened her glass, twice. I even held her gaze when she told me how shitty Daddy had just been for cutting down her college fees. Regardless of her family problems, Zoë was a quality fox. And here was I, closing in fast. Only for her to turn interrogator by going back to films again.

'What's your favourite?'

'Mine? God. I don't know. *Sweet Smell of Success* has to be pretty high up there. Anything starring Big Tony.'

'Tony?'

Maybe she was even younger than I had first thought.

'Curtis,' I said. 'Tony Curtis?'

Still she looked at me blankly.

'*The Great Imposter*? *Wild and Wonderful*? *The Defiant Ones*?'

Zoë shook her head on every prompt.

'As in father of Jamie Lee.'

A shy grin told me she was up to speed.

'Now we're on the same wavelength,' she said. 'I'm a girl, you have to put everything to me in the context of a relationship.'

'A *relationship*? Is that what you're looking for?' It was a reaction to the word, really. As if it had just tried to bite me. Desperate not to let the story of my love life leap out and lay waste to the moment, I leaned in to the cup of my hand. Clamping my jaw in the process.

Zoë moved in too, said, 'Depends where I wake up in the morning.'

My recovery was miraculous, and I was right there for her when she asked me for a cigarette. I took two, lit one for her, slipped the filter between her lips. Stayed so close she was obliged to exhale from the corner of her mouth. Just as a shadow fell between us.

'You should come with a government health warning, Reynard.'

I recognised her voice, and the nervous giggle. Damn it, I even recognised her shadow. Pulling right back from Zoë, I looked up and there she was.

'Christine.' I switched my cigarette from one hand to the other. 'God, you look good.'

She looked better than good. My ex looked pretty much transparent underneath the silver sheer slip dress she was wearing. For a moment I actually thought I recognised her black lace underwear. A present to myself the previous Christmas. Even her hair fell in such a way as to signpost the fact she was practically naked, and yet it was me who felt exposed. Vulnerable. Deeply alarmed, too. For Christine was just staring in my direction, looking slightly stunned. I knew she was basically stuck for something to say. That she'd come across with the best will in the world, and then blanked under pressure when Zoë and I both turned to face her. But I also knew that it didn't look too great. Not from where Zoë was sitting. The fox looking back at me in a new light now. Harsh and unforgiving. I tried to stand, hoping to disarm the atmosphere with an introduction, but the rim of the table prevented me from rising more than a couple of inches off the cushion.

'This ... this is Zoë,' I stammered, and a pained expression crossed my face. 'We were just talking about, um, relationships.' It was too late. I was going down fast. My sense of allegiance in a tailspin, I sank back on the seat and heard myself say, 'Not ours, obviously.' I couldn't breathe. Couldn't do anything but watch Christine turn nervously to the girl I had so badly affronted.

'Oops,' my ex pulled a stupid face. 'Rebound alert.'

I grimaced at her gaffe. So did Christine. Her subconcious may have just found a short cut to her mouth, but I could tell it was simply for want of something to say. My ex didn't possess a malicious bone in her body, and as I willed her to relax I realised it was only her body I'd really lost. What I needed now was tact on tap. Quick wits and class. In other words, I needed Christine to vanish, and steal the scene she was fast creating.

'Oh yes,' she declared suddenly, as if some great unseen presence had just whispered in her ear. 'I wanted to apologise about the other night, Ren. I know you didn't mean to pester, and I'm sorry I reacted so badly.'

'Pester?' spluttered Zoë, and looked at her in disbelief.

Christine turned to me again, bounced the same expression my way. I felt like sinking under the table. Escaping somehow from the paralysing tension my ex had brought upon herself, and then shared with us both. But before I could even attempt to move out Christine had focused on my scratches. I could see it on her face, what she was thinking. A chance to save the moment. And that was when I knew that I was finished.

'Congratulations,' she ventured. 'I've just seen Sweet, downstairs. He told me you're doing some cat food commercial. When will we see it?'

Weakly I explained that it was for the overseas market.

'How exotic!' cooed my ex, entirely oblivious to the girl now scowling across from me. 'I'm glad things are looking up so quickly.'

'Thanks,' I muttered bitterly.

'Love to chat more,' she said, evidently relieved to be drifting away.

'*Goodbye*, Christine.'

'Enjoy your drinks!'

By then, however, there wasn't actually anything left. Just the melted cubes in Zoë's glass which she upturned into my lap. Fortunately the drama went unnoticed. For in that very same moment my dealer reappeared at the top of the spiral stairs, one giant hand clamped round the scruff of a deeply shaken-looking suit.

The management, I presumed.

8

'Cats are often thought to interact more readily if there is only one tom in the territory.'
http://www.purradise.com/purrfect10.html

In a late-night poll of online males, not a single one listed HONESTY in their Virtual Vitals. I know, because I checked the Vault. Buzzwords such as SEX and FUCKING featured heavily. Not only in 'Interests' but 'Occupation' too. Surprisingly, ROCKET SCIENCE returned one screen name, though further investigation placed the term in typical context:

Screen Name:	**LIKRIK**
Real Name:	Ricky
M/F:	You callin' me a poof?
Age:	25
Marital Status:	I do wives
Location:	The Arsenal!
Occupation:	Tool Hire
Interests:	Girls who go down! Especially Asian Babes
Watch Word:	'Fuck rocket science. Let's fuck!'

To ensure some impartiality, I ran the same check on the female net contingency. HONESTY came up plenty. A virtue, sought in vain by so many. FUCKING was also a contender. As in 'no FUCKING men'. Interestingly, MEN itself returned a number of variations on the same theme: 'MEN don't bother me.' 'MEN, get a life!' 'Not into online MEN.' 'Only woMEN please.'

Following up a growing suspicion, I ran a search on LESBIAN, but was informed that there were too many online at that time to list. As a compromise, I tapped in BI FEMALE, and watched my computer crash.

Cyberspace. A new frontier for girls who could get boys in the real world, it seemed, but who now wished to find each other. A chance to get intimate first without getting physical. To connect without connecting. Such technology, I realised, was tailor-made for the closet female community. It relied on words to seduce. An art form which was lost on men. It just didn't click with us. We needed visual stimulus. As I waited impatiently for the system to restart, I began to wonder by extension whether it was these same women who had created the endless strips of online red-light websites. Was Internet porn just a means of distracting the macho majority, while the ladies got together on a one-to-one?

A bottle of sweet sherry helped me digest the question. I had nothing else in stock at the time. Which was around three in the morning. Indeed, it only came to light when I remembered to search the rack under the sink. The same place where I also stored the floor polish and toilet bleach. At the time it seemed the best place for it. An unwanted gift from a previous party. My twenty-fifth, if I remembered rightly. The kind of ropy old alcohol that kicks around for years, and finally gets sunk in a moment of desperation. Like the evening I trudged home from the Pandemonium with a damp crotch and a crisis of confidence.

Back in the club, I had tried my best to follow my dealer's advice. I was cool. I was confident. I was interested in her, and I was *honest.* Up to a point. And yet as a reward for all my efforts, I had a shirt which needed dry cleaning and a feeling that my ex was going to influence my life for some time to come.

I couldn't just forget about Christine. Not as Sweet had suggested. OK, I could delete her screen name from my Cyber Circle. I could even take solace in the fact that her online exhibitionism would never net her a more decent man than me. But I couldn't just wipe her from my memory. Only time would put things in perspective for me. And if Willie was right about women, that they didn't want to hear about my problems, then I was destined to stay out of the game until I could perform like the best of them.

My virtual efforts seemed pointless too. There was no point even trying to be a player in cyberspace when most of the foxes were pursuing a different game altogether. I raised my Vitals, sat back for a moment, and took a long last look at the loser I had created:

Screen Name:	Ren125733
Real Name:	Reynard. Ren, for short. Rennie at a push
M/F:	Male
Age:	27
Marital Status:	Single, as if I need reminding
Location:	London
Occupation:	Thesp
Interests:	Women, if they'll have me
Watch Word:	'Still searching . . .'

'What a sap,' I muttered to myself. 'Even I wouldn't want to date me.'

Did I really think a woman would be interested in a Quick-E with Ren125733? He didn't have much to offer, I realised now. Apart from a long sob story. I thought of all the other Rens out there. All 125732 of them. Every single one more charismatic than me. Even if they were just a bunch of primates.

Anyway, it was over. Time to bow out of the game.

I tapped into the field containing my name, and began to erase. From the last letter back to the first. Then I rolled down to the next field, the one that declared my sex, and there, in the blink of a cursor, I saw another side to me.

'I wonder . . .'

This time I didn't delete. As an exercise, a mere act of curiosity, I made an addition. A precursor to my masculine status. Seeing the result on the screen looked weird. Funny. Freaky.

M/F: **Female**

To complete the experiment, all I needed was a new name. Renee seemed only natural. I made the amendment and hit enter. The update confirmed, I promptly buried my head in my hands.

'What the fuck are you doing?' I asked myself, and immediately closed down my computer for the night.

I needed the sleep. Though you never realise these things until you wake up.

The next morning, I opened my eyes to a cathedral of light. Sunshine flaring through the skylights, illuminating my space. I put coffee on the ring, the Chairman of the Board through the speakers and myself in the bath. I felt refreshed. I felt beautiful. From the inside out. Really I did. As sweet as Sinatra Himself. Like a man with a future, not a past. One going places, too. I was expecting a car from the studio within half an hour. Something low-key, I guessed. Tinted windows, maybe. Nothing more. I imagined the Persian being chauffeured there in a limo, but was in no mood to bear grudges. Not today. The first of many dedicated to positive thinking. There would be no alcohol. No narcotics. No listening to my dealer. I would be deaf to his rules of engagement. Blind to his plan of attack. All talk of getting over my ex by getting off with someone new would hereby be ignored. Life involved so much more than the pursuit of women. And though I couldn't actually think of anything at the time, I pledged to work up a few ideas just as soon as I had wrapped with the cat.

I knew my resolve would hold when I clocked Sweet's bag of seeds and passed on the temptation to abuse a few. I still had no idea what they were, or what kind of kick they would bring. The previous night, with my appetite for self-destruction at its most intense, I had toyed with the idea of smoking some or infusing the lot into a tea. Now, my only inclination was to plant the damn things. Which

I did. In an old disk box, using soil scooped from the square outside. I positioned it on the sunny side of my hard-drive, convinced I had done the right thing. Once I'd killed off my ridiculous Virtual Vitals, the last legacy of my sorrier self, we would both be free to push our way up to the top.

As I logged on, I wondered what had possessed me to fool with my virtual gender in the first place. In that hour of darkness, I had done something dumb. Something silly. Something soon to be erased. Something that would have been cast from my life for ever, had I not been informed of post waiting.

One glance at the sender's screen name was enough for my hand to scurry for the mouse.

    email to: Ren125733
    from: BiRuth
    subject: still searching?

The bi bit made my heart race. I opened it immediately, unsure what I was supposed to be searching for.

    Hi Renee,
    Saw your Vitals, hun. Wondered whether you'd had any joy yet. Fancy
    some female guidance? bi for now, Ruth xxx

I felt guilty as hell. As if I'd opened mail sent to the wrong address. I even had to order up my damning Vitals to remind myself who I was supposed to be.

    Screen Name: Ren125733

    Real Name: Renee

    M/F: Female

    Age: 27

    Marital Status: Single, as if I need reminding

Location:	London
Occupation:	Thesp
Interests:	Women, naturally
Watch Word:	'Still searching . . .'

'Oh Jesus,' I whispered. 'What have I done?'

With just a simple online sex switch, I had gone from sounding like a pitiful young man to a pitiful young lesbian. One who pretty much begged me just then to erase her from existence. This time, I didn't bother wiping out each field. I just hit Delete All, and watched my female incarnation vanish into the virtual equivalent of a black hole. It was done. It was clean. It was kind. I now had no Virtual Vitals. Just a screen name. If anyone wanted to contact me now, they would have to know me personally.

A moment's silence followed. Not in respect. But relief. It would have extended a lot longer, had a Quick-E not flared upon my screen.

Quick-E to: Ren125733

BiRuth:	Boo! ;o)

A wink. The semi-colon read sideways. This fox knew her netiquette.

Quick-E to: Ren125733

BiRuth:	I took the liberty of adding you to my Cyber Circle last night.

Two messages in as many seconds. I had never been so hit upon in all my time online. I thought about logging off, running away from the intrusion. But this BiRuth seemed so keen. I just couldn't pull the plug on her.

Ren125733:	I'm flattered.

The truth? I really was. It was also the right thing to say.

| BiRuth: | Pleasure, hun. xx You seen my Vitals? |
| Ren125733: | Gimme a second . . . |

I couldn't help it, but on reading through her details I was slightly disappointed. Then again, my last lesbian encounter dated from my school days, when a mate let me peek at one of his dad's specialist magazines. It had been a formative experience, but sadly one which left me with high expectations of a Scandinavian nature.

Screen Name:	BiRuth
Real Name:	Ruth
M/F:	Redhead bi fem
Age:	Dirty thirties
Marital Status:	Understanding husband
Location:	London
Occupation:	This one
Interests:	Girlies
Watch Word:	'Stop me and bi one'

I flicked back to the Quick-E box. Already there was a new line waiting for me.

BiRuth:	Like it?
Ren125733:	You bet!
BiRuth:	Perfect match, eh?
Ren125733:	Your husband doesn't mind?
BiRuth:	Hub's cool. As long as I'm safe.

Ren125733:	So you've done this before?
BiRuth:	Try stopping me! U?

Sideways symbols and now shorthand. I might have been up to speed on the virtual lingo, but I was in no position to take the lead. Not with someone this assertive. I decided to play it coy. The wallflower approach.

Ren125733:	Not yet. Never done anything like it before in my life.
BiRuth:	Curious, right?
Ren125733:	Only since I went online.
BiRuth:	It's a girl's world, hun. Go with it.
Ren125733:	So what happens now?
BiRuth:	Tell me something about u that I don't know.

For a beat I considered telling her the truth. Levelling the playing field by switching back to my natural side. Holding out hope that this bi would still want to play ball. But then my curiosity really was growing by the second. Unwilling to risk being knocked back by coming clean, I conjured Christine in mind and proceeded to paint a picture of her.

Ren125733:	I've just finished with my boyfriend.
BiRuth:	You're bi! I like you even more!
Ren125733:	It was a bit of a shock for him.
BiRuth:	Men deserve a taste of their own medicine. Did he treat u badly?
Ren125733:	No. It was about me really, not him.
BiRuth:	Always wise to tell them that :o)

I pursed my lips and kept typing.

Ren125733:	Anyway, enough about him.
BiRuth:	OK, let's talk about your Vitals.
Ren125733:	What about them?
BiRuth:	Have u found what you're searching for?
Ren125733:	Maybe.
BiRuth:	My offer still stands.

My heart was galloping now. This wasn't right, but what made it even more weird was the fact that I was beginning to feel a bit turned on. Charged up by the course of our conversation. Even my keyboard felt sensual to the touch. Something I had never appreciated before. Certainly not as a man, at any rate. I was even beginning to think in a different way. Going against my natural instinct to seize an offer before it was withdrawn, I found myself wanting to *tease*.

Ren125733:	I could certainly use a sensitive pair of hands.

Five. Ten. Fifteen seconds passed, and I feared that I had overstepped the mark. But then BiRuth got back to me, with a question I could only answer by slipping into Christine's shoes once more.

BiRuth:	Do u look as sweet as u sound?
Ren125733:	Oh yes. Actually I've just bought a new dress. A see-thru number, to celebrate being single again.
BiRuth:	Tell me more, hun.
Ren125733:	Let me see, I'm tall. Very athletic, with great hair that I can style to fall right over my knock . . . breasts.

Knockers. What was I *thinking*? That kind of boob I couldn't afford to give away. If I was to get any further, I would have to get right inside the head of Renee. Think more like a lady and less like a man. Still, BiRuth seemed more attentive to content than style.

BiRuth:	Hun u r the 1. I like a well-groomed girl.
Ren125733:	Glad you're impressed.
BiRuth:	Can I ask u one more thing?
Ren125733:	Shoot.
BiRuth:	U won't be upset?
Ren125733:	Ask me anything.
BiRuth:	Are u shaved?

Instinctively I rubbed my chin, then stopped still when I reinterpreted her question from a female point of view. Within the space of a few minutes, I had become so intimate with a woman that she felt able to question my pubic state. I was embarrassed things had gone this far, but thrilled we might go further.

Ren125733:	Well, that's for me to know.
BiRuth:	And me to find out?
Ren125733:	Maybe.
BiRuth:	I think perhaps we should meet.

BiRuth certainly knew what she wanted, but I was still reeling over the shaved thing. Be honest, Sweet had said. Don't be so shy about your sexual needs. This was one thing coming from a man. But when the tables were turned, I wasn't sure whether I should have been flattered or furious. Desperately I tried to think what a fox like me would say.

Ren125733:	Would you respect me afterwards?

BiRuth?	After what?
Ren125733:	After sleeping together.
BiRuth:	Easy, hun, I think we should meet for coffee first!!

Damn. Did I sound like a slapper? I moved on quickly.

Ren125733:	Sorry, new at this game.
BiRuth:	Don't worry about it. I like a forward planner.
Ren125733:	So where would we meet?
BiRuth:	Somewhere public. Just in case. How about Cafe Ragueneau in Soho?

I thought ahead. Not just for her safety, but mine too.

Ren125733:	Will your husband be there?
BiRuth:	He watches out for me, but I'm a free agent.
Ren125733:	How will I recognise you?
BiRuth:	Leave it to me. I know a bi when I see 1.
Ren125733:	OK, when?
BiRuth:	I'm free this evening.
Ren125733:	Half seven?
BiRuth:	Date! :o) xxxxxx

I was euphoric, and clapped my hands together over the keyboard. Right then my maleness didn't come into it. Blinkered to the outside world, online was all that mattered. This bond I had formed with a total stranger. The words we had exchanged through cyberspace, culminating in a time and a place to meet. All my previous insecurities seemed suddenly insignificant. Here was a woman who *wanted* me. A delusion which was brought to an abrupt end by the sound of a car horn blaring.

My pick up had arrived. Reality was waiting. Within a few hours, I would be expected to sell cat food to a continent that very probably regarded the animal itself as a delicacy. I logged off in a hurry, blushing in the wake of what had just happened, and wondered whether I was seriously cut out for the part.

9

At the studio, I sat in my dressing room without uttering a word.
Indeed, I felt no obligation to strike up any small talk when the
make-up artist leaned in close with the lip gloss. The very same
vision that had reduced me to a silent mass of self-doubt over
recent days. This time she wore her long black locks folded up
into a loose knot. The kind of knot I would normally fantasise
about pulling free. A knot that crowned the sort of gypsy look
no red-blooded male would dream of moving off their patch. Yet I
was above such distraction this time. Desensitised even to the navel
piercing that peeked over the rim of her hipster threads. A gold
ring. Possibly twenty-four carat. Frequently she came close enough
for me to test it between my teeth, but my brain didn't have room
to register the thought and heat up my cheeks. She was the most
phenomenal-looking fox I had ever seen. The way she looked. The
way she moved. The way she *breathed*. Everything about her was
perfect. But in the wake of my online deception I was consumed
by more immediate matters.

Like how I was going to handle a date with a bisexual woman.
One who was expecting me to be a she.

When the producer came to collect me, I considered coming
clean to her. In view of our previous chat, I thought maybe she
was someone who would understand. The problem was I couldn't be
sure which website she had meant me to visit. Maybe she genuinely
figured I could find enlightenment among cat fanciers. It was one
thing to reveal that instead I had checked out some girl-on-girl
chat room. Quite another to admit I'd then tried my hand as a

woman myself. So instead, when she asked me if I had followed up her recommendation, I said, 'My computer's out of action. I'm strictly offline.'

We were on our way down to the studio at the time, and the producer chose not to follow up my response. Judging by her offhand manner, I figured perhaps she just didn't care. I should have been fraught with doubt, my self-esteem a scuppered wreck. And yet the fact that I had connected with anyone at all served to keep me focused.

If I had got this far with BiRuth, I thought, then what could stop me going all the way? Sure, the initial revelation might be a bit awkward, but once my date got over the shock she'd see that I was sane. And available. Under the circumstances, wouldn't it make sense for her to hit that switch inside her and make do with a man?

I nurtured the idea throughout my time in front of the camera that morning. Even though I had to retake the final shot. Three times. The director was eager to glean a genuine air of submission from me when my co-star showed its claws, but it was hard to achieve while feeling increasingly more optimistic. Despite the delay, we were wrapped by lunchtime. After shopping for a few provisions, across the road from the studio, I decided to ask my driver to drop me off at the flower market. I wanted to savour Sweet's reaction when I pulled up with my news.

'You plank,' he yelled. 'Don't *ever* fucking do that again!'

'What?' I asked, palms spread. I had only just stepped onto the pavement behind his stall, and this was how he greeted me.

My dealer exhaled sharply, and removed his hand from inside his puffa. I wasn't sure if he had just been reaching for his heart or something heavier. By the way the tension vanished from his face I feared it might have been the latter.

'In my line of work,' he snapped, waving derisively at the car as it turned out of Columbia Road, 'a smoked-out motor says one thing to me.'

'That your best friend's finally made it?' I quipped, but Willie was far from laughing. I apologised. Quickly. I hadn't meant to look like a drug lord, I assured him. Though I had meant to impress.

'You scored with the fox from last night?' he asked, suddenly calming right down. 'Even with a damp lap?'

'Not exactly, no.'

I told him about my forthcoming date. How I had met BiRuth online and agreed to meet her that evening. My dealer responded by whistling for his apprentice.

'Cover for me,' he instructed the boy, then turning back said, sotto, 'Did you do anything with those seeds?'

'No,' I began, but Sweet was onto me before I could finish.

'Well, something's made you lose your bitch mind! What possessed you to set up a date with a woman like that? She's after pussy, Reynard. Not plonkers!' My dealer was turning heads again. I sometimes wondered how he managed to stay in business for so long.

'But it's not like she's completely off men.' I ushered him into the canvas gap between his stall and the next. 'She swings both ways.'

'She'll swing for you, all right! If I was in her position, I'd fucking flatten you.'

'But Willie, you're not a fox with a penchant like hers. You don't think like one. You don't operate in the same way. You have no idea of their needs.'

'So you're the recognised expert on the bisexual lifestyle, right?'

'No,' I said, and opened the plastic bag I was carrying. I handed him the book I had just bought. Flushed some when he read out the title.

'*Bisexuality For Beginners.*' My dealer looked at me gravely, and then flicked through from cover to cover.

'There aren't any pictures, Willie. It's not that sort of book.'

Ignoring me, he held the tome by its spine. As if checking to see if something might fall out.

'You bought this? In daylight?'

'I said it was for your mother.'

Nothing. No reaction. My dealer didn't even twitch. This was serious. He re-examined the cover, an apple with a bite taken from both sides. Then he jabbed a finger at the author's name, and his forehead buckled into a single crease.

'A.C. Découcher. What kind of name is that?'

I snatched the book from him, annoyed at his lack of support, and turned to the biographical notes. '"A.C. Découcher was born in 1965, and is an active campaigner for bi-rights."'

'So? Girl or boy writer?'

'It doesn't say.'

My dealer shook his head at me, like some surgeon faced with a flatliner. He glanced back down at the bag.

'What else you got in there? *Self-Help For Sad Men?*'

It was a little book of make-up tricks actually. An impulse buy from a counter display. As I saw it, a little inside knowledge might give me something to talk about if I ever found myself in a make-up chair again. My dealer tried to peer inside. I twisted the handles so he couldn't see.

'Give me a break, Sweet. At least I'm getting out there. "Be a player," you said. "Show the foxes you want to party."'

'Luring a bi babe on a date under the pretext that you're a woman too is not partying. That's gate-crashing.'

'But it has to be worth a try,' I argued. 'If you weren't such a blagger we would never have got into the Pandemonium last night.'

'I had an invite, Reynard. Always do. I just pull strings for you.'

'But my foot's in the door here. She *likes* me. She said so herself. As long as I keep it up when we meet, there's no reason why she won't settle for the male version of me.'

'So you've spoken?'

'Online. Yes. This morning.'

'What did you discuss?'

Awkwardly, I said, 'Bi things.'

Sweet William shot me a quizzical look. I held his gaze for a second, then crumbled.

'All right,' I confessed. 'She asked if I was shaved.'

My dealer grinned. A huge, expansive grin bracketed by two fat cheeks. I could see his next question ticking over.

'Don't ask,' I warned him. 'Don't even think it.'

'What can I say?' Sweet said instead. 'If you can't see what a ridiculous game you're playing, then you deserve everything you get. She's *bisexual*, Reynard. That doesn't make her a nympho. And even if she was, let's say you struck lucky, it's not going to keep your candle lit for long.'

'Why not? She might have some friends.'

'Which is the problem. Because with two sides to her sexuality, how can you be sure she'll ever be satisfied by you alone? As a man, there are things you can't provide. So even if you did get it together, think how insecure you'd feel every time a fox walked by and you both followed with your eyes.'

'Who's to say she'd exclude me?' I levelled the book at him. 'I'm sure A.C. Découcher has something to say about your view that bisexuals can't be faithful to one person.' I decided to withhold the fact that Ruth had said she was married.

Willie scoffed at me. 'Theory and practice. Two very different things. Like fantasy and reality. One of which you've left behind, Reynard. For God's sake, you don't even know what this BiRuth looks like.'

'I have an idea in my head.'

'Let me guess. Tall. Slim. Blonde. *Panting* for sex, maybe?'

'She's a redhead, actually.'

'Don't get fly with me, bitch. You know what I mean.'

'BiRuth said she can recognise a bi when she sees one. Why shouldn't I?'

My dealer glanced heavenward. 'I was wrong about you getting out more,' he said. 'You were right all along. You need to stay *in*. With no connection to the outside world. Somewhere you won't bother other people until you realise this whole plan is going to hurt everyone involved, including yourself.'

I was getting nowhere. The only thing moving on was the time, taking with it my fast-thinning patience.

'I was hoping you'd be pleased, Sweet. That maybe you'd admire

73

my initiative. Because I've tried it your way, and all it got me was a dry-cleaning bill.'

'My way doesn't involve messing with people you don't understand.' My dealer sounding gruff again. Squaring up to me now. 'My way won't leave you feeling like a short-sighted shitbag.'

A fleck of spit hit my eye, but I didn't flinch, or back away. Not after an outburst like that.

'I don't even know why I listen to you,' I declared, and jabbed at his breastbone. 'You talk about foxes but I've never seen you put your words into action. You're always on the sidelines, Willie. I've never seen you *chase*.'

'Enough, Reynard,' he warned me. 'You're still upset over Christine.'

'Christine is another thing,' I snapped back. 'You know what, I think you sent her across to see me in the Pandemonium.'

'Will you stop it? Coming on like this, already.'

'I think you knew Zoe was puckering up to kiss me at the time. So you get my ex to mess up my chances because I'm going places without you.'

'Says the man who wants to be a woman now.'

'Is that the problem here, Willie? Have I touched a nerve because I'm trying something a little different? Reinventing myself in a way that makes you uneasy? You got something you want to share? Something you want to get off your damn back? What is it with you and women?' I asked, almost yelling now. 'Just whose side are you on?'

Whatever he was about to say, my outburst served to stop it. Instead, my dealer levelled his gaze. Narrowed his field of vision. Looked at me like he was looking right through to the tarpaulin behind. As if I had just revealed something about myself which he always suspected. All of a sudden, just as Willie had warned, I felt like a shitbag.

'Sweet, I didn't mean anything by that.'

But Willie was finished with our conversation, and had already turned to go back to his stall.

'Really, I'm sorry. I don't know what's got into me.'

He stopped at this, but didn't turn, the man who had stood in for my parents all these years, and I wondered if I was about to lose him too.

'Whatever it is, Reynard, see it through. Just don't come back to me until you've got it out of your system.'

10

'The bisexual community is invisible. Until you show an interest in joining.'
A.C. Découcher, *Bisexuality For Beginners*
Each Way Press, San Francisco 1995

The vibes weren't right from the moment I arrived. Cafe Ragueneau was far smaller than I had anticipated, seating only a dozen customers. That all the corner tables were occupied only conspired to tighten my nerves. A kind of waiting-in-the-wings anxiety which had sprung from my spat with Sweet. Loitering there on the threshold, without a computer to hide behind, I felt vulnerable, exposed, ridiculous. As if I was wearing a sandwich board that displayed the damning details of my Virtual Vitals.

Hard as it was to look around without appearing like a nutter off the street, it seemed that nobody else was weighed down by the same burden. If BiRuth was already here, I thought, she had certainly hidden herself well. And even if she did have an eye for a bi female, I could hardly expect her to stand up and wave *me* over.

This wasn't a blind date, I realised now. This was blind stupidity.

A tide of misgivings flowed through my mind, but I knew that if I let them push me back I would just feel worse about myself. In a bid to steady my resolve, I took a window seat beside the door, then ordered up a pot of tea and some cake.

'Cake's finished,' the waitress informed me. 'We're closing in fifteen minutes.'

'Just tea will be fine then.'

'Pot for two?'

'Whatever,' I said, anxious not to attract more attention to myself.

The place was pretty full. Even at this time. Shoppers seeking refuge from the streets. Two deflated-looking cycle couriers. Both male. A woman with a cream and custard blue crew neck that matched the Pest Control van parked outside, and a posse of students whose massed collection of empty cups suggested they had been there all day. The shoppers were closer to sixty than thirty, and ringed by bulging supermarket bags. Not the kind of thing one would carry to a date. The students were way too young, and I was just beginning to get seriously concerned about the rat catcher when the door chimes tinkled. I glanced across to see not one but two candidates walk in and then fan out for separate tables. The only tables unoccupied in the cafe. These women looked very different, I noticed, when I finally got it together to act natural. Apart from the fact that they were both around the target age and could each be described as redheads.

'Just what I needed,' I said quietly, partly to myself and also to the waitress as she served me.

Suspect number one had natural auburn corkscrew curls and was my kind of fox. Leopard skin mules. Thigh high skirt. Three quarter length coat favoured by class act strippers. She asked for an iced tea. It came quickly, and she watched me watching her take a long, leisurely suck on the straw. Suspect number two, meanwhile, had gone directly for the free seat on the far side. She wore Doc Marten boots. Camouflage pants. Scuffed leather jacket favoured by class war advocates. Her army issue buzz cut was as red as you could get, even if it was from a bottle. She ordered coffee. Black. No sugar. Then she saw me watching her and scowled. I dipped into my tea, discovered to my cost that it was boiling hot.

I was confused. Deeply so. In appearance, I expected BiRuth to occupy the middle ground. Somewhere that sent out signals to both parties. Neither of the women up for consideration fell into that category. I was faced with a pair of sexual extremists. One guaranteed to get a man hot under the collar. Another dressed in a way that left me cold. But what the hell was I expecting? I needed to consult my manual some more. Get the view from the inside out. But flicking through a book about bisexuality was not an option. Not in public. Not unless it was me who wanted to be judged by the cover. Indeed, it was appearances that demanded my attention when two more customers walked into the cafe. First a close-cropped polecat with ears ringed like curtain rails, and then a sober-looking man in a pinstripe. The fox with the iced tea let the straw fall from her lips and smiled. She stood up, but the suit went the other way, and into the arms of GI Jane. I turned my attention back to the fox. She certainly looked pleased to see the polecat. I didn't see either couple leave, however. I was too busy digging deep for my wallet.

Sweet, I feared, was right. I really didn't understand the rules of this game. I wasn't even qualified to be a player. Worse, I had lost a friend for the chance of this futile trial. If Ruth was here then she was invisible to me. Drawing solace from a cigarette, I managed to stretch out my tea for a further five minutes. Still I prayed she would make a late arrival, even as the cafe began to empty out. Finally the waitress flipped the closed sign on the door, and I lost all hope. Even the woman with the van didn't seem interested in me. Certainly not when she got up to leave. Then again, the focus of my attention had shifted from her to the customer sitting at the table behind. The one whose presence had previously been obscured from me. At first I thought it was a wraith. A ghost-thin thirtysomething with a shock of white hair and little round glasses. Someone who looked far older than the years he had lived. A man who regarded me with a terrible air of familiarity.

'Renee, I presume.' His voice was weak, but it crashed over me. I felt revulsion, shame, indignation and fury but, above all, *relief*.

'You're Ruth, aren't you?'

We both stood up. As he made his way to my table, I wondered briefly whether I should brace myself for a fist fight. He didn't look like he was going to swing for me, however, though I did hesitate before shaking hands.

'So,' I said sourly. 'Is this something we need to discuss? Or shall we just pretend it never happened and go our separate ways?'

'Gentlemen,' the waitress called across the cafe. 'We're closing up.'

Ruth pushed the chair back under the table. 'I could use a stiff drink,' he said. 'How about you?'

I wasn't happy with his choice of words. After all, we barely knew each other.

'I'll be straight with you,' I told him, on the way out of the cafe. 'I'm not gay.'

'Not even bisexual?'

'Not with men.'

'Then, sister,' he smiled, gesturing at a pub opposite, 'we have a great deal in common.'

My date could talk. Having ordered us a couple of bitters, Ruth served up his story from the start. His screen name had been in existence for some time, he began, but formerly it belonged to his wife. A bit of fun, so she told him. The opportunity to exercise the dormant side of her sexuality. Virtually, of course.

'It was a thrill for us both,' he explained. 'I would watch over her shoulder while she hooked up with women who felt the same desires. Curious bisexual females. The net's heaving with them, Renee.'

'Tell me about it,' I said, wishing he'd stop calling me that.

'Sometimes she revealed things via the keyboard that even *I* didn't know about her. For months I watched her flower. Role-playing a fantasy under my watchful eye. Even when she appeared to lose interest, she still performed for me. Using our computer, as I saw things, to bring us closer together.'

I lit a cigarette, uneasy about being taken into such close confidence. For it seemed to me that BiRuth had shored up this story for some time. Like I was the first person to hear it flooding out.

'So, what happened?'

'I came home one evening and found she'd taken things offline without me.' He tailed off to attend to his pint, focusing ruefully on some imaginary point midway between us. I imagined BiRuth waiting up for his wife. A single light burning in a house enshrouded by darkness.

'Must have been a long night for you.'

He quit gazing into nothing, and turned his eyes on me. 'It still is.'

I suggested a chaser, turning to the bar before he could refuse. I had heard enough. I couldn't face him any more. Not now I knew why those orbs of his were so sunken. Sadly, the Scotch I ordered served only to fire him on.

'She just disappeared from my life,' he lamented. 'It was as if the virtual world laid claim to her. She didn't call. She didn't write. She didn't email. All I have left is her screen name.'

'And a hot set of Vitals,' I offered sympathetically.

'If only it would help me meet a woman who knows her.'

I felt bad. Like I was the only one who had been dishonest about myself, somehow. We had very different motives, but right then I was deeply embarrassed about mine. More so when BiRuth looked up and asked me if I had come across a real bi redhead during the course of my online travels.

'Christ, no!' I said quickly. 'I was telling the truth when I said I've never done anything like this before.'

'You're not the first bloke to try,' he told me, and took a slug from the shot glass. 'Although I've never met one who's had the balls to take the masquerade offline. The kind of man who makes out he's female usually regards a lesbian cybersex session as the ultimate triumph. Going for the real thing is something else entirely.'

'I'm not like the others,' I argued. 'The only reason I gave up as a man was because the women of the web assumed I was just one more sad bastard. This way, I figure I get a chance to prove I'm genuine.'

'By pretending to share their persuasion?'

'I prefer to see it as empathy,' I reasoned, and took shelter behind a cigarette when BiRuth's hollow cheekbones tightened.

'So what happens when you step out as a heterosexual male? How were you planning on spinning it to me, had I been the woman you were waiting for?'

I pulled on my smoke for inspiration. 'You tell me,' I said eventually. 'You're so experienced.'

This time, his gaze failed to spook me. If I wanted to be a halfway dyke online, I thought, then no man had the right to stop me. Even one who had been there before with the love of his life, and lost her in the process. I finished my drink. It was time to leave this husk of a husband.

'I'm sorry about your wife,' I said, 'but you're wrong about me. I'm under no illusion that every woman needs a good man to make her see straight, and nor do I get my kicks from fooling anyone. I gave it a shot tonight because I've been rejected every other way, and this was all I had left.'

I turned for the door, only to come full circle when BiRuth said, 'You have to make the most of yourself.'

I furrowed my brow. Pulled hard on the cigarette.

'If you're going to succeed,' he continued. 'then at least make an effort before you meet. Do something with your Virtual Vitals. *Sell* your presence. Demand some attention, but don't just accept the first offer like you did with me.'

'I'm not that easy,' I protested.

'No, you're good. You fooled me, but you have a lot to learn.'

'You really think I can do it?'

He shrugged, switched his glass from one hand to the other. 'My wife was just like you when she first logged on. That's why I made contact. Because you reminded me of her. Unsure of herself but eager to please, however probing the question.' I dared not touch my chin, despite a sudden itch. 'In time,' he continued, 'she learned not to reveal all until she really felt a connection. It earned her respect. Something I wasn't giving her. To my cost I guess it finally found her the perfect partner. But if you want to follow in her footsteps, Reynard, you have to find a voice. Learn to sing before you fly. And get a scanner too.'

'A scanner?'

'Everyone likes to see a face eventually. Obviously not yours, but something to keep her keen while you work on her heart. Just *never* send a porn shot. Too obvious. Male giveaway.'

'Why are you telling me this?' I asked.

BiRuth returned his glass to the bar, and extended his hand to me. 'Because I never know who you might meet. The more eyes looking out online for my wife, the more chance I have of finding her for real.'

We shook on it. I understood.

'Before you go,' I said, and held his grip, 'just how do you recognise a bisexual female when you see one?'

Smiling briefly, he said, 'Back in the cafe, when you saw me, something clicked between us, didn't it? You knew I was the woman you were waiting for.'

'I guess.'

'Then you have your answer.'

Had he winked at me, I would have clocked him. As it was, I felt a renewed sense of confidence in my alter ego.

'Good luck, girl.' He floated from my grasp. 'Don't let the side down.'

'I'll do my best,' I assured him, and glanced at my watch.

If I hurried, the computer store would still be open. I looked up again, for I wanted to ask if he could recommend the best scanner for the job, but already BiRuth had vanished. His absence suddenly creeped me. Even his empty glass had gone, and though the barman was now filling the washer, I was left with the idiot feeling that I had imagined the whole encounter.

I stubbed out my cigarette, mindful of the fact that there was no hash left back at my space. Still, I figured a straight head was what I needed. Even before I began to inch my way through the scrum, in fact, I had set my sights on logging on.

11

*'Good make-up shouldn't aim to transform the way
you look, but it must enhance the way you feel about
yourself.'*
Verity Pepper, *Make Up a Million*
Essence Editions, London 1998

I laboured deep into the night, forgoing snacks, cigarettes, even the overhead lights. Illuminated by the computer screen, I worked with a passion on my Virtual Vitals, trying out different names, interests, occupations. Reinventing, rehearsing and refining. Leaving no room for misinterpretation. Making her unmistakable.

On occasion, in my pursuit of authenticity, I would consult the Découcher manual. My bi-ble. Yet ultimately I was guided by the words of advice I had picked up on the way. It may have been my baby, but other people were responsible for its conception. My dealer. BiRuth. The producer, even. Despite their very different opinions, I hoped they would be proud of me eventually. A prospect that became ever more realistic as I continued to breathe life into my online creation. Preparing for her imminent arrival.

The net was a no-man's land. That much was clear to me now, and it left me little option. If I wanted to find a new woman and attempt to win her round, then first I would have to become one myself. A little underhand, maybe, but this brave new world was in its infancy. A World Wild West. Lawless and morally ambivalent. A digital wilderness that would see the strongest survive. Where only males like me who crossed the divide would conquer. Those left behind? They had basically signed themselves up for their own extinction. It was only a matter of time.

Overhead, for all I knew, a storm could have been massing. Were rain to patter upon the skylights, I would have continued to work oblivious. Hunched there over the keyboard. Frowning in concentration, muttering to myself on occasion and once even cackling with glee. As my grand design approached completion, I was indeed beyond distraction. Although come midnight a ragged shock of lightning might have turned my head high. Just as my modem shrieked and a unique presence was finally delivered to the virtual world.

She was here. She was mine. She was *me.*

Screen Name:	**NuBiFem**
Real Name:	Ask and I might tell
M/F:	100% fem
Age:	27. 5'11. 36–26–36
Marital Status:	Free
Location:	London
Occupation:	I get bi
Interests:	Online fun, offline frolics
Watch Word:	'Men, don't bother me in this world'

NuBiFem. New Bisexual Female. An incandescent trinity, so I thought. Coming together like a lush lipstick kiss across the monitor. Steaming up the screens and girding up the loins of any fox out there with a woman in mind. Ideally half a mind, I should stress, for that's where my alter ego came into her own. It was beautiful, just thinking of the times that lay ahead. If I had lost it in one realm, I would find it here in the other.

I felt like a new dad, though I couldn't broadcast my news. Not until I had found a pretty picture to slip into my new scanner. If her Vitals were anything to go by, however, I was sure she would be an irresistible fox. Even thinking about stepping into her cyber slingbacks proved too much at the end of this long session, so I got up to switch on the lights and grab a fag from the packet on my coffee table. Flicking through a copy of *Staple* while I smoked didn't help take my mind off things. After stepping out of the computer store, I had stopped in at the newsagent next door and bought the first issue. The magazine was pretty much an endless centrefold of end-list babes. The kind of content that quite brazenly appealed to men of the lowest common denominator. Two good reasons why I was confident about selecting a face no sophisticated bisexual woman would have come across before.

In particular, I had my eye on a shot of some cable TV kids' show presenter. That she wasn't splayed into some post-watershed pose appealed to me. As did her lack of any apparent Scandinavian breeding. What's more, the photograph had been deliberately styled to appear like an amateur snap. Slightly out of focus. No balance or hidden depth. Just your basic catch-me-at-home-in-my-catsuit kind of look. She was ideal. The one for me. Not too glamorous or unapproachable, pornographic or pristine.

Truly the bi next door.

I set about tearing out the whole page, but in my haste I nearly ripped her head off. It was a close call, and as I searched out a pair of scissors I was reminded of BiRuth's advice. Take things slowly, he had said. Learn to sing before you fly. And so, after safely scanning the image onto my hard-drive, I considered switching off for the night. Not least because my neck and shoulders ached after being at my desk for so long. I stood up again and stretched, then resolved that if I turned in now I would just end up lying awake. I couldn't close my eyes. Not now I knew she was here. Her picture filling my screen. I was exhausted, but she was looking right at me. Pleading with me to sit down again. Pouting when I resisted, then smiling wickedly when finally I swayed and let her out to play.

12

*'Introduce a new cat to the household by confining it to
one area for a while.'*
http://www.purradise.com/purrfect10.html

I was ten when I first dropped my shorts for a girl. Sadly, Becky
Vogler reneged on the promise to show me hers and instead fled
tearfully to her mummy. At twelve, Tasha Park would secure her
reputation as a teen bitch by telling everyone that she had opened
her eyes during our first snog to find me 'staring at her like a serial
killer'. While we reconciled our differences at a party the following
Christmas, my bid to further the festivities was cut off by her at
the panty line. Losing my virginity to her older sister should have
righted the injustice, only fifteen seconds didn't count as sex in her
book. Just sad, as she said so cuttingly. I would have to wait until
drama school before I got a chance to work on my performance,
and from there things slowly improved. By the time I slept with
Christine, I was a natural. Not perfect. Just experienced. As far as
I could see, my rite of passage was complete. The milestones in my
sexual history lay behind me. Clipped and chipped, maybe. But at
least there was nothing new for me to leap over. Nothing more to
botch on my first attempt.

Then I stepped online in my virtual heels, a man in digital drag,
and promptly tripped over two Quick-E's. In my eagerness to please,
I just didn't scrub up to the image I had hoped to project. If
anything, I felt like a tennis lesbian. More Billie Jean than sexy bi.

Quick-E to: NuBiFem

VulVal:	Wow! Some Vitals. I can almost smell you.
NuBiFem:	You can?

VulVal:	What are you wearing?
NuBiFem:	Catsuit. No panties.
VulVal:	Actually I meant your perfume.
NuBiFem:	Oops. Can we start again?
VulVal:	Sorry. Bye.

'Your loss,' I muttered, mostly to myself, just as the second shot bounced over my side of the net.

Quick-E to: NuBiFem

Megs11:	Tell me more, hun.
NuBiFem:	Want to know what perfume I'm wearing?
Megs11:	Easy. Why don't we start with your name.
NuBiFem:	Renee.
Megs11:	OK, so what perfume are you wearing, Renee?

My fingers hovered over the keyboard, ready to fire off an answer, but nothing came to mind. Nothing since my adolescence, at any rate. A time when perfume ads could take me to a place where only bigger boys said they'd been. When I finally got there with a girl, I guess I lost the scent. Principally because I didn't have to worry about how to remove it at the end of a date. Unlike the rest of her outfit. Later on, Christine would always atomise herself on a daily basis, but even then I couldn't say what notes she sounded. I might have funded her fragrance supply, but my selection was informed by one overriding factor: price. If it cost a lot, she would like it. Which wasn't much help to me now. I focused on the cursor. Alarmed that it wasn't blinking on the screen any more so much as steadily counting me out. I had to give this bi something. Any name would do. Even if it was the schoolboy in me who did the typing.

| NuBiFem: | Tramp. |

Megs11:   What? Me or the brand?

NuBiFem: How about if I said both?

'Smooth,' I assured myself, and rubbed my hand together.

Megs11:   I'd say you have a lot to learn.

NuBiFem: So teach me, doll.

Megs11:   Sorry, don't do remedial classes.

I closed the window, resigned to the fact that I had screwed up two chances. I really did have a lot to learn. Only this time I couldn't afford to make more mistakes. I would have to think on my feet. No matter how unsteady I felt. I drew a long breath, and knew I had to go on. Backing out was not an option. Not now that I had proved my online presence could attract the right attention. It was just a question of living up to my Vitals. And so in the wake of my wobbly start, I set off along the virtual highways and bi-ways in a bid to build my character. Pulling in at contact websites where women were looking for women. Sitting in silently on meet markets all over the virtual world. Listening in on Sapphic chat room conversations. Determined not to falter. To walk, this time, before I talked.

Twenty minutes was all I needed to compose myself, in mind and made-up body. Indeed, when I finally ascended to the all girl heaven of purradise.co.uk I felt like a new woman.

I couldn't say what kind of reception I expected. Internet technology hadn't quite evolved to communicate a round of applause. Even if it had, the sum total of three screen names would have mustered no more than a slow hand clap. Who knows, maybe most bi girls were in bed before midnight, but at least it meant I could slip into the chat room quietly. Acclimatise myself to the lifestyle.

I studied the list. Cpl4fem, HailMary and LezGyrl. The latter aroused my suspicions. Too obvious, I thought. Indeed, one click into LezGyrl's particulars convinced me that another impostor had arrived before me. I only hoped I didn't look as transparent as he did.

Screen Name:	LezGyrl
Real Name:	Who cares?
M/F:	Pammy lookalike
Age:	Barely legal
Marital Status:	Fuck that
Location:	My bedroom
Occupation:	Rug Muncher
Interests:	Swapping xxx pics.
Watch Word:	'Is that a mirror in your panties, cos I can see myself in there!'

If her Virtual Vitals aroused my suspicions, LezGyrl's line of conversation in the chat room unmasked her for the he 'she' was.

LezGyrl:	Come on, ladies, give it to me.
HailMary:	Leave us alone.
Cpl4fem:	Get real, Lez
LezGyrl:	I've got some hot shots to swap. 2girl. Amateur. The works
HailMary:	Sorry, not with u.
LezGyrl:	Oh come on! You dykes love this kind of thing.
Cpl4fem:	Give it up, get offline.
LezGyrl:	(_ X _)
Cpl4fem:	What's that?
LezGyrl:	'Kiss my ass.'

Cpl4fem:	You wish.
HailMary:	Sad. Sad. Sad.
LezGyrl:	(_ _!_ _)
Cpl4fem:	No more, please.
LezGyrl:	What's up? Don't recognise you're own FAT butt?

Witnessing one of my kind abuse the net like this made me angry. I was about to confront the guy via Quick-E when I received one myself. I glanced at the list. It seemed a new girl had joined the throng.

Quick-E to: NuBiFem

RoxiNYC:	What a jerk!

A moment passed before I realised that she wasn't talking about me.

NuBiFem:	There's always one.
RoxiNYC:	Nah, they usually bring their mates.
NuBiFem:	All boys together, eh?
RoxiNYC:	Damn right! LOL!
NuBiFem:	LOL?

Was this a lesbian thing? A code I should know? When she didn't respond I worried that I might have given myself away. In a bid to find out more about her, I clicked on her Vitals, only to find she hadn't filled in the form. I was going to abandon the girl, get away from a conversation that had kicked off so uncomfortably, when the answer to my question flashed up at me.

RoxiNYC:	Laugh Out Loud. You really are Nu aren't you.

I smiled. She seemed nice, but I needed to know more.

NuBiFem:	Why no Vitals, hun?
RoxiNYC:	I find it can attract unwanted attention.
NuBiFem:	From guys?
RoxiNYC:	You got it. So what do you want to know?

This time I kept the truth to myself. Played the ball back easy. Gave her a chance to get on top.

NuBiFem:	Whatever makes you feel comfortable.
RoxiNYC:	Let's see. I'm 21 in net years.
NuBiFem:	Net years?
RoxiNYC:	You never heard of net years?
NuBiFem:	I'm a fast learner.
RoxiNYC:	OK, your net age is your real age minus three, or five if you're pushing 30.
NuBiFem:	Why?
RoxiNYC:	Why not! Take advantage of the anonymity in a nice way.
NuBiFem:	So you're 24 in real life?
RoxiNYC:	What else can a bi do to stay young online?

I laughed. She had style, but I wasn't here to make friends. Besides, her screen name worried me. Notably the NYC bit. This was a British-based website. Naturally, anyone in cyberspace could come in, but I couldn't come out too far.

NuBiFem:	Something tells me you're American.
RoxiNYC:	Indeed I am. A girl from Nu York City.

'Marvellous,' I muttered bitterly. 'Just what I'm looking for.'

Having moved into the global village, it appeared I lived on the wrong side of town. All of a sudden, the prospect of taking things further with RoxiNYC seemed pointless. Especially when a second window eclipsed our conversation. One with a more immediate proposition.

Quick-E to: NuBiFem

HailMary:	**Hot Vitals! xx**

I transferred my cursor, and quickly started typing.

NuBiFem:	**How hot are yours?**
HailMary:	**Why don't you take a peek ;o)**

I scanned through her details, then bit into my bottom lip. Just so my smile wouldn't spread off my face.

Screen Name:	**HailMary**
Real Name:	Nun of your business
M/F:	All female
Age:	29
Marital Status:	Already have a Man in my life, thanx
Location:	Upskirts of London ;o)
Occupation:	Being a good girl
Interests:	Wicked things
Watch Word:	'Protect me from the women I want'

I liked the theme. I liked the way she winked in symbols. She sounded kinky. Unlike Roxi, this bi lived a little closer to home. I was about to ask Mary to be more specific about her whereabouts, but it appeared she had her own agenda.

HailMary:	Wanna see a pic?
NuBiFem:	Sure.
HailMary:	I'm wearing my favourite outfit.
NuBiFem:	Me too. Can't beat a tight catsuit.
HailMary:	I like bad habits.
NuBiFem:	Swap ;o)

I only had to wait a second before my post bag filled. I opened up the email. Downloaded the attached picture file marked 'Mary001'.

What could I say? She was dressed as she had promised. Straddling a wooden chair, and sporting a costume hitched high enough for me to take the Lord's name in vain. I had only ever witnessed strippergrams from the back of a baying audience. Never before had I been a guest at a private party. Thanks to the camera flash, this one also possessed a pair of demonic red eyes. The loose crooked smile was clearly not of this world either, but I liked her look. I also believed there might be more to see. My hopes raised by the fact that the shot was numbered 001. As if it was the first from a revealing portfolio. The way HailMary then reacted to my own offering, I figured I'd find out soon.

HailMary:	Wow! U look divine! xx
NuBiFem:	I'm flattered. So, where are you?
HailMary:	Where do u want me?

This, I realised, was an invitation. A chance to get intimate with a total stranger. To embrace each other from a distance for a scroll in the online sack. *Cybersex.* The virtual Grail. HailMary sounded like a veteran. I hoped she would break me in easily. It was, after all, my first time.

NuBiFem:	Let's start in the bedroom.
HailMary:	Mmm. I'm wet already.
NuBiFem:	Me too . . .

I played it submissive. Let Mary use her imagination on me. Complying without comment as she stroked my hair. My earlobe. My neck. My breasts. What struck me most was the time she devoted to each stage. Talking me through her every action. Teasing. Licking. Stroking. At one point I even left my chair to track down my cigarettes and fix myself a drink. Even then I didn't miss much. I returned to find my online partner had just about reached my belly button. Every now and then, I would hold down the letter M. Sound the right noises for her benefit. I could have moaned in another way, but asking her to hurry up would have given the game away. As a bi fox, I was in ecstasy. As a hetero man, I was bored. When it came to sex, virtual or otherwise, it just wasn't in my nature to be patient. This was one lesson in lesbianism I hadn't anticipated. Foreplay, to my great disappointment, was *everything*.

After fannying about like this for a good thirty minutes, I took it upon myself to climax for the last time. By then, I must have been heading for double figures.

NuBiFem:	Mmmm Mmmm, I'm coming.
HailMary:	U mean cumming.
NuBiFem:	I'm nu. Go with it.
HailMary	Ooooh!!!! U taste so sweet!
NuBiFem:	Oh God!!!!

I was typing swiftly now. Driven not by lust, however, but a desire to get the act over and done with. I had expected some buzz. A voyeuristic thrill. Yet the reality seemed so meaningless and mechanical. I had lost my virtual virginity, and in keeping with the real thing I felt awkward, sheepish, let down and used.

Unlike HailMary, who seemed suddenly concerned by my last exclamation.

HailMary:	**Say it again, sister! Tell me u mean it.**
NuBiFem:	**Mercy! Lord, I can't take any more!**
HailMary:	**If only I could believe u.**

Had I really faked it that badly? Quickly, I assured her she had lifted me to new heights.

HailMary:	**Then we should definitely meet.**
NuBiFem:	**For coffee?**
HailMary:	**For sex. Maybe coffee after.**

I should have been thrilled. It was a result that justified my online existence after all. Yet I felt a growing sense of unease about the whole encounter. By the way HailMary had ravished me, she was certainly female, but she just seemed so driven. So desperate. As if she was prepared to take on anyone. I decided I should have some standards.

HailMary:	**You're welcome to drop in any time.**
NuBiFem:	**It's a tempting offer, but I'm not sure.**
HailMary:	**:o(**

The sad face. She had to play the sad face on me. Not only did I have my reservations about her, I now felt guilty about holding back. After everything we'd been through, I couldn't just walk away. I clicked back through our exchange. Re-read the details of our online union. She was certainly an attentive fox. Clitorally speaking, I might have learned a few things too. I figured what the hell. If she lusted after men as much as she did women then she wouldn't be disappointed when she saw me for real.

NuBiFem:	Where shall we meet?
HailMary:	My place. You want the address?
NuBiFem:	Shoot.

I reached over my keyboard, tore a sheet from the jotter, then promptly crumpled it into a ball.

HailMary:	Saint Scholastica's Retreat, you know it?

'Christ Almighty,' I whispered.

HailMary:	Hope u don't mind a hard mattress xxx

'You really are a nun!'

HailMary:	Plus you'll have to go before prayers. We start at four in the morning.

This was one revelation I did not need. If there was such a thing as virtual Hell, I was surely destined to languish there. I had just been deflowered online by a sister of mercy, and here she was booking me up for a second coming. I couldn't handle any more, and I closed the Quick-E box without even saying goodbye.

My bathroom seemed like a sanctuary, but washing my hands and face didn't leave me feeling much cleaner. If anything I felt even more grubby when I dared venture back to the screen. For there I found someone waiting for me. Arms crossed, I imagined. Tapping her virtual foot.

RoxiNYC:	Sorry, was I boring you?

Seeing her there was like finding a friend. I needed to confess my sins. Some of them, at any rate. With a quick cut and paste, I brought Roxi up to speed on my ungodly affair. Copied her into the whole damn tryst. So what, I thought, if I was making myself out to be cheap as a woman. My sights didn't stretch across the Atlantic, and I needed a confidante.

RoxiNYC:	She's good though, don't you think?
NuBiFem:	You know her?
RoxiNYC:	HailMary? Every bi's received her blessing.
NuBiFem:	LOL.
RoxiNYC:	Whatever would Mother say? Apparently It's her Internet account. A direct link to the Vatican by day. The road to temptation at night.

Again she made me smile. Despite the distance between us, I felt relieved to be in her company again. Having exorcised Mary's window from my screen, the main chat room returned to my attention. I noticed LezGyrl was still hustling for pictures, offering two for one with the nun. I figured he could find out the truth about her for himself. Hoaxer and heretic together.

RoxiNYC:	Can I let you into a secret?
NuBiFem:	Sure.
RoxiNYC:	I find cyber a bit cheesy.
NuBiFem:	Me too! Not my style.
RoxiNYC:	I like to see who I'm sleeping with first. Check I'm not being conned
NuBiFem:	?
RoxiNYC:	Too many sad men pretending to be women.
NuBiFem:	Tell me about it. Bastards.
RoxiNYC:	I wish they'd just be honest. I like a man as much as the next bi, but he's gotta be straight right from the start.

I should have come clean there and then. Unmasked myself while I had the chance. I actually typed out my confession. Admitted I was a man. Then hesitated before sending. I needed this girl, I realised. It was a shame that she was so out of my reach geographically. But as an insider, Roxi could prove to be useful to me. Someone I could lean on for advice. A bi-stander in my bid to find the right fox.

So instead I told her that I sympathised. For what it was worth, I added, some of these men probably felt a tinge of guilt about what they were doing.

RoxiNYC:	You think so?
NuBiFem:	It's only natural.
RoxiNYC:	Online, I can usually tell when a guy's pretending to be a woman.
NuBiFem:	How?

I needed to know. The information would be invaluable. I drummed my fingers on the edge of the desk. Waited for Roxi to enlighten me. In the chat room itself, LezGyrl still appeared to be hawking his shots. HailMary, meanwhile, was present but silent. Engaged, I guessed, in a litany of Quick-Es with another poor innocent like me. The place had really filled up since my arrival, and as soon as I learned how to hide any telltale signs of maleness I would make my introductions. Roxi was certainly taking her time coming back to me, however. In fact the chime that sharpened my focus on the screen also marked the arrival of another Quick-E. To my annoyance, it covered her window entirely.

Quick-E to: NuBiFem

Cpl4fem:	The answer to my dreams!

I sighed, and rattled off a quick response.

NuBiFem:	Can we talk later. Bit busy.

Cpl4fem:	One quick question.
NuBiFem:	Go on.
Cpl4fem:	U looking for a meet?
NuBiFem:	Maybe.
Cpl4fem:	Adult fun and friendship?
NuBiFem:	Sounds good.
Cpl4fem:	Great! What toys are you into?

Visions of Action Man flashed into my mind, complete with lifelike gripping hands. But I knew what this girl meant, and it had nothing to do with teddy bears or tea parties. Doctors and nurses, maybe. Only without the doctors, I thought, as I typed what I thought she would want to read.

| NuBiFem: | The bigger the battery the better. |
| Cpl4fem: | It sounds like we'd play well together. |

It certainly did. All I had to do was give her the word.

NuBiFem:	Hun, I'd be happy to share with you.
Cpl4fem:	I've got one special toy I know you'll like.
NuBiFem:	Do tell.
Cpl4fem:	If you're a good bi I might even let you play with it first.
NuBiFem:	Sounds hot. What's it called?
Cpl4fem:	My husband.

'My God!' I declared. 'What kind of slut do you think I am!'

| Cpl4fem: | He'll be gentle with you. Or is that genital. LOL. |

I grimaced at the screen, though her invitation helped me make sense of the name. Cpl4fem. Couple-For-Fem. Not this one, I thought, and blanked out their request.

Underneath, I discovered RoxiNYC had also been busy.

RoxiNYC:	Check my new Vitals. So you know a genuine bi when she takes an interest. xx

I acted quickly, spurred on by her kisses.

Screen Name:	RoxiNYC
Real Name:	Roxi, stupid.
M/F:	Female
Age:	21 ;o)
Marital Status:	Free spirit
Location:	Closer than you think
Occupation:	All work and no play makes Roxi a dull bi
Interests:	Romance – if such a thing still exists!
Watch Word:	'Why can't more girls be like you?'

I took it personally. Felt myself blushing.

NuBiFem:	Do you really mean me?
RoxiNYC:	Unlike you, I don't just talk to anyone!
NuBiFem:	I'm flattered, I think.
RoxiNYC:	Give too much away too quick, you end up with nutters like HailMary. Or worse!
NuBiFem:	There's worse?
RoxiNYC:	Sure. Had you kicked off by asking me what I

	was wearing, I'd have marked you down as a guy straight away.
NuBiFem:	That's worth bearing in mind.
RoxiNYC:	Just say no, hun. Take your time getting to know who's behind the screen name.
NuBiFem:	I think I've learned my lesson :o)

Part of me wished I had cybered her blind. At least she wouldn't have taken me into her confidence like this. Already we had talked to the extent where it was almost too late to come out as a man. Especially when the girl appeared to hit on me.

RoxiNYC:	What counts is that you kept it clean. I like that in a woman ;o)
NuBiFem:	I'm glad I passed the test. I'll let you know how I get on.
RoxiNYC:	But that's not why I'm drawn to you.

This line, following on so quickly she couldn't have read what I'd written. My back tracking had to get better. As did my choice of bisexual females. A girl this good, and she lived across the Atlantic. How unlucky could a guy get?

NuBiFem:	I'm nothing special. Honestly.
RoxiNYC:	All I know is you're different, somehow. And I like it.
NuBiFem:	xxx

I didn't want to ask what made me stand out. It was a weakness I would have to work on alone. Concentrate harder on projecting myself as a regular bi. Quickly I scrolled back through our conversation, looking for the fluffs. As I did so, I began to see this whole encounter as a dress rehearsal. A chance to get things wrong with someone far away, before getting it right here on my doorstep. Returning my cursor back to the tail end of our chat, still debating whether I should ask, I flexed my fingers over the keys and found myself typing it anyway.

RoxiNYC: D'you want to swap pics? Nothing dodgy. Just like to put a face to the screen name.

NuBiFem: Sure.

I drew up an email, attached the scan of the *Staple* pin-up, figuring it wouldn't hurt to gauge her reaction. Find out whether, bi-wise, I was as hot to trot as HailMary had said. I held out for an objective opinion this time. As we lived on different continents, there didn't seem much point in false flattery. Unless, I smiled to myself, it turned out she was an air hostess. Which would be a result on many counts. I prepared to send, upon which my flight of fancy dropped right out of the sky.

RoxiNYC: Be nice to see a real pic. The catsuit chick is such a fake.

One click and she would have had it. So too would my chances of getting another response from her. I lifted my fingertip from the mouse button, exhaled sharply, went for the words instead.

NuBiFem: ?

RoxiNYC: It's just started doing the rounds.

NuBiFem: It has?

RoxiNYC: If you haven't got it yet, you will soon. The models always go far in cyberspace ;o)

NuBiFem: LOL.

Laugh out loud? Had I done so on this side of the screen it would have been shot through with nervous panic. One time I had sent my picture out, and this is what happens. People taking liberties with my property. Passing themselves off as me. I cursed HailMary for her treachery, then the real culprit made himself known.

Quick-E to: NuBiFem

LezGyrl: **Wanna see me in a catsuit? Mail me your filthiest shot and I'll let you take a peek!**

'Christ, I'm second hand now!'

Stung by the deceit, paralysed by indecision, I punched out the window, to be faced again with Roxi.

RoxiNYC: **Problem, hun?**

Problem? Hell yes! I had to buy some time. Say something while I got it together.

NuBiFem: **Just trying to attach the pic. Hold on!**

RoxiNYC: **Technology, eh? Never a man when you need one!**

For a beat I contemplated pulling out and getting offline, but I knew I would live to regret it. As BiRuth once said, I had a connection here. Long-distance, maybe, but I didn't want to lose her now. Not unless I wanted to arouse her suspicions. Have her put out the word on me. I spun out of my chair, and mentally continued spinning as I raced to think of a solution. I had an old family album under my bed, but knew I couldn't bring myself to mail a picture of my mum, God rest her soul. I wasn't so worried about showing her disrespect as showing myself up. A bi with a Farrah Fawcett flick and flares? Not even retro chic, but the genuine article. I thought not.

Which was why I went straight for the bin bag. Rescued the best photograph I could find and slipped it into the scanner.

It had been my favourite, one time. Until the subject in the shot decided my services were no longer required. Christine. The summer before. Paxos. Greece. Leggy ex-girlfriend posing at the water's edge in vermilion pink bikini. Simmering smile. One hand on tilted hip. It had been a hot fortnight, I recalled, as the scanner combed the shot.

RoxiNYC: U do have a pic, don't you?

The image began to materialise on my screen. A portrait of my past love which I prayed would save my immediate future.

'Oh yes,' I said to myself. 'I've got the shot for you.'

NuBiFem: Sending . . .

As I delivered, so I received. A picture of Roxi, I presumed. One I would have opened immediately had she not got in there first. Christine, it seemed, spoke a universal language.

RoxiNYC: What a body!

NuBiFem: Thanxxx

RoxiNYC: I mean it, you look so . . .

NuBiFem: What?

RoxiNYC: . . . so real

NuBiFem: Is that good?

RoxiNYC: Even better. I wish we could meet.

This was it. The time had come. I could take the charade no further. She was smitten, that was evident, but with no chance to put things right in the real world, it seemed cruel to leave the girl pining at the digital shoreline. What's more, Christine's effect on her had left me feeling a bit short-changed. It was me who had put in the graft to sweeten up this bi. All my ex had done was pose for a photograph. Did looks count for everything in a woman's world too? I hoped not.

Indeed, I prayed that she would go easy when I revealed that there was a little bit more to me.

> **NuBiFem:**   **Roxi, there's something I need to get off my chest.**

As I waited for her to respond, I clicked on the email she had sent me. Attached was a high definition picture. Heavy on my memory. Slow to download. One that opened up in a big mosaic of pixels and gradually began to define itself.

> **RoxiNYC:**   **Actually, I have a little confession to make as well.**

For a moment I thought Roxi was going to tell me *she* was a guy. The picture hadn't got beyond a blur. Just in case she was a bloke, I decided now was not the time to get in first. I held back from the keys, wishing my processor was that little bit faster.

> **RoxiNYC:**   **It's about my whereabouts.**

> **NuBiFem:**   **What? Where are you?**

Her Virtual Vitals were still open. I clicked on the corner of the window. Brought it to the front of the screen:

> **Location:**   Closer than you think

'How close?' I asked myself, and switched back into the message:

> **RoxiNYC**   **London.**

'*What!*'

> **NuBiFem:**   **!!**

> **RoxiNYC:**   **Moved here a few years back.**

It was some confession. Not as major as mine, perhaps, but I reacted as if I had been playing it straight with her from the start. Which, in some ways, was true. The shot still had some way to go, but I could just make out a three-quarter-length image of a female form. I should have been relieved, instead I was rigid in my seat.

NuBiFem:	You said you lived in New York???
RoxiNYC:	I didn't. Just said I was from there.
NuBiFem:	Why pretend otherwise?
RoxiNYC:	You had me down as unavailable, but still you talked. I'd say that's a mark of a good woman. Second only to steering clear of cybersex!

I looked to the skylight, seeking a moment to focus. If there had been a downpour, it was over. The night was studded with satellites and stars.

RoxiNYC:	So, what do you think of me? ;o)

Another chime. This time to confirm the download had been successful. I folded away the Quick-E blocking my view, and everything was revealed.

'Oh my God!'

Roxi. In all her glory. A vision I could have never imagined.

RoxiNYC:	Please don't go quiet. I'm getting twitchy here. You haven't even told me your confession!

She wasn't naked, I should say, but my bloodstream still turned tide. In fact there was nothing suggestive about her pose whatsoever. It was just a regular shot of a smiling fox in a tight T-shirt and no bra. Just like the woman of my real-world dreams.

The make-up girl from the cat commercial. The one who had been totally unresponsive with me in the dressing room, but who was now here online, pushing to take things further. With me. A *woman.* In all the chat rooms in all of cyberspace, she had to pick mine. I was shocked. Spun out. Seduced all the more by her spell. As a bi fem it was fate, and for a moment I forgot myself.

RoxiNYC: Don't be shy. You can tell me.

My hands floated over the keyboard, but I didn't pay attention to my typing. Yes, I had a confession, but not the one I had planned before she hit me with hers. Distracted by her image, it was my heart dictated the words. Expressing a sentiment that hadn't identified itself to me until I rattled it out to her now.

NuBiFem: I'm in love with you.

I was. Truly. At first sight, too. Which wasn't now but way back. Right from the moment she had appeared to me in the dressing room, in fact. Only I didn't know it at the time. All I knew was that I had been tipped right back when I first saw her, and my world hadn't levelled out since. Now I had a name to put to that fabulous face. Roxi.

RoxiNYC: Are you for real?

OK, it had been an impulsive admission, especially as I hadn't found the courage to even *talk* to her during make up, but online it was just so easy. I didn't feel like a blurter. Not like I would had this been a physical encounter. We were intimate but also anonymous, and my words filled the space between us.

NuBiFem: I couldn't be more certain.

Having come so close we could have kissed, I realised now that I couldn't go back. I had to make this Roxi mine. It was her next response that awoke me to the practicalities.

RoxiNYC: We should speak.

'Shit,' I hissed, and rubbed my sockets with the heels of my hands. It was late. I hadn't touched a drink since my meeting with BiRuth. My drug supply had been cut off at the root. And yet once again I was intoxicated. Oblivious to the consequences of my actions.

RoxiNYC:	What's your number? Can I call?

She liked me. She had said as much. But it wasn't all me she wanted. I thought of Christine, and Roxi's response to her picture. Evidently we shared the same taste in women. One more thing we had in common. Another reason why I couldn't let the opportunity go to waste. There had to be a way I could come out that somehow wouldn't ruin my chances with her. But not tonight. I was too tired. This thing had exhausted me. I couldn't think straight. Or rather, I was too far gone to think anything *other* than straight. All I could do was give Roxi my telephone number and sleep on the situation.

NuBiFem:	How about tomorrow? I'm bushed.
RoxiNYC:	I'm not. LOL. Far from it, in fact.

Had I raised the whole shaved issue once again? I was about to say I wasn't that coarse, but even a line like that was up for misinterpretation. As indeed was the whole evening. One web venture I couldn't see floating in real terms. I had to get some sleep. Dream up some way to bail myself out. Grateful as I was for the small concession she then gave me:

RoxiNYC:	Are you free in the daytime?
NuBiFem:	Sorry, strictly office-bound.
RoxiNYC:	Then I'll call you after work. Say six?
NuBiFem:	Great. Look forward to it!
RoxiNYC:	Bi for now xxxxxx

I laid out a repeat row of kisses, but by the time I blew them downline she had vanished. All that remained was her picture. Roxi, gazing at me as the catsuit once had. She really was a beguiling bi, and I saved the shot under Favourites. Next, I opened up a blank email. Addressed it to Christine. Marked it urgent. Then found I didn't know what to say. After staring at the screen for a minute or so, I realised I would have to call my ex. Speak to her properly. Be ready to react. Ready to beg, if necessary. After wrecking my chances with Zoë in the Pandemonium, I figured she owed me. Instead of abandoning the email, however, I substituted her address for another. One belonging to the only other presence in my Cyber Circle at the time.

Tony Curtis.

The man himself.

A Hollywood legend who wouldn't know me from Adam, or Eve, but I took his screen name as a sign that he was watching over me. Here in my time of crisis, omnipotent and inspirational. With a leap of faith on my part, it seemed like he was *there* for me. Ready to hear my prayers.

Was I doing the right thing? With great reverence, I keyed in my predicament. Asking also whether Marilyn Monroe had treated him any differently when he was dressed up like a doll on the set of *Some Like it Hot*. I didn't expect a solution. Didn't even expect a reply. But at least I had been honest with someone. And that in itself was the salve my conscience needed that night.

13

'Next strike a balance, or risk falling from the wire.'
A.C. Découcher, *Bisexuality For Beginners*

'You did *what?*'

I took a swig from my morning coffee, then went through the story again. It was no surprise to me that Christine found it hard to take in. To avoid further confusion I avoided the difficult words this time. Kept things nice and simple. Boy meets girl. Girl is bi. Girl thinks boy is girl. Boy calls ex for help.

'Well, I'm appalled,' she said finally. 'How would you feel if someone messed with your feelings like that?'

I knew only too well, but this was no time for a fight. I switched the phone from one ear to the other, and faced the window gallery. Under the tree canopy in the square outside, a derelict was feeding the pigeons with bread from a cheap carrier bag.

'That's why I'm calling you,' I told her. 'I need your help to break it off.'

A pause. A sigh. Then, 'How?'

'All I'm asking is that you're here to pick up the phone when she calls.'

'What will I say?'

Like Christine had never gone cold on someone before.

'Don't worry about that,' I assured her. 'I'll be here to talk you through it.' I watched one pigeon break from the flock and hop closer to the tramp. He crouched before the bird. Tossed more crumbs in its path.

'I'm desperate,' I told her, to no response. I guessed my ex agreed. 'If she finds out I'm not a woman, it means I can't try it on as a man.'

'I see. I think.'

'I finished our relationship on your behalf,' I reminded her. 'Just see it as a return favour.'

'I don't know. You're asking a lot.'

I was about to give up. My ex was right. It was a ridiculous request. I should have been embarrassed. Ashamed of myself. Had it been any other girl on the other end of the line I would have been dying on my feet. But Christine and I were history. Recent history, maybe. But it changed the way I could relate to her. Left me free to make a prat of myself without compromising our relationship. Just then a brief but frantic squawk returned my attention to the window. The tramp with the bag was walking briskly from the square. I couldn't see the pigeon. Only a scattering of feathers. I had to see this through. It was just a question of patience.

'I guess it's my way of dealing with losing you.'

I had called Christine at the office. Caught her early before she booked up for the day. Until now, our conversation had been accompanied at her end by the chatter of keyboard keys. This time, I earned her full attention.

'You're doing this because of me?' she said.

I smiled to myself, and quietly confirmed that I was.

'And you just want me to cool things off for you, right?'

'That's all.'

'As a bisexual woman.'

Finally, she was up to speed.

'Can you be here at six?' I asked. My knuckles went white around the receiver. I squeezed shut my eyes. Willed her to hop into my bag.

'I have to go,' she said eventually, and promptly hung up on me.

'You can't do that!'

Immediately, I hit redial. Punching the button so hard it probably detonated a charge somewhere. Her answermachine kicked in.

'Come on, Christine. Don't freak on me. It'll be easier than it sounds, I swear. You can do it!'

Frustrated that she hadn't intercepted, I tried her office switchboard instead. Begged the receptionist to put me through. She, too, left me hanging there. Keeping me on hold for a minute before relaying the half-arsed excuse that Christine was out to lunch.

'Tell me something I don't know.' I shut down the phone. Puffed out my cheeks and sighed. It was time to face up to the fact that there would be no one else at this end but me.

In my space that day, every clock conspired to tick louder than usual. Each time the hour hand completed a circuit, my nerves seemed to wind round with it. Towards the end of the afternoon, I had paced back and forth so much that the varnish appeared to be coming off the floorboards. Having considered every means of escape, all I had achieved was a major headache. Mentally burrowing under the problem so many times that eventually the roof caved in on me.

Roxi was going to phone soon, and I was going to hurt her. Our connection would be severed, whether I picked up or let it ring.

Eventually, as the sun began to sink on me, I decided to let my own answermachine do the talking. It was the coward's option, but the only one guaranteed to break the news to her without bottling half way through. I knew exactly what I was going to say. I was also pretty certain about the way she would respond, too. Reluctantly, I pressed the record button.

'Don't hang up, Roxi,' I began. 'I'm afraid you have got the right number. Obviously this isn't the voice you wanted to hear, and for what it's worth I feel like a shitweasel. I know you've been hit on by men like me before, but I didn't do this to hurt you. I swear. If anything, I'm the one who's lost out. That's all I wanted to say.'

I couldn't bring myself to say goodbye. It sounded so final. In some ways, I wished I'd never put myself in the position to even say *hello*. Together in the dressing room, I had learned to live with the silence between us. It left me feeling awkward, maybe, but never this bad. Online, as NuBiFem, I had unwittingly broken the ice with Roxi, and promptly come closer to her than I could handle. Which was when I decided it was only right that I retrieved my screen name from cyberspace and put her out of my misery, too.

My modem was beginning to irritate me. It sounded like a fag hag. Shrieking in that attention-seeking way. Creating a big fuss over my arrival online. All I had wanted to do was slip in quietly, retrieve my Vitals and run. Instead, within seconds of logging on, my screen was obliterated by Quick-Es. Advances from women who had searched the Virtual Vault for a nice bi like me, added my screen name to their Cyber Circle, and then kept a weather eye on the list from that moment on. Ready to pounce when it finally announced my online presence. Watching so many little windows reminded me of bacteria proliferating in a Petri dish. And yet I was the scum here, nobody else. I couldn't face staying on for a second longer, stopping only to download one single email to read offline. Nothing from Tony, naturally, but an email from my agent. Apparently the fruits of my cat food fiasco had delighted the Far Eastern client. Such was their enthusiasm for the animosity between myself and the moggy that they had revised their marketing campaign. Indeed, they planned to use us both for a whole series of advertisements. Once again my agent had acted on my behalf. Confident that I would be free for a couple more shoots. I should have thought of the money, but my mind was on more immediate implications.

Like the fact that my phone had just started ringing.

Another shoot meant more make-up. More make-up meant more Roxi. If she recognised my voice on the tape, and confronted me during the session, I knew I'd come away with more than just a cat scratch.

'Speak to her,' I reasoned with myself, and wheeled out of my seat. 'Be a man about this.'

Only I couldn't find the phone. The fucker was absent from the cradle, and the signal hadn't yet reached the handset. After balling out the receptionist I had obviously dumped it some place. Panicking now, I just couldn't remember where. I had an extension beside my bed, but as I rushed across the floor the original began to pick up the signal. I stalled, disorientated, turned one-eighty and saw it there. Right back where I had started, on the desk beside my keyboard. The ringing stopped as I reached it.

I jabbed the receive button, killing the machine as it prepared to betray me. With mounting dread, like a man about to put a bullet through his head, I put the phone to my ear.

'Betcha didn't think I'd call.'

Roxi. Had to be. Like, how many other foxes did I know who sounded like Lois Lane? More to the point, how many foxes did I know period? I tried to speak. Really I did. I faced the window and drew breath. The truth was in there, but it wouldn't come out. Not because I couldn't bring myself to talk, but because my attention flew from the phone to the figure racing under the trees through the square. I only exhaled when she emerged at the gate, paused to wave up at me, then sprinted across the street. *Christine!* She had made it. My voice was here.

'Hold on,' I shrilled down the line, a ridiculous falsetto, and threw open the door to my stairs.

'Give me the phone,' she said breathlessly.

Christine was dressed for business, but she hadn't been briefed. She rested her hands on her knees, as if she'd just sprinted here all the way from work. Either she'd failed to flag a taxi, or left the decision to help me out to the very last minute. Not for the first time, it placed her commitment under question.

'You're in no state to talk,' I hissed, masking the mouthpiece with my palm.

'Neither are you.'

She had a good point. We looked at the phone, then at each other.

'OK, just go easy. Keep it simple. Keep it brief.'

Christine exhaled deeply and took the handset from me. I was reluctant to let it go and when she finally won possession and pressed it to her ear I knew the reason why. The intense concentration in her eyes, shutting me out by focusing on the floorboards, it was like watching a kid with a sea shell. One who couldn't believe what she was hearing. Who didn't know how to respond. My ex was so tense I could see I was in trouble. Big time. Standing there, just inches away from her face, I was desperate for the words racing through my mind to somehow spill from her lips.

'Roxi?' she said, and snapped her attention to me. 'Sorry about that. Jehovah's Witness. Always come round at a bad time, don't they?'

I frowned. This wasn't in my script. Besides, when was there ever a good time?

'Anyway,' Christine continued. 'Where were we?'

Frantically, I mugged across the message that I'd only just picked up.

'I mean last night,' she said. 'Where did we leave off?'

My ex, I realised, was talking to us both. Only I couldn't get a silent word in. Not while Roxi had her ear.

'We did?' said Christine, grinning now. 'Why, thank you. You're pretty hot too.'

Hot? How could she say something like that to another woman? That kind of thing was boy talk. *My* talk. Christine hadn't even seen Roxi's picture, yet here she was making assumptions on my behalf. I grimaced at her, drew my finger across my throat, but her stare had an unfocused glaze. My ex was looking at me but paying me no attention. Too busy listening down the line to notice. I had to hear what was going on, and made for the bedside phone. When I picked up, intercepting Roxi's voice, I realised I had missed something major.

'It's true,' she disclosed. 'Sometimes in public too.'

What? I glowered across at Christine. She winked at me, finger-tipped the mouthpiece and said, 'Girl things.'

My ex was enjoying this, though her smile slackened off when Roxi pressed her further.

'Anyway, you know why I'm calling. To find out if you meant what you said.'

This time it was Christine's turn to throw the imploring look. Roxi could only be referring to one thing, I thought. And yes, I had meant it. I nodded at my ex, and mouthed three words across to her: I-Love-You.

Christine looked at me quizzically, and pointed to herself.

'Not you!' I hissed. *'Roxi!'*

She looked a little hurt by this, but relayed my sentiments all the same.

'Of course I meant it.'

Cradling the second phone between my shoulder and ear, I gave my ex a big thumbs up. I may have felt like an air traffic controller faced with a soon-to-ditch aircraft, but it was vital I maintained a positive front. Even if the needles were beginning to spin.

'Then tell me again,' said Roxi. 'So I can hear you say it.'

'I love you.'

'How much?'

Again, Christine palmed the phone.

'How much, Ren?'

I shrugged. Unsure what to say that wouldn't offend one party as much as it flattered the other.

'A little?' she suggested. 'A *lot*?'

Nervously I felt the back of my head. What could I say?

'I just do,' said Christine, winging it in the wake of my silence.

I felt like butting in, and telling Roxi myself. Confessing that I had already come close enough to her to be sure. That her presence bewitched me, and silenced me too. Something I had never experienced before. So soon. So naturally. Only I didn't know how my ex would react, and I needed her now more than ever. Besides, Roxi had other reasons for asking:

'What about you? Anyone ever said they loved you?'

Silence from Christine, like it was so long she couldn't remember. I felt a tinge of guilt.

As if to refine the question, Roxi said, 'How about a man?'

'Sure. I guess.'

'Not under duress, though. I mean unprompted.'

'Oh, definitely.'

'What goes through your mind?'

Christine with her gaze levelled right at me now. Thinking back to our own time together, I suspected. Especially when she said, 'You mean when he springs it on you?'

'Uh huh.'

This time it was me who looked at the floor.

'A guy comes out with a line like that, I'd say he wants me on my back.' Roxi's throaty cackle turned my phone ear puce. 'Sometimes, I wonder if they think it's a password,' Christine continued, then got real when I came up glaring. 'But not always.' Up tight and now out of control, my ex and her mouth under the spotlight. Then Roxi spoke again, and I was suprised to hear her voice had lost its cautious edge.

'I'm glad you turned out to be genuine.'

'Oh good,' breathed Christine, sounding horribly relieved.

'When I saw your words appear on my screen last night, I thought one of two things.'

'Go on.'

'Either I'm chatting online to a man who's desperate for sex, or I've chanced to meet the most honest woman in cyberspace.'

My ex took this with both brows cocked like rifles.

'Glad I didn't disappoint,' she replied.

'Well, you certainly have balls.'

Christine managed to squeeze out a thank you before clamping her mouth and shaking for a second.

'I mean it,' said Roxi. 'I'm talking to a girl who comes out of nowhere to say she loves me, and I don't even know her damn name!'

My ex recovered her poise, but sadly not her wits.

'It's Christine.'

I pressed my free hand to my forehead and flopped back on the bed.

'Well, Christine, you're the boldest bi I've ever had the pleasure of not yet meeting.'

'You want to meet?'

I shot bolt upright.

'Sure,' said Roxi.

'What the fuck are you saying?' I was clasping the mouthpiece with both hands now.

Christine had done likewise with her phone, only I was the one looking stressed here.

'Just checking I heard her right.'

'Say no, then. Say you're sorry for screwing up her day. Say you realise now that you overstepped the mark. Say you have to go. Say your boyfriend's here. Say anything!'

'You are not my boyfriend.'

'And *who's* decision was that?' I countered, then remembered the phone in my hand. I lifted my palm away from the mouthpiece, surrendering to her control of the situation. As Christine prepared to return to the conversation, I could sense she was more relaxed with Roxi than with me. Something about the way she cuddled up to the receiver smiling to herself as she said, 'Let's do it . . . Tomorrow night? Great!'

I dropped my phone. Aghast as my ex made the arrangements. Astounded when she finished the call and looked at me like I was the one in trouble here. 'I'm curious, that's all.'

'Curious?

'About your taste in women, Ren.'

'I can't believe it, you've set up a *date*!'

'For you to go through this charade, and then come right out and say you love her too, I'm thinking she must be pretty special.'

Christine was right. Roxi was special in every way known to man. Or woman. Watching my ex palm down the aerial, I realised I had never met a fox like her.

14

'Don't even think about concealer until you're happy with the foundation.'
Verity Pepper, *Make Up a Million*

My special shirt was waiting to be taken to the cleaners. It felt like my love life had already gone there. As I didn't possess a back-up shirt, I decided to keep things simple. Black box jacket and jeans. I was getting ready to shadow Christine to my own date, so it was important to keep a low profile. To appear like the kind of barfly who looks at home alone. A drinker at the no-chance saloon.

I stood a man's length from the mirror, but couldn't muster the spirit to keep my shoulders square. The outfit was fine. It was my body that disappointed. I pressed my hands flat against my breasts, and wished somehow they could inflate for one night. Nothing outrageous, of course. I wouldn't feel comfortable with Dolly dimensions, and Roxi didn't seem like the kind of bi who went for busty women. My thighs, however, could pass muster as they were. Rangy on a man, maybe, but shapely on a female. If only I had the hips. Then I turned side on, examined how my jeans hung from my flat shapeless ass, and knew that I was asking for a miracle.

There was no alternative. Christine would be the one to see this through. Having bungled her way into an evening out with Roxi, all I could do was keep my distance and hope she followed the brief better than she had the first time.

'Was it too much to take in?' I had snapped back then. 'When I asked you to cool things off with her, which little bit didn't you understand?'

My ex had glowered at me defiantly, then brushed the lint from the sleeve of her suit.

'I have a life to rebuild too.'

'Then take up an evening class!' I yelled. 'Leave Roxi to me.'

'I just thought it would be nice to meet her.'

'So did I! Only thanks to you she's otherwise engaged.'

'Ren, we're meeting for a drink. Like sometimes you go out with Willie for a drink.'

'That's different.'

'Why?'

'We're guys.'

'So?'

I looked out at the square for a beat. The dusk was turning to darkness under the trees. A light came on in the building opposite.

'So there's no . . . potential.'

'Potential? For what?'

'You know what I'm talking about.'

Christine with that smile. The one that broadcast what she was really thinking.

'Why not?' she said eventually. 'You and the big guy.'

'Because we're just friends, all right! I'm straight. Sweet's in love with his flowers. Hell, we're not even talking to each other right now because of all this. But Roxi's bisexual, Christine. She goes for both sexes. You fit into one of those categories. So do the maths. Even if you're only going to make a new friend. There's *potential*.'

'Darling,' she said, and catwalked towards my computer. 'There's potential in us all.'

My ex, talking like she was the experienced one. Winding me up in exchange for her help. I half wondered whether she was being like this because I had found someone else first. Granted, in a weird kind of way.

'I'm coming with you,' I told her.

Christine leaned over my desk, coolly switched on my hard-drive. 'No you're not.'

'It's my date,' I reminded her. 'And you never can be too careful when it comes to meeting people offline. Roxi may not be who she says she is.'

'I can handle myself, thank you very much.'

'Like you demonstrated so ably on the phone? Christine, if you found that hard to handle, how it's going to be when you're faced with her for real?'

A beep, and my monitor opened its eye.

'Why don't you let me find out for myself?'

'You don't even know what she looks like,' I countered. 'You need me.'

But Christine wasn't listening. She had the mouse in her clutches, and one objective on her mind. 'Is this her picture?'

'That's private!'

The screen framed the shot before I could stop her. But it wasn't Roxi who made an appearance.

'Blimey,' said Christine with a start. 'Is she a nun or a stripper!'

By then I was right behind her, leaning over to assume control of the mouse.

'Both,' I said.

We studied the screen, almost cheek to cheek.

'Tell me that's not Roxi.'

I smiled, closed down the image and relaxed a little myself. 'Like I said, you need me.'

We agreed to meet five minutes early. Roxi had suggested that they hook up at a cybercafe in the centre of town. It was a good choice, I thought, as I left my space that evening. One of those wired-up joints where a single man like me wouldn't attract special attention. I couldn't quite bring myself to wear a backpack, however, even though I knew it would guarantee my invisibility among all the homesick antipodeans that were usually drawn to such places.

'Just don't breathe down my neck,' Christine had requested. 'If I know you're listening it'll only put me off.'

'You won't even know I'm there,' I assured her. 'With any luck, Roxi won't want to stay long anyway.'

'Why not?'

'You're blowing her out, remember?'

'Am I? Oh yeah.'

'*Christine!*'

I didn't take kindly to being teased, but in her heart I figured she wanted to do the right thing. It was the brain to mouth connection that left me feeling twitchy. The slightest pressure and something inside her would threaten to short again. Which was why I didn't let on that I knew Roxi on a professional basis. It would just complicate things, for Christine at any rate.

Just to be sure my ex put in the effort, I decided I ought to show her some appreciation. A goodwill gesture. One that reminded her how important it was that she didn't screw up. Sweet William would understand. We may have fallen out as friends, but he remained a florist and the customer was always right.

'Bitch, look at you.' Willie said this without actually looking. 'All dressed down and nowhere to go?'

'Actually,' I said, 'I'm on my way to a date right now. Met her on the net two nights ago.'

Sweet's neighbouring traders had long since packed up their stalls, leaving the street littered with crushed stems and clods of soil. Only Willie worked late on this beat, the man doing most of his business after dark.

My dealer brushed a petal from his puffa, said, 'As what?'

'As me,' I confirmed uneasily. 'We're meeting in a cybercafe.'

'As a bloke?'

'In a sense.'

'So now you're deluding yourself, too.'

My cheeks spoke for me. I peered into the rose bucket at my feet, pretended to be interested in the crisp wrapped tokens of affection Sweet would later hawk around the restaurants and hash dens of East London.

'This poor girl's expecting to meet another fox, isn't she?'

I confirmed that she was, and began to wish I'd gone for chocolates instead.

'Sweet, just give me some flowers and I'll go.'

'Flowers?' he repeated, and rolled his eyes. 'Like that'll make it better when she finds out you're a guy? Sheesh, you gotta whole lot to learn about women.'

'At least I try, Willie. Now hit me with something impressive. Something that shows I'm serious about this.'

My dealer reached for a mixed bunch. I couldn't be bothered to object.

'What you really need is a wreath. Seeing that you're about to attend your own funeral.'

'Very funny. How much?'

'You hit lucky tonight, you can have it for free.'

'Fine,' I said, and withdrew my hand from my pocket. 'Just don't expect me too early tomorrow. I may have to catch up on some sleep.'

'Whenever you're ready, Reynard. Whenever you're ready.'

I took the flowers and left. It was only on the bus into town, however, as a heady bouquet drifted out from the mouth of the wrapping, that I realised Willie had surprised me again. So pungent was the smell that I was obliged to open the fanlight for fear of attracting attention. I knew it was skunk weed before I'd even managed to retrieve it. Had I asked for this? Even hinted at it? I thought not. Even so, I found myself in possession of some premium shit. A calibre of cannabis that could incapacitate even hardcore stoners. This time, I wondered whether Sweet had slipped it to me in preparation for the date, or its aftermath.

Every computer terminal in the cybercafe was flanked by a mouse pad and a drinks coaster. The place was humming. Busy too. Banks of customers tapped away to themselves. Every one communicating feverishly without a single word passing between them.

I arrived early. Intending to get acclimatised before Christine pitched up, and prepare myself for Roxi's arrival. Except it appeared my ex shared my anxieties. Even before I joined her, I could tell by the beer bottles that she had been here for some time.

'You're drunk. I can't believe it!'

'Just warming up,' she protested, and saluted me with the bottle in her hand.

'For what?' I noticed that she hadn't even switched on her monitor.

Christine didn't seem to care, focusing instead on the flowers under my arm. 'You going on a date?'

I could have brained her with the bunch. She looked up at me, her gaze holding true as she swayed slightly on her stool.

'Are they for me, or Roxi?'

'Christine, get a grip. She'll be here any time.'

'So get the drinks in.'

I grabbed the bottle from her hand, set it way out of her reach.

'Why are you doing this to me?' I hissed furiously.

'Doing what?'

'Letting me down all the time. Disappointing me. What's with you at the moment?'

Without warning, she leaned forward and kissed me. Just a peck. But forceful enough to knock me back a pace.

'I'm sorry, Rennie.'

I was about to weigh in again, when I noticed that her eyes were filling up. Seeing her crumble like this made me feel bad. Really bad. I put my arms round her, tried not to tense as she hugged me tight. At the same time I twisted a glimpse at my wristwatch. If I didn't settle her in the next few minutes, I knew my unease would double.

'Hey,' I said soothingly. 'I'm not angry. I'm just nervous for you. I know you can do it. Christine, you're a natural. All you have to do is be yourself. Believe me, she'll get the message.'

She pulled away, smiled bravely at me. 'Do I look OK?'

Did it *matter*? As it was, she looked fabulous. Long French pleat. Short plaid skirt. Mid thigh stockings. Like a convent girl gone bad. I took a slug from her beer.

'You will set the stage for me, won't you? Find out if she likes actors. Creative types.'

A barmaid stepped in to clear Christine's empty bottles, frowning at the mess around the keyboard. Then she switched on the screen, as if to say 'log on or leave.' Christine dabbed at her eyes, smiling now after this brief lapse in composure. 'Don't worry,' she said. 'I know what I'm doing.'

I handed her the flowers. 'I bought them for you. Honestly.'

Even though I had removed Sweet's hidden extra, the bunch still reeked of hash. My ex put her nose to my offering and sourced it immediately. 'So you and Willie made up?'

'That depends.'

'On what?'

'On whether this whole scam works.'

My ex laid the flowers alongside the monitor, and for a second I thought she might surf.

'Go take a seat,' was all she said next. 'It's almost show time.'

I glanced around the cybercafe. Spied a spare terminal on the other side. Working there, I could peek round the screen every now and then. Check on the situation without being seen.

'One more thing,' I heard her say.

'Yeah?'

'What does she look like?'

'Roxi?' I smiled to myself thinking about what BiRuth had said. 'Don't worry. She'll find you.'

I took Christine's beer with me to my station. Drained it dry while logging on. At the same time I glanced along the row, and couldn't help wondering how many men present were posing online as women. A couple of surfers midway down from me I dismissed immediately. One had a *Rough Guide to London* with him. The other wore a Rock Café T-shirt. I wasn't able to read the location, but I was pretty sure he had come half way round the world to buy it. Not that their appearance disqualified either of them. It just gave them a clear reason to be here. At the far end, however, a sun shy youth with a hook nose and jester's jaw was engaged in bouts of frenzied typing. These were cut by long, lingering pauses. Moments in which he would lean in close to the screen, as if willing some response to appear. I marked him down as one. A classic LezGyrl.

Turning my attention to my keyboard, I wondered how often it got cleaned. At the same time the geek with the nose, he just gets up and leaves. No post cyber chat. Nothing. I tucked in my chair as he passed by, thinking what a creep to leave his online partner like that, and only looked his way once more when the cafe door creaked open again just after it had creaked shut. Immediately I fenced off my face with my hand, and watched through the gap between my fingers. For my date had just arrived.

Roxi.

Her royal bi-ness.

Grace and perfection in her features. Elegance in her every step. Silence in the court around her.

And a handmaiden in her wake.

She had a friend! A fox but not like Roxi. Oriental, I thought. On one side but maybe not the other. Pretty all over, nonetheless in a milk-skin, moon-face way. After swapping a few words with Roxi, she retreated to the bar at the back of the cafe. The chaperone, I figured. Nothing more. As far as I was concerned, the girl from New York City was incompatible with anyone else but me.

'Christine?' I heard her declare.

At this my ex popped up from behind her monitor, smoothed her skirt and beamed. Roxi extended a slender hand, but switched it for Christine's light embrace. I frowned. Compressed my lips. If my stand-in was seeking to look authentic, she risked looking even better than the real thing. 'Calm down,' I muttered. 'Ease into the part.'

Hearing this, a slicker at the station beside me smirked in solidarity. 'Taking a walk on the wild side, huh?'

Another bi fem. With that kind of line, he had to be. Like I needed another.

'Not now,' I said quietly, my gaze still trained through the gap between our screens.

'Want some help from a pro?'

'No. Thank you, I'm fine.'

He leaned in regardless, studied my monitor. The mint masking his breath had holes in it. I wondered how many hours he had languished in his office for it to get so bad. I couldn't say I saw myself in him, but the fact we shared the same online pursuit made my skin crawl. I felt disgusted at us both, and hoped he'd just leave me alone. Pretend I didn't exist.

'What's your screen name?' he asked, and flashed another grin at me. 'Mine's MollyCuddle.'

This time I turned to glower at him squarely. Seeing my expression, every upturned line in the joker's face turned south.

'Oh dear,' he said, weakly. 'You mentioned easing into the part. I assumed maybe you were like me . . .'

'What?' I snarled. 'A bisexual female, perhaps?'

'No, no,' he countered quickly, his voice quavering now. 'I'm strictly lesbian.'

A moment passed before he realised what he had said, cringing at his own haste. I was itching to turn and see how Christine was getting on, but this guy needed dealing with first. Not least because I was appalled to think people might be equally disgusted if I ever let slip about my own virtual venture. Calmly, I enquired how long he had been this way, and watched him inch back from me.

'It's just a phase,' he squeaked, showing me his palms. 'I have a family.'

I sighed heavily, and consulted my watch. 'Thirty seconds from now, I plan to stand up and out you, OK?'

Panicked, he retreated to his station and raced to sign off.

'Buck up, Molly,' I encouraged him. 'Time waits for no man.'

Jolted by the very mention of his screen name, the slicker abandoned the procedure altogether, grabbed his bag and hurried away.

'Bi,' I called brightly, and watched him crash through the door.

All along my row, heads glanced his way and then mine. At the bar, even Roxi's chaperone glanced over her shoulder. A few others looked up from their screens, but a couple on the far side of the cybercafe didn't seem to notice at all. So engaged were they in conversation, I was free to glare right at them.

15

'Spare a thought for your tom during the mating season.
He must vie for the female's attention, and risk a few
scratches if he dares to advance out of turn.'
http://www.purradise.com/purrfect10.html

If a guy goes cold on a fox, he'll often just date her anyway. At least until a better opportunity arises. Of course the poor girl suspects that all is not well. Experience has conditioned her to question every move he makes. She just can't quite accept the guy could be so low until it actually happens. A fox backs out on a guy, meanwhile, she faces up to the issue. Does the decent thing and says so, even if she can't explain why. It's not going to work, she tells him. Case closed. Until that evening in the cybercafe, however, I had never witnessed one fox go cold on another. How did the dynamics of a girl on girl romance play out? Who assumed which role? Watching Christine relate to Roxi, I began to worry that such a relationship was impossible to finish. Once she loosened up, my ex could be naturally inclined towards brutal frankness, but what if my date was programmed to mistrust every word she heard?

I admit, my view was somewhat blinkered. With several rows of computer hardware coming between us, I could only see the top of their heads. Even so, I just knew things weren't going my way. No one tends to giggle when a potential fling founders, or order up drinks as a toast to the end of the affair. Seeing the barmaid arrive with yet another bout of beers left me feeling even more anxious. For alcohol mixed too readily with Christine, and she had already had a few. Any more would have a disarming effect. In fact, my cover could easily be blown. If my ex ever got involved in espionage, the enemy wouldn't have to bother injecting her with expensive truth serums. They could just buy her a pint and press the record button.

'Why don't you tell her?' I muttered to myself. 'What's going on over there?'

Straining to hear a line or steal a glimpse, I convinced myself that Christine was losing it like she had on the phone. Steadily drifting out of her depth because she didn't know how to swim for shore. I had to throw her a lifeline. Somehow sling her a cord across the cafe before my date pulled her under. Physically, there was no way I could raise her attention. Not without alerting Roxi's chaperone. There she was, at the bar at the back of the cybercafe. Sitting side on with her legs scissored high. Relaxing with a martini and a stogie that could smoulder for days. I dared not make assumptions about her sexuality, but it was clear to me she was dug in for the duration. Here for Roxi, should things go wrong. Which they would, I pledged once more, and quickly left my station to get myself another longneck.

I arrived at the bar a safe distance from her, and began to count out my small change. Starting with the coppers. As I had hoped, the barmaid took one look at the mounting stacks, and seemed suddenly driven by the need to go pick up empties. A moment after she was out of earshot, I made my move.

'Damn computers,' I sighed, addressing the crisp boxes at the back of the bar. 'Always crashing at the wrong time.'

As I expected, the chaperone shot me a cursory glance then turned back to her drink.

'Ever happen to you?'

This time, she looked back and saw me waiting for her reply.

'It's as if they can read your mind,' I said. 'Like they sense when you're doing something really critical, and screw up just to remind you who's in charge.'

She shrugged, reached round and tamped her cigar in the ashtray. 'I don't have much time for technology.'

'Is that right? Cyberwidow, huh?'

'Cyber *what?*'

'Who is it?' I asked, and turned to face the computer banks. 'Which one of these anoraks have you lost to the Internet?'

A cool smile. She sipped her drink. 'It's not like that,' she said, and motioned to the far side of the cafe. 'I'm here with a friend.'

All this time I'd been keeping a cautious eye on the girls. Ready to turn my back should either of them pause for breath. Even from this angle, Roxi would have to spin right round to see me. She'd also have to deal with Christine's flowers which, I noticed, were resting across her lap. I wondered who valued them most.

Still facing the bar, the chaperone said, 'She's on a blind date. Some woman she met online.'

'A *woman*,' I said, like it was news.

'Lucky for her, I'm sure you'll agree.'

I glanced over my shoulder for a moment. My date was telling some story with the help of her hands. Christine, nodding enthusiastically. Leaning in like she might miss out.

'Is it on?' I asked.

'If it isn't, she'll call me in and we'll leave.'

I narrowed my gaze. 'Twenty quid says it's off.'

She looked at me suspiciously. 'In coins, or legal tender?'

'Whatever you got,' I told her. 'Are you in or are you out?'

A short pause followed, and for a horrible moment I half wondered if she thought I'd been alluding to her sexuality.

'You seem very confident,' she said finally.

'I should be. Your friend's hitting on my ex.'

This time she faced right up to me, but where I had hoped to see alarm I saw only the glint of defiance.

'So?'

'So I know what she's like,' I said, and circled a finger round my temple. 'Want to leave me the money and go rescue her? Or would you prefer to waste time while I show you the scars? Eighteen months together, I try to bail out and she comes at me with the bread knife.' I lifted my brow, grabbed the rim of my T-shirt as if to do the same, and was relieved to see her return to her drink. I followed her in close, conspiratorial. If she wanted to know more, I planned to fabricate a tale that made my ex sound so unstable it was a wonder that she dared to wear heels. Instead, get this, she produces a fat clip of folded purple notes from her purse.

'Fifty says Roxi can handle her.'

'*Fifty?*'

'Fifty,' she repeated. 'Partly because I'm wise to what Roxi can do to a woman, but mostly because I'm keen to know whether it's a man or mouse I'm dealing with here.' I tried hard not to look outclassed. Sensing myself on a losing streak as one corner of her mouth stretched into a smile. 'Come on, baby, what's it to be?'

Her name was Tallulah, so she said. According to her story, Roxi was an old friend, and, briefly, a wild experiment. One she didn't regret but wouldn't repeat, but which had brought them closer together. I said that Christine had been a commitment. One I really should have got committed. We smiled politely and shook hands. Tallulah sported long, manicured fingernails, painted crimson like her mouth. She wore her hair in a sheer black bob, with one side pinned behind the most delicate ear I had ever seen. She was drinking a vodka gimlet. One part lime juice, two parts vodka, and a teaspoon of sugar. I knew because I asked. She said it was a drink to be savoured. I wasn't so sure about the cigar. At first I thought it was an affectation. Until I saw her roll the smoke from her mouth. Going by the money on the bar, it seemed she also liked to gamble. My pride dictated that I had to accept, even though I didn't carry that kind of money.

'If you don't intervene,' I warned, 'Christine will eat her for breakfast.'

Tallulah peeled another note from her wedge. 'Roxi has a voracious appetite.'

One hundred pounds. For a beat I considered nipping across to the cashpoint, then wondered aloud what the fuck we were doing.

'We're talking about our ex-girlfriends,' I reminded her. 'Not race horses. Call it off before someone gets hurt.'

Another fifty fell over the first two.

'What's wrong, baby? Worried she can't go the distance?'

I looked up and saw Tallulah grinning at me, the cigar already clenched victoriously between her teeth. Desperate as I was for Christine to pull out, I couldn't back down now.

'Well?'

'You accept credit from strangers?'

Tallulah unplugged the stogie and said she did. If the price was right.

'Then another fifty on top says mine leads yours home tonight.'

She dropped the extra note, let it go like she could afford to let the whole clip fall. 'Roxi always calls the shots.'

I had no choice. As much as I wanted it off between the girls, it was on between Tallulah and me. We shook hands once more, this time to secure a wager, then turned to discover that both of us had missed the damn finish. Indeed, it appeared that I had already blown my biggest gamble of the evening. A realisation that left me gawping across at the workstation, unable to blink, barely able to breathe.

Roxi and Christine had gone.

'I've lost,' I whispered, and looked back at her as if to seek confirmation.

'All bets null and void,' corrected Tallulah. 'Neither of us won.' She retrieved her fifties, then batted a glance at the tarnished pennies in front of me.

'I'd let you buy me a drink,' she said. 'But I think perhaps we should go Dutch.'

16

'Your first time may feel like a welcome release, but it could also leave you feeling traumatised.'
A.C. Découcher, *Bisexuality For Beginners*

I expected to find Christine waiting for me. Hugging the wall outside the cybercafe. Looking a little uneasy. Anxious to make up for the fact that I had just been obliged to drink to her happiness with Roxi's minted minder. I also expected to see her standing at the mouth of the tube station, and at the exit twenty minutes downline. As I trudged through the puddles across the still, moon-silvered square, I half expected to see my ex waiting for me on the step. At the very least, I anticipated a note under my door or a message on my answermachine. My email was out of bounds, I realised, on skipping the light switch and making for my desk. For my online creation was supposed to be on a date. Without me. The man who pulled her strings. Standing there in the nocturne shadows, I surrendered to the fact that there was only one other place Christine could be. At the same time, I noticed that in the pot beside my computer, Sweet William's seeds had finally started to germinate. Weird looking shoots, palsied and pale, peered out from the soil at me.

I had expected so much, but not this. Christine had really done it. She had gone with Roxi. Another woman. By my design and my direction too. Somewhere in this city, I thought, two girls were making out without me.

'Fuck it all,' I said to myself. 'What have I done?'

With the spots off, my space felt more cavernous than ever before. Darkness filled every recess. Infinite and absolute. Only the skylights provided any source of illumination or perspective. As if all but the floor had flattened out like a cardboard box, exposing me to the star-crossed vaults above. I felt empty and excluded, isolated and insecure.

I couldn't face consoling myself with the dregs from the sweet sherry bottle. Instead, I opened up the bin bag and rooted out an old cardigan that Christine had left behind. I remembered how snug she looked inside it, and hoped the same feeling might rub off on me. It still smelled faintly of her perfume. Whatever it was, in my mind at that moment it was Tramp. I even granted k.d. lang some air time, believing that it might shed light on her way of thinking. Nothing helped, however. The music failed to speak to me, and the cardigan proved way too tight across the shoulders. Plus it was pastel, and I didn't have the hips to carry off the sash.

Snuffing the torch song from my speakers, I shook off the extra layer and slumped onto the sofa. Maybe I'd just had the volume up too high, but suddenly the silence seemed so profound. No distant drone of traffic. No scavengers in the bins. No drunks serenading themselves home. Nothing. Just the creak of the world on its axis. I settled back a little further, and faced up to the cosmos once again. Watched the big wheel turning without me, hoping for a sign. If my girls were the mothership, I was mission control. Anxiously awaiting news of their safe re-entry. BiRuth would understand, I thought. He had been faced with a similar communications blackout once before. Was still going through it, in fact. Until I had relocated my so-called-body, however, I couldn't risk making my voice heard online. Sweet William had said my connections deserved to be severed, and maybe he was right. For here I was in limbo. Shut out from one world. Shut off from the other.

I leaned forward, pulled the coffee table closer and sighed. This was it. The moment had arrived, as foretold by my dealer. And why not? I just couldn't cope with the situation while feeling so straight. Retrieving his skunk weed from my sock, I stripped off three, four, five then six skins. Then, with great reluctance, I embarked on the construction of an apocalyptic joint.

Girls have never had it so good. Time was, a boy claimed all the glory. At work and also at rest. Nowadays, it's girls who excel. In everything. At school, she's a sponge. At home, she's a rock, and a comet in her career. Boys, on the other hand, are bad news. Good for nothing but serial failure and self-destruction. From steering stolen cars into walls to driving beer bottles into faces, we've turned the fuck up into an art form. Where once a proud father might crash from the labour room to announce the birth of his son, today he'll shuffle out looking shattered for all the wrong reasons. After all, what future lies ahead for his lad? What prospects does he face when girls are bagging all the best things in life? Including, it seemed, each other.

My completed spliff looked more like a telescope. Determined to stay positive as I sparked it up, I pondered how good it must feel to be a twenty-first century fox. In some ways, I decided, it seemed the most desirable thing a man could wish to be. Especially now it meant you were more likely to have sex with them too.

Sliding down the sofa, I launched a stream of smoke into the gloom and wondered how long it would be before Christine knocked on my door. I predicted that whatever it was that had tempted her to take off with Roxi, guilt would eventually bring her back down to earth. And I would be here. Kurtz-like in the shadows. Awaiting her presence. Ready to debrief her. Several tokes later, I even started to think the whole episode might improve my chances with Roxi. Having sated one side of her sexuality, surely a bi would crave a change of scene? As I had a shoot the next morning, I would be in a prime position to pick up where my ex had left off. Christine might have stolen the show on this, the opening night, but ultimately, she was nothing but the warm up act for the real me. The main man. I took a final hit on the joint, in awe of the insight and perception that had come from getting caned like this, and was immediately consumed by a profound desire to eat Pringles.

17

*'Aim to merge light and dark shadows with a flat
blending brush, particularly under the eyes.'*
Verity Pepper, *Make Up a Million*

By the time I hit the hotseat in the studio next morning, my appetite had deserted me. So too had the courage behind all my convictions. Waiting alone in the dressing room, I felt strung out, tense and twitchy. As if I expected some Nazi dentist to walk in at any second, not make-up. The skunk had left me feeling like I'd been hit by an elephant tranquilliser, and I didn't need a mirror to remind me that I wasn't at my best. Sweet William had already claimed that pleasure. After Christine failed to show up at my space, my early-morning reconciliation with him only served to make me feel even more unsure about myself:

'Tell me the fox wasn't responsible,' he said, while counting out change for a punter. Some withered old white-hair stooped over a Senior Shopper. 'Tell me you look like you do because it didn't work out.'

I wasn't prepared to open up to him about it just then. Not in the presence of a pensioner. Even if she did look deaf. I also had something for him, and wanted his full attention. The money sorted, Sweet William leaned across the counter and passed her a single potted geranium. She reached up high with both hands, her head still horribly bowed, and received it like it might spill.

'Enjoy,' he said, as she stashed it away.

I switched my attention from my dealer to the mute old lady. Sweet's manner with her, it just didn't seem right being this fresh. I stood back smartly to let her dodder into the crowded drag, avoiding her glance when she mumbled her thanks.

'You didn't,' I remarked, filling her space at the counter. 'Did you?'

My dealer zipped up his money belt, and confirmed that he had. 'I know it's not pretty,' he said with a shrug. 'But if I turn away the crack whores they'll only come back and rob me.'

'That's OK then,' I said dryly.

Only Sweet acted like he wasn't being funny. Like he meant business. I turned again to look for the old lady, but she had gone. As if somehow she had picked up her pace as soon as I stopped watching her.

'Jesus, you did!'

'Appearances can be deceptive,' he replied, and swept the counter clean. 'As well you know.' Sweet William, speaking gravely, like he was in a position to lecture *me*. Still, it reminded me why I had stopped by.

'Willie,' I said hesitantly, and produced the roses I'd been hiding behind my back. 'I'm sorry about the way I behaved. Some of the things I said, I didn't like myself much afterwards. I want to make it up to you.'

My dealer regarded the flowers as if they were the last thing he had been expecting. Which was why I had picked them up on the way over.

'Apology accepted,' he growled, then loosened up with a smile. 'How much did you pay for these, then?'

'Less than I would from you,' I said. 'But you get better service here.'

'Plus gratuities.'

'The finest.'

'As the size of your pupils testify,' my dealer observed, and began to peel off the wrapping. 'So are you going to tell me why you look like you've been up all night?'

I informed him I had been hoping for someone to get in touch.

'Don't tell me your Internet girlfriend failed to show up for the date?' Willie, feigning surprise as he said this.

'Oh, she showed all right.' I paused to clear my throat. 'Only she didn't see me exactly.'

'No?' he said, distracted, having just plucked something off one of the petals. I waited for him to finish examining it, but cut him dead as he cursed me for bringing him greenfly.

'She saw Christine.'

Silenced, my dealer binned the whole bunch without once taking his eyes from me. As I filled him in about the photo switch and the phone call, his brow folded up then flattened out again. Like his brain had struggled to swallow the whole story.

'She was supposed to cool things off, Sweet. Then set her up with me as a man. Recommend a nice guy she knew, that kind of line. Only things moved beyond my control.'

'How out of your control?'

'I'm not sure. They left before I could find out.'

'That's out of control,' confirmed Willie, then drew breath as he considered the implications. 'You mean they left together?'

I nodded.

'In the *lesbian* sense of the word?'

'Looks that way.'

'On the way out, did either of them slip a hand inside the other's back pocket? They always do that, girls together. I guess because they can.'

I told him that I didn't know. My back had been turned at the time.

'Right, like it was getting boring to watch.'

'Actually, I was sorting a bet.'

'No!'

'It's true.'

'Get outta here! Who with?'

'Her chaperone.'

'Jesus wept!'

'It's complicated. I didn't intend to make money out of all this.'

'Did you win?' my dealer asked, incredulous.

'Neither of us saw them leave. But if Christine made the first move I would have been up two hundy.'

'Man,' he declared, and pressed the heel of his hand to his forehead. 'You're a piece of work. This fox must be a piece too.'

I could have told him that Roxi stimulated my senses more than anything he could sell me. That I had seen her face in the stars all night. Her voice in the birdsong that roused me in the morning. The warmth of her presence in the sunshine on my back. Only I didn't think Sweet would believe me, so I stopped short after her name and just agreed. She was a piece. My dealer, however, appeared to expect the kind of thing I'd held back. He regarded me pensively. Made me feel like a plant in need of repotting.

'You like her don't you?'

'No. I just get a kick from fixing up my ex with girls I fancy.'

'I mean, you *really* like her,' stressed Willie. 'This isn't just a rebound thing.'

'It's real for me,' I said. 'But I can't speak for Christine.'

Sweet William folded his forearms. Under the puffa, he was wearing a Whitney Houston tour T-shirt. I could only assume it said 'Security' on the back.

'You know, I often wondered about your ex. Always asking for orchids out of season.'

'Come on, Willie,' I reasoned. 'Christine's basically in between men.'

'You make her sound like a sandwich.'

'Mark my words, she needs a man.'

'To give her a decent filling? Is that what you're implying?'

'No, but—'

'Don't go down there. Keep your dick out of this.'

'All I'm saying is Christine isn't serious about Roxi.' Even as I shared this with Sweet, I could see I no longer had a voice in this conversation.

'Because if you're wrong about her,' he insisted, 'if she gives up on men altogether then you're bound to feel responsible. Like you were the one who made her realise there are more rewarding ways a girl can get her oats.'

I compressed my lips, and glared at him. 'Like I said, we did not have a problem with the sex. I measured up fine in that department.'

'Let me ask you this then,' he said, and spread both hands. 'If size doesn't matter—'

'Which it doesn't,' I cut in.

'Then how come they make vibrators so damn big?'

I frowned at him, glanced distastefully at the gap between his palms. 'Vibrators you get in all sizes.'

'Sure you do,' he said. 'From about *ten* inches upwards.'

'Behave.'

'I defy you to show me a dildo that couldn't be used to cosh a man.'

I thought about this for a second, sensed my conviction waning, then tried a different tack. 'Sweet, everyone knows it's what you do with it that counts.'

'Right,' he agreed, at last. 'And how many speeds do *you* come in?'

'Speed is irrelevant. Time and attention is what counts.'

He glanced at his watch. 'How long did you say Christine had been awol?'

'*Thesexwasfine!*' I snapped. 'What they're doing is different, alright!'

'Easy, tiger,' my dealer acting surprised all of a sudden. 'I'm just trying to help you through this. It's tough, being the guy who can't compete. I sympathise, really. But you got to deal with this somehow. Find your way, just like Christine.'

'Christine has not found her way,' I insisted. 'The only thing she needs to find is a way to apologise to me. I just wish she had the decency to face me about it. My guess is she's too embarrassed.'

'Or busy.'

'Willie!'

'Just covering every base.' He shrugged, then paused to lick his top lip. 'You think maybe they're still . . .'

'Enough, Sweet,' I snapped. 'This isn't making me feel any better.'

'But if she's really sold on this Roxi fox, then you'll have to do the decent and let her roll with it.'

'No way. I saw her first.'

'And how do you plan to stake your claim? Grab her by the hair and drag her back to your cave? You don't even know where she lives.'

'No, but I know where she works.' I glanced at my watch. I had arranged for the studio car to pick me up from the market. It was due in a matter of minutes. I told Willie about the forthcoming cat commercials. My chance to make over with Roxi. 'I'm just going to sit back in the chair and let her see what she's missing.'

'Strike while the fox is hot, eh?'

'She rates honesty, Willie. Said so herself. At least I get the chance to start afresh with her. As the real me. Which is more than Christine can manage now.'

My dealer rubbed the bristles on his chins. 'Say I was in with Roxi, not Christine. If it was me dating her, would you make a move then?'

'No,' I said instinctively. 'Of course not.'

'Why? What's the difference?'

'You're a guy.'

'So?'

'Code of honour, I guess.'

'Just because you lost out to a fox, the principle remains the same. Leave them be, Ren.'

'Christine stole Roxi from under my nose!'

'She did not. She just got in there before you.'

'By using me. Using my charm. My damn words on the screen!'

'So you can spell good, Reynard. How does that affect her performance in the sack?'

'But Sweet, I can give Roxi more than that. She's drawn to my personality online. All I need is the chance to be me face to face.'

'Just bide your time. Find out what's going on in the background before you make a move you might regret. If Roxi's on a roll with a beautiful doll fox like Christine she's not going to be interested in rolling with you right now.'

'Like I said, they are *not* rolling.' I would have continued to stand my ground, but Sweet looked set to jump the counter all of a sudden. The purr of an approaching engine put his alarm in context for me, and I quickly turned to acknowledge my car's arrival. We couldn't see through the tinted windows, but it pulled up to frame my reflection clearly enough.

'I have to go,' I said. 'Do I really look like I've had a bad night?'

'Appalling.'

'So how should I play it?' I asked, backing across the pavement now. 'Stay silent like last time. Let her think that in my mind's eye I can see her in the buff?'

The driver stepped out to open my door. Sweet William, keeping his eye on him all the way.

'Be a friend first,' he said as I ducked inside. 'Not a fuckwit.'

'Hi,' I said to my reflection. 'How are you?'

I abandoned the rehearsal right there, and scowled at the dressing room mirror. How could I possibly open with that kind of line? Knowing what I did.

'Hey, there!' I tried again. 'Remember me?'

Once more I stopped before I could even picture her response. Just in case it lived up to my worst expectations. With so much of her time unaccounted for, I couldn't be sure what Christine might have let slip. If she'd squealed about my role in the date, then there was every chance Roxi would never forget me. God, I thought. Imagine. Maybe she wouldn't say anything until she had me good. Let me think I was way in with her as she made me look pretty. Then stick me with the mascara pen. I breathed in from the diaphragm, lounged back in the chair a little, and decided to try something a little more friendly than friendly. Just to exercise my options. Build up my fast fading confidence.

'Hey, hot stuff!' I said, and fired a finger pistol. 'Look at you.'

It was only as the imaginary smoke settled that I realised I was no longer alone. For there she was in my mirror. My make-up date. My dream. Wearing a powder-blue slip dress and a smile that said she had heard every damn word I just said.

'Looking good yourself,' said Roxi, and closed the dressing-room door with the sole of her shoe. She was carrying two coffees, and set them both down on the shelf before me. 'At least you will once I've finished up.'

'What do you plan to do?' I asked nervously.

Roxi reached for her drink, and I braced myself for a scalding.

'I mean to bring out the man in you,' she said, and paused to take a sip. 'Now sit back and let me work out where to start.'

18

'Cats respond well when you're on the same level.'
http://www.purradise.com/purrfect10.html

Exactly how much pressure can a man take? Not just mentally or physically, but sexually too. I'd heard of one instance where these three central characteristics can be measured simultaneously. The buckling test. A standard scientific procedure for evaluating the effectiveness of impotence treatments. Sweet William had told me about it one stoned session round at my space. Claimed he knew a guinea pig who had volunteered for the trial. Qualified because he couldn't get wood. At least not without the aid of a needle, a pump or a pill.

Under strictly clinical conditions of course, the good doctors get you up and running before a kilogramme weight is placed upon your head. The head that arguably contains no brains. If your manipulated member stays pointing skywards then it's smiles all round. Even if the drugs don't work at least you get to pick up a cheque along with your trousers. It's an unenviable experience, though not intolerable, I argued. Not when you think of the poor bastard required to test the *test*. With no chemical assistance, he's the one faced with the real trial, and my dealer had agreed. In fact neither of us could imagine the kind of additional weight placed upon the fully functioning dummy enlisted to authenticate the findings. Unlike his fellow volunteers, it's not just his virility he'd be forced to expose to the crescent of clipboards but his strength of spirit too. For if the slightest doubt or insecurity creeps into the equation, then the pillars that support the purpose of his very existence could come crashing down.

She meant to bring out the man in me. That's what Roxi said, and as she tilted my chin so I faced her directly, that's exactly what I feared. Like I was about to be submitted to her own brand of buckling test. Had she turned up in a white coat I would have felt no more intimidated. Mentally. Physically. Sexually. I was at her mercy in every way. If Roxi knew of my involvement in her date with Christine, I certainly wasn't going to fathom it in the dark pools of her eyes. I felt like a small boy contemplating whether or not to dive into unknown waters. Fearful that I might drown in the impenetrable depths, or crack my skull on hidden rocks. The weight of uncertainly began to bear down. More so, when she blinked and said, 'What are we going to do with you?'

'Pardon me?'

'You have a nice face,' she said, turning it one way then the other like she was sussing out the best side to slap. 'But you sure don't look after your skin.'

A moment passed before I realised I was still alive. That perhaps she didn't know anything about my hand in her affairs. My relief was tempered only by the fact that she was right. Having spent much of the night keeping vigil, I looked like I felt. Desiccated. Inside and out.

'When was the last time you moisturised?' she asked.

'Um, I don't actually.'

'Typical.'

'I am?'

'Men and moisturisers. What's the matter? Afraid it might turn you into a *girl*?'

She continued to scrutinise my skin. One word. That was all it had taken, and already I felt an unseen weight bear down on me.

'Is it terminal?' I joked weakly.

'If anyone can save you,' she said, 'I can.'

Smiling at last, Roxi put her coffee on the shelf and turned her attention to her make-up box. It opened up in tiers. I was reminded of my ex. Hoped she hadn't done something similar. Next, Roxi took a glazed cylindrical bottle and shook it up and down. A toner of some sort, I guessed. As she did so, a bang slipped loose from the folds of her hair. Then another. I gripped the arms of my seat, desperate to avoid being crushed by the visions this moment brought upon me. So what if she had let her hair down with Christine last night, I reasoned with myself. It didn't make her any different, so why did I feel so intimidated by my own imagination? Next Roxi pressed a cotton swatch to the mouth of the bottle and immediately I saw her kissing my ex. Their lips locked together. Bodies entwined in a naked embrace. Shaved like a pair of pencils.

My brief for the shoot was as simple as it was undemanding. Having fallen out with the moggy in the first commercial, it was the turn of my on-screen partner to fork the food into the bowl. This time, however, the cat would watch her lovingly, while I skulked in the background and watched in envy. Like I cared about who the manky-looking wormball loved the most. It was a shoddy storyline. As thin as the muck I had been hired to endorse. According to the producer, whose appearance in the dressing room I actually welcomed at that moment, my role was to amuse as well as inspire.

'You're the clown here,' she told me, the clipboard tucked under one arm.

'Oh, cheers.'

'I mean it, Ren. It's important the viewer laughs at you. Not with you. Particularly the men in the audience.'

'Why?'

'In Korea, housewives tend to be the primary purchasers of pet food. The manufacturers are hoping these commercials might persuade their husbands to pop a tin or two in the shopping basket.'

'So you see me as a role model?'

'Not quite,' she said. 'We think they'll watch you, then switch off knowing they can do better.'

It was my cue to switch off too. The producer standing right behind me. Outlining how the ad campaign would climax in the third instalment and stuff. Seemingly unaware that I was barely listening. Her antagonistic attitude I could take. But not while Roxi was working so closely on me that I could feel the fabric of her dress brush my ear. Somehow, all talk of hitting my mark was rendered insignificant by the thought that just hours earlier the fingers rubbing Vaseline into my lips might well have been rubbing something else. Another pair of lips I didn't dare think about for fear of being squashed. I wasn't in a position to ask what went on after she and Christine had left the cybercafe, but everything about Roxi screamed post-coital.

'Don't let your coffee go cold,' she reminded me, when the producer left for the studio floor.

Seizing a respite from the pressure, I leaned forward and reached for the cup. It was then I saw the ripples in my drink, and realised how obviously my hand was trembling. Quickly I returned the coffee to the shelf. Sinking back into the chair without having taken a sip, looking like someone who couldn't handle the heat.

'It was nice of you to think of me,' I said, hoping she hadn't noticed.

Roxi moved behind me, stood where the producer had been. Looked right at me in the mirror. 'I don't think I could function without caffeine.'

She couldn't? Instantly, I wanted to know why. Was the coffee part of her daily routine, or had her overnight activities left her feeling fatigued? Just dwelling on the question made me dizzy, and when she rested her hands on the crown of my head I thought I just might blast the mirror with bits of breakfast.

'You seem a bit on edge today,' she said. 'Is everything OK?'

'Sure,' I countered quickly. 'Why wouldn't it be?'

The pressure on my head vanished, and I realised how abrupt I'd been when Roxi raised her hands in submission. 'Sometimes actors get nervous, is all.'

'Ignore me,' I said, wishing this hadn't happened. 'The last few days have been kind of stressful actually.'

'Oh?' Roxi returned her hands to my head. I hoped she wasn't into mind reading or anything.

'A friend of mine just came out of a relationship,' I confessed. 'She's been leaning on me to help her through it.'

'That's sweet,' she said, and without warning began to knead my scalp with her fingertips. In the mirror, I watched my eyebrows rise and sink in turn.

'Do you have any idea how good that feels?' I asked.

'Shiatsu. Ancient Japanese art. It's a great way to relieve stress. I can feel the tension in the meridians here. You're one uptight bunny.'

'Where did you learn to do it?' I asked. 'They don't teach this to nit nurses.'

'Trained as a masseuse back home. Quit two years ago and got into this game. Still, I like to keep my hand in.'

A masseuse. She got better by the minute. Whatever it was she was doing under my hair, nothing Sweet William fed me had ever been so disarming. Which was perhaps why my guard dropped so quickly.

'Tell me, Roxi, when did you leave the Big Apple?'

The fingers stopped. 'You know my name?'

'The production list,' I said quickly, aware that if I opened my eyes she would see me in a blind panic. I squeezed my lids a little tighter. 'I always like to know who's handling me.'

'Well then, how did you know I was from New York?'

I could hardly say that I knew so much more about her. That I could tell her Internet age from her real age. That she appreciated men to be honest from the start, just as she liked her women to be straight about their sexuality. All I could do was draw upon my acting skills like never before. Nothing dramatic. Just cool as I could keep it.

'Recognised your accent,' I said finally. 'It's unmistakable.'

'Very observant,' she replied, resuming the massage. 'You must have worked there for a while.'

I should have said Broadway. Six-month stint. Maybe with the Rostand musical. As the leading man, not the understudy. In view of the scrape I had just escaped, however, I played it safe and told her I watched a lot of TV. *Cagney and Lacey.* That sort of thing.

'You like *Cagney and Lacey*?' she said, brightening some. 'I'm their number one fan.'

'Correction,' I said, glad to be moving on. 'Number two. After me.'

'You're kidding! Who's your favourite?'

I told her I liked the one with more meat on her bones.

'I've never been able to decide. Harvey's a doll, but I've always got time for Sharon Gless.'

'Figures,' I said under my breath.

'Sorry?'

'Oh, nothing. So what's the appeal?' I asked. 'I only really tune in because it makes me feel so much better about the amount of alcohol I drink.'

'You're right,' she said. 'They do get thirsty on that show.'

'Like, how many times do you see Ponch and Jon put away bourbon on the job like that?'

'You like *CHiPs* too? Boy, we have so much in common.'

We did. More than she could ever imagine. But as we continued to debate the finer points of alcohol abuse in American cop shows, I actually felt myself bearing up under the load. For we shared a passion for something other than my ex, and this helped me relate to her. As me. Reynard. By the time she got back to finishing off my make-up, she was even calling me Ren. It was only as I went into my theory about Starsky being a closet teetotaller (he *always* did the driving) that I was reminded of my situation. When Roxi lifted the back of her hand to her mouth and yawned.

'Excuse me,' she said, and reached for the blusher. 'Didn't get home until late last night.'

That was it. I didn't stand a chance. All manner of Sapphic images began strobing my thoughts, and I feared this buckling test was close to completion. Roxi on Christine. Christine on Roxi. Both of them dressed as nuns. Red eyes from the camera flash when they turned to pose for me. That the make-up artist herself was actually right in my face was enough to make me blush. Much more so than she intended, and there was nothing I could say to excuse it. From that moment on, slowly but inexorably, the lengthening silence became a chasm between us. Only this time, I genuinely did have one thing on my mind.

Had she done it? Had Roxi really got physical with my ex? I

was burning to know again, now more than ever before. Pulverised by my own thoughts. Crushed by her close proximity. I suddenly decided that if she wasn't going to give it up direct then I would find out some other way. The moment presented itself when Roxi came back round to work some wax from my hairline to the nape of my neck. Driven to escape this self-torture, I succumbed to a call I couldn't resist. I figured Roxi was too busy up top to notice, but then she pulled back with a start.

'Did you just do what I think you did?'

'No.'

'You did!'

'I didn't,' I protested, my voice up by an octave.

Roxi. Fire in her features now. Poised to flare at any time. 'Damn it, Reynard, you *sniffed* me.'

I had. Caught with my nostrils peering down her cleavage. It hadn't taken much. Roxi had done most of the leaning in. An inch out of my seat was all I had needed, but it was clearly an inch too much. In that one deranged moment my animal instinct assumed control over my better judgement. I had inhaled deeply, then let it all out in one flimsy denial.

'Hay fever,' I said, and pinched my septum as if it was giving me grief.

'At this time of year?'

'Must be a cold then.'

She shook her head. Immune to my excuses.

'Cocaine. Didn't want to say anything. You know how it is.'

Roxi said she didn't. Didn't believe me. And there I was. Clean out of excuses.

'OK,' I confessed. 'You smell great. Really fantastic. I know I sound like a sap but your perfume knocks me out.' I wasn't bullshitting her now. It was an understated fragrance. Fuck knows what it was, but it was nice, and I was hoping she'd be pleased that I had picked up on it. Indeed, when she spoke next she was calmer. A little guarded, perhaps. But definitely flattered.

'I guess I'll take that as a compliment.'

'Pleasure,' I said, relieved to be out of danger.

'Except I'm not wearing any.'

I froze. There in the chair. My eyes locked on Roxi as she turned unabashed to tease my hair in the mirror. The hinges of my jaw straining to close. Which they did, when I realised I had got my answer. Not the one I wanted, perhaps. But I could deal with the consequences later. Now I knew for sure that she had been with Christine, for it was her perfume I could detect. A hint, maybe. But that was enough. I didn't need to know its damn name. What I knew was they had mingled.

'Sorry,' I said. 'I shouldn't have overstepped the mark like that.'

'Don't worry about it. Most men never even comment on a perfume. They just buy it.' Roxi finished fussing with my hair, and stood back to examine her work.

'So,' I said, choosing my words carefully, 'is anyone buying you perfume at the moment?'

'Not yet.'

'Not yet?'

'OK,' she said. 'I just met someone. But it's early days. Haven't got to the perfume-buying stage, that's for sure.'

Another mental flash. Christine stepping up behind my make-up artist. Sliding the straps of her slip dress from her shoulders.

'So what stage are you at?'

Roxi stopped looking at me in the professional sense, and glared at me instead. Immediately, the vision of my ex kissing her bare neck vanished. Leaving me with nothing to face but the consequences of my indiscretion.

'You mean are we sleeping with each other?'

The room went white for a beat. Had she meant it? Surely not. Much as I would have welcomed an answer, I recovered sufficiently to dismiss my inquiry.

'I'm sorry. None of my business, right?'

'You got it,' she said, and untied the gown I was wearing. 'Why do guys always have to know about the sex bit? What's wrong with romance, eh?' Had a smile not formed around her opinion, I might have just abandoned the whole shoot. As it was, she left me grinning sheepishly.

'What I meant to say was I hope it works out. Romantically speaking.'

'Sure you do,' she said, and dusted me down with a powder brush.

A knock at the door just then. Followed by a disembodied voice. My two-minute call.

'You're on,' she said with a wink, and invited me to stand. 'Let's just say I'm sure you'll be the first to know if things firm up between us.'

I left the chair quickly, hoping a thought wouldn't follow me. For what could possibly firm up that wasn't attached to a man?

'I really didn't mean to be nosy back then,' I said anxiously.

'Hey, no sweat. It makes a change to work on someone who's actually prepared to have a conversation. Normally the talent just sit here in silence. Treat me like I don't exist.'

Said the woman who had recently become the axis for my world.

'Are you always this forgiving?' I asked, hopefully.

'Why fall out when we're gonna be seeing a whole lot more of each other over the next few days.'

'We are?' I said, then realised she was talking about work. 'Oh yeah. Of course. The ad campaign. Looking forward to it already.'

I studied my reflection, but quickly found myself watching Roxi instead. She stood right beside me, her attention turned to the mirror too, and did what I had seen in my dreams. She slid the pin from her hair. Her locks fell like a balm. Transforming her appearance so dramatically I actually turned face on to admire her. Away from the mirror, the dressing room seemed to shrink. Like it was only built for one. The main attraction. Roxi. Lipstick in her hand now. I felt like her biggest fan.

'Going anywhere special?' I asked.

Without looking at me, as if her mind was on other matters, she said, 'Just meeting a girlfriend for lunch.'

19

*'Be attracted to more than one person, but sexual
with only one.'*
A.C. Découcher, *Bisexuality For Beginners*

Girlfriend. Girl. Friend. What did Roxi mean? As a woman, she could have been talking about very different things. For when a fox says she's meeting a girlfriend, it doesn't necessarily follow that she's sleeping with her too. She could just as well be referring to her best mate, in fact, so why was it different for guys? What was it that made the boundaries so much more clearly defined for us? That's where I went adrift. Were I to mention to the film crew that I had hooked up with my boyfriend before pitching up at the studio, people would look at my relationship with Sweet William from an entirely different perspective.

I dwelled on the issue throughout the shoot. Managing without any effort whatsoever to appear grimly sidelined while the cat cuddled up to my on-screen missus. She wasn't my type. The only thing bigger than her ambition was her hair. Possibly also her breasts, which seemed a tad too fake for me. As did her affection for the camera, and my former co-star too. Right from the first take, she was all strokes, tickles, nuzzles and hugs, and the damn thing *adored* her for it. Honestly, it was a sickening sight. Almost sexual. Made me feel even more redundant than ever before, and I was glad when the whole thing finally wrapped. According to the producer, my star turn was scheduled for the shoot the next day. 'A real scene stealer', as she put it. Managing in the same breath to make it sound like something I really wouldn't want to do. I pretended to listen, but I was looking right through her. Didn't even bother asking how this next commercial would link into the last. After three and a half hours of mooching around on set, I was more interested in getting back to my dressing room than sucking up to someone who evidently talked to men like she did to children.

Disappointingly, I found myself obliged to remove my own make-up. It was then that I began to wonder whether Roxi's lunch appointment had extended into dessert.

When I finally swung clear of the the studio doors, I discovered it was hissing down. Rain like glass shards. Shattering on the pavement as I hurried across to my waiting car. I was relieved to find the driver didn't regard the journey home as an opportunity to test my opinion from left to far right. It made a change from the kind of political diversion I always had to put up with on standard taxi rides. This guy was silent as he drove me back, and I was glad for it. Pleased, too, that the rush hour had yet to choke the roads and delighted, finally, to pass Christine just before we turned into the square. I didn't ask to stop like my heart just had. Preferring instead to let my ex find me frowning outside my space. On seeing me there, sheltering in the narrow porch, she slowed her step a little. Waiting for a sign that it was safe to approach. I nodded at her solemnly, then faced up to the harsh, unforgiving skies.

'Turned out shite again.'

Still keeping her distance, Christine said, 'It wasn't forecast, that's for sure.'

I returned my attention to her. Hands in my pockets, but less of the weather in my expression now. The rain had plastered her high cut fringe to her forehead. Framing the trepidation in her face. She blinked at me. Looked like she was lost. I pulled the keys from my pocket. Turned for the door.

'You'd better come in.'

Christine clearly hadn't dressed for the downpour. To be frank, she seemed better prepared for playgroup. Honestly, she looked like a four-year-old. Hair pulled up in fluffy-banded bunches. Pink and white stripe crop top and pedal pushers. That her wet clothes clung to her body put her in a very different class, however. I decided to hold off on my offer to find her a towel. Just until she had revealed a little more to me.

'You want to talk about it?' I slung my keys on the coffee table, and turned for her response. Thinking, did I even have to ask? Hugging herself, avoiding my eyes, Christine said, 'I think it's too late, actually.'

I watched a drop glide off her nose before exploding right in front of her.

'Damn right it's too late!' I snapped. 'It was too late last night, when you decided to leave me like a lemon in the cybercafe.'

'Gooseberry,' she said, looking up sharply.

Like it mattered.

'What?'

'Gooseberry. When you're with a couple who'd prefer to be alone. I think the word you meant to use was gooseberry.'

'No, I meant lemon.'

'You're confusing your fruits, Ren.'

'Don't talk to me about being confused!' I was stalking around her now. 'Don't even talk to me about fruits, for that matter.'

'I understand why you're cross.'

'Cross! I'm *furious*! But mostly at myself, Christine. Idiot that I am, I kind of hoped you were clear about the plan. Talk Roxi out of the date then make way for me. But no, I went wrong because I never dreamed you'd take a piece of my pie.'

'It wasn't like that.'

'I just hope she tasted as nice as I imagined.'

'Stop it, Ren.'

'And since when did you go for women?' I added, standing behind her now barking like a drill sergeant. 'Is this like a teen dream come true, or did you just basically decide to make my week really crappy? Finish with me one day. Turn bisexual the next.'

'I am not bisexual,' she said abruptly. 'It means more to me than that.'

'Don't even say it.' I raised my finger. Almost laughed at where this was going. 'Christine, you're no more of a lesbian than I am. And believe me, I know my capabilities.'

'Don't do this.'

'Was I really so bad that you lost all faith in men?'

A sob. Then her head bowed into her hands. Shoulders shuddering.

'Do I regard that as a yes?' I asked bitterly.

Her bunches swung one way then the other. I still wasn't sure how to take it. Or what I was doing pressing her to confirm my greatest fear.

'I hate it when I'm the one who does all the talking.' My voice lowered now. 'You make me feel even worse than I do already.'

But Christine wasn't listening, and shook away my hand when I tried to console her. I backed off a little, then figured maybe it was a good time to fetch that towel.

I spent a good couple of minutes in the bathroom. Took the opportunity to remove the last trace of pan stick from my face. Even cleaned the scum line from the sink. All the time hoping that when I stepped outside again, Christine would have pulled herself together. I hadn't abandoned her to make her feel worse. Some kind of punishment thing for shutting me out of the deal. OK, I was a bit mortified by how batchelorised my bathroom had become, but that wasn't why I chose that moment to tidy up. I just found it hard to handle the opposite sex when they fell apart like this. I couldn't help thinking Roxi would have been right there for her. Wouldn't any woman? Comfortable with handling such a crisis. Understanding. Empathic. Natural. *Sisterly*. I opened the door slightly, just to see if I could hear my ex still crying, but instead heard her being counselled by k.d. bloody lang. I peeked out, saw Christine at the window gallery. Clutching the controls for my sound system. Staring mournfully at the square.

'I thought you loathed this album,' she seemed to say when I handed her the towel. A clean one from the cupboard, of course. I swapped her for the controls, then tempered the volume so I didn't have to shout back.

'I was hoping it might grow on me,' I told her. 'But I guess some things you can never get into.'

She pressed the towel to her face, then dried her fingers one by one.

'So,' I said. 'What happened?'

'It wasn't Roxi,' she said quietly. 'It was me.'

Right, I thought. Where had I heard that one before? But now was not the time to remind her.

'Would it help if I just listened?'

'What is there to say? I've made a mess of things.'

I told her that was my forte. She laughed. Despite herself. I suggested it might be a good idea if I put the kettle on. She talked as I waited for it to boil.

'Since last night,' she said, 'one thing stopped me feeling totally liberated and elated.'

'What?'

'You.'

'Oh.' I didn't know what else to say, except, 'Sorry.'

'No, *I'm* sorry. I just couldn't help myself. For a long time, Ren, I've been feeling like something was missing in my life, but I didn't know what. Then I met Roxi and realised this was it. An opportunity I couldn't afford to pass. Only now I've ruined everything.'

'For me, maybe. Why you too?'

'I've just had lunch with her.'

'I know.'

'You do? How?'

'Educated guess,' I told her, hoping to elicit more details about the night before. 'I had a feeling you girls would be hungry.'

Christine balled the towel a little tighter. 'Why couldn't I have just held off a couple of days? Played it cool for a while.'

'That's a man's job,' I said. 'Girls don't blow hot and cold. They just simmer. Makes them irresistible.' It also made them unreadable, but she didn't need to hear that.

'I might have handled things better if I'd waited.'

'Since when did waiting improve *our* approach? All that stuff about blokes not calling for two, three or four days, it doesn't stop us sounding like saps when we finally pick up the phone. You did the right thing,' I assured her. 'You seized the moment.'

'I blew it,' she replied. 'I had so much to say, but I couldn't find the words.'

'Christine, you have to learn to relax with people. God knows,

I wish you could have been more chilled when you finished with me. If only you'd explained that you felt this way about women, I wouldn't have been left to go online in search of my own answers.'

That my ex was relating to me here without a hint of unease left me feeling unsure if I should be flattered or flattened. Regardless of her feelings for me now, Christine contemplated what I had just said with a look that said do not disturb.

'Back then I couldn't even say how I felt about myself,' was what she revealed. 'Meeting Roxi changed that, but it's as new to me as it is to you, and that's what caught my tongue at lunch. I just hadn't had time to make sense of it, let alone get my feet back on the ground. From the moment I arrived at work this morning, in fact, my whole life seemed so different. Like I'd shed a skin overnight. On the way to meet Roxi, I even thought people were looking at me in a new light.'

'Might that have something to do with the fact that you're dressed like a minor?'

'But it felt good,' she continued, ignoring my remark. 'I liked the new me.'

I took two matching cups from the cupboard. Flung a tea bag into each.

'And Roxi?' I asked. 'Did she treat you differently? Was that the problem?'

'Far from it,' said Christine. 'She was just as warm and enthusiastic as she had been all night—'

'*All* night?'

'But seeing her again, across the table, Ren, it brought everything home, what we had done. That it was no big thing for Roxi just made it even weirder. Here was the woman who was responsible for transforming my life, and I couldn't even find the words to tell her.'

The kettle began to whistle. Rising in pitch and intensity then dying when I took it off the hob and poured.

'So you did, then.'

'Did what?'

'Do I have to spell it out?' I asked her, spooning out the sodden bags. 'You know. *It*. The business. You slept with Roxi.'

'Reynard!'

'What? Like I can't ask whether I'm supposed to have scored on my date last night! It was me, I'd be out there telling everyone.'

'Because you're a boy. Girls are a little more discreet.'

'Bollocks. Girls just wait until we're not listening.'

'Same thing.'

'OK,' I said, backtracking now. 'Maybe it is, but don't I have a right to know some details?'

'Please, Ren. What I did to you was unforgivable. But knowing any more won't help you understand why I had to do it.'

'Why not? Why won't I understand? Because I'm a man?'

'Because you're my ex, and I don't want to hurt you more than I have done already.'

I flipped the spoon into the sink and told her she should try me. Christine held my eye, then took her tea and walked back to the window again. Outside, the rain had slackened off. Falling in drifts, now. Defining the breeze.

'She did most of the talking.'

'That must have been a relief,' I said to myself.

An awkward silence, then another shy concession. 'I can tell you she gives a good massage.'

'Really,' I said, flatly. 'How good?'

'The best, alright.'

'And after that?' I asked, still holding out for more. 'What happened after the warm up?'

Christine spun round at this, and for a second time that day I was right down at the wire with a woman. In a place I had no business to be. 'You really want to know?' she snapped. 'We had sex! And it felt like the most natural thing in the world.'

'Thank you,' I said, then promptly felt my heart fall into my feet. 'That's all I needed to know.'

Christine had only confirmed what I had already sussed out from Roxi. But to hear her actually say it left me feeling torn in two. Like a man whose wife has just confessed her infidelity, I felt fired up by an impossible desire to learn more without hearing another word.

'Alright,' I said hesitantly. 'Maybe you could just give me just the highlights?'

'Don't push it, Reynard.'

'But you can't leave me like this. It'll kill me.'

'I am *not* going into any more details,' she asserted. 'I have too much respect for Roxi, and no desire to impress you.'

'So you think I might be impressed?'

'That's enough, Ren.'

'One more thing, then. A compromise, if you like. Then we'll leave it. I swear.'

Christine revolved back to the window, sighed some and said, 'Go on.'

I cleared my throat first, but it didn't stop my voice from sounding all weasel-like. 'How many orgasms are we talking about here?'

My ex made out like she hadn't heard me.

'Just give me a figure, Christine. Something to compute.'

'You mean something to compare,' she muttered.

'Don't be ridiculous,' I protested too quickly. 'I just want to know that you weren't disappointed.'

'Oh no,' she said wistfully, and for a moment her thoughts seemed to travel elsewhere. 'Not any more.'

I finished my tea, hoping it would fill the hollow feeling inside me. Eventually, I said, 'There'll be another time, I'm sure.'

She turned from the window. Her head followed quickly by her body. 'Ren, I made love to another woman. A *woman.*'

As if I needed reminding. Twice.

'For what it's worth,' I said, 'the first time I had sex with one, it left me feeling a little strange. But I soon found my feet, and I'm sure you will too.'

'Yeah, but you can talk under pressure. You know how to say all the right things.'

'So it seems.'

'Anyway,' she said dismissively, 'none of it really matters now.'

'So you had a bad lunch,' I reasoned. 'It's not like they refused your credit card or anything.'

'It was worse than that, Ren. Honestly, Roxi made such an effort to put me at my ease, just as she had the night before, but this time it was all conversation and I couldn't deal with it. I couldn't eat my food, I could barely even look at her. In the end I guess she thought I was trying to tell her something. She made her excuses before coffee, while I just sat there feeling stupid. Really stupid.'

I walked across to the window gallery. Stood beside my ex and looked out at the square with her. By the way Christine's voice had just trailed, I figured she was about to flood again.

'You mean you felt like a lemon?'

Another sob. This one hidden inside a guffaw. The next buried in a hug from me.

Just then, maybe we both needed to be close to someone.

20

'Enhance your good points to detract from your flaws.'
Verity Pepper, *Make Up a Million*

Christine didn't ask to take a shower. She just broke off and stole one. Said she needed to warm up. A month or so earlier, I might have persuaded her to share a bath with me instead. As it was, she looked like she needed some time alone. Even if my hose attachment didn't measure up to much. Still, the image kept me company while I sat down at my desk and logged on. As her. NuBiFem. The dirtiest of stop outs. For now that her physical incarnation had slunk back to me, I was safe at last to step out online and ensure that she would never escape again. My modem made a stuck-pig kind of protest, but I was adamant. If my ex and I were to move on as individuals, then all this nonsense had to stop bringing us together.

Strange, then, that I should feel a rush of excitement on seeing that she had post. Nothing from Tony. Naturally. But an unexpected email, nonetheless.

sender: VSQ

title: Warning from the Viagra Snatch Squad

I was intrigued. It didn't seem like spam. The junk mail of the cyber age. Spam invited you to improve yourself. Financially. Emotionally. Physically. Pornographically. Spam arrived under a tabloid shoutline. A one in a million chance to become rich, happy, attractive or blind. Virtual money shots in every sense. But this unopened email was different. Sinister and threatening, but tempting me all the same. Certainly more enticing than the prospect of ordering up my Virtual Vitals and then holding my finger on the delete key. Behind me, I could hear water slapping.

I had a couple of minutes. Enough time to lay to rest my online incarnation. Or so I thought.

> **email to:** NuBiFem
> **from:**　　VSQ
> **subject:**　Warning from the Viagra Snatch Squad
>
> ---
>
> Hey, Hun Bun,
> Been watching you recently. Nice style. Very convincing. For a *guy*!
> Now be a good boy and stop being a girl. You have until midnight to destroy your screen name and Virtual Vitals.
> Consider this your only warning, creep.
> The Viagra Snatch Squad xxxx

I read the note once, and wondered if it would have had more of an impact arriving by hand. Pieced together from cut up newspaper headlines. At least that way I might have had something to take seriously.

'This is a joke,' I assured myself, tickled by their name but not their manner. For where was the law forbidding men to go online as women? And who the hell would know that I had done so anyway? As I saw it, cyberspace was somewhere you could live out your fantasies and nobody would be any the wiser. A kind of digital dreamscape. Nevertheless, I figured whoever was behind this email deserved to know they were messing with more than the average LezGyrl. Stabbing the keys with my forefingers, I began to punch out a short response. Halfway through telling this clown exactly where I planned to dump the demand, however, my computer beeped at me indignantly. Again when I hit another key. I glanced up, and saw the reason why. It felt as if she had slipped the note in on my desk top then stepped smartly out of range.

> **Quick-E to:** NuBiFem
>
> ---
>
> **RoxiNYC:**　　Am I disturbing?

Was Roxi disturbing? Fuck, yes. I hadn't slept properly for days.

Couldn't eat or think clearly either. Since meeting her, in fact, the only things that hadn't appeared to suffer were my acting abilities.

NuBiFem:	Not at all. Just dealing with my emails.
RoxiNYC:	Christine, we need to talk.

I still found it hard to get my head around the fact that I was speaking for my ex. I even considered calling Christine from the bathroom. But then I reflected on how far she had gone without me, and my instinct told me to quit dithering and say something.

NuBiFem:	What's on your mind?
RoxiNYC:	You. Me. Us.
NuBiFem:	Any one in particular?
RoxiNYC:	If I can be frank for a moment, I actually logged on to forget about the first and last.
NuBiFem:	Oh dear.
RoxiNYC:	Make some new friends. Move on before I get hurt.

I sensed a break-up coming. A chance to make a fresh start. All I had to do was stand aside as Christine, and be sure that I was waiting there for Roxi. The only problem was I felt numb just thinking about it. Like *I* was being dumped here, not my ex.

NuBiFem:	Is that what you want? A split?
RoxiNYC:	No! I thought we had something good going together. But at lunch it was clear you were trying to tell me otherwise.

I imagined them together at the table. Roxi trying to keep things together. Christine with her eyes in the bread basket. Bad vibes hovering like an unwanted waiter.

NuBiFem:	I didn't mean things to turn out this way.

I sat back for a beat, and wondered who was talking here. Me or Christine.

RoxiNYC:	If you're having second thoughts, just say.
NuBiFem:	On the contrary. You're the best thing that's happened to me since I discovered boys.
RoxiNYC:	Is that a compliment?
NuBiFem:	You've had such an effect on me, the truth is I just don't know how to be myself in your presence.
RoxiNYC:	I'm very flattered.
NuBiFem:	And I'm just sorry I couldn't put this into words for you earlier.

It occurred to me then that in some ways neither myself nor my ex were responsible for the words up there on the screen. She, I realised, had found her own voice. NuBiFem. Distinctive and unique. At odds with my own, maybe, but expressing my kind of feelings. In fact only she could handle the kind of disclosure that followed. Christine would have zipped right up, while I would have risked coming desperately undone.

RoxiNYC:	You definitely knew how to be yourself last night.
NuBiFem:	I did?
RoxiNYC:	You know you did ;o) I've never had sex like that before.

Neither had I, but I couldn't tell Roxi. Even so, I knew not to play it like a man this time. To push for more detail. Seek an action replay. Or confirmation of my sexual prowess.

NuBiFem:	I must say I feel a little dazed today.

| RoxiNYC: | Dazed? I'm so exhausted I've had to take the after-noon off work! |

'Christine never had that effect on me,' I muttered to myself. It was the sound of taps spinning shut that reminded me who I was again.

NuBiFem:	I'm glad I didn't disappoint.
RoxiNYC:	Me too.
NuBiFem:	And I'm sorry if I seemed cranky earlier. You have to remember this is all very new to me.

Then Roxi revealed something that made me glow. It had nothing to do with Christine, and yet it had everything to do with her.

RoxiNYC:	It's funny how I feel more comfortable with this.
NuBiFem:	With what?
RoxiNYC:	Talking with you here.
NuBiFem:	Same with me.
RoxiNYC:	At lunch the most exciting thing we talked about was the rain. Right now, I don't even know what's going on with the weather outside! Only one window can interest me at the moment, Christine, and that's the one I'm facing. Chatting online to you.

I glanced up at the skylight. It was clearing up nicely.

NuBiFem:	OK, let's make the most of it.
RoxiNYC:	How?
NuBiFem:	Tell me something about you that I don't know.

A smile crossed my face as I asked her this. I thought of BiRuth. Recalled the thrill that grabbed me when the very same question cropped up on my own monitor. I hoped it would have the same disarming effect on Roxi. An invitation for her to be as intimate as she wished, without me seeming forward or pushy.

> **RoxiNYC:** What can I tell you? There's not much about me that you haven't seen.

On the contrary, I thought. There was plenty.

> **NuBiFem:** Shall I start?

> **RoxiNYC:** Ladies first ;o)

Roxi, making light of a moment in a way that I couldn't find funny. If anything, it simply fuelled the need in me to type now as myself. Building on the climax to our formative online encounter, when my feelings for her were revealed to us both. Three little words, that was all it had taken to trigger this avalanche in me. Tapped out in silence, but reducing me to rubble on every level. Since then, I revealed, I only had to whisper her name to myself and a tremor ran right through me no sensors could hope to measure. I told her these things because I could. Because the Internet had given me this chance to express myself to her. And that if she forgave me for my offline insecurities, and believed I was speaking from the heart, then perhaps she would know that this was the real me.

I spoke as I typed, this time. Reading out my eulogy as it appeared. Sending it to Roxi, sentence by sentence. First a paragraph. Then a page. By the time I had finished, I was short of breath.

I leaned back, spent, but quickly began to tense once more. For Roxi didn't answer. Only my conscience responded. Berating my enthusiasm. Questioning the wisdom of such candour. What had I just done? Who the hell did I think I was? Me or my ex? Yes, I was coming across as Christine, but would a woman play out her heart in the same way as a man? The longest minute of my online existence passed before the script inched up again.

> **RoxiNYC:** I guess it's my turn to reveal a little bit more of me.

'If only,' I muttered wistfully. 'But I'll settle for anything.'

RoxiNYC: I could tell you some stuff but it isn't very interesting.

NuBlFem: Try me.

And she did exactly that. Tried me so hard I had to read back twice to take it all in.

RoxiNYC: My star sign's Libra, but I don't read horoscopes. Way I see it, only thing rings true for me is my desire for balance. Parents still together. Which is a blessing, in view of my astrological temperament. Neither aware of my sexual preference, however. Not ashamed. Just never found the right moment. OK? How am I doing?

'Fine,' I said, and it seemed like Roxi had heard me.

RoxiNYC: Let me see ... Lost my virginity with a boy at 15. Again with a girl at 16. Melissa. High school friend. Didn't know she felt that way until I kissed her. Nor did I for that matter. Two days later, she's dating Gregory. Major hockey jock. Nickname, Gregory Pecker. Clung to him like she was frightened of falling into an abyss. First to get married. First to get divorced. First to get therapy. Guess I went into denial too, but in a different way. Dated a string of guys. All short term. Some good. Some not so good. Some great. But none so great as Miss Estella Gleam. Student relief teacher. In more ways than one. Just a two-week affair, but the best learning experience of my life. After her, I found my feet with girls. Graduated with good grades in all the wrong subjects, but I was happy. Understand?

'Oh, I do.'

RoxiNYC: Moved into an apartment on the Lower East Side. Male flatmate. Leon. Pastry chef. Never brought his work home with him, sad to say. Met the rent by working as a chambermaid. Waitress. Window dresser. Eventually trained to be a shiatsu masseuse. Loved the job. Not the clients. Finally sacked for assaulting an investment banker. Jerk expected me to relax him all over. Married. Two kids. No prospect of any more, thanks to me. The night I lost my job, I slept in Leon's bed. Next morning, moved my stuff across into his room.

'Leon,' I said mockingly. 'I hate him already.'

RoxiNYC: Sublet spare room to my little sister. Perfect arrangement in view of sky high rent. Until I came home one day to find that she was Leon's dish of the day. Walked out on the spot. Struck by a desire to run away and start over. Old girlfriend lived in London. Tallulah. One-night wonder turned soul mate. It was her encouraged me to move here two years ago. Signed with make-up agency. No formal qualifications, but no complaints either. Work on commercials. Pop promos. Fashion shoots. Sometimes on the continent. Favourite country, Italy. Once powdered Leonardo DiCaprio's nose. Winona Ryder's, too. Only regret, that I never sorted things with my sister. That's it really.

A moment passed before I thought about typing back. Everything Roxi had revealed served to make me want her more, but above all I was thinking about Leon, and what a dick move he had made.

NuBiFem: Is there anything left I don't know about you?

RoxiNYC: Well, there is maybe one thing . . .

'What?'

RoxiNYC: I don't normally do serious relationships.

'Ah,' I said, thinking perhaps she'd be up for grabs again soon. Still, I was careful to go the opposite way online.

NuBiFem: Oh :o(

RoxiNYC: Not with women, I should say . . .

Even better. Now my hands curled into little grips. Poised to lift in victory. So she still had an eye for a man. Favoured them, even.

RoxiNYC: . . . but with you, Christine, I could be persuaded.

Head in my hands for a moment, then reluctantly back to the keyboard.

NuBiFem: Are you sure? I wouldn't want to push you.

RoxiNYC: You're not.

But what if I did? I wondered. Could a fox have too much of the same thing? Part of me wanted to step up the pressure. Anything that might sway Roxi away from my ex. But then I had to keep telling myself that I wasn't really speaking for myself here. Sure, I could make out Christine was a crank, but I just wasn't that two-faced.

NuBiFem: So would you like to meet again?

The question appeared in black and white, and for a moment I still wondered what would happen if I became a bit more bossy. A demand to meet right now, perhaps. And if not, *why* not? That kind of advance wasn't just pushy but potentially psychotic. But no, I played it like a good girl. Then Roxi's reply came back at me.

RoxiNYC: How about tomorrow?

'God, you're keen!' I sat back with a start, surprised by my own voice. 'What's wrong with waiting a couple of days?'

As a man, my instinct would have been to set a date to set the date. Arrange to connect again a bit later, and sort out the details then. The cursor marked my thoughts, counting down to the moment I pulled my chair closer. I couldn't quite take in what I went on to type, but I went all the way to the bitter end. Hitting send before I had a chance to change my mind.

NuBiFem: **Tomorrow sounds great xx**

I was staring at the screen, taunted by my own words, when a door squeaked open behind me. Bare feet padding across the floorboards. Now was not a good time for my ex to discover exactly how strong her feelings were supposed to have become, so I told Roxi I had to go. Tying up the details with her just as a pair of hands began to mock massage my shoulders. I logged off and looked round to see Christine wearing a sweater and a pair of old jeans rolled up to fit. My ex. Freshened up and dressed as me.

'Thanks for that,' she said. 'I'm feeling so much better now.'

As she spoke, her mobile began to ring. Calling out from somewhere under the brightly coloured heap of clothes I could see just inside the bathroom.

'You'd better answer that,' I said, turning with her. 'No one keeps Roxi waiting.'

Christine wheeled back to me, looked at the computer for a beat, then the filament behind her eyes brightened up a hundred watts.

'She wants to talk? To *me*?'

I nodded bravely. Even forced a smile.

'I've already done that for you,' I informed her. 'She just wants to know when you're free tomorrow.'

21

'A cat will pick up on your displeasure if you hiss at it.'
http://www.purradise.com/purrfect10.html

I felt OK. I felt *good*. Two women had found one another thanks to me. At least, that's how I attempted to spin it to myself when Christine danced from my space. I had gone online to sever some links. Logged off having strengthened them further. Alone at the window gallery, I watched my ex skip through the square, then quietly uttered the mantra: 'Bollocks, bollocks, bollocks.' For the truth was I felt bad. Mad. *Miserable*. Things weren't going OK for me. I didn't feel good at all.

I flopped into bed really early. Not that I had intended to get horizontal so soon, but after a couple of gin and lemons, each with just a squeeze of tonic, the world kind of tipped that way. Still, I was conscious enough to remember that the producer had told me to expect the car early next morning. I hadn't asked why. I didn't care much either. The only significance to me was that I would be seeing Roxi again. And that was the thought with which I cuddled up and closed my eyes. It was here, in my head, where she kissed me. A moment where my heart raced ahead of my senses, and my chances of getting any shut-eye receded further into the night.

email to: Tony Curtis
from: NuBiFem
subject: It gets worse :o/

Dear Tony,
Can I call you Tony? Not sure if you've had a chance to read my earlier email, but I thought you should know there's been some developments. Just in case you were thinking of getting back to me.

This bi fox, Roxi? She's really sold on my ex-girlfriend, even though I'm the man behind the woman, as it were. Anyway, I could have finished this relationship today. We spoke online, me doing my girl routine, but one thing led to another and, well ... you know how it is. So now they're meeting up again, all thanks to yours truly. And the closer I bring them together, the less room there is for me.

I know, what a schmuck, right?

It's almost twelve o'clock here. I guess that makes it late afternoon with you. My head certainly feels like it's in another time zone. Shame I can't zip down the wire in person. Join you for a drink by the pool. Any way to wind down would be good. I just quit my bed because the sheets were trying to mummify me. Ever been in that position, Tony? I don't suppose so. A guy like you must get the full eight hours. No worries keeping you awake so bad you have to get up and go online. I couldn't get into the insomniacs chat room, mind you. The place was rammed. I considered checking into Purradise, the all-girl website I mentioned once before, but I have to say my confidence as a woman has faded recently. Not just because of the Roxi thing, but because I've had a crank email warning me off. Does that count as having a stalker? I hear it can boost an actor's earning power. I'd ask my agent, but you know what they can be like about returning calls.

Anyway, thanks for listening and do stay in touch.

Reynard

PS – I'm not a stalker myself! Just read this over, worried it might sound a bit weird and cranky. All I need is some sleep, and I'm sure I'll be myself again.

From their own bed, in the disk box by the computer, my dealer's seedlings watched me working the keyboard. I was impressed by how far they had come. The stream of warm air that flowed from the side vents on my hard-drive had evidently helped them to thrive. Already they stood about two inches tall. Formed like little shepherd's crooks with swelling buds for heads.

'Onwards and upwards, fellas.'

I wished they were able to say the same about me. In fact, any form of conversation would have been welcome. I had persuaded myself out of bed because I wanted to talk. To download my predicament onto someone outside the situation. Get things out of one system and onto another. To this end I was disappointed not to find Tony Curtis hanging out in my Cyber Circle. Being late afternoon in Bel Air, I had figured this was a good time zone for him. A chance to get out of the sun and catch up on my news. Then I got realistic, and figured a hero of his stature had other things to do. Better things than me. Still, it felt good to update him. More rewarding than it did to be reminded that another side of me was still in demand. Courtesy of my Virtual Vitals. By the time I finished up with TC, in fact, NuBiFem had received two propositions I couldn't ignore.

The first was from a starter bi looking for tips. Ask someone else, I said in a message back to her. Someone genuinely able to follow things through. Someone who could reach the stage where the online legwork became a physical thing. Someone, I wanted to say, who wasn't weighted down and doomed by the sex between his legs.

I was just wishing her all the very best of luck when the second missive arrived like a brick through my Windows.

Quick-E to: NuBiFem

VSQ   Hey, hun bun! What's this? Last minute fling before the clock strikes twelve?

VSQ. Viagra Snatch Squad. The crank. Unlike my response to the earlier email, I felt a little chilled this time around. For someone to know I was online meant I had been entered into their Cyber Circle. My space felt suddenly invaded, though I still didn't see what authority she had to make me leave the virtual ball by midnight.

'So turn me into a pumpkin,' I murmured.

NuBiFem: Who are you?

VSQ: A representative from the Viagra Hit Squad.

NuBiFem:	**Male or female?**
VSQ:	**Female. Only way to be.**

A lesbian, I thought. Had to be. And an angry one, too.

NuBiFem:	**What do you want?**
VSQ:	**The right to meet other women without being duped by phoneys like you.**

I tutted and sighed. For I hadn't logged on to be lectured. If she wanted a battle of the sexes she had picked the wrong time, the wrong place, the wrong person. In fact, she had picked the wrong medium entirely. For a threat on the net was nothing. A virtual gesture. What could she realistically do? Email me into submission? I glanced at the keyboard. Considered the kind of response that would be unforgivable anywhere else. Which was why I went ahead with it.

NuBiFem:	**Alright, you got me. I'm a man.**
VSQ:	**I knew you'd come out to us.**
NuBiFem:	**Can I go now?**
VSQ:	**If it means you'll stop bothering women online.**
NuBiFem:	**Guess I'd better tuck up right now then.**
VSQ:	**Glad to hear it.**
NuBiFem:	**Care to join me?**
VSQ:	**?**
NuBiFem:	**Get yourself some deep dicking. See the light.**
VSQ:	**Oh grow up!**

NuBiFem:	But it's what you expect straight guys to say, isn't it?
VSQ:	You disgust me.
NuBiFem:	Only because I don't conform to the stereotype.
VSQ:	I know where you live.
NuBiFem:	Grab a cab, hun. I'm horny as hell.
VSQ:	Hoxton Square. Nice place.

Suddenly my amusement turned to alarm. Even the mouse in my hand seemed to shrink. This wasn't supposed to happen. This was the Internet. Nobody knew your damn name here. Let alone your damn *whereabouts*. Anonymity was everything. The oxygen needed to survive. My computer beeped ominously. My throat was tightening already.

VSQ:	You got post, hun bun.

I opened it quickly. Found a line of xs and a file attached. A picture, I discovered, as the pixels began to arrange into something recognisable. Taken on a long lens from somewhere inside the square. A shot of a sorry-looking man gaining entry into my space.

A picture, I realised, of *me*.

NuBiFem:	What the fuck is this? Are you following me?
VSQ:	Give it up, Ren. Or we'll give it out.
NuBiFem:	Give out what?
VSQ:	Hit this and see for yourself.

It was a hyperlink. The Internet equivalent of a teleport machine. A short-cut-click to any website in cyberspace. I levelled my cursor over the magic word, and found myself in new, uncertain and very definitely hostile territory.

WELCOME TO
The Viagra Snatch Squad
HOMEPAGE
Tracking the Web's Most Wanted

Underneath, a picture gallery began to form. A dozen black and white thumbnails filling in turn with what I guessed to be a dozen wanted men. Some captured walking into bars, others caught skulking out of cybercafes. One loading a car with shopping bags. Another eating lunch in a park. Men doing everyday things. Nothing out of the ordinary. Only the screen names emblazoned under each shot suggested otherwise. SexiPegs. AmbiSandi. VelvetMel and that idiot MollyCuddle. Lezgyrl was there. Even BiRuth, photographed at the head of a bus stop queue. The man looking like he had been waiting there patiently for a hundred years. Looking like he really ought to be picked up by the Reaper not the Routemaster.

Only one picture was missing. The final frame in the gallery coming up empty. A provisional reservation, I realised, depending wholly on me.

> **VSQ:** You're next on the hit list, hun bun.

I didn't doubt her word. I just didn't think I deserved to be set up like this.

> **NuBiFem:** You're wrong about me. It's a complicated situation.
>
> **VSQ:** All men say that, Ren.
>
> **NuBiFem:** Really, I'm not getting anything out of this.
>
> **VSQ:** They say that, too.

I was angry, unnerved and increasingly panicked. This wasn't a game any longer. The last thing I needed was membership of a club for people with not one shadow but two. That was for celebrity actors, not no-marks like me. Tony Curtis was bound to have encountered a few for real. Fans of his films, most probably. Unblinking types, who followed him around as if he held the key to the meaning of their existence. But then Tony Curtis was someone. I wasn't worthy of the attention.

NuBiFem: What if I continue?

She didn't respond for a second, and suddenly I felt quite vulnerable. As if at any moment a string of dykes in balaclavas might abseil through the skylights.

VSQ: First we alert your victims, then we exact our pun-
               ishment.

NuBiFem: How?

VSQ: You'll just have to wait for the snatch. You're used to
               waiting for that, aren't you? :o)

'Marvellous,' I sighed to myself. 'A stalker with a stand-up routine.' I wasn't laughing, however. Her surveillance shot of me had already soured this whole exchange.

VSQ: One minute to midnight, Ren. One strike is all it
               takes.

Way out west, far beyond the lofts and rooftop gardens, some-where in the guts of the city, a familiar chime began to count me out. Even before Big Ben fell silent, however, I had made up my mind about things. Indeed, I had gone so far as to log off and even shut down my computer. Yet my Virtual Vitals remained untouched. Live online for anyone who wished to look me up. Not a statement of intent. Just a stubborn salute.

Nobody told NuBiFem where to get offline.

Having made my decision, I didn't question it once, Deep inside, I just knew that it was the right thing to do. If anything, these threats had stoked my determination to stay in the game. Sure, the risk of defeat increased now I knew my moves were being watched, but I had already taken the biggest gamble by becoming a player. Fronting for a woman in a way that had already cost me my self-esteem. I was cleaned out. Left with little to lose. Just an outside chance of winning something priceless. So the odds didn't look good, my ex seemed as sold on Roxi as I was, but whatever this so-called Squad held close to their chests was nothing compared to what I held deep in my soul. And nothing they could do would make me give it up. *Nothing.*

I took A.C. Découcher to bed with me. Read for a while, but I didn't absorb much of it. Online, I had got myself all fired up as a fem. But if I was to get anywhere with Roxi, it was vital that I focus on the times we connected for real. Working on her in the dressing room while she was working on me. As a man, I wondered, could Christine really see me as competition? We both offered Roxi different things, after all. Even if I did have to help her out a bit. I switched off the lights, thinking maybe things would work out for us all. Only the darkness didn't settle and blanket me as expected. Instead, my space appeared to open out to the night time world once more. Stars through the skylights like all-seeing eyes. Moonspun shadows all around. Hiding things I couldn't see.

For a while I just lay there, barely daring to breathe. The silence measured by my heart. Each beat more forceful than the last, until eventually it was thumping so bad it could have put dents in my chest. Indeed, it seemed as if the whole building was shaking when I finally mustered the courage to zig zag across to the window gallery and drop down every blind.

22

In the dressing room next morning, I regarded the costume my
producer picked out and realised why I had been called in early.

'It's a blouse,' I said tersely. 'Nobody told me I had to wear a
blouse.'

My producer insisted she had informed me of the decision
yesterday. Directly after the shoot. Once on set. Again as I whisked
through reception. Apparently I had even estimated my size for her.
Having watched my on-screen wife bonding with the cat, the viewing
audience were now expected to believe that I would be driven to
dressing up in her clothes in a bid to fool it into feeding from
me. As if any man would want to go to such lengths for a moggy.
According to the producer this was state-of-the-art slapstick. In a
state, I wanted to say, where Benny Hill still dominated prime-time
schedules.

'The client has high hopes for this campaign.' The producer
hooked the garment back on the rail as she said this. 'They reckon
it'll make the brand a household name.'

'All it will do,' I said darkly, 'is brand me as a twat.'

She glanced at me witheringly, then unzipped a holdall at her
feet. 'Only in Korea.'

Ignoring her comment, I reached out to feel the fabric between
my thumb and forefinger. It was a hideous synthetic. Elasticated
waist. Puffball sleeves. White on blue polka. It even smelled of
mothballs.

'You're not serious, are you?'

'Deadly,' she replied, and looked it too. 'You've got five minutes to get dressed before Roxi arrives to pretty you up.'

Just hearing her name brought me out in goosebumps.

'Can't anyone else do me?' I asked weakly.

My producer hoisted the bag into the empty chair, ignoring my unease while evidently revelling in it too.

'Let's see,' she said jauntily, and began to disembowel the contents. 'There must be some things in here that'll put you in touch with your feminine side.'

I couldn't go through with this. I so wanted Roxi to see the real me, and here I was being asked to choose between sheer and fishnet stockings, mules or sky high heels. I had already resigned myself to the appearance of the padded bra and inserts. But nothing could prepare me for the gaff.

'What the hell's *that*?' I asked.

It was a three-way harness of some sort, though I wished I hadn't asked when my producer held it against her waist.

'It tucks you in,' she said, lifting her eyes to savour my response. 'Keeps you flat.'

She told me what it was called. Explained that the strap hanging free pulled tight between the legs. Said a transvestite friend had lent it for the shoot.

I extended a finger and said, 'That thing has been worn *before*?'

'I'm sure he won't mind if you want to hold on to it afterwards.'

'I'm calling my agent.'

She followed me out of the dressing room. All the way to reception. Even stood behind me while I dialled his number.

My agent told me to wear the damn frock. It wasn't even nine o'clock, but it sounded like he'd had a bad day already. He even hung up on me. I talked to the dial tone for a second, then made out it was me who put the phone down first. When I turned round, my producer was right there in my face.

'We're not happy about this,' I said sourly.

She looked at me like she already knew. 'But you'll do it.'

'I don't have much choice. But the gaff stays in the dressing room.'

'That's fine. No one will notice.'

'What's that supposed to mean?'

She pretended not to hear me. Ticked off something on her stupid clipboard instead. 'It's going to be a great day, Reynard. We're so looking forward to seeing your transformation.'

'Evidently,' I muttered, and was promptly foiled in my attempt to peer forward and see what she was writing. Not only did the producer take two steps back, she also took the opportunity to check me out. Brazenly giving me the once over, with both cheeks sucked right in. Nobody had ever done that to me before. I felt suddenly self-conscious.

'Things won't seem so bad when you get into the part,' she assured me just then. 'I'm sure it'll come naturally to a guy like you.'

This wasn't the work of the Viagra Snatch Squad. It couldn't be. The humiliation was way too harsh. My crime didn't merit such punishment. I deserved to be dressed down, not up. Standing in front of the make-up mirror, squeezed into a blouse two sizes too small for me, I tried to remind myself that it was just a job. That nobody was out to get me, and that countless actors had been through worse in pursuit of their dreams. Look at Tony, I thought. Look at *Tootsie*. Any other time I might have accepted the situation. Focused instead on turning in a performance to the best of my abilities. The trouble was my ambitions had changed in recent days. Switched from the professional to the personal. My sights were focused, sure enough, but only for an audience of one. Hearing footsteps approaching outside, I hurried into my seat and tried to appear as relaxed as possible. Which wasn't easy when my bra strap shot apart and my tits went into a seesaw.

'Bollocks,' I muttered.

Roxi breezed in behind me. 'Everything OK?' she asked, as if it was no surprise to see me dressed like a Hairy Mary.

One of the foam inserts had popped free. I chased it down the inside of my blouse, smiling at her awkwardly when I used my other hand to intercept it between my legs.

'Women's problems,' I said finally, and showed her the cause of my discomfort. 'I'll get used to it.'

She registered the insert, and nodded sympathetically. And yet something at the edges of her expression told me she was ready to share the joke. I tried to smile for her, but it didn't work out that way. Roxi with her long locks flowing freely this day. A Rapunzel to my haggard witch.

'Here,' she said, moving close behind me. 'Let me try.'

She began to unbutton the back of my dress. I assumed she would stop midway, find the straps and mesh them back together. Not spread the whole blouse off my shoulders and peel it down to my waist.

I didn't know where to look. Didn't even know whether I would survive another second as she tended to each cup. Refitting the inserts so each one sat straight, and even standing back to appraise them. It was unbearable. Obscene. Not what she was doing, but the sight of me and my pigeon chest. By the time Roxi had me cooped up again, I had broken out in a sweat.

'Thanks,' I said falteringly. 'At least one of us knows how to handle a pair of breasts.'

She caught my eye in the mirror, stood tall right behind me.

'I meant your own,' I covered quickly, but immediately wished I hadn't. 'When you grow up with them I suppose you learn to fit a bra with your eyes closed.'

'I guess you're right,' she said. Resting one hand on my back, she leaned forward and pulled the light cord. Lit the ring of bulbs that framed us both. 'Though I've never liked wearing one much.'

I tried not to think about that one, knowing the effect it would have on me, and was relieved when she turned for the clothes rail. I took a deep breath, anxious to restore my calm. It was the sight of my own chest heaving that stopped me exhaling so readily.

'How do women live with them?' I asked quite sincerely and rolled one shoulder after the other. 'Mine's giving me friction burns already.'

When Roxi came back to me, I was pleased to see that she was smiling.

'Want me to slacken it off a little?'

'I'll be fine,' I said, and crossed my arms protectively. 'If I get my boobs out again you might mark me down as a cheap tart.'

She beamed at me in the mirror. Tied the gown round me. 'Now there's a first,' she said. 'A man with standards.'

Just hearing her say this was enough to shore my spirits. That the gown covered up my ridiculous costume was a bonus. Protecting not just my blouse but my sense of purpose too. At Roxi's bidding, I relaxed back in the chair. Watched her open up the make-up box and rest the lid against the mirror. Free from my own reflection, I actually began to feel myself again.

'This may take a while,' she said. 'Let me know if you want a break.'

If Roxi wanted to take all *day* that was fine by me. I closed my eyes. Submitted to her makeover like she was some kind of healer. Savouring the charge coursing through me whenever her fingers made contact with my face. An electric connection, every time. God, I *yearned* for her to touch me more. To use her whole body, if necessary. This time around, I actually welcomed the silence that settled. In some ways I hoped it would mean she could read the one thing on my mind. To see that I was crazy for her. But Roxi remained oblivious to my vibes. Evidently lost in her own thoughts, she even began to hum.

I didn't recognise the tune, but it sounded suspiciously like something k.d. might have penned.

'Someone sounds happy,' I said eventually.

'Oh, sorry, is it bothering you?'

'Not at all,' I lied.

She stopped nevertheless, and reached for a pair of tweezers.

'What are they for?'

'Plucking,' she said. 'Is that OK?'

If Roxi wanted to pluck me, I wasn't going to object. It was worth it just for the treat of having seen her lips articulate the word.

'I'd like to thin out the middle, that's all.'

I tilted my face up for her. 'Too werewolf, right?'

She leaned in to examine me. Hovering there like some celestial surgeon. 'It's not so bad,' she said, 'Just needs a little definition.'

Tell me about it, I thought to myself. I was after the very same thing. A little definition. Like some clarity about her and my ex. Could Roxi really be serious about Christine? Or was it just something she had persuaded herself to say after my online ode to her.

'So,' I said, as she came in close. 'Any news from the romance front? You promised to update me . . . *ouch!*'

'Whoops,' said Roxi. I could have sworn the hair root that came away in her tweezers had a fleck of flesh attached. 'Think I need to concentrate here.'

I rubbed the space between my eyes. Registered the fact that she seemed quietly amused, then realised she had done it on purpose.

'Point taken,' I relented. 'I'll let you get on.'

The next few tweaks were nothing. In fact I even started to enjoy the whole process. For it meant I was free to gaze right into Roxi's eyes without feeling like I was broaching her personal space. I even wondered if she was beginning to take more interest in me. Glancing down from her work on occasion. Even putting a question my way.

'Ever dressed up as a woman before?'

I could have answered her immediately, but she turned to switch the tweezers for a compact and brush. When she came back, I said, 'Never. Not my style.'

She shrugged, and returned to lay my foundation. Had Roxi harboured any suspicions, I was glad they were cleared up now. A moment passed before she spoke again.

'I used to have a boyfriend who was into it.'

'A boyfriend?' I said, and felt my ears go red.

'Never in public. Only when we were fooling around.'

I pictured Leon the pastry chef. All lemon tart and lipstick.

'And you didn't think it was weird?'

'Not at all. I admired the fact he wasn't one of those guys who went into denial about it. Kind of turned me on.'

A short silence followed while Roxi dusted me down. When she turned for the blusher, I suddenly remembered something.

'Actually, I did try on a pair of women's panties once.'

'Yeah?'

'Old girlfriend dared me.' I tried not to think of Christine. Not because I feared it would trigger another mental riot of girl-on-girl action, but because she hadn't actually dared me to wear them at all. In fact I wasn't sure my ex even realised she had left a few garments like that behind. Remnants of our relationship that were mercifully confined to the bin bag now, but which had served to remind me of her in those first few days of despair.

'How did it feel?'

I didn't want to say that I had worn them on my head.

'Different,' I said instead, and looked directly into her eyes. So direct Roxi stopped sweeping my cheeks and pulled away. 'Is your new date into dressing up?' I was pushing my luck, I knew it. Asking her to be out with me. But this time she had invited the question. Having opened up for her, it was only right that she respond in kind. I held her gaze. Unwilling to let go.

'Yeah, she likes to dress up,' said Roxi, quite suddenly, and there she was holding *my* gaze. 'Gotta bold sense of style too.'

She. She had said it. *She.*

I didn't know what to say. I didn't know because I already knew. Not just about Christine but also about her clothes sense. It meant I couldn't even pretend to be surprised by her admission. It would look utterly fake. So fraudulent that Roxi would pick right up on it. I tried to look away. Pretend it had gone over my head. But by then it was way too late. She was waiting for me to say something. Acknowledge her somehow.

'A bold sense of style, eh?' I was braced for her to belt me, but I couldn't stop here. So I smiled at her cheekily and said, 'Maybe if I had a decent wardrobe, people might say the same about me.'

Not a glimmer from her at first. Then a spark of a smile. Slow burning to begin, but quickly spreading my way.

'I like you,' she said finally, and closed in with the eye pencil. 'Guys usually turn weird on me when they find out I'm bisexual.'

It was an awkward moment to go quiet on each other. That word just kind of resonated with me. Partly because she'd been so open.

As if she was testing me further. Which was why I forced myself to keep looking into her eyes when she traced under mine, waiting for her to focus back on the conversation.

'So is she nice?' I ventured tentatively, when Roxi moved on to the mascara.

'Who?'

It occurred to me that I didn't know what to call her.

'Your . . . special friend.'

'My what?' She leaned away. Her brow hitched high, inviting me to try again. To say the word before she was prepared to speak about her.

'Okay,' I said, and paused to work it up. 'Your *girlfriend*. Is she nice?'

'Nice?'

'As a person,' I stressed awkwardly. 'This isn't easy, Roxi.'

'It's not meant to be,' she said. 'No one ever made it easy for me. Most people assume I just can't make up my mind. Some treat me like I'm going through a phase. The worst kind think I'm open to persuasion.'

My whole body stiffened at this. Quickly I took her back to the question. Asked if I would like her.

'Everyone likes her,' she assured me, and then something mischievous sharpened her smile. 'Though I doubt she'd see much in you.'

Another rent in the conversation. Roxi making me pay for being so persistent again. Leaving me to wonder why the fuck I was even asking her about someone I had slept with for eighteen months.

'So,' she said. 'Seeing anyone yourself?'

I opened my mouth, relieved to be moving in a different direction, and immediately found myself in another corner.

'Yes,' I said. 'Actually no. Yes and no.'

Roxi with the eye shadow now. Deciding between two shades. Taking the kind of time I wish I had just used for myself.

'Meaning?'

'Just that I've met a girl I like. But nothing's happened yet.'

'So make it happen. What are you waiting for?' She opted for oyster over silver, began to dust it on.

'It's complicated.'

'Why?'

'I'm not sure she likes me.'

'Work on her then. Get to know her better. If the vibes are right, she'll soon let you know.'

'I can't. She's involved with someone else.'

Roxi moved across to my other eyelid. I closed them both for her.

'You know what?' I heard her say.

'What?'

'Maybe you could use some help finding someone a little more eligible.'

'Maybe,' I said.

She stopped brushing. I opened my eyes.

'You're really smitten, huh?'

I glanced across at Roxi. Tried to look like I appreciated her sensitivity.

'I guess I am.'

'So what makes her so special?'

'I wouldn't know where to begin.'

'Oh, come on.'

'Really, I'm not sure I could single out one thing.'

'Looks or personality?'

I chewed on my lip. Decided for the first time that morning to chance a little honesty.

'I'm supposed to say personality, aren't I?'

A smile crept out across her face. Broadened as I looked at her quizzically.

'I can't deny it,' she confessed. 'I'm a sucker for a beautiful woman.'

'Tell me about it.'

'It gets me into real trouble, though.'

'Leap before you look?'

'No,' she said. 'I always look first, but sometimes I forget to listen.'

I laughed with her. The pair of us tuned to the same wavelength.

'Especially if she's got good calves,' added Roxi. 'If she's got good calves I'm all hers.'

Christine had *great* calves.

'I would agree with you there,' I said. 'I'm definitely a leg kind of person.'

'Legs beat butts, any day.'

'You think so?' I said, impressed by her candour. 'In heels or bare feet?'

'Heels have to be a perfect fit to qualify. Nothing too tall.'

'You're right. Lacks grace.'

'Just enough to stretch the muscles so they sing.'

'All the way to the top,' I said, smiling now.

'Ain't that the truth.'

For a beat, we each withdrew into our thoughts. Probably taking with us an image of the very same woman. Then Roxi broke away for some lip gloss, and it occurred to me that I had finally made the connection I so desired. An offline bond with a major babe. Something I had initially dismissed as impossible. Outclassed, as I believed I was in every way. And yet something here didn't feel right. In fact, it felt wholly wrong. Then the reason dawned on me. Sure, we were talking intimately. Just as I had hoped. But we were relating to each other about girls here. Bantering like a couple of *blokes.*

'On the subject of impressive calves,' she said, coming back to me now with a deep rouge, 'did you see the football last night?'

I compressed my lips without being asked. Waited for her to finish painting them.

'It's not my thing,' I told her. 'Actually, football bores me rigid.'

Roxi adopted a look of horror. Cracked on that I was a heretic.

'I know,' I said, grinning now. 'Not cool for a man to admit.'

'Damn right! What kind of guy do you think you are?'

'You tell me.'

Roxi looked at me squarely, as if checking I shaped up symmetrically, then stepped to one side.

'You know,' she said, and closed down the make-up box. 'I think you'll turn out fine.'

With the lid out of the way, my reflection pretty much leapt from the glass and attempted to mug me.

'Jesus wept!' I gasped, fighting back the urge to shriek.

'Like it?'

I couldn't form an opinion. Roxi had done a professional job. Fulfilled her brief to the final fake freckle. But for me to say anything, it would have been like passing judgement on a total stranger. One with bee-sting lips, cherry-pink cheeks and startled, italicised eyebrows.

'Hold on one second,' she said, and went to search inside the holdall at my feet. 'One thing's missing.'

At first I thought she had a dead poodle in there.

'Oh no, please!' I appealed to her, then groaned as she tried to shake some life into it. 'Is that strictly necessary?'

The wig fitted as if it had been made for me. Or a barmaid past her prime.

'There,' said Roxi, teasing out my silver bouffant. 'The very model of a man.' Which was nice of her to say, but not even a joke could ease the fact I looked worse than a drag act. I didn't even come close to passing muster as a trannie. In terms of style and finesse I shared more in common with a fucking *panto* dame. It reminded me of the ridiculous palaver awaiting me on the studio floor. For the first time in my professional life I felt a pang of stage fright. Just thinking about the reception I would get from the camera crew was enough to make my toes curl.

'Will you come with me?' I asked her. 'Hold my hand for a while.'

'Sorry,' she said. 'Brunch date. Gotta be in reception at ten.'

I tried hard not to look disappointed or even think about Christine. Covered up by leaning forward a little to let her untie my gown. This time, however, I had to be sure.

'Girlfriend or girlfriend?' I asked.

Roxi whipped off the gown, revealing my blouse and an unseemly pair of legs.

'Girlfriend,' she said.

Even in tights and heels, I knew that I couldn't compete.

23

Believe me, I would have been more comfortable dressed as a man-sized penis. I once met an actor at an audition who actually claimed to have played such a part. Some Dutch sex education video. Required him to don the pink foam body suit, then head-butt his female counterpart in a futile bid to gain entry. Apparently the money made it worthwhile, though the whole project had come close to disaster when nobody noticed the poor sap fighting for air just after the condom was fitted. I was reminded of his story as I ventured into the corridor, snagging my dress on the door hinge. For I had never felt like such a complete cock in my whole life. It wasn't a life-threatening role, but I seriously feared I would die of shame.

I arrived on set a little early. Nevertheless, the entire crew appeared to have skipped their tea break to welcome me. Ignoring the jeers and wolf whistles, I clopped behind the cameras and lowered myself into a low-slung sofa. Trying to sit elegantly in something so lacking in support was a complete bastard. My blouse rode way too high, while crossing my legs just exposed even more of me. Only my shoulder bag, carefully positioned on my lap, saved what little modesty remained.

'Got a problem?' I snarled, as one of the sparks tripped into a mince. 'Or do you just fancy me?'

Even the producer couldn't resist a dig. While the cat was being filmed for cutaways, she came across and asked me whether I'd like a coffee. Then cracked up when she asked how sweetly I took it.

The very model of a man. That's what Roxi had said, and I clung to the comment like I clung to my shoulder bag. Maybe she hadn't been joking, I reasoned. Maybe she meant every word. In view of my impending role, however, I figured she could only have been talking about my balls. About the courage I had shown while my masculinity was systematically stripped away. Even when she presented me with the full Rocky Horror in the mirror, I had resisted the urge to flounce. And if it was this quality in me that had impressed her, then I was prepared to see the part through.

But only just.

Providing nobody else knocked me a wink or blew another bloody kiss.

All I wanted to do was sit there on the sidelines and clear my mind. Wait for my call without being treated like a piece of meat. It didn't help that my mobile began bleating, right in the middle of a crucial take. By the time I found it at the bottom of my bag, everyone was looking at me. Even the cat.

'Hi,' came the voice, high as helium. 'Free to talk?'

It was Christine. I glanced at the studio clock. It was two minutes past ten. She was running late. Roxi would be waiting.

'What's the matter?' I whispered. 'Are you OK?'

'I'm fine. But I'd be lost without you.'

I frowned into the phone. Hunkered down so I could speak a little more freely. 'Tell me where you are then, I'll give you directions.'

Silence on the line. Not even a crackle.

'I'm in the kitchen. At home.'

'What?'

'I've just fixed myself some toast. Why?'

'What's wrong with you! It's gone ten.'

'Calm down,' she said, sounding hurt. 'So I've had a late breakfast. But I'm on flexitime at work. Is it a problem if I like to lie in a little?'

I told her the problem was this end. Roxi was expecting to do brunch with her. Right now.

'Brunch?'

'You know,' I said impatiently. 'Not breakfast. Not lunch. Something in the middle.'

'I know what it is,' was how she replied. 'But I'm not doing brunch with Roxi. We arranged to go clubbing tonight. I only phoned to thank you for setting it up.'

I thought this through, then doubled back to the previous night. To the online threat I had dismissed. The vow to blow the whistle on me if I didn't wind up being a woman.

'Fuck,' I said to myself, killing the phone as I scrambled from the sofa. 'The *Squad*.'

Let me tell you, running in heels is a major bitch. Trussed up round the ankles, forced up on my toes. I was all forward motion and no balance. Still, it didn't stop me hurtling breathlessly into reception. Scattering a cluster of couriers and causing Roxi to spin round.

'Don't go,' I cried, and almost tripped into her arms. 'I'm begging you.'

Before Roxi had even drawn breath, a figure turned through the revolving doors behind her. A woman in a boiler suit with a baseball cap pulled low. I couldn't see her face properly, but she didn't look like Maintenance. Whoever it was certainly saw my face, however, and wheeled full circle for the street.

'What's the matter with you?' snapped Roxi, and tried to push me away. I let go of her immediately. Stuttered an apology. I glanced up again, but the woman had gone. 'You look fine, Reynard. Don't panic. Your face won't slide. Even under the lights.'

'I'm really worried.'

'Don't be. Didn't I say you looked fine?'

'You did,' I said hesitantly, increasingly aware that I couldn't go back now. At the same time, the smell of leather and sweaty Lycra began to close around me. Even the couriers, it seemed, were keen to know what was with the flouncer. 'Actually, Roxi, it's not me I'm worried about.'

'Well, who then?'

I glanced around uncomfortably. Saw no option but to say, 'It's your girlfriend.'

Now it was Roxi's turn to look uneasy. Her attention flicking left then right, before glaring back at me. 'What about her?'

I tried to think of a way to explain things without making my interest in her sound deeply unhealthy. 'It's just not a good idea for you to see this particular one right now.'

'Why not? She's just a friend.'

I sensed the couriers drifting back to the front desk.

'A *special* friend?' was how I put it to her, as quietly as I could, and suddenly there they were again, facing right back at us.

'Someone I got talking to on the net yesterday,' said Roxi, and spelled it out so calmly that I knew a storm would follow. 'But I am not planning on sleeping with her, if that's what you mean.'

'God, no!'

'Then quit being a jerk just because I told you some things about me.'

This was bad. This really wasn't going well. Not only did we have the couriers back with us, they were flanking us now on either side. All of them waiting for me to explain myself. The man dressed as a woman, pestering this poor girl about her private life. Gripping Roxi gently by the elbows I said, 'For the sake of your relationship I'm asking you not to see anyone else right now.'

'My *relationship*?'

'With Christine. If you meet up with another woman, I just know she'll take it the wrong way.'

As one, our audience swung their attention from me to Roxi.

'I never told you my girlfriend's name.'

'You didn't need to. I know her.'

'You do?'

'Intimately,' I said, and played the same hand I had played with her chaperone.

I told her that we used to date, Christine and me.

Roxi didn't say anything. Didn't move. Didn't even breathe. Just looked right at me. Even when a voice crackled over the intercom and summoned me back to the studio floor. I had to go, and the couriers stepped back smartly as I turned. Tottering back through the corridor, I knew that there was nothing more I could do. Except give silent thanks when Roxi caught up with me.

'Maybe I'd better stick around after all,' she said, looking dead ahead. Not even glancing at my make up. 'Just in case I've missed something.'

24

Sweet William stayed cool when my car home pulled up by his stall. He didn't reach inside his puffa. He didn't bolt away. He only looked uneasy, in fact, when I lowered the mirrored window an inch.

'Kill me,' I said flatly. 'Give me your heaviest shit. I'll smoke it.'

My dealer stepped into the gutter, then leaned in close. I felt like I was on one of those safari drives, where the gorillas get a bit too curious.

'Man, what happened to your face?'

I pursed my painted lips and frowned. All I wanted to do was score, get out of the blouse and go soak in the bath. After that, I planned to skin up the kind of reefer that would have the same effect as a lobotomy. I might have foiled an attempt by the Squad to put Roxi in the picture, but covering my tracks had cost me dearly. So I asked him again. Pleaded for something to help me forget it all for one day. My dealer shifted his attention to the driver up front. Caught him watching us in the rear view. Then stared right at the man as he scrambled to shut the glass partition.

'Who did this thing to you?' Sweet looking at me now, sounding quietly outraged. Like I had come to him cut up and bleeding. Not made up like the bride of Ronald McDonald.

'I don't want to talk about it.'

'Yes, you do,' he growled. 'Be a good boy and tell Willie from the top.'

So I told him. No question. Ran the window right down before his expression blackened any more. Then took him back to the studio floor. Returning to the scene between Roxi and me. No fancy lights.

No camera. No claws and no applause. The shoot was over by then. The crew had all gone home. Just the two of us centre stage at that time. House lamps illuminating the moment when I lied through my teeth about my ex-girlfriend. Begging her to believe no conspiracy existed between us.

'I knew Christine had met someone,' I explained to her. 'But I swear I didn't even know it was a woman until yesterday afternoon, when she turned up on my doorstep in tears and poured out her heart to me.'

'We'd just had lunch together.' Roxi's tone informed me she'd put that one behind her. Didn't want to be reminded. I had my work cut out here.

'When she mentioned your name, said you were a make-up artist, I put two and two together.'

'Came up with three, right?'

'Not at all,' I protested, and tried to look hurt. Anything to wear down that scowl of hers. 'I think it's great, you and Christine, really I do, but none of this adds up for her right now.'

'How so?' Roxi, shifting from one foot to the other, wanting to know more.

'Meeting you has been a revelation for her. But it's all so very new. She's just unsure of herself, Roxi, and what she means to you.'

'I could've told her over lunch, if she'd loosened up a little.'

'That's why I encouraged her to get on the Internet and talk it out. Build up some confidence with you that way, and get things back on track.'

'You give good advice,' she said, and uncrossed her arms. 'The way Christine couldn't bring herself to look me in the eye, I had her down as an overnight bi. Going with a woman one time because she's heard that everyone's doing it. They're the hardest to get over,' she finished. 'Can break a girl's heart so badly.'

'You don't have to worry about Christine,' I grinned. 'I think I put her off men for ever.'

Light in our conversation here, and not from the rig above. My ex hadn't asked me to dig for details, I added just to clarify. I told Roxi that in the dressing room I had been acting alone. Just doing what any ex-boyfriend would do under the circumstances. It was then that I chewed my lower lip a little, and admitted that I still cared for Christine. As a friend. That she remained as special to me as Roxi had become to her, and that all I had wanted to do was be sure she wouldn't get hurt. Roxi listened to my spin, consulted her thoughts for a second, then asked me not to mention the brunch date thing.

'I was on a low when I logged on after the lunch. This woman I met in a chat room, she understood me.' Roxi paused for a moment, then took me deeper into her confidence. 'It's so easy to open up to people online. Even total strangers. After one or two exchanges, they suddenly seem like family.'

'I can imagine.'

'She was the one who suggested we meet,' Roxi continued. 'I told her it would be good talking to someone who knew what it was like to have a girl go weird on her after just one night. But if she wanted anything more, she sure wasn't going to get it from me. Especially as Christine logged on just after, and spelled out her feelings so clearly.'

We both smiled. A little grimly on my part, but I covered it up by saying, 'Next time, turn to me. I know plenty about girls who go weird without warning.'

And that was how we finished up. Our conversation ending on a high, for Roxi at least, when I assured her she could trust me. In her position, I said, I too would have wanted to talk. So this brunch that never happened, it was a secret safe with me. Why worry Christine now things were good between them? In return, I asked for one small favour. Nothing much as far as Roxi was concerned, but privately it meant I could at least salvage something from the situation. A little security, in view of the fact that someone was out to unmask me. That was what I hoped when I asked if she could devote her online time to one woman only from this moment on.

'It would mean so much to Christine,' I said. 'A sign that you were serious about this relationship.'

This relationship. This relationship that was me but not me. This relationship that had become something I could never finish.

Roxi even thanked me as we parted in reception, but I assured her there was no need. Providing she kept this chat to herself, I was happy.

'I know Christine too well,' I stressed. 'She'll think I'm interfering.' I was pleased that Roxi agreed without question, though I had very different reasons for keeping my ex in the dark. If she knew I'd also been speaking offline on her behalf too, I feared the pressure could prove too much and all kinds of confessions would come tumbling out. I turned for the door, thinking I had got away with this. Thinking I had taken care of everything, just so Roxi wouldn't know the truth and cut me out of her life. Everything, that is, except me.

'Want to know what I think about it all?' I stopped right there, came around slowly. 'I think Christine lost out on something special when she finished with you.'

The end of the scene was in sight, and she had to floor me with this. Despite everything, it was a brave face I adopted when she kissed me on my cheek. Didn't even slip when she said I'd been a star. Though it was a face that promptly turned to stone in the back seat of the car. Set like my make-up as we inched our way through the traffic. Crawling slowly here, to my back seat confession with Sweet William.

'So there you go,' I complained to my dealer. 'You think Cupid ever shot himself with his own arrow? Because that's how I feel right now. That's why I need your help, Willie. Say you'll sedate me. Stop me thinking what a good thing I did for Christine just to save my own skin.'

My dealer had listened in silence, one massive forearm filling the open window. The driver hadn't moved either. Didn't even dare blip the engine.

'I know what you need,' said Sweet finally.

'You do? Thank God.'

'A good cleanser.'

Willie matched my glare for a beat, then told me he'd be right back. I watched him have a word with his boy, before marching my way once more. Zipping his puffa so high the fastener vanished under his lowest chin. But instead of slipping me some dark narcotic through the window, he yanked the whole door back on its hinges and hauled me into the street.

'What the fuck are you doing?' I complained, and tried to twist my wrist from his grip. 'Look at me, I'm dressed like a *woman*. I can't be seen out like this!'

'Shut it,' snapped my dealer, and began to drag me through the busy market. 'You're *my* bitch now.'

Nobody stopped us. Not one person stood in Willie's way. Even the cars braked sharply when he clomped across the road, dragging me in his wake. It must have looked like one hell of a domestic. With my wig askew and both legs laddered, I tried with all my might to free myself. My protestations turning even more frantic when a bus pulled up just yards ahead and my dealer broke into a lumber.

'Sweet!' I screeched, heels dug in as he pulled me on board. '*Talk* to me! What have I done? Where are we going?'

My dealer shoved me into the nearest seat.

'Call it an outing,' he said, and stood over me menacingly. 'My treat.'

'Couldn't I at least get changed?'

Sweet clamped my jaw, and squeezed it so my mouth went mushy. 'One more squeak from you, Reynard, I'll spank you so hard you won't sit down for a decade.'

I could barely bring myself to look at the row of stunned passengers opposite. Most of them hurried to get off at the next stop, while the conductor elected not to approach for a fare. Those who joined the bus took one look at the pair of us, then scurried upstairs. By the time we arrived in the heart of town, the top gallery was standing room only, while Sweet sat opposite me with his huge arms spread across four deserted seats.

'Willie,' I pleaded, my voice trembling now. 'Can't we go home? This is madness.'

It was late afternoon, but as ever, the streets were clogged with tourists. Every time we stopped for the lights, a new rank of faces looked once then twice through the glass. One even took a damn photo. Sweet William didn't seem bothered, but then he wasn't the one in the frame.

'How does it feel?' he growled, as the flash went off in my eyes. 'Being a minority interest.'

'How do you think?' I muttered weakly, attempting to shield my face.

My dealer stood up, grabbed my puffball sleeves, and pulled me from my seat. 'Perhaps we should get a drink,' he said. 'Give you a break.'

'A break?' I repeated, stunned by the very suggestion. 'Sweet, I've had all I can take in a bus. You want to take me to a *bar*?'

'I know the perfect place. But you'll have to sign me in as a guest.'

'I don't belong to any club.'

Sweet William straightened out my wig, then clasped my elbows and gave them a little squeeze. Just enough to prove that he was capable of crushing the bones inside.

'Not a problem,' he said, and led me from the bus. 'You qualify for temporary membership.'

The club was tucked down one of those narrow alleys flanked by tall buckled buildings and dangerously deep basements. Sheets of newspaper coming at us like tumbleweed. Graffiti on the walls. The kind of alley that serves as a cut through by day and a cut throat by night. The sun had already pulled out as Sweet William escorted me through, but at least I didn't have to worry about the risk of being jumped. Not with my dealer leading me by the hand.

'Where are we going?' I whined. 'My toes are fucking killing me.'

I wasn't prepared for Willie to stop so abruptly, and cursed again as I blundered into his Hulk-like frame.

'Here we are,' he said, and turned to rap on a battered metal door. We both stood back. Then Willie weighed one arm round me. 'Just act the part, we'll be sipping frozen daiquiri in seconds.'

'Part?' I said, feeling squashed by him now as well as demoralised. 'What part?'

I was about to tell him that I didn't even know whether I liked daiquiri when a bolt shot back inside. First one. Then another. And as the door opened out, I began to realise what was expected of me. There was no neon sign to indicate what kind of club this was. No flyposter. Nothing. But then it all became clear just as soon as we stepped over the threshold. The bouncer who signed us in wore a standard black tux, with a white shirt tight enough to see the muscles underneath. I kept my head down. Hoped no one looked too closely at me while my dealer paid for us both. Money changed hands. Lots of it. A protracted creak as the notes got folded away. I glanced up at the bouncer again, but I couldn't tell if it was the fabric or her biceps making all the noise. Even Sweet wouldn't want to haggle with a heavy like her, I thought. Or her female colleague. Equally pumped, and just as intimidating. Hair pulled back like a Sumo, keeping a bead on me behind her yellow-tinted wraparounds. Without a word, she opened the door that led downstairs. Too scared to even thank her, I seriously began to fret that my dealer was about to sink us both. I didn't dare air my suspicions, however. Not until we were well out of earshot.

'Is this what I think it is?'

'Welcome to the Venus Squeeze,' said Willie, and in the same breath I found myself moving freely. Down towards some double doors and the muted melody of a lounge piano. 'Man, this is going to be so far up your street it'll hurt to leave.'

'Willie, it's a *lesbian* club. How many straight clubs have dykes like that on the door?'

'Who says they're dykes?'

'Well, I didn't fancy yours much, and I hope to hell she didn't fancy me.'

'There you are making assumptions again, about the club too.'

'Are you out of your mind?' I hissed. 'Wake up and smell the oestrogen!'

'Bisexual women are also welcome here.' He thumbed his chest. 'And their partners.'

'Partners!' I stopped dead. *'Partners?'*

A hand on my wrist at this, and a digit to his lips. 'Be cool,' he said calmly. 'Be natural and nobody will hassle us.'

I pulled free and invited him to look at me. Just in case Sweet had forgotten I was wearing a big girl's blouse.

'How can I be natural? Dressed like *this*?'

'You're doing fine,' he asserted, and ushered me onwards. 'If you weren't such an outstanding actor we'd be back out in the twilight with no other place to go.'

I knew of a place to go. East from here. Back to my space. Lock the door. Close the book. Mission unaccomplished. That morning I had stepped out as a secret admirer. A man who hoped to quietly attract a bisexual woman from one side across to the other. Back then, and all through make-up, I really did believe that I was getting somewhere with Roxi. I had earned her trust. She liked me. I was her model of a man. But thanks to forces beyond my control I had become her confidante. A compromise that had drawn me just a little too far into the open for my liking. Far enough, it seemed, for my self-righteous bloody dealer to yank me off my feet and decree that I should go further. Now, at the end of what had possibly been the worst day of my life, I was being asked to see things from the far side of the sexual spectrum. A place so far from home that I was now dependent on my guide for survival.

While Sweet William sorted the drinks, I found myself the nearest table and wished I was invisible. The bar itself was in the round. A spot-lit circle in a square. Surrounded by a close-knit pattern of very different-looking women and the odd loose stitch of a man. Guests like Willie. Not impostors like me. I took stock of my position for a minute or so. Looking away quickly whenever someone glanced my way. But nobody let their gaze linger. No one stared. No one started. No one *bothered* me.

By the time Sweet set my cocktail down on the doily, I had figured out why we were here.

'A thank you would be nice,' he grumbled, squeezing into the seat right beside me.

Stirring from my thoughts, I couldn't decide if he was talking about the drink or the whole damn date. Nevertheless, I thanked him. Begrudgingly. He raised his glass. Waited for mine to catch up.

'Cheers,' I muttered. 'You git.'

'To the last great romantic,' he suggested instead.

I took a slug to the back of the throat, mindful of the pineapple slice as it slid around the rim of my glass. Beyond caring how it looked.

'Did you mean that?' I asked him.

Sweet tasted his in a different manner. His cheeks billowing one way then the other like he had a big fish in there, chasing its own tail. 'Every word,' he said finally, and put his fist to his mouth to mask a burp. 'But you gotta give up on this Roxi fox now, else you'll turn into a tragedy.'

I juiced the air between my teeth, glowering at him side on. 'We've been here before, Sweet.'

My dealer hoisted his brow, looked around the club, and corrected me without saying a single word.

'OK, but you have to admit I've given it a good shot.'

'The *best*,' he said, and leaned in close. 'Reynard, you took things further than any other man I know. Further than I thought possible. But now she's met Christine it's gone far enough.'

'But nothing's happened between us.'

'And nothing will. Roxi doesn't want a man right now, and you have to respect that fact. Otherwise you're no better than the dumb fucks who make someone feel uncomfortable just because they're different.'

I leaned back for a moment. Took my thoughts that way too. Retracing every excruciating step I had taken since I first tottered from the studio dressing room. A journey I didn't wish to repeat. Just then my attention got turned by a gale of laughter from a couple at the bar. Two women sharing a private joke. Looking relaxed. Off guard. Looking like the very best of friends. They certainly didn't need someone like me looking at them. So I looked at Sweet instead.

'I'm not like that,' I assured him. 'Not any more.'

'Good man,' he said, and rattled down the ice cubes from his daiquiri. I swear I witnessed each one pass unbroken down his throat. 'You want another drink?' he asked when he finally broke off for breath.

Mine was still half full, but I finished up. Swilling the last of my daiquiri just as Willie had, then shook my head from side to side.

'I'm ready to go.' I rose from my seat. 'Though I just want to fix my face first.'

'Smart move,' Sweet William agreed. 'I'll meet you out front.'

I headed for the ladies', but only because there didn't appear to be a gents'. Once inside, it took me maybe a couple of minutes to sort things. Without any make-up remover, all I could do was fill a basin then scrub with soap until it all came off. Every last trace of Roxi's handiwork. The wig went into the bin, too. Followed swiftly by the heels. It made things less of a hassle as I eased myself through the fanlight window and reached up for my dealer's hand. Even freed up my feet to push off the frame and let him haul me high. The only person who could take the full weight of a man like me and deliver him safely back to the world outside.

25

'Talking to those who have been through your experience
will help make sense of your emotions.'
A.C. Découcher, *Bisexuality for Beginners*

With the morning sun on my back, and a good night's sleep
behind me, I stood outside the door to Christine's block and
waited for her to buzz me up. I felt good. Really I did. Looked
OK, too. A little fish-eyed maybe, and with a nose so long my
face seemed set back on the opposite side of the street, but then
I was checking my appearance in a convex camera lens. One of
those sinister state-of-the-nation intercom systems that allows you
to vet any visitor before deciding if you wanted them in. Unless a
mute dwarf happened to call round, of course. The speaker stopped
my thoughts from working on that one. Crackling like a crisp packet
before a startled, over-amplified voice burst through.

'Roxi?'

I frowned, and stepped back an inch so she could get a better
look.

'Oh, Ren. Sorry.'

The buzzer went. I pushed open the lobby door, and jogged up
three flights of stairs.

It wasn't the print on her T-shirt that arrested my attention. Nor
the dun-coloured face pack. The latter was a regular thing with
Christine, though the T-shirt was something new. An oversized
number sporting two of those interlinked gender motif things. I
had never worked out which was male and which was female. The
circle with the cross underneath or the arrow pointing off it. Still, I
didn't need to ask now. Not with two crosses in front of me. How
very fem, I thought. Under any other circumstances I might have

ribbed her new passion for girls. Covered up for my losses by poking fun at her gain. But my mind was on other matters. For my ex was standing in a flat which appeared to have been picked up and given a brisk shakedown.

'Jesus,' I declared. 'When did this happen?'

She plucked a cushion off the floor. Whisked it home to the sofa. 'Last night, I think.'

'You *think*? Where were you?' I stepped over a wine bottle, and righted the yucca plant. The soil had spilled right out across the carpet. Just like the wine, in fact. I could only think she had been robbed.

'I was here.'

I quit slotting magazines back into the rack and looked aghast at Christine. She yawned in the face of my concern, cursed as her mud pack fissured and picked her way to the bathroom. It was then I conceded that she didn't look as traumatised as one would expect. Like, how many burglary victims cleaned up their face before their flat? I followed her down the hallway, but she had already shut the bathroom door behind her.

'Are you OK?' I called out after a minute. 'You're not hurt or anything?'

'A little dazed,' came the reply. 'But I'll be all right after a soak.'

To my left, I noticed her bedroom door was wide open. I had been there many times, but never seen it reduced to such a state.

'Are you insured?'

'For what?' Christine swept from the bathroom, padded into the bedroom. I followed close behind. 'I know a few things got broken, but I just haven't had a chance to tidy up. Roxi only left half an hour ago. Give me a break, Ren.'

'Roxi did this?'

Even through the fresh layer of clay, I could see Christine looked suddenly sheepish.

'I guess we were both a bit responsible.'

'You two have a fight?'

'No,' she asserted, and the face pack, still wet, accommodated her loping grin. 'Far from it.'

I stole a second look around the room, going giddy this time as

I took it all in, and wondered exactly how two women could cause such damage. Whenever I had slept with Christine, I regarded it a triumph if the duvet finished up on the floor. But a whole damn *dressing table*? That was just taking the piss. It was as if she and Roxi had taken it in turns to stand on the bed and spin the other one round like a wrecking ball.

Gazing reflectively at the scene, my ex said, 'I guess things might have got a bit out of hand.'

This time, I really didn't feel like pressing her for the whole story. Instead, I reminded myself why I had come here in the first place.

'Christine, this has to stop.'

She took a second to digest this, then swung around to face me. 'It's my bedroom.'

'Yeah, but it's my screen name, and I can't do it any more. I can't talk to Roxi, making out I'm you.'

That got her. The clay around her temples, the stuff which had survived from the first round, it began to splinter a little.

'I'm not sure I can manage alone,' she said.

I forced myself to check out the legacy of their latest encounter. Said she'd managed all right without me so far. 'Maybe one day you can repay the favour,' I told her. 'But from now on, she's all yours.' I was ready to leave. Ready to get on with the rest of my life. Except my ex wasn't going to let me out of hers so easily.

'Roxi told me all about the chat I never had with her. The one on the Internet, while I was in the bathroom?'

'What about it? At least you got a second slice of the pie.'

Christine said, 'I couldn't believe some of the lines you came up with for her. Things you never once tried on me.'

'I'm an actor. It's what I do.'

I walked across to the window. Hoped Christine couldn't see me blushing.

'All night she kept reminding me what I was supposed to have said. Even in bed, Ren.'

'Thanks, Christine. Spare me the location detail, OK?'

'What I'm saying is your online thing with Roxi, it really clicks with her.'

I shifted my attention to the curtain rail. Anything not to think of the implications. It hung at an interesting angle. One which I could only describe as approaching vertical. 'That's why I want out of this relationship,' I said next, thinking there was no good time to be doing this. 'If you want to keep seeing Roxi then you have to do so on your own terms.'

A silence from Christine. A moment to think ahead. For a note of panic to rise up with her response. 'You know what I think? I think you're jealous.'

'Oh come on!' I turned to reason with her. 'I'm doing this for you as well as me. I want out for both our sakes.'

'You can't have Roxi, so why should I?' My ex was mad, but a pro with the mud pack, accusing me like this while barely moving her mouth. 'That's how it is for you, isn't it? A man who has a problem because he's missing out.'

'You're tired, Christine. You don't know what you're saying.'

'I never do with you!'

This time, it was me who didn't know what to say. I was hurt by her outburst. Not just because my ex probably had a point, but because I hadn't wanted things to end this way. In a mess, like her flat. With Christine eyeballing me so fiercely that I could see no option but to sink my hands into my pockets and turn for the door.

'I should go,' I sighed. 'You obviously don't need me to clean up for you any more.'

'Fine by me.'

'Bye then.'

'Close the door on your way out.'

Only I didn't even get a chance to open it. Got into the front room. Got my hand as far as the handle, in fact. But a buzz from the intercom phone stopped me going all the way.

'Want me to get that?'

'You've managed quite enough of my life, thank you.'

Christine huffed her way round me like I was a major obstacle. I backed off as if it was an even bigger imposition. My ex watching me as she picked up the receiver. Me watching the wall-mounted monitor beside her as the picture faded in.

It had to be Roxi. I knew it was her even before the contrast settled. I knew because when the voice at the other end came through Christine's face pack cracked wide open in response. Stress lines splaying across the clay. Feathering her cheekbones. Forming great faults across her brow. She looked at me, a disaster waiting to happen, and for a second it seemed as if Roxi was looking at her, there on the screen in black and white. Christine turned the phone so the mouthpiece pressed into her collarbone.

'I can't let her see me like this,' she said imploringly. 'I look a complete state.'

'That didn't seem to bother you earlier,' I snapped. 'How come it's fine for *me* to see you in a face pack and not Roxi?'

'It's different, all right? Just different.'

Roxi leaned in again. The way Christine reacted next, it was as if the receiver on her shoulder had let out a little shock. She held out the phone to me. Switching her attention from me to the monitor and back to me again.

'Why don't you just ask what she wants?' I suggested calmly. 'Surely she's not come back for seconds?'

My ex turned away from me, consulted the phone, then came right round all cobbled up in the cable. 'She's left her purse.'

'So let her come in and find it. Don't mind me. I'll go and wait on the next floor until she's gone.'

'I *can't* see her, Ren! Not like *this*.'

Christine, imploring me to come up with an excuse. Stricken with the kind of terror I had only ever witnessed before in my dealer when the stall next to his got raided. Trading without a permit, as it turned out, but I guess Willie's worries had been justified. My ex was just over-reacting, I thought. What was so wrong with being under-dressed? It wasn't as if the pair of them had much left to hide from each other. I was going to walk, regardless. But then her lip went into a wobble, and I resigned myself to one last favour. Pinching the bridge of my nose, I considered Christine's options for a moment, and said, 'You're sick.'

'What?'

'Tell her you're sick. Trust me.'

Christine looked at me as if I was trying to be funny. Poised to pick up on the slightest hint of a snigger, then put the phone back to her ear and told Roxi she was sick. In the monitor I watched Roxi say something back. Something Christine dutifully relayed to me.

'She wants to know what's wrong.'

'It's love sickness.'

'*Ren*, what shall I say?'

'What I told you.'

'Love sickness sounds stupid. How about chicken pox?'

'Stupid?' I reflected, choosing to ignore her own suggestion. 'Did Cicero regard it as a stupid matter? Did Shakespeare strike it from his script? How about Casanova? Gustave Flaubert? Tony Bennett? Barry White?' As I counted off the masters on my fingers, both women appeared to be watching me with equal bemusement. Christine here in front of me. Roxi there on the wall. Unaware once again of my presence in between them. 'Love sickness is a *deadly* serious affliction!' I emphasised. 'The only affliction to strike both heart and mind. Early symptoms include a loss of appetite and a disarming sense of euphoria. It's a combination that goes on to badly compromise the sufferer's ability to function properly. She doesn't want to eat. She doesn't want to go to work. She can't explain how she feels, or work out how to cure it. All she wants to do is put on a face pack, maybe listen to some music in a different light, and set her sights on the next date. That's how love sickness would seem to me, if I were you, of course, now tell her all about it.'

On the monitor, I noticed that Roxi appeared to be looking high up the wall of the block. My ex, meanwhile, was still looking my way but with her mouth agape now. A voice just then, calling out anxiously. The accent a long way from home.

'Christine? What's with the silence? Is everything OK?' Christine's first reaction was to stare in disbelief at the receiver and then at the screen, but Roxi was no longer in the frame. Nor was she speaking into the intercom. I thumbed across the room, turned her attention to the window, to where I guessed her girlfriend was waiting three storeys below.

'Take a deep breath and tell her how you feel,' I said. 'You can do it.' She untangled herself from the phone and hurried across to open the window. There, she inched forward to take a peek and then pulled back smartly. I pictured Roxi sitting on the side wall of the municipal gardens. Legs crossed at the ankles. Twisting a daisy between her fingers maybe. Waiting for Christine to get her act together.

'What was the first bit?' she whispered across to me.

'Think how it is to be lovesick. Open your heart to her. Embroider. *Embellish*.'

Christine pulled a face on all three counts. And yet when she turned to address Roxi I felt sure she would redeem herself. Use my sentiments as a springboard for her own. Tossing out words like confetti, as if from an ivy-clad balcony and not the ex-council block it actually was. Which seemed kind of fitting, I guess, when she cleared her throat and said, 'I'm just feeling a bit pukey.'

'*Pukey*?' I hissed. 'That's all you can say?'

Christine glanced over her shoulder, and I expected to see abject terror in her face. But only the clay remained cracked. Underneath, in fact, she seemed utterly composed.

'You do love her, right?'

The pause, it lingered just a beat too long. A silence broken only by Roxi calling her name once again, and followed by Christine who whispered, 'Clearly not as much you.'

Never before had I heard her speak so accurately. To say what she meant with such certainty and devastation. That only one of us felt this way. I had fallen for Roxi in a flash, and here was Christine exposing the extent of my blindness. A woman who had left me, as she always maintained, to find herself.

'So it's *lust*?' Struggling to keep my voice down now, I flung my arm round the room. 'This is just a physical thing for you?'

'I don't know what it is just yet.'

'Whenever you're ready,' called Roxi from outside, this dream who had divided us.

'Now I understand why you won't see her,' I hissed. 'You feel the need to look your best because that's all you're prepared to give! Except Roxi wants more, and that's where I come in, isn't it? To say all the right things for you? Not because you can't find the right words, Christine, but because you haven't got the *heart* to say them.'

'That's not true—'

'Prove it, then.'

We scowled at one another. Breathing bull-like through our nostrils. But as hard as I stared at my ex, all I could think about was Roxi. Half holding her gaze, I fumbled for my mobile and then punched in a number from memory.

'Ren, is this really a good time?'

I didn't answer. A second passed before Christine's home phone began to ring. 'That'll be the cavalry,' I said. She looked startled again. 'Don't worry, it's nothing you can't handle.'

Roxi's purse lay on the carpet between us. I dropped to one knee and lobbed it across to Christine with my free hand. 'Throw it to her. Then pick up.' This time, she listened to my instructions. Even stood down with a smile. Nothing knock-out, but recognition for my services.

'Thank you.'

At the window, my ex held out the purse for Roxi and let it fall without showing her face. With the phone still ringing she followed it up by saying, 'Let me answer this, and I'll be right back.'

A soft thud. A silence. Then Roxi's voice once more. Tempered now by a note of resignation. 'OK, I'll be here.'

'It's your mother,' I said calmly into my own mobile, when Christine picked up. 'No, even better. It's your *grandmother*. She's not well. You'll have to take this.' My ex, looking at me across the room as if she'd just heard a heavy breather. Both of us with our phones pressed to our ears. 'Go ahead,' I said. 'Tell Roxi you'll be in touch later.'

I watched her edge back to the window, and repeat what I had just said.

'Your grandmother's sick too?' I heard Roxi ask.

Christine glanced over again, but this time she spoke without a prompt.

'She has gout. The way I'm feeling now, she's the lucky one.' I smiled to myself. Christine cracking a joke like that. Maybe there was hope for them both.

'So what is wrong with you,' Roxi called back. 'What's with the sickness all of a sudden?'

'It's love sickness,' my ex said finally, her back to the frame now, staring straight at me.

'Boy,' called Roxi, sounding relieved at last. 'It must be serious.'

'You can't imagine,' she replied. 'Took me by surprise, too.'

'Is it infectious?'

Christine said she thought it was catching, and for a second I thought she might identify me as the carrier. Then Roxi's voice again. Playful, this time. In on the so-called-act. 'Maybe I'll drop you an email,' she said. 'Let you know if I'm starting to show the same symptoms.'

'An email from you could be just the tonic.' Christine paused as if to consult me again, then decided to go with it anyway. 'I'll get right back to you, hun.'

The look she gave me when she said this, I just knew she assumed I would comply. That she expected me to go back to my space and carry on with her correspondence. Even *enjoy* it. As if our fight had been something about nothing. A lovers' tiff, of sorts. And what was with the *hun* crap? Christine talking the talk like it was her mother tongue. Certainly looking like she'd been there, I gave her that. Even come back wearing the damn T-shirt. I had to get out of her flat. Away from this bi-osphere before it became a totally alien environment to me. Back to my own breathing space. Yes, I needed a tonic. But I wanted vodka in mine. This thing was over. Finished. Behind me. There would be no more emails. Not any more. Wherever my ex was heading, it was time we parted company.

'Where are you going?' asked Christine, still talking into the phone, when she saw me head for the door.

'Away from here,' I told her, with such a note of finality that she followed me out. Watching me from the rail as I shut down my mobile without saying goodbye.

26

*'Always carry the means to fix your make-up in
emergencies.'*
Verity Pepper, *Make Up a Million*

By the time I stepped out into the street, Roxi was nowhere to be
seen. For a second I stood there. Hands on hips. Eyes shut. Face to
the sun. Feeling like a man who had pulled up in a marathon way
before the tape. But then I didn't feel defeated because I hadn't really
qualified to set off in the first place. Not in this race. A strictly female
affair. Right from the start it had turned the undertaking into an
impossible task. A novelty act left staggering at the back with knees
like butter curls. A joke that wasn't funny any more.

In this light, my decision to give up seemed nothing less than
courageous. Leaving Christine to forge ahead without me wasn't
easy, but at last I was free. And in more ways than one. On top
of my own personal liberation, the cat's people had insisted on a
rest day. A message from my agent that I regarded as great news.
According to the feline psychologist, after a long week under the
studio lights my co-star was beginning to display signs of distress.
After filming the day before, it had slunk back into its cage and
refused all food and water. I sympathised. Really I did. Nobody
had consulted me about my own mood, but then I knew that I too
would benefit from the next twenty-four hours. Mentally, physically,
but above all sexually. I would take time out from them all. At last I
had time to myself. To be no one for anybody. Time to make the
most of being me.

I opened my eyes, just a little, and was pleased I was carrying
shades. For it was shaping up to be a dazzling day. Even the breeze
was behind me as I headed into the city. A day devoted to good
things. A day for cashing cheques, the first in months from my agent,

and for trying out new threads. A big band kind of day. One that put a swing in my step and my shopping bags. Like some maestro and his music men were right there with me. Partying on every street corner. Kicking up a storm with nine fine horns. It was that kind of a day. A day so good I really didn't want to go home, though it was only when I flopped back into my space that I confronted the reason why.

The late sun sliced through the blinds, still drawn and quartered from the previous night. Dust motes turning in the rafters of light. Swayed by my return. I bumped the door shut behind me, and immediately felt like I had sealed myself in. The whole place felt stuffier than ever before, in fact. Slow cooked in my absence.

I dumped my bags, and then fingered my way through a fine selection of white lilies and scarlet dahlias I had picked up from the porch. A present from my dealer, going by the blim of dope I found inside. With such a contrasting bloom, I couldn't be sure whether it was intended as an apology for the hell he had put me through, or applause for the decision it had persuaded me to reach. That there was probably just enough hash to skin up a toothpick spliff made me wonder whether Willie should have bothered at all. I was about to bin the bunch, but found I couldn't quite bring myself to do so. It seemed like a waste. A lost opportunity. Minutes later, having slotted Sweet's flowers into a carafe, I conceded that in fact it wasn't his drugs that would have the greatest impact on me.

All day I had kept myself busy. Filled my time by showering myself with gifts to keep me feeling good. Now I was back where I started, however, things didn't feel so fine. Slumped in the sofa, captivated by the dazzling floral arrangement on my coffee table, I was forced to face up to the one thing I had been trying not to think about.

Roxi. A woman I had pledged to forget, and who in turn had become the centrepiece of my existence.

The fox hadn't even set foot in my space, but still it felt empty without her. I should have felt this way when Christine finished with me. Instead I felt worse because of who she had taken up with.

Smoking the joint didn't alter my outlook one way or the other.

Didn't do a damn thing, in fact. The bastard burned so fast I barely got a chance to drag it down. All I had time to do was accept that once it singed my fingers there would be nothing left to come between me and my monitor.

She said she would send an email. Reveal how she was feeling. It was something I needed to see if I was to log out of Roxi's life. Like anyone on the bum end of a relationship, I wanted to know all the details. Tie up any loose ends and create some kind of *closure* for myself. Even if Roxi wasn't aware she'd even opened anything with me.

Settling down at my desk, I figured this was where I should have finished up my day. Not washed out on the sofa, hoping for a turn in the tide. Seeing how Sweet William's seedlings had progressed made me feel a whole lot better. A joy, in fact, to see that they had grown another inch. Some had even sprouted a skirt of leaves, while many of the buds were swollen and even starting to split. I was so impressed that while my computer booted up I actually watered them for the first time. My only concern was the angle at which they had grown. Inclined as they were towards the air vents, as if shying away from direct light. I turned the disk box round, and made a note to myself to rotate it on a daily basis. For it was important to me that they finished up straight. It just made sense to me at the time.

I had mail. But I wasn't at liberty to read it because I couldn't actually get to the bloody mail box. My female creation might have been in existence for just a matter of days, but her Virtual Vitals had clearly been looked up more times than a lap dancer. Within seconds of logging on, the Quick-Es had begun to splat open like flies on a windscreen. LadiByrd. FilliShave. S8Mimi and FlyBi. All of them had entered my name into their Cyber Circles, then pounced on me when I appeared. NuBiFem. New Bisexual Female. An online presence who promised so much, these women were virtually *throwing* themselves at my feet. I responded by deleting each and every one in turn. Zapping away like I was playing some Sapphic version of Space Invaders. Working through all comers in a bid to reach my goal. Roxi's email. Hovering at the back of my browser. Partially obscured but clearly titled, 'The Contents of My Heart'.

The contents of my own heart surged on seeing this. One click away from my prize, however, and a window opened up that I couldn't ignore. Not with our history. Our common bond. Our secret.

Quick-E to: NuBiFem

BiRuth: How's it going?

It was going nowhere, but I didn't want to get into that. Not right now. Having soared into cyberspace fuelled by Ruth's words of wisdom, I could hardly tell him that my ex was now in charge of the mission.

NuBiFem: Going OK. Nothing to report, really.

BiRuth: Oh, come on, with Vitals like yours? The women must be queuing up.

They were. Even as we spoke I clicked another one away.

NuBiFem: Actually I'm about to retire from the scene.

BiRuth: Rash words for one so young.

I was desperate to open up Roxi's email. That's all I wanted from this session. I kept glancing at the title, longing to get inside and read what made her tick. But every time I moved the cursor across, my online mentor would drag my attention back again.

NuBiFem: I've made up my mind. After this session, I'm coming out as a man again.

BiRuth: Not you as well.

'As well as what?' I asked, and typed exactly that.

BiRuth:	It seems our presence has stirred the wrath of the sisters.

I knew who he was talking about before he had even typed the name in full. The Squad. The Viagra Snatch crank e-caller. When BiRuth invited me to visit the website, I informed him I had already been there.

BiRuth:	Ah, now I understand why you want to bow out. You're not the first to find yourself under surveillance. At least six of my contacts have been frightened off as a result.

I told him I wasn't frightened. That nobody was forcing me offline. I was quitting for personal reasons. Nothing more. Even so, BiRuth seemed unconvinced.

BiRuth:	Of all the fake women in this game, I have more faith in you than any other man.
NuBiFem:	This was never a game. Not for me.
BiRuth:	I know. I sensed you were for real when we met. That you didn't regard cybersex as your ultimate goal set you apart from the others. Your commitment impressed me. You possess the drive to see things through.
NuBiFem:	I'm finished, Ruth. It's over.
BiRuth:	I still believe you can find what you're looking for, Ren, and maybe find what I'm still seeking too.

I pictured BiRuth, alone at his console. Lost without his wife. Stuck between two worlds. A keeper at the gates.

BiRuth:	You're my eyes and ears, my son. You can't give up on me now.

As much as I pitied the man, he just didn't fit into my agenda. For I had an email to read. A pressing desire to download all there was to know about Roxi. Maybe even shift it ceremoniously into the waste basket. When another window opened on my screen, however, my frustration began to spill from my lips and onto the keys.

Quick-E to: NuBiFem

VSQ	Hey, hun bun. You owe me a lunch.

'Oh, not you *again*!'

NuBiFem:	Stick your lunch, and pick on someone your own sex.
VSQ:	I'd love to. If men like you stopped making it so hard for us to tell the difference.

I switched windows. Clicking out of one private conversation, clicking into another. There, I informed BiRuth that the Squad were online.

BiRuth:	I know.
NuBiFem:	You do?
BiRuth:	I have the screen name listed in my Cyber Circle, but I've put a bar on incoming correspondence from them. Anything they send to me bounces right back.

I was aware of my mail controls, I just didn't think it was a good idea to ignore women with a beef like theirs.

NuBiFem:	Actually, Ruth, I think this outfit mean business.
BiRuth:	Nobody could make my suffering any worse, Reynard. I have nothing to lose. Except you.

I stressed that my mind was made up. That I was bowing out from the scene. But BiRuth wasn't having any of it. Nor was he alone in his persistence. For in the adjacent window, cut off from the course of my exchange with him, the Viagra Snatch Squad continued to harangue me. Irate that I had thwarted their attempt to get to Roxi. Furious that I should be back online. Threatening my social destruction unless I submitted to their will.

VSQ: Log off, hun bun. Listen to your head, not your dick.

BiRuth: Stay online, Ren. Trust your instincts.

I watched these two opposing forces vying for my attention, and wondered what it would take to shut them up. It was beyond me how Luke Skywalker put up with this kind of crap without telling all involved to just fuck themselves. Unlike him, however, I had already lost my princess. All I wanted to do was gather something to remember her by and then go. Bow out and leave my own personal O-Bi Wan to fight these sexual stormtroopers on his own terms. As it looked like neither of them would stop and listen, I fired off a quick email to Tony Curtis instead. A thank you note, really. For he had been very patient with me, but I was going and I planned to be some time. After that, I informed BiRuth that it had been a learning experience, copied it over to the Squad, and cleared their windows from the screen. At last, I was free to read Roxi's email. Open up the one thing that mattered most to me just then.

email to: NuBiFem
from: RoxiNYC
subject: the contents of my heart

Dear Christine,
I promised I would write. Having had a day off work to think about things, I've realised what it is about you that keeps me coming back for more—

'Fuck!'
This was not a good time for a Quick-E to dominate my screen.

Another box. Another bisexual. Another woman drawn to the fox in me. This one adopting an approach I had now seen many times over. It was all becoming so tiresome.

Quick-E to: NuBiFem

PlayMissT   Hey, baby! When your name appeared in my Cyber Circle I just had to come and say hi.

I didn't give a damn whether she wanted to come and do things to me with whipped cream or a mint in her mouth. Whoever she was, my only concern was that her greeting eclipsed Roxi's email. Which returned to my attention once I'd dealt with this unsolicited Quick-E with one deft click on my delete button.

... I'm in love with you, Christine. Catching fast, isn't it? Physically, you're just wild and you know it! The way you move, the way you moan, the way you touch me—

The way this bi returned with another Quick-E . . .

Quick-E to: NuBiFem

PlayMissT: It's a real surprise to see you online.

Now it was my turn to moan. Just not in the way I guessed my ex had responded to Roxi.

PlayMissT: Makes my heart race, contacting you here.

'Well, fancy,' I said sourly, and clicked her out of Roxi's way once more.

... But it's your mind that really blows me! Literally! Those times we speak online I sometimes felt closer to you than I do when we're making out. Some of the things you say leave me feeling—

Quick-E to: NuBiFem

....

PlayMissT: Weird!

'Oh, Will you give it up, girl Go back to your people. I'm a *bloke!*'

PlayMissT: I can barely get my head around the fact I'm even talking to you.

Three windows she had sent me. Three times I had blanked her completely. Still she came back for more. Even as a man I had never been this desperate. Maybe women just didn't pick up on the vibe like they did from us. Reluctantly, I spelled it out.

NuBiFem: Listen, hun. I'm flattered by your attention, but I'm not really looking for anyone special right now.

PlayMissT: Glad to hear it!

NuBiFem: You are?

PlayMissT: Let's face it, Roxi wouldn't like it if she thought you were playing around behind her back.

'Roxi!' I said out loud, and sat right up in my chair. 'You know Roxi!'

NuBiFem: Who are you?

She told me her name was Tallulah. A name I had heard once before. Only this time it had more of an impact. Like a cloud of cigar smoke had mushroomed through the screen and into my face. Making me smart all the more when she added that Roxi was her flatmate.

NuBiFem: Does she know I'm online? Is she with you now?

PlayMissT: No. She's downstairs.

'Thank God!'

PlayMissT:	In the kitchen with Christine.
NuBiFem:	What!
PlayMissT:	You just dropped by.

'Fuck!' I cried, clasping my forehead.

PlayMissT:	Which is odd. Because when Christine came in she wasn't packing a laptop with her.

I wasn't sure which way to go. Whether to come clean or cobble up some other story. Paralysed by indecision, facing Tallulah on the information superhighway, all I could do was watch her headlights grow bigger.

PlayMissT:	So I'm wondering how she can be offline with Roxi, and online talking to me at the same time. Any ideas, 'Christine'?

Briefly I considered reinventing myself again. As my ex's female flatmate, maybe. An ali-bi with access to Christine's computer. That was it! I even began tapping out my plea, until Tallulah's window on me was itself overshadowed by yet another Quick-E.

Quick-E to: NuBiFem

BiRuth:	Trust me, Ren. You can do this. Follow your instinct.

I could virtually hear his words play out in my head. Could see him sitting opposite me in the cafe again. A man with all the presence of a hologram.

Quick-E to: NuBiFem

VSQ:	Watch yourself, hun bun. We're certainly watching you xxx

I closed my eyes for a second, searching for some space to think, before returning to delete the two windows with a decisive double click. There was no room on my shoulders for either of them. I also wiped the line I was composing for Tallulah. The flatmate spin seeming suddenly very foolish indeed. Instead, I responded with a question. Upfront and direct, offering to show her my hand.

NuBiFem:	If I reveal who I am, will you promise not to say anything to Roxi?
PlayMissT:	Perhaps.

I went with my instincts, but not as BiRuth would wish. Without even looking at the keyboard, I let my fingers run through a familiar pattern.

NuBiFem:	Reynard. Call me Ren.
PlayMissT:	From the cybercafe? All mouse and no trousers?
NuBiFem:	Afraid so, yes.

I glanced at Sweet William's seedlings. Looking to them for support, almost. Except now it seemed like they were leaning *away* from my computer not because I had turned the disk box but because they couldn't bear to watch me any longer.

PlayMissT:	Meet me there in thirty minutes.
NuBiFem:	What about Roxi? Will you tell her?

I waited a full minute for Tallulah to get back to me, before conceding that she must have left already. I followed suit. Shutting down the computer without logging off or saving mail for later. An illegal operation, maybe. One that could potentially corrupt the hard-drive, but it wasn't the crime that concerned me as I scrambled to leave my space.

27

'Cats will learn tricks, if they know there's something in it for them.'
http://www.purradise.com/purrfect10.html

She was there before me. Sharp suit and slingbacks. Same bar stool. Same drink. Maybe even the same stogie. Tallulah by name. Tallulah by nature.

'Sit down, baby,' she said. 'And shut up.'

I did as I was told.

'What are you drinking?'

I asked for a daiquiri. She ordered two vodka gimlets. Ice for mine, not hers. I decided it was probably not a good idea to argue, or even appear to *think* she looked cold enough.

'In a moment,' she said calmly, 'you can tell me all about it. If you like, you can tell me that you're misunderstood. That you respect women really, even the ones who are gagging for it. The bisexuals, right? Those whores who want it so bad they'll even screw their own kind.'

'It's not like that,' I protested.

Tallulah raised her finger. Glowered at me. I ducked into my drink.

'You can tell me whatever you want real soon. And baby, I'll listen. I will. Every word. But before you start, just in case you think I'm another soft touch, I want you to know that I've probably heard it all before.'

'I don't think you have.'

She reached for the ashtray beside me. I leaned away from the bar. Just to give her a clear shot.

'All men are the same. You're no different from the rest of them.'

'That's not fair.'

'OK,' she said, and straightened up to cross her legs so high I suddenly had to find my own source of nicotine. 'Try me.'

So I did. Through several drinks and double the smokes. I told her all about myself. All about my relationship with Christine. Not just the one she had broken up because of her, but the one we had gone on to form because of me. Because I had fallen for a woman under false pretences, and she in turn had fallen for my stand in. I swore that I never meant to hurt or humiliate Roxi, and vowed I never would. In fact our online trysts had demanded such honesty and candour that I could never step out of the shadows. Not now I had laid my feelings bare to her. Encouraged her to believe I had given her everything. Things had gone so far that removing the screens was out of the question. She would know me too well, wouldn't she? This woman who didn't know the half of me. Could I really expect her to want it all?

Throughout my explanation, Tallulah's expression remained well below zero. A look so chilling I kept one eye on her cigar, in case she stubbed it out on my knee. I barely knew her, and yet I went so deep that I finished up feeling as drained as my glass. On the way I begged for her to make this our secret. Reminded her that I wasn't even fighting for a romance of my own. I was out of there. Back in as a man. All I wanted now was for two women to make the most from my mistakes. Get something right where I had gone wrong. What was so bad about that? I sat back and shrugged, my arms spread wide. Only then did she stir to say, 'Typical.'

I let my hands fall back in my lap. 'I'm sorry?'

'Typical,' she said again, and paused to draw on her cigar. 'Man walks away from a mess of his own creation, thinks he's doing everyone else a favour.'

Smoke in my face again, but by then I was beyond insult.

'That's all you can say? After everything I've told you. That I'm a *typical* man?'

'Seems so,' she replied, and examined her scarlet talons.

'And that really is the best you can do?'

She glanced up, cut me a frown from under her fringe. Quizzing my question, as if I'd run out of time with her. My audience with her complete. But I wasn't done yet. I was quite prepared to improvise.

'Reynard, we're through.' She waved at me like I was a bad smell. 'Go and do whatever boys do when they're feeling sorry for themselves.'

I stuck it out. Stayed right there on the chair. 'I just thought you could at least match me for imagination. Honour my efforts by being a little more . . . creative.'

'Baby, I know this is humiliating for you, but there's no need to get this upset.'

'Maybe I should run through some examples,' I suggested, just loud enough for some of the nearest surfers to turn from their terminals. 'For instance, instead of calling me a typical man, which is a gross generalisation, and one I hope nobody would ever dream of using to describe a woman, you could have given more thought to your insult. Maybe accused me of being *hopeless.*'

'Hopeless?'

'You've never come across a hopeless man? Let me show you.'

I shot my cuffs. Cleared my throat. I didn't really know what I was doing, but I knew exactly where I wanted to go. I slid from my stool, clasped her wrists and projected my voice so Tallulah wasn't the only one who would hear me.

'Honey, I'm only asking you to iron one shirt. Mum never taught me how to do it. I can do the back bit but the sleeves are beyond me.'

'What are you talking about?' she hissed, aware that people were now paying some serious attention. 'Are you tripping?'

'OK,' I said, and flopped to the floor 'How about *helpless.*'

The sound of many keyboards falling quiet served to open out my stage. I had performed in front of an audience many times before, but none so captive as this.

'Shweetie,' I slurred, lying on my back with my arms outstretched. 'A pint with the lads, that's all I had, I shwear.'

'Get up,' snapped Tallulah, then smiled uneasily at the growing ranks of dumbstruck cyberpatrons.

'*Aggressive?*' I sprang to my feet and lurched at the front row, simian-like and seething. I had everything clenched. Fists. Teeth. Arse. A bound-up ball of fury that saw those within range retreat behind their monitors. 'Come on then,' I yelled. 'Who'll have some? No one ever seen a man lose his rag for no reason? Beat someone senseless for "looking at him funny"? Well, step right up and I'll show you how easy it can be.'

There were no takers. A couple near the back seized the opportunity to head for the exit when I tossed my head back and laughed like a crazy.

'*Funny* man. Everyone loves a wise guy, Tallulah. Heard this one? What's the difference between an airship and three hundred and sixty-five blow jobs?'

A flicker of disgust crossed her face, but I wasn't going to let her off. In one long resigned sigh, she said, 'I don't know. What is the difference?'

'One is a Goodyear.' And then grinning for the audience. 'But the other is an *excellent* year!'

A stifled guffaw. Somewhere up at the back. The shark smile vanished from my face, consumed by a scathing stare. Over by the door, a young blade with a goatee looked at his trainers.

'Reynard,' said Tallulah. 'You've made your point.'

'Wait,' I said, charged by another idea. 'Here's a classic. *Desperate* man!'

'Don't do this,' she pleaded as I fell to my knees and begged her to let me back into her life.

'She meant nothing,' I implored her. 'Honestly, every time we did it I pretended I was with you.'

'*Reynard!*'

I paused for a second. Caught her eye. Then winked mischievously.

'*Ignorant,*' I suggested, and asked her why she was so uptight.

'I'm not.'

'Yes you are. And at the same time every month too. It's unacceptable, Tallulah. Pull yourself together.'

'Enough!'

'*Insensitive,*' I followed up quickly, and suggested her clothes looked a little tight-fitting recently. Especially round the hips.

'You need help.'

'All I'm saying is you should be using a cooler wash, Tallulah. A lower setting won't shrink stuff so quickly.'

'Very clever. Please stop.'

'*Persistent,*' I proposed, regardless. 'OK, so you're too tired for sex. What if I wait until you're asleep?'

'You're disgusting.'

'Far from it,' I said. 'I'm *outrageous!*'

'Don't,' she begged as I prepared to moon my audience. A cheer went up from somewhere, but my trousers didn't come down.

'I have a better idea,' I said, rebuckling my belt. 'Let's take a request.'

I had just enough time to turn my gaze across the rows before a disembodied but disgruntled voice told me to sit down and stop being an idiot.

'Ah ha!' I cried, and my forefinger shot up. 'The *idiot* man.' I glanced behind me, saw Tallulah with her hand cupped over her eyes. 'Ladies and gentlemen, there's not much I need to do to illustrate that kind of guy. You know why? Because by all accounts, and by my own admission, you're looking at one.' I turned one way then the other, so everyone got to see me. 'The all original idiot-male. Right here for your disapproval. A real prize prick, as I'm sure you'll agree.'

A titter of laughter. Then a whistle went up like a firework.

'To finish,' I declared, aware that I would have them soon, 'the *typical* man!'

I heard Tallulah groan behind me, but still I grinned like an impresario. Counting down to the moment when I adopted a Laurel-like look of confusion. Tickling the crown of my head, I addressed the cybercafe once more:

'Do you know, I'm all dried up for ideas. Would anyone care to improvise this one for me? Is there a typical man in the house? A man prepared to stand up and say: "Yep, I'm so sadly predictable you could set your watch by me!"'

It was one of those moments when everyone was watching, but nobody made eye contact. Least of all the men

'You, sir!' I said, spinning round to point at the first unfortunate. Gap teeth and T-shirt, khaki pants and cauliflower ears. When he realised I was addressing him directly, his whole face appeared to contract. 'What about you?' The guy behind shook his head before I even finished. 'Are you a typical man?' I asked the piercing freak at the terminal beside him, and got the same response. I stepped back to bring Tallulah under the spotlight. 'Can you see one?' She pursed her lips so tight they lost colour. 'Typical, isn't it? Never one around when you stop to look.'

'You've made your point.'

I dipped my hand in my pocket. Opened out my wallet and flipped my credit card onto the bar. 'I wonder if this might lure a volunteer?' I faced into the spotlight once more. 'Would we get a better response if I asked if there were any typical men here tonight who also happened to be a bit parched?'

A sudden stirring proved me right. More so when I said, 'And how about the ladies? If there was a free drink at stake, would any of you be willing to be described as typical chicks?'

By now, *everyone* in the cybercafe was looking my way. Silently straining to win my attention.

'You've been a marvellous audience,' I announced. Gesturing now like I was ready to embrace them all. 'Enjoy a round of beers on me!' I bowed my head, measured the silence with both hands. Then slowly came back beaming as the scattered clapping picked up into applause.

Tallulah looked up from the floor. Looked at me. Looked around at the audience calling for an encore, and finally acknowledged my performance like it hurt to join her palms together.

'That'll cost you,' she said, when the noise finally subsided.

I reclaimed my stool. Reached for the last of my gimlet. I needed another, but I would have to wait. The barmaid was too busy filling a tray with longnecks.

'A small price to pay, under the circumstances.'

Tallulah nodded as I spoke. Rolled her eyes when I finished.

'All right,' she said. 'So I'm deeply sorry I said you were a typical man.'

Barely half a minute after my final bow, and already everyone had returned to their consoles. Each one shut off from the next like battery hens. Quietly pecking at their keyboards again. Returning to their virtual habitat. Which I hated to admit was kind of typical for a place like this. I wouldn't have been surprised if they were all gathered in a chat room now, discussing what had just happened offline.

'I might not be able to justify my behaviour,' I told Tallulah, 'but I'm tired of being stereotyped for it. Just because I've got a dick doesn't mean I act like one all the time.'

She smirked, failed to freeze it before it spread into a smile. The Ice Queen was melting. I raised my glass to her. Toasted my own front too. For my performance had been as cathartic as it was improvised. One which had served to rid me of a building frustration. I felt revived. My self-respect restored in some ways. That Tallulah hadn't just stuck a knee in my nuts and walked was a relief too.

'So what now?' she asked.

'Your call,' I said. 'Roxi's happy enough with Christine. Christine's happy enough now she's found herself. Personally, I can't say I'm totally happy with the arrangement. If I'm honest it's going to cut me up every time I see them out together. But if that's how it's going to be, I'll take it like a man.'

Tallulah's cigar had been smouldering in the ashtray throughout my little drama. She retrieved it, and I swear the coal started glowing before she had even taken her next puff. It was a good sign, I thought.

'Roxi means a lot to me. I don't like to see her get hurt.'

'At least we share the same view about one thing.'

'So you'll keep away from her?'

I surrendered on the spot. 'She's in Christine's hands now.'

'And what about your web presence? Will we see any more of NuBiFem?'

Now I shot her a look that said she couldn't be serious. Half amused. Half horrified. Like she didn't really expect an answer. But then her eyebrows cantilevered, and I could see they weren't going to come down without me.

'After everything that's happened? You think I'd go back online for more of the same?'

She shrugged. Said it was only a question.

'Get real, Tallulah.'

'Some men might.'

'Not me.'

'At least you realise it could never work.'

I pulled back from the conversation. 'I didn't say it could never work. I'm just through with trying, that's all.'

She returned to her cigar to consider this one.

'Log on as a bisexual female,' she said suddenly and smoke streamed out like a jet from an unmanned firehose, 'the only thing you'll pull is grief and disappointment.'

'I would have got there with Roxi,' I insisted. 'Even without Christine I could have talked my way into her heart. In time, she wouldn't have given a damn whether I was male or female.'

'Crap. *Typical* crap. In fact only a guy could delude himself like this. To think any girl would want to go to bed with a guy who's seduced her online as a woman. It's ridiculous. You're living in a dream world.'

I thought of all the screen names who had thrown themselves upon my screen. Quick-Es from wanna-bis. Lost girls looking my way for direction. Surely someone out there would consider going the distance with me.

'You may think it's a fantasy,' I said. 'But sometimes dreams come true.'

'You really think so?'

'I *know* so!'

Immediately, I wished I hadn't stressed the point so hard. Gripping the stogie between her teeth, Tallulah narrowed her gaze at me and set about patting down her pockets. I didn't like the fact that she appeared to be grinning now. Nor the reappearance of the money clip. So fat this time it could have used an index at the back.

'Don't,' I pleaded with her quietly. The barmaid was just setting out on my round, and I seized a beer from the tray. Took a slug to keep my mouth from drying. 'Not again.'

Tallulah stripped out a mint-fresh fifty, paused to assess my reaction, then went back for another three.

'A real man would put his money where his mouth is.'

'A *real* man? What the fuck is a real man?'

She laid the two hundred on the bar. 'You tell me, baby. I was kind of hoping I might be speaking his language.' As she spoke, the stack doubled in value. 'Money does talk with you boys, doesn't it?'

'Put it away, Tallulah. Whatever you have in mind, you can keep it there.'

'Five hundred says you can't do it,' she said regardless, and two more notes went down. 'Show me the man who makes out he's a woman and still scores with one that way, I'll show that man a monkey.'

'You really think it's impossible, don't you? That there's no way I can pull it off?'

'Baby, the only person getting pulled off here is you.'

'What does that mean? You think I'm a tosser, don't you?'

She batted her gaze at the cash. 'Prove me wrong. So long as nobody else gets hurt, my money's good to go.'

I dismissed the offer with a cursory wave. 'This is ridiculous.'

'It is,' she said, and doubled the offer. 'So do you need me to carry on?'

'I can do it, no sweat. But I'm thinking you only want to see me humiliated because I made you feel like a fool just now.'

'Oh yeah,' she sneered. 'I won't be able to look another anorak in the face for a week.'

A grand lay on the bar. One thousand pounds. Now it was my turn to worry that people might be watching.

'Can I ask what you do for a living?'

'Sure,' she said, and promptly walked her fingers through another ten sheets. 'I work in the City.'

'Doing what?'

'I trade in futures.'

The stack on the bar rose by five hundred. I leaned in to shield the mounting stack. Pretty soon I was going to have to agree just to get her to stop.

'Tallulah!'

Another five hundred. I tried not to look at the money. I tried not to look but it was beginning to suck me in.

'Prove to me you're a real man, Reynard. Easy money, for a guy like you.'

I bit my lip. Chewed over the situation. She was right. It was easy. And there was lots of it, too. If any man could do it, I was the one with all the qualifications. Walking away from this wager might earn me a clean conscience, but even the cat deal wasn't paying this kind of cash.

'You'll need evidence,' I pointed out. 'It's not like I can bring you along to watch.'

'Oh, I wouldn't be so sure. I've seen a few things in my time.'

'No way. That's one audience I don't need.'

'Like you're even going to get that far.' Tallulah still filleting the money clip. Building up the bet. 'But if it does, I'm sure a resourceful guy like you will find a way.'

I told her nothing surprised me any more. She said the only thing that would surprise her now was if I won the bet. Looking at the fortune on the bar, it had got to the point where I couldn't afford to fail if I took her up on it. Couldn't afford to turn it down either. I wiped my mouth, and wondered how much further she would go.

'If I agree to seduce a girl as a girl,' I said quietly, 'and I'm not saying I will, but if I did, then I'd be doing it as a matter of principle. Not love. Not lust. Just honour.'

'Yeah, right.' Tallulah just carried on counting. Laying it out like a croupier. Like the dough wasn't hers. Like she didn't care how I sold it to myself.

'I'm prepared to take this up to five thousand,' she said coolly. 'Right here. Right now. You can see all the money if you want, but you know I've got it, and as you're kind of uncomfortable dealing with this kind of sum in public, I'm suggesting we just cut to the quick and shake on it now.'

Nervously, I assured her I wasn't worried about the money. I was just worried about what someone might do to me at any moment in order to *get* to the money. I glanced over my shoulder, half expecting to see the whole place had been repopulated by thieves and murderers.

'So is it on?' she asked.

I faced back to the bar. Found Tallulah waiting on her feet for me. Another note down, and I thought about Roxi. About Christine. About two girls together and one man out on a limb. Their romance had cost me a great deal, but left me with nothing. So maybe this would settle things, I thought. An introductory fee, of sorts.

'How long is the bet good for?'

'Shall we say until the end of the month?'

My mouth moved through the figures, counting silently from one day into the next. I didn't have far to go.

'That's little over a week!' I declared. 'I doubt I could even pull a *straight* girl in a week.'

'I'm only trying to keep your misery to a minimum,' she said. 'But we can make it the end of next month if you think you can stand it.'

'Your generosity knows no bounds,' I said disdainfully.

Just then, the barmaid returned with an empty tray. She took one look at the money and whistled.

'Want me to carry on counting?' asked Tallulah. 'I'm down to tenners from here, but I'm happy to go all the way. If that's what it takes.'

'And you won't say anything to Roxi. About me.'

'My silence can be bought, yes.'

I thought about Sweet William, next. About the fact that he was right. That what I had done was wrong. I figured my dealer would slaughter me if he knew I was set to continue with the pretence. But this was different, I reasoned. My status as a man had been called into question. If I was to go online as a fox once more then it would be to defend my masculinity. A matter of honour. Nothing more.

'OK,' I muttered. 'We have a deal. It's on.'

'Good man!' she beamed. Tallulah reached for her glass, but I caught her wrist as she raised it for a final toast.

'Just put the damn money away first,' I hissed. 'It's not big or clever!'

As an alarm call, it worked. For she put her drink down again and did as I asked. Gathering every stack, squaring it all off on the bar, then feeding the lot back into the clip.

'You're absolutely right,' she agreed and, with the money safely out of sight, looked directly into my eyes. '*Obscene*, isn't it?'

28

'The last people you come out to are often those you love the most.'

A.C. Découcher, *Bisexuality For Beginners*

'You're real quiet this morning,' she said. 'Something on your mind?'

I surfaced from my thoughts with a sharp intake of breath. Focused on my reflection in the mirror. Found Roxi waiting there for me. Hands on my shoulders. Concern in her eyes. I had been a long way down at the time, way beyond the shallow stuff.

'I'm fine,' I replied. 'Trouble sleeping.'

I had been in make-up for fifteen minutes now. Preparing for this, the final shoot. Yet nothing but pleasantries had passed between us. The state of the coffee. My open pores. The way the weather kept turning. Topics I didn't have to think about while I considered my position. Not with Roxi any more. But with every other fox like her. I had nearly six weeks to find one. A little more than a month to make it as an online bisexual woman and then triumph as a real life man. Ever since accepting the challenge, I'd felt tense and uneasy. As Roxi sensed when she gave my shoulders a little squeeze.

'Reynard, are we cool, you and I?'

'How do you mean?'

'About Christine. About the other day. This whole situation.'

'Sure we're cool. No problem.'

'I mean she is your ex-girlfriend, after all. I'd hate to let it come between us.'

'As if,' I said, and smiled perhaps a little too bravely.

As if. If *only*. Without Christine, I really believed Roxi could have been mine. Indeed, without Tallulah things might have been very different. Despite my promises, just seeing her again here in the studio was enough to make me realise that I couldn't simply switch off my feelings for her. A woman whose very presence threatened to shatter my resolve. Her honeyed skin. Fairytale hair. Generous mouth and easy smile. It all conspired to bewitch me. Even the stories she had spun about herself online seemed like legend here in this domain. Everything about Roxi, in fact, I was beginning to see in everything around me. In the car on the way to the studio I passed her several times, though she was someone else when I turned. At traffic lights I even saw her in a cloud above the city. Just the snub of her nose, nothing more, but enough to keep me watching the skies for the rest of the journey. Like BiRuth before me, I was fast becoming a haunted man. And yet it was something I was going to have to deal with alone. For a start I might have been a little more forthcoming when Roxi let me go and said, 'How about you fill me in on *your* love life? Any movement with that girl you're sold on?'

I shook my head. Said I didn't think it was going to happen.

'Not keen to move in on someone else's territory, huh?'

I closed my eyes and held my breath while she brushed my face with powder.

'It's nothing to do with her,' I said when she had finished. 'It's me.'

Roxi broke off to sip her coffee. I felt bitter enough already, a stew of my own making, and didn't bother reaching for mine. Returning to her work, she said, 'Maybe it just wasn't meant to be.'

'So everyone keeps saying.'

Her fingertips under my chin just then, inclining my face to meet hers.

'Don't get morose on me. You're a good looking guy, Reynard. You won't be single for long.'

I told her I only knew unavailable women.

'Then I think I know what your problem is!'

'I very much doubt that,' I grumbled.

'You're too nice.'

'Too *nice*?'

'Sure. You're easy to get on with. You're good company. But

above all you're not a threat. Kinda neutral. And that appeals to girls who already have a relationship. Girls who don't need the hassle.' Girls like Roxi, I thought, feeling more like a gay best friend than a secret admirer. 'Don't take this the wrong way,' she added, having hesitated for a moment. 'But things might be different if you sent out a few signals. Asserted yourself more. You know? Let it . . . hang out a little.'

Another ten minutes remained before I was due on the studio floor. Compared to this, the shoot would be a breeze. It was the campaign climax. Straight to camera. Brand in hand. An appeal to the cat owners of Korea. Buy this crap. Let your pet see you in a new light. Turn your man into a pussycat, too. That was the sell. Not hard. Just hopeless. Still, there was no frock required this time. No fight with the feline. Just a suspicious sideways look from my screen wife. I didn't even have to learn any lines, for the whole thing was going to be dubbed. I could probably say anything, providing my mouth moved for a few seconds. I love ponies. Bring on the revolution. Your toys break too easy. *Whatever*. It would come out on screen as an insane staccato babble that would mean nothing to me. But whether I could sign off on a genuinely upbeat note depended wholly on this moment here in the dressing room. For I really wasn't sure if I could last much longer without breaking into little bits. Any more well-meaning advice from Roxi and her finishing touches to my appearance would only go to waste. *Too nice*. That's how she saw me. I did my level best to contain the truth, but the mirror wasn't alone in picking up the strain all over my face.

'I've offended you, haven't I? I'm sorry, I don't know you well enough to start shooting my mouth off like that. You're just fine as you are, Ren, Don't listen to me.'

'It's OK,' I said. 'In fact you're right. I could probably do with being a bit more ruthless.'

'You don't need to go that far,' she smiled, twisting up a lip salve now. 'There are way too many men like that already. If you want to get somewhere with a woman, you just gotta be more open with her. More articulate with your feelings.'

'I'll bear that in mind,' I said.

'Take a leaf out of Christine's book.'

'Huh?'

Roxi lifted her attention from my lips. I suddenly wished it was glue she had just applied down there. Sealed up my big mouth instead of simply glossing the cracks.

'Reynard, she's a *romantic* at heart! You know that, surely.'

'You're right,' I said quickly. 'She is.'

'The very best,' argued Roxi, but then her gaze fell away from mine. 'Sometimes.'

I could see where this was going. I could see because without my online assistance Christine probably wouldn't even have merited a 'sometimes'. Unwilling to get into this conversation, in view of the fact that 'sometimes' risked turning to 'never' now I'd signed off from their relationship, I drew breath to insist that Christine was a winner. So incisive. So focused. So *passionate*. But Roxi got in before me. Leaned back against the shelf and took things one step further.

'Can I ask you something personal?'

I folded my arms to think about this, though I knew I didn't have any alternative.

'Go ahead.'

'What did you see in Christine? What attracted you to her most of all?'

I was about to say her personality. The way she could articulate a thought or say all the right things with perfect timing. But then I remembered I had been here once before with Roxi. Calves conquered all for us both. Everything else came second, even if it was all bullshit. I saw no other choice but to level with her.

'I guess it was a physical thing.'

She nodded, like it was the only answer she was prepared to accept. In the mirror behind her, I could see that the clock still had another seven minutes to go. I willed the hands to spin faster.

'Did you love her?'

'Sure,' I said, but it sounded so dud I had to follow up. 'Alright, I thought I loved her until she finished with me.'

'And Christine? What was her take on you?'

'The same, maybe. You'd have to ask her.'

'You didn't talk it over? About your feelings for each other?'

'Like I said,' I replied, bristling slightly. 'It wasn't that kind of relationship.'

An uneasy silence opened up between us, and then suddenly it was Roxi's turn to glance at the clock.

'We should be finishing up,' she said. 'Do something with your hair.'

I watched her scoop a slither of wax from the pot. The time she took just rubbing it in her palm, however, it was clear her thoughts remained with Christine. That she couldn't move on without seeking advice from me. The ex-boyfriend.

'You know, she talks to me.'

'Well, that's great,' I assured her, as if I'd been waiting to hear the news for ages. 'Maybe she's finally found her soul mate.'

'I'd like to think that,' said Roxi, and looked back at me now. 'It's just she doesn't talk all the time. Not like we do online. Where it first started between us. That's where she really opens up, Ren.'

'She stresses easy, you know how Christine can be sometimes.'

'Yeah, but it's almost as if the chemistry changes when we meet. Like the physical side takes over. It's fantastic, what we have, but I know she can offer so much more. I just don't know how to bring it out.'

Holding my hands up under the gown, I told her she was speaking to the wrong person. 'As a man, I'm supposed to appreciate it when a woman *doesn't* talk too much.'

A restrained smile, followed by a spark in her narrowing gaze. 'Then maybe it's something she picked up from you.'

'I'm sure you'll set her straight,' I said, and immediately regretted my choice of words. 'What I mean is she'll shake off her bad habits.'

'And learn to be a good bisexual?'

That word. From her. Anyone else, it wouldn't have stung me so.

'I really wouldn't know.'

'But you'd sure like to, right?' She was addressing the man in me. The typical one, too. Prone to blunders like the one I'd just made. But in view of my wager with her flatmate, Tallulah, I figured I needed all the inside information she could give me. So I went with it. Why not? I thought. The conversation had come this far, why back out now?

'I guess I'm as bi-curious as most blokes, yes.'

'Oh really?'

'In a totally het sense,' I asserted, ignoring her wry smile. 'I mean, you see things from both sides. In my view that puts you in a better position than most women to tell a guy what he has to do.'

'To get a girl?'

'What else is there?'

Roxi with that smile again. Amusement and intrigue in the way she looked at me. 'And you think I can help you?'

I thought of Christine, and met her in the middle. 'I think maybe we can help each other.'

We had a deal. It was *on*.

Abandoning my half-done hair, Roxi plucked a tissue from the box beside her, and said, 'So where do you want to start?'

'The basics, with my track record.'

'Sex?'

'Easy,' I cautioned her. 'I'm a guy, we don't talk about these things so directly.'

'You don't?'

'What we do is allegory. Anything to get the info we need without having to admit we know nothing. Cars is a good cover.'

A smile played round her lips as I said this. A smile that questioned whether she really expected me to talk in these terms. I was only half joking, but then Roxi suddenly looked set to give it a go and my instinct was to let her.

'OK. So. Sex and cars. So, do you drive?'

'Sure. But I couldn't do both without a high risk of crashing.'

Balling the tissue. Rubbing the wax from her hands. Roxi, waiting for me to get with my own game.

'Ever driven abroad?'

'Outside the M25?'

'I mean abroad,' she grinned. 'Some place they drive on the right.'

I told her I had been to Los Angeles, once, a couple of years ago. Against the advice of my agent, I added, who correctly foresaw that I would come home without having seen a single casting director. But yes, I confirmed I did get to drive on the other side. Just didn't get to enjoy any valet parking.

'And how did you find it?'

'LA? Soul-destroying. Even the bellhops had better representation.'

'Reynard!'

'Alright, so I stalled twice getting out of the rental lot, nearly filled my pants negotiating a space on the freeway, but it got easier.'

'But you didn't have to start from scratch, is what I'm saying.'

'The basics were the same,' I conceded. 'But some of the road signs were *totally* alien.'

'Maybe you weren't there long enough,' she suggested. 'A couple more trips you'd recognise all the signs without having to think. It's then you start to relax and even enjoy the ride. That's how it was for me, anyway.'

'Can I ask you something more?'

'Shoot,' she said. 'This is fun.'

'Would you say your natural affinity was for driving on the left or the right?'

One dark eyebrow went up, but thankfully the rest of her expression retained its air of amusement.

'Are you asking,' she said slowly, 'if I prefer men or women?'

I shifted in my seat. Tried to get comfortable. 'I suppose I am, yeah.'

'Then I would say that depends entirely on the motor. Sometimes you get behind the wheel and you know instinctively how to handle it. Doesn't matter if it's a left or a right hand, it's still a dream to drive.'

'Come on, you must have a preference.'

'Reynard, I'm a bisexual. Not a motoring correspondent.'

'Humour me.'

'OK,' she said, boldly like I'd asked for it. 'Let's just say I haven't been on the road much since I came here, but when I have it's been on the left. Is that allegorical enough for you?'

'Perfect,' I said. Then thought some more and wished I hadn't started down this road. 'So when you say left you mean women?'

Roxi looked to the ceiling and laughed. Then came back down to spell it right out. 'I mean woman, *singular*. I mean *Christine*. At this moment, she's all I want. Maybe it'll work. Maybe it won't. But I never think beyond the relationship I'm in at the time.'

'But you'd consider a man, hypothetically?'

'Are we still talking in cars here?' she asked playfully. 'I'm not sure I can do hypothetical and allegorical. We'd have to bring in metaphors then, agree on the difference between, say, a Ford and a Lincoln.'

'Just give it to me direct,' I conceded. 'I don't even know what a Lincoln looks like.'

'In that case I would say the way I'm drawn to someone depends on lots of things.'

'Like what?'

'Well, firstly sex doesn't always come into it.'

'It doesn't?' I said, surprised.

'I mean sex as in someone's gender.' Roxi clarifying this for me with a look that said I should listen. 'It can mean as much or as little to me as the way they tell a joke or hold a fork. But then I can't speak for everyone. I know some bisexual women who consciously switch from one to the other, or keep both going at the same time. I know some who cross over once in a blue moon, and some who stick with women but can't quite bring themselves to accept they're lesbian. Everyone's different, Ren. We all want different things, just as you do.'

'Yeah, but you stand a better chance of getting it than me.'

'Because I'm bi?'

'Because you're amazing, I was going to say.'

Her eyes moved from mine. Looked uncomfortable coming back. I sort of wished I'd kept that one to myself. This wasn't supposed to be about my feelings for Roxi, though it had everything to do with her.

'To answer your question,' she said eventually. 'I don't consider myself a lesbian, just because I'm involved with Christine. I see things more fluidly than that.'

'All right,' I went on. 'But even though you're focused on a woman right now, a man could still turn your attention?'

'What is this?' she retorted. 'I can understand why you're curious, but you make it sound like an *obsession.*'

I could hardly confirm that it was. That the stakes raised by Tallulah actually demanded I attempt a conversion. Coming on to a fox like a bisexual female. Getting off with her as a man. That was the challenge I faced. What made this chat even harder for me was the fact that Roxi was the only woman I wanted. Either way, I had pushed her far enough. It was time to turn the tables. For me to shine a light on her love problems, and hope I could still find some answers of my own.

'It's Christine I'm thinking about.' That was how I spun it. 'Just trying to see things from her perspective. Work out what's holding her back with you.'

'So what does it matter whether I favour men or women?'

'It would matter to me, if I was her.'

'You seem very sure.'

'Damn right,' I said. 'If you had a major thing for guys, I'd question your commitment.'

'As a girl?'

'As Christine is what I mean. As someone new to the scene. Someone used to driving on one side of the road, not both. In her position, I might be a little cautious about committing. Just until I was absolutely sure I wasn't just a phase you were going through.'

'I don't go through phases, Reynard. I know what I am.'

'So, have you slept with more men or more women?'

Roxi looked at me like I'd just propositioned her. Which, I kind of had. My thoughts, they just bypassed all security checks, and broke free. It was too late to shoot down the question myself.

She said, 'Are you taping this or something?'

'No. Of course not.'

'Then what are you like?'

'Just trying to think how I would see it,' I asserted for her once more. 'If I was a woman dating you.' All I could do was pray my probing would make it. That a question as crass as the one I had run with could reach and breach her borders without tripping off sirens and searchlights. Had she slept with more women than men? Coming from a guy, it sounded feeble. From a girl, as I had pitched it, I figured I was in with a shot.

A moment passed, then the tension left the corners of her mouth, and I knew for sure that I was through.

'Men, I suppose, but that doesn't mean I'm more inclined towards them. It's just the way it played out.'

I nodded sagely, and did my utmost not to follow up but I did. It was inevitable. I just had to. If only to get a handle on things. As a man, I needed numbers.

'How many?' she repeated after me, but not as quietly. 'No more than average.'

I touched a fingertip to my lips. 'So what are we talking about here? Ten? Twenty-five? Fi—'

'*Fifty!* You think I've had fifty guys in my bed?'

'Fifteen?' I threw in weakly. 'I was on my way down again.'

'Come down to eight,' she suggested. 'And I'll resist the temptation to break your nose.'

'Eight guys.'

'That's what I said. How about you?'

'Me? *None.* Jesus!'

'Women, Ren. How many women?'

'What's that got to do with the way Christine sees things?'

Roxi said, 'Let's just say it's my turn to be curious.'

'God,' I blustered. 'I've never considered the notches in my bedpost.' Which was a brazen lie, and she knew it. Pensively, she touched a finger to her own lips. Kept her smile from spreading too far.

'Ten? Twenty-five? *Fifty?*

I didn't know what to say. Certainly less than fifty. Sadly, less than eight. Five was probably a more realistic figure. A very precise one, in fact. But I couldn't let on until Roxi had quantified her own female count. I just couldn't. It didn't feel right. That's all.

'It's hard to say,' I muttered to myself, and glanced at her like I needed prompting.

'I've slept with five women, Reynard. OK?'

'Probably about the same for me, too,' I offered quickly.

'Christine makes six.'

'Oh,' I said, and wished my call to the studio floor would come quickly. The truth was out. I was dealing with a fox who was sexually more experienced with women than I was. I had never felt more inadequate in my life.

'Although two of those girls kinda happened at one time. So I guess that brings it down to four.' Whether or not Roxi said this just to be charitable, it didn't make me feel any better. She folded her arms, and an arch smile crossed her face. 'Does that put you in the picture now?'

'Almost,' I replied. 'I got one more question.'

'For Christine?'

'For me. I just want to know what you look for in a man.'

'Well,' she said, 'great calves aren't as high up on the list.'

'I'm serious.'

She shrugged. Her grin fading into something altogether more sincere. 'Same as any woman, really.'

'And that is?'

Roxi opened her mouth to speak, then looked right over my head. 'Hey there!' she beamed. 'What's the matter, lost your flat keys?'

In the mirror, a familiar figure shut the door behind her. Instinctively, I sank into my seat, but she was looking right at my reflection. Virtually frosting the glass with her stare. Tallulah by name. Nemesis by nature. This time sporting a pink stetson and patent leather trench coat. I figured she had the day off work. If not, I was in the wrong career.

'I wanted to meet the star of the show,' she said to Roxi, as if I wasn't there. 'You talk so much about him I just had to come and say hi.'

Roxi made the introductions, almost like she was proud to bring us together. I tried to free my hand from under the gown, and felt like a compere fumbling for the parting in the stage curtains. It was Tallulah who spared me, and told me not to worry. She could see I was in a fix, she said. Didn't want to interfere with preparations for my big moment. Then Roxi in her innocence served to stoke my sense of panic even further.

'We were just talking about girls, actually.'

'And cars!' I added hastily. 'Girls and cars. Stupid guy shit. Nothing serious.'

Roxi looked a little surprised, as if there was no need for shyness in front of someone so close to her.

'He was asking what women look for in a man,' she said, addressing Tallulah. 'Any ideas?'

Without once taking her eyes off Roxi now, talking like I'd left the room, Tallulah said, 'That would depend on the kind of woman he's hoping to find.'

'I was going to say that too,' said Roxi.

'Providing he doesn't try to be anyone other than himself,' she finished, 'I'd say he could get whoever he wants.'

Stuck between the pair of them, feeling about as attractive as a blancmange, I raised both hands under the gown and stopped them both from going any further.

'Thanks, really. That's very helpful. I'd be lost without you.'

Roxi looked right over me again, crinkled up her nose for Tallulah. 'He's a doll, isn't he?'

'A real honey,' said Tallulah, humourlessly. 'The genuine article.'

By now I was looking at my shoes, at the tips poking out on the foot rest. Just waiting for her finger to point at me, the man behind Roxi's woman. But perhaps Tallulah felt I was on the way out as it was, for she backed away instead. Said she would wait outside the studio while Roxi finished up with me. Smoke a cigar. Intimidate some more little guys maybe. All right, she didn't actually say that bit, but I heard her clearly in my head.

'I'll only be a couple of minutes,' said Roxi. 'You can wait here if you want.'

To my great relief, Tallulah declined the offer. 'I really think I should leave you to it,' she said, then caught my eye in the mirror. 'Good luck with your search.'

'Thanks,' I said, thanklessly.

'Keep me posted, won't you?'

'I'm sure you'll be the first to know.'

The door had barely shut behind her, however, when it opened right up again. In that same moment, my sigh of relief extended into an unharnessed groan.

'Ready to do some stroking, Reynard?' The producer smirked at Roxi. I hoped Roxi was being polite when she smiled right back, and didn't actually find her funny. 'We're going to miss you when all this is over.'

'Not as much as I'll miss you.'

'You've got two minutes,' she said, her mood turning brittle all of a sudden. 'Maybe you could do something with your hair?'

Roxi mugged a face at me as she left, much to my comfort. 'Don't worry about her.' She reached for the wax once more. 'She's not your type, believe me.'

I smiled, and submitted to what I conceded would be her final touch. Roxi working her fingers through my mop. Smoothing me down. Shaping me up. Sweeping away all hope I had left of putting her out of my mind.

'Thank you,' I said, as she teased her fingers to the nape of my neck. 'For everything.'

'It's my job. But it's been a pleasure.'

'And an education for us both.'

'I mean it,' she insisted. 'For once I looked forward to coming into work this morning. I can't believe you're about to leave knowing how many *women* I've slept with, but at least I know the same thing about you. So I guess that puts us on a level pegging.'

'Not quite,' I countered. 'You've still got one more notch on your bedpost than me.'

Holding back her smile, Roxi beckoned me to stand. Reached round to untie my gown. It appeared that the bow had slipped into a knot, however. So tight, it seemed to take an age to undo.

I smiled awkwardly, then turned my attention to the mirror behind her. Saw myself looking over her shoulder, Roxi's arms round my neck. Mine lolling useless at my sides. Desperate to embrace her.

'Good luck,' I heard her say, and suddenly I felt my cheek warm where she had kissed it. All I could do was look back into her eyes, falling deeper into the depths until her hands moved out to my shoulders, my breathing slowed, and I could go no further. Whether it was me, or whether it was Roxi, I will never know. The moment seemed to draw us both in. Defined by the closing space between our lips. Faltering as the gown slipped free and fell between us. A moment abandoned by us both.

'Roxi, I . . .'

'You should be going,' she said, and turned away. 'Everybody's waiting.'

'Yes, you're right,' I replied too quickly, aware once again how little space there was in this dressing room. How little air there was to breathe.

I reached for the door handle. Stunned by what had just happened. Numbed by how it had ended. Roxi right behind me. Next thing the door was open, but I knew that I just couldn't walk away from this. Not without keeping some kind of connection.

'About Christine,' I said, without looking round. 'I think maybe you should stick with the emails for a while. Give her a chance to realise how lucky she is to find a woman like you.' Slipping into the corridor now, cold air on my face.

'Reynard!'

I turned and there she was. Alone there in that room. Big eyes sparkling all of a sudden. Swimming at the rims. Roxi, looking at me like I was leaving her life for ever.

'Thank you.'

'No need,' I said, and returned her smile. 'The pleasure's all mine.'

29

That night, she went online once more. Just briefly. Blinking in to send an email and then disappearing before anyone even noticed her presence. It wasn't much, but it was inevitable, really. After everything that had happened, I knew she would send something. Seek out the intimacy she yearned for so much in the real world. Connecting in the only way she could. By going down the line. Across the network. From one terminal to another. Out of sight, maybe, but very much in mind. For that was all she could do, being me.

NuBiFem. New. Bisexual. Female. A man consumed by the woman of his own creation. One who could have walked back into that dressing room and seized the chance to embrace Roxi for real. But in taking her into my arms I would have risked losing her for good. Christine, for one, might have had something to say. It hadn't taken much for her to reveal all physically. I figured stealing her girlfriend would easily persuade her to reveal everything else. Then there was Tallulah to consider. What would she say if Roxi stepped out with me? No bi was out of bounds when it came to our stupid bet, but if she regarded it as cheating and blew the whistle on me then I'd stand to miss out on both prizes. It left me with no choice. If I wanted to get close to Roxi then this was the only way left. A labour of love, dressed up as a favour for an old flame, and a means to an end for me. That's how I saw it just then.

email to: **RoxiNYC**
from: **NuBiFem**
title: **A moment of truth**

Writing as Christine, breaking my vow never to email Roxi like this again. I could almost hear the voice of my ex, in fact, reading as I typed.

> These are the words that desert me whenever we're together. The things I want to say but can't. I love you. Unconditionally and absolutely, but in a way you can never know.

> Meeting you has tilted my world in a new direction. Off-kilter from the norm, but in a way that every revolution leaves me feeling both unsettled and exhilarated. You've put me in a spin, Roxi, but I promise I'll find my feet soon. All I ask is for time to readjust, and faith in my commitment to you.

I signed off with the letter C, pecked out four X's then hit send like it was the fifth. A dispatch that followed on so quickly from my kisses because I couldn't bear to see them on the screen.

The window vanished. Sucked into cyberspace. Coursing through the virtual veins, rushing for the backbone of the web. There, it would replicate and divide. The original winding up in Roxi's mailbox, a blind copy with Christine.

Afterwards, I felt much better for being so honest with my emotions and much worse for hiding them behind another name. Similarly, I was flattered that my words stirred Roxi into visiting my ex the next evening, and frustrated that it wasn't me who buzzed her in. I knew because I was watching. Still keeping my distance, but this time from a bench in the rose garden opposite Christine's block. I had been there for hours. Oblivious to the soaks and the dispossessed as they gathered for the night. My focus fixed three floors up. Drawn there in the first place because in her reply Roxi had thanked me for my candour and confirmed she would call round. A message I had dutifully forwarded to my ex, assuming she would use my change of heart to her advantage, but which again she failed to acknowledge. And the longer my mail box remained empty, so my concerns grew that Christine was out in more ways than one. That's how I foresaw things, and that's why I had been drawn to come see for myself. Fearing that at any second Roxi would storm from the building. Leave both our lives and never come back. Eventually, however, the light in the bedroom went off and I knew for sure that she was still in. More so than I wished to imagine. A bottle passed my way just then. A gesture of solidarity from one lost soul to another.

I came close to wetting my lips with it, to wash away that ghost trace of a kiss, though some forty days and nights would pass before I finally gave in. Lost in my own sexual wilderness, this was how I cut my time:

Firstly, I went hunting. With the survival of my pride at stake, I pursued Tallulah's wager with a vengeance. Wouldn't any man in my position? Knowing Roxi's whereabouts meant I was free to retreat to my space and head out online. To make headway in a world of words and pictures without fear of being caught there by the woman I was supposed to be with. It didn't distract from my longing for her, but it had to be done. Even Christine would have no idea what I was doing in her name. The first of many midnight excursions that saw me bring out the bitch in my bi.

I didn't have to look long. The Quick-Es came to me. This time, I considered each invitation carefully, and if I replied I went by the book. I talked the talk. I toyed and teased. I *tantalised*. With advice and experience on my side, I soon came to read all the signs from a hundred yards. Blanking the no-hopers and the obvious blokes. Cybering only when necessary. Where the prospect of a real world encounter seemed likely. That night I virtually had sex with my first married woman. A naughty bi forty called 0Tbi4T, who was happy to share her bed with anyone and everyone, so she said. A bed based in bloody Vancouver, she later revealed. I almost billed her for the battering my keyboard had endured before that little detail slipped out. My hopes picked up soon after, however, when

I received an offer I just couldn't delete. MayBi was her name, and what appealed about this debutante was the way she hedged her bets.

Quick-E to: NuBiFem

MayBi:	I'm basically straight, OK?
NuBiFem:	So what are you looking for?
MayBi:	I just want to find out if I like women as much as men.
NuBiFem:	Fine by me.

MayBi certainly knew what she wanted. She was cool. She was confident. She was keen to meet.

She was so damn nervous when I clocked her in the Cafe Ragueneau next day that I knew I couldn't go through with it. Seriously, there was more tea in the saucer than there was in her cup. She seemed so delicate and afraid that every time the door chimes clinked behind her she would catch her breath and look right through me. The terror in her eyes magnified by her spectacles. Too scared even to turn and see if it was her date who had just walked in. Sitting at the table opposite her, as I had been long before she arrived, I knew that I couldn't go through with it. To stand up, let her down, and hope she would still come round.

It just wasn't me.

Not like my correspondence with Roxi. Now that really was me. In everything but name. Having abandoned the cafe and slunk back to my space, I finally got a call from Christine to thank me for helping her out. A little late, perhaps. But at least I could take heart in the fact that not all my efforts were going to waste.

'I wasn't sure if you would do it,' she said. 'What can I say?'

'Nothing. Why start now?'

I heard Christine laugh nervously. After a brief pause, she cleared her throat. Instinctively I held the phone a little tighter. 'What you said about wanting to stop—'

'Forget about it,' I cut in. 'I shouldn't have sprung it on you like that. Seeing your flat, I just reacted badly and I'm sorry.'

'Don't be,' she insisted. 'It's not right, you speaking for me any more.' I told her the subject was closed. I was happy to help. Happy also to be on talking terms again, as I went on to say. What I didn't say was that my good deed in keeping their relationship alive would make up for my dirty deed with other women like them. That's how I saw it. A means of redeeming myself in my own eyes. Providing I could get Christine to work closely together with me.

'I'll need to know about everything you get up to together,' I told her. 'I want details on a daily basis.'

'Reynard, what are you asking from me here?'

'Not *that*,' I stressed. 'Just the times and places you plan to meet. Meals you've eaten. Things you've seen or heard. Conversations I wouldn't otherwise know about. Special moments. That kind of thing.'

My ex considered my offer for a moment. 'If I thought you weren't getting anything out of this,' she said finally, but I had heard enough.

'Christine, just keep me posted on your offline activities and I'll take care of the mail.'

Taking care of the male in *me*, however, wasn't proving so easy. That I felt no desire to pursue women in the way I had pledged was a problem, but the prospect of losing out to Tallulah pushed me on. Slipping home each night from my vigil outside Christine's apartment, I continued to log on and keep looking. To improve my focus, I even followed BiRuth's lead and barred the Viagra Snatch Squad from bothering me. On further reflection, I also barred BiRuth himself, anxious as I was to make my online time my own. Having filed their screen names on my Browser Blacklist, any incoming communique from them would immediately get bounced away. I felt better as a result. A bullet-proof bi. Even Tallulah's PlayMissT was denied access. She would hear from me once I had proved her wrong. Hell, I became so blinkered that I didn't even bother tending to Sweet's seedlings. Just let the lot creep up my monitor. Tiny tendrils anchoring themselves to the vents, before opening into a wall of tiny purple flowers. I had never seen anything like it. Not least the strange fruit which began to appear through the foliage. No bigger than a grape, but shiny like an apple. Whatever it was, I didn't care. I was beyond distraction, counsel or warning. Beyond *reason* at times, too. As Queen Bi, I knew exactly what I wanted from each late-night session, and would log off only when I had enticed a fox to lunch with me the next day.

Online, over Quick-Es, my dates could barely contain their hunger to meet me. Who could blame them, after all? I was a babe. Calves cut from the finest cloth and more. So deep did I slip into character, I almost forgot who I was. Until I came out in the cafe, that is, and the appetite just deserted them. All bets off and a bill for one.

I met nice girls. Girls who had never dared to explore their feelings about women until now. The kind of bi fox I hoped might be relieved when I showed up instead. Not burst into tears on the spot.

'Creep!' sobbed Angel24f, then grabbed her coat and walked out on me.

I met bad girls. Girls who were easy with women on the web. The kind of bi fox I hoped might just make do with a man when I turned up instead. Not push back her chair and show me up in front of everyone.

'Jerk-off!' screamed MizzFizz, then grabbed her glass of mineral water and emptied it in my face.

I met *nasty* girls. Girls who gorged themselves on sex as if they might starve without it. The kind of bi fox I hoped might be so insatiable that she would have whatever was served to her. Not slap me round the chops so hard it stung for a day.

'Wanker!' yelled OralSue2, then grabbed her overnight bag and stormed from the cafe.

I had never enjoyed auditions. They made me nervous. Fear of failure and all that. After three weeks of misery and humiliation, my dislike threatened to become a phobia. I was almost too scared to turn up at the cafe for fear of another showdown. It got to the point where I would be sitting there in the corner, with one eye on the window, just waiting for the ground to shudder and pedestrians to flee. I could see it clearly, the havoc heralding her appearance. An attack of the sixty-foot switch hitter. Spearing cars with her stilletos on her way to a date with me.

I should say that I wasn't rejected out of hand. I did turn down a couple of candidates myself. And wisely so, I thought. Just the boiler suit kind of bisexuals, you understand. Now I know that doesn't sound too good, but PC counted for nothing when it came to my personal safety. This wasn't me being a pig, just prudent. Quite simply, I didn't fancy chancing my luck with any woman who looked remotely like the one who had attempted to do brunch with Roxi. I would have settled for any of the others, however. I really wasn't in a position to be picky. Frankly, I was getting *desperate*.

Only my dispatches to Roxi saw me through this dark, dispiriting time. Stopped me giving up in the face of daily rejection. Not that she knew, of course. About me or my bone-headed bet. Blissfully oblivious, her emails shone out from my screen. Lighting up my face. Bringing out what was left of the best in me. Online, we embraced and explored the things that really mattered. Love. Life. Happiness. And offline every evening I would watch in clandestine as Roxi made the most of them all.

With Christine.

I sat behind them on buses and in cinemas. Ate takeaway in the drizzle while they dined in fancy restaurants. I sheltered under bridges as they canoodled by the riverside. Became the first person to ride the London Eye without once marvelling at the view. The couple in the next pod along being all that I wanted to see. Everywhere they went, I followed. Even if it meant daring to ask cabbies to tail the car in front. But always I found myself back in the rose garden. Waiting there for the light to switch off and that bottle to swing my way.

30

'Cats who behave as if "spooked" are often just venting built-up emotions.'
http://www.purradise.com/purrfect10.html

The desire to quit grew stronger with each day. The only time I got out was to size up women in cafes or shadow Roxi through the streets. It made me feel less like a real man and more like a sick man. The kind who needed help. In any shape or form. Every night the drink beckoned, but in this state I knew that route would only bring me ruin. Drugs would have been good, but I figured my florist and dealer would take one look at the shambles I had become and start digging around to uncover the root of my problems. A root worth five thousand pounds to me, if only I could get it to flower.

Midway through this madness, I succumbed to an unexpected temptation.

I had just stepped in from another date with the girls. By which I mean a cosy night in for them and a bracing night out for me. I was tense. I was tired. Under pressure and unfulfilled. And though I was just weeks away from losing a pile of money, all I could think about was Roxi. It was as if she had become a drug to me. Turning my life into a contradiction. For I craved any contact with her, but I yearned to break free. I loved her, but I hated myself for it. She was all I wanted, but ultimately it would kill me. I even followed the inflexible rituals of a junkie. Shedding my coat at the door, as I did every night, and then shuffling across to my computer. Booting it up then sitting back while the modem unleashed the woman in me. Normally, I used the moment to prepare for the part. Often summoning up the scan of the catsuit model, as if to see what I might look like. An immaterial girl, I know, but it helped me focus my thoughts. Maybe I was too far gone this time, because instead

I was drawn to the shot of Roxi, my very own virtual Madonna, and I faced her as if she were here before me.

I didn't have anything to say that I hadn't said already. Everything else was unspeakable. All I wanted was some time alone with her. And yet the only inspiration I could muster from this moment was to find a way out from it all.

Which was why I succumbed to the fruit.

For ages I had watched it slowly ripen. There in the foliage smothering the west wall of my monitor. Swelling like a pregnant belly. Flushing from green to a pinkish red until suddenly it looked fit to eat. I plucked it from the plant without thinking. Popped it in my mouth, and was pleased to find it tasted supremely sweet. Chewy, too. A divine kind of candy, I thought, as my modem fell silent and the Quick-E's began to blister. It certainly made the subsequent trawl more palatable, and I deemed it a well-deserved treat. After knocking back a couple of hopefuls, I even talked myself into taking an entire break. Fetch myself a glass of water to quench my building thirst. Smoke two cigarettes in succession, if only to blunt the pang in my guts.

I did wonder about what it was I had just ingested, but by the time I returned to the screen I had other matters to consider. Like my nightly update to Tony Curtis. Another aspect of my ritual. Fulfilling my need to fill him in on all the things that hadn't happened to me. Having basically followed the same routine every day, my email to him pretty much panned out to be a carbon copy of the previous note. And the one before that. In fact the only change appeared to be the date. Moving ever closer to my deadline at the end of the month. This time, however, in a startling break from the norm, I found my thoughts kept springing off the end of each sentence and into a syrupy void. At one point I couldn't even remember what I had written. Even though I virtually knew it off by heart. Such was my struggle to think straight that it came as a relief when I finally pressed send. As I did so, I wished that I might have something fresh to bring to him the next day. Something better than the stomach cramp that hit me in the same instant. When my browser window began to buckle before my eyes, and everything went white.

No dream.

No wild, revealing hallucinations.

Just a blank. A big zero. Nothing to report.

Sunshine. Punishing mid-morning light. That's how it was when I came to my senses. I lifted my head from the desk. Let my sticky eyes and my stickier brain adjust to this apparent shift in time. Going by my wristwatch, I had been out for almost eight hours. By extension, I realised, I had been online for the same duration. My screen might have gone to sleep on me, but the line was still linked to the web. The meter still ticking over.

'Damn it,' I muttered. 'Another wasted session.'

Only this time I hadn't even got a lunch date out of it. The Quick-E's I dealt with by just shutting down the application, but the mail I downloaded for later. I really couldn't face wading through the lot just then in search of a suitable candidate. Nor did I even want to *think* about how much it had cost me in call time. Probably about as much as a new pair of shoes, I thought, as I logged off and looked down. For I thought my toes had felt a little free, and it was then I discovered the reason why.

The stitching around my brogues, it had literally fallen apart. Both of them were ruined, in fact. Totally written off. I had got them in a sale but nobody told me they were seconds. Honestly, it was like someone of monster proportions had squeezed into them or some-thing. As for the state of the soles, I resolved never again to cut across the grass in the square as I had the previous night. It was a detour I had only recently taken to making on my way back from Christine's, but I'd obviously cut one corner too many. They were caked in mud and God knows what else. I even picked off a ticket stub for London Zoo. My only consolation was that I felt remarkably refreshed. Passing out in front of the keyboard, my body had obviously been desperate for some time out. Shutting me down to recharge and rejuvenate. Like when the phone started ringing, I darted from my seat with the kind of zest I hadn't shown in weeks.

'At last,' she said. 'You've been engaged for ages.'

It was Christine, and even though I'd been out of contact for some time I doubted she had tried very hard to get through. Lately, my ex had slipped on her promise to keep me abreast of her relationship with Roxi. Her emails to me had dropped from one a day to one every couple of days, tailing off through the previous week to precisely nothing at all. Still, it hadn't stopped me keeping up my correspondence with her girlfriend. If anything, Roxi had been receiving more emails from me than ever before.

'So how are you?' I asked. 'Good date last night?' I took the phone across my space, dropping my shoes into the bin as I passed it.

'Not bad, I suppose.'

Not bad? In my view just being with Roxi was a treat in itself. Her tone, however, suggested otherwise.

'But not good, right?'

'I gave her a good send-off, if that's what you mean.'

'Why? Where's she going?'

'Abroad. And she's already gone.'

'What?'

'For a week.'

'Why?'

'Work. Some photo assignment, apparently.'

Christine sounded bored by my questions, but I had to know.

'Where?'

'I don't know,' she snapped. 'Read her post.'

'But she never mentioned going away.'

A sigh, then, 'Reynard, you know more about Roxi than I do. She told me she'd put the details in an email. All she said to me was France.'

'Hold on,' I said, and padded back to my desk.

I scrolled through my unread post. My eyes trained to pick up the one screen name which meant so much to me. RoxiNYC. The bi fox from the Bronx. She had indeed sent me email. This morning, it seemed, while I was out of it.

email to: NuBiFem
from: RoxiNYC
title: bon voyage!

Hi Sexy,

Thanks again, for another fantastic night. In some ways it's a relief to
be going away. At least I can catch up on some sleep! ;o)

Anyway, I'll be away for a week from today. Flying down to Gascony,
near the Spanish border. Some spread for *Staple*. You know it?
New men's magazine. Popular with a lot of guys right now. Anyway, they're shooting a spread about the region. It's called 'Fine
food, fine wine, fine women', or something. So that's three good
reasons to go!

But I'll promise to be a good girl. The only thing I plan to take to bed
is my laptop, so mail me every day, you hear me!

Kisses to your honey bud – Roxi xxxx

'Kisses to your *what*?' I asked, having read the email down the
line to Christine. 'Did we really need to know that?'

'It's an email to me, remember.'

'So what's wrong with "see you next week"? Jesus! You'd never
catch a guy sign off with kisses to anyone's honey bud. Wherever it is.'

'That's why guys never write it.'

She had a point, but not one I wished to clarify all of a sudden.
Instead, I printed off the email, and asked how she felt about Roxi
going away.

'Fine,' said Christine abruptly, like the subject was closed. 'I was
only calling because we saw Sweet William today and he was asking
after you.'

'Is that good or bad?' I asked. 'Last time he took an interest in
me I nearly died of shame.'

'He's got tickets for a club.'

'Don't say the Venus Squeeze,' I said nervously. 'You say the
Venus Squeeze I'm hanging up.'

'Hardly,' she laughed. 'Somehow I don't think you'd get beyond
the bouncers there.'

'You'd be surprised,' I said. 'And since when did you start going anyway?'

Christine, ignoring my question, said, 'Look, why don't you go and see him. Willie says you haven't been to see him in ages. He says if you leave it any longer he's going to take offence, and you don't want to do that, Reynard.'

'I'd better get round there,' I said, turning my attention to my monitor. 'I need to see him about something too.'

The plant had truly hard-wired itself to my machine. With my free hand, I pinched one of the stems and pulled hard. The foliage stuck fast, but the monitor swivelled round.

'So will you do it?' asked Christine.

'Do what?'

'Email Roxi. Like she asked?'

'Sure,' I said. 'If I went quiet on her now, she'd only think something was wrong.'

A silence from her end of the line. I felt like I was waiting to hear an echo.

'You're right,' my ex agreed finally. 'I'll leave it in your hands, then.'

31

*'Bisexual hell: that feeling of limbo when torn between
two people of the opposite sex.'*
A.C. Découcher, *Bisexuality For Beginners*

Later that morning, having showered as best I was able, I made my way to the flower market. I walked with a spring in my step, but that was probably down to the fact that I was wearing a pair of ten-year-old trainers with pumped-up soles. Not my first choice of footwear nowadays. Unlike my battered and broken brogues, however, these had at least proved they could go the distance. It was my first unplanned excursion in weeks. A break from the old routine. A merciful release, indeed. The sun was shining. A black cab even stopped to let me cross the road. I felt good. Truly I did. Much better about things, in fact. The combination of a fulfilling sleep and the news of Roxi's foreign assignment had broken her spell on me. Brought me back to reality, even. For it made me realise that she had a life aside from her relationship with Christine. Something I had forsaken lately myself, and paid a hefty price. I also contemplated my thing with Tallulah. Sure, there was a great deal of money at stake, but then my sanity was more precious to me than my sense of pride. The problem would be finding the cash. The space was bought and paid for, but my cash flow was still a problem. I knew one person who had the funds, of course. Someone who was generous to a fault. But giving him a reason for the loan was out of the question.

Sidling up to his pitch, I found Sweet William talking once again to the mute old duck with the Senior Shopper. I hung well back this time. Retreating even further when she three-point-turned her way out.

'She's going to have to find some other place to score,' he said, shaking his head as she shuffled away. 'I know she's on a pension, but she's breaking my balls on the price. A man can only go so low.'

'Can you *go* any lower?' I asked him, watching her snail away. 'At her time of life, she shouldn't have a weakness for anything harder than Werther's Originals.'

'I agree,' said my dealer. 'But you don't fuck with anyone when they're carrying a shiv. No matter what time of life they're at.'

'She's got a *knife*?'

My dealer made like a gunslinger. 'Ever see *Taxi Driver*? That scene where De Niro gets tooled up with the blade? The one that rails out from his sleeve?'

'No way,' I said derisively. 'She never did!'

Willie bust the move in question. I found myself facing two stained ochre fingers. Sweet had a lot of lilies on sale today, but then he liked to smoke a lot too.

'Wanna go ask her yourself?' he asked. 'Go ahead. Tap her on the shoulder. She turns around and questions whether you're talking to her, you take my advice and run!'

I looked in her direction again. Watched her struggle to get the trolley off the pavement. She did seem kind of stiff around the wrists.

'I can't believe what I'm hearing, Willie. That's too crazy for words.'

'You think that's crazy.' He paused to hoist his money belt back round the mountain of his waist. 'What do you say to the zoo thing?'

'What zoo thing?' I asked, wheeling his way.

'Last night. Someone got in and fucked with the animals.'

Against all will and reason, I suddenly found I couldn't look my dealer in the eye. That ticket stub, stuck now in my mind.

'Fucked in what way, Sweet?'

'Who knows?' he shrugged. 'Keeper reports seeing some lunatic loping across the lawns this morning.'

'Not the wolves?'

'Worse,' said Willie grimly. 'There's a search. They find he's been kipping in the Web of Life.'

'The Web of what?'

'Life, Reynard. As in the food chain exhibition? It's a building houses cockroaches. Amoeba. Shit like that. Now what's going on there? A man gets his kicks from cuddling up with animals, you would've thought he'd go for something a little more sheep-like. Know what I'm saying? What kind of sick mother feels at home with the bottom feeders?'

'Maybe he got lost,' I offered weakly.

'Yeah, right. In the *head*.'

I decided to abandon pressing my dealer about the seeds. The implications were just a little too heavy-duty. Waving the subject away, I said, 'Christine says you wanted to see me.'

My dealer didn't reply. He appeared to be looking at some imaginary point midway between us.

'Willie,' I snapped. 'Will you just forget about the zoo thing. Let it go!'

My dealer blinked and shook his head. His jowls winging one way then the other. 'Sorry about that,' he said. 'You mentioned your ex and I started getting visuals of her new fox friend.'

'Roxi? You met her?'

'Christine introduced me to her when they dropped by this morning. On the way to the airport or something.' He drew breath to whistle his appreciation. 'Boy, you missed out there.'

'Thanks, Sweet,' I muttered. 'I am aware of the situation. In fact I'll probably never forget it.'

'So let me take your mind off things.'

'Actually, Willie, I'm going to pass on drugs for a while. I think I need to straighten out a little.'

My dealer grinned, slipped a hand inside his puffa, came out with two laminate passes.

'Another month,' he said. 'Another magazine launch.'

'Yeah? What's it called?'

'Dunno. Usually, it's the same as the last but with the letters in a different order. Does it matter? What counts is that you're free tomorrow night.'

'Is it at the Pandemonium again? I hate the Pandemonium. Last time I was there, I got a vodka martini in my lap. Plus it's always a fight to get upstairs.'

Frowning now, my dealer leaned over his counter and slotted one ticket into my shirt pocket. 'Quit being a gimp, and show some gratitude.' Willie patted my shirt pocket, then finished with a play slap to my cheek. 'Bitch, without me you wouldn't even know what upstairs *looked* like.'

'Thanks, Willie.'

'Don't mention it, man. Now, what are you drinking?'

'Vodka gimlet,' I said, and turned to see who was here.

This was in the Purgatory Room, next evening. It didn't look like anyone had left since the last time. Low lights pooling each table. Cigarette smoke hanging in veils. Bouncer at the spiral stairs and a dealer in a quilted number that I didn't dare criticise. Maybe the balloons in the net were different, hanging over the masses on the other side of the soundproofed wall, but the faces down below certainly looked the same. Beaming but blank. Swelling and subsiding to the same seamless sea of beats. In fact the only other thing that appeared to have changed was me. The cowboy shirt had gone. Run out of town by a new set of threads. A killer sharkskin. Tailoring so sharp that moments earlier I had spiralled up the staircase sure that when I surfaced I would cause a stir. As it turned out I just got it in the neck from Sweet. Even as I eddied my way around the final few steps I could see him at the rail. Looking over the side at me. A face like Ahab.

'How long does a girl need to dress up?' he had asked, tapping his watch.

'I know, I'm late. I apologise.'

'What was it? Another bad hair day to add to your decade?'

'Nothing like that,' I said. 'Just got caught up in an email.'

A fat finger stopped under my nose. 'No funny business, I trust.'

'Willie, am I laughing?'

The finger relaxed along with the frown. 'Maybe not,' he grinned. 'But tonight you lighten up, all right?'

It was then that my dealer had ushered me between the tables. Then that I thanked him for being a friend. Everything would have stayed just dandy had I asked for a different drink.

'Vodka gimlet?' sputtered Willie, and his pug nose crumpled up. 'What kind of drink is *that* for a man?'

I told him a friend of mine had introduced me to it, which was when my dealer's eyes narrowed right up.

'Only person I know drinks Vodka gimlet is a girl,' he said. 'Frostiest fox I ever met. Only ever buys snowdrops from me. Never accepts the change.'

'Forget the gimlet.' I ducked back to the bar as I changed my mind. Hoped he wouldn't bring up her name. 'Give me whatever you're having.'

My dealer followed me round, and before he even looked like asking, two highballs came our way. Willie whacked his back in one, wiped his mouth, and said, loudly, 'You sure you're through with being a pussy bumper?'

Suddenly I felt like everyone around the bar was looking at me. The freak with his big fat friend. I laughed nervously, looked around for some way of defusing the situation, and was relieved to spot a familiar face.

'Hey,' I declared, looking over Willie's shoulder. Anxious that she shouldn't see me. 'Look who's here. It's Zoë.'

'Zoë?'

I pointed her out. Sitting alone in the same booth as last time. Strapless black dress. Honey hair clipped back to one side. Thankfully unaware of my presence.

'Isn't that the fox who dumped her drink on you?'

'She had her reasons.'

Sweet twisted back to face me. 'So what are you waiting for, man? Bring her another one, just stand well away while she decides what to do with it.'

'I can't do that.'

'Bitch, it's a gift. A second chance! *Look* at her!'

'That's just it.'

'What?'

'I have a problem with the signs.'

'How so?'

I shot my cuffs, cupped the air to demonstrate. 'Women know what we want, right? You said so yourself.'

'There's no hiding it from them,' said Sweet. 'We were born to be obvious.'

'So why can't women be more obvious too? Sometimes I can't be sure they're even *interested* in men.'

'That's because you been hitting on them as a woman, Reynard. Trying to speak the native lingo.' Willie paused to gulp back a belch. 'Man, I can just about ask for directions in French, but I'm fucked if I understand the answer.'

A moment for me to contemplate this, then, 'OK, then how do you ever get to your destination?'

'By asking in plain English. Why make a prick of yourself with a language you don't understand? Keep speaking your mother tongue, it doesn't take long to find someone who can give you what you want.'

I glanced at Zoë again, but this time she was looking right at me. There in the booth. One arm crooked on the table. Body squared my way. I shot behind my dealer. Looked up at him in a panic.

'She's seen me. What does that say to you?'

'Well, does she look pissed off?'

I nudged another look, and was surprised to see her perk up into a smile.

'She smiled. I can't believe it, she smiled at me.'

'Then in my interpretation I would say she must be pleased to see you.'

I peeked out again, only to be knocked back by a wink.

'Jesus, Willie, she's *delighted.*'

'Oh dear.'

'What?' I asked, but by now my focus was on Zoë. I lifted my hand from my knee. Rolled her a little wave. She glittered into a grin.

'I think you should leave it, Reynard.'

I glanced back at my dealer, to find he was looking over *my* shoulder, over towards the washrooms. I moved to look his way, just as someone brushed by me. A woman I knew too well.

'Hi, boys,' said Christine without stopping.

Stunned, I watched her slip into the booth beside Zoë. Squeeze right up like it cost money to take two seats. It was only then that my dealer turned back and shrugged.

'So sometimes you get the wrong directions.'

I had arrived late at the club because of Roxi. Because I hadn't been able to leave without sending one more email. A quick fix, that was all. Telling her how the distance between us made me feel closer somehow. That she had moved into my thoughts and brought her own furniture too. I told her that I couldn't find my way around my own head any more. That I needed her back here just to help me function properly. All this I did in Christine's virtual hand, to make the time apart more bearable for us all, and here she was. The girl in question. My ex. Snugged up so close to another girl I had to cough to get her attention.

'Ladies,' I was standing at the table now. 'Could I have a word?'

Zoë saw me first, but it didn't stop her giggling at something Christine whispered in her ear.

'It's kind of important,' I added.

My ex broke away reluctantly. 'What's up?'

'What's *up*?' I hissed, but managed to cool it sufficiently to ask for a moment alone.

Christine looked between the two of us. 'Alone with who? Me or Zoë?'

I didn't react. Stayed right where I was, fighting to keep it all in. My compressed lips quivered only slightly, but enough to persuade my ex that she should slide out from the booth.

'Keep my seat warm,' she grumbled. 'This won't take long.'

I left Zoë with an acidic smile. 'Don't go spilling your drink,' I told her. 'If there's one thing Christine hates it's a damp patch.'

It was Sweet William who said I should talk to her. Find out what was going on. I had hoped he might make himself scarce when I made the approach. Go check out the house plants or something. As it was he held firm at the bar with another highball for company. All I could do was usher Christine into the corner, and keep my voice down low. Which was hard. On account of the fact that all I wanted to do was yell at her.

'What the hell is wrong with you?' I hissed. 'How do you think Roxi would feel if she knew about this?'

'I'm just having some fun, Reynard. Lighten up.'

'Lighten up? Do you know how much you mean to her?'

'Sure,' she countered. 'I'm always the first to be copied in.'

'What does that mean? You don't appreciate what I've done for you?'

'Let's be frank here,' she retorted. 'It's you who's got what Roxi really wants.'

'Are you serious? For the last few weeks I've been slowly killing myself precisely because you're the one who can give her all the things I can't.'

My ex shook her head. 'She's in love with you, Ren. As me.'

'And I'm in love with Roxi. As you.'

We both fell quiet for a beat. Christine searching my gaze to see if I saw things her way. I could barely believe what I had revealed in response, and just knew what my ex was thinking. Even before she said, 'It doesn't leave me much, does it?'

I sighed. Pressed my hand against the wall beside her and let my head sink low. It hadn't left her much, and I had to explain why. That Roxi was my make-up artist. That I had forged a connection with her there.

'We've become close, Christine, but you have to believe that's as far as it goes.' I paused to consider the irony in what I was about to say. 'She's seeing someone else, after all.'

My ex listened impassively. Like there was nothing else for her to add. Like it was my affair now. Only I felt as if I was being dumped again. This time from a relationship that wasn't even mine.

'You've run away with this thing,' she said eventually. 'Taken it much further than I ever intended.'

'I had no idea.'

'Only because you never really asked. You've always presumed to know what I'm thinking. This time you were so busy speaking my mind, you didn't stop to listen.'

I glanced back at Zoë. The fox just sitting there begging for some company.

'You can say that again.'

'I never fell for Roxi in the same way you did,' she reasoned. 'For me, it was about trying out something new. About trying to make sense of feelings and desires I'd never had a chance to make real before.'

'So my emails to her? All this time, they never reflected how you felt?'

Christine composed her thoughts for a moment. 'In the beginning, I was genuinely overwhelmed by her. Just as you were. What's more, your correspondence worked like an aphrodisiac. It really turned her on to me, and for that I'm truly grateful, but that's where our feelings parted company. For me it was passion, not love. That's what I realised, after a while. Eventually I just wasn't prepared to lie through my teeth and say it like you wrote it.' My ex, making more sense than I had ever heard before. Talking as I guessed she always could, had I given her the right opportunity.

'So what's all this about?' I thumbed over my shoulder. 'You certainly got further with Zoë than I ever did.'

Christine smiled shyly. 'Who knows?' she said. 'I'm still trying to work out who I am before I work out who I want.'

I rubbed my hand across my face, aware that it was time to wake up to a few things. 'What are we going to do about Roxi?'

Christine shook her head. 'Making the kind of commitment you both expect from me right now is the last thing I need.'

'Then it's over, isn't it?'

Christine bit into her lip.

'Well?' I said, leaning in closer now.

My ex glanced over to the booth, then up into my eyes again.

'It is for me,' she replied. 'I just can't speak for you.'

Sweet William insisted that he hadn't heard a thing. I wasn't so sure. When I joined him once more, I found he had lined me up with a short. Whisky. Straight, no ice. I kicked it back, brooded for a moment as Christine left with Zoë, then asked him what the hell I should do.

'About what?'

'Willie, you know damn well what went on back there. The only reason you're not going to give me a hard time is because you know I'm perfectly capable of doing that for myself.'

He shrugged. Reached for my cigarettes. 'Way I see it,' he said, and flared a match from a brick on the bar, 'you got two options.'

'That's exactly what I don't have,' I muttered. 'I'm not a bisexual babe.'

Willie pulled on the cigarette like it had a pinhole for a filter. 'Option one,' my dealer counted out a pudgy digit. 'You get very, very drunk with me, right now. So utterly sauced that for one night you can't even remember Roxi's name. Let alone think about how you're going to handle her.'

'I knew you'd been listening.'

'Christine was right,' he continued regardless. 'Roxi's your lookout now, man. You care for her so much that you got her into this relationship, it's your responsibility to get her out.'

'So what's option two?' I asked.

I expected another finger to come down. Instead the first one curled back to join the others in a fist. 'The second option, Reynard, is I beat the crap outta you for being such a big swinging dick and ignoring my warning in the first place.'

I considered my options quickly, before setting my empty glass on the bar.

'Better give me the same again.'

32

My first concern as I came round the next morning was that the drink had loosened my tongue. Sweet William may have been sympathetic towards my situation with Roxi, but my wager with Tallulah was another matter. For a minute I just lay there, running diagnostics on my horizontal body. Checking for signs of the beating I would have inevitably received from my dealer had I been foolish enough to fill him in. Everything seemed to be functioning normally, however, from my toes up to my nose. I did sense some pain behind the eyes, but I figured that had been self-inflicted. Tentatively, I lifted my cheek from the floor. Then opened my eyes just long enough to realise I wasn't actually on the floor. I wasn't even in my space, for that matter, but sprawled on the bench in the square.

'Jesus,' I groaned, and swung my feet onto the ground. 'What happened?' I sat there for a second, my head slumped into my hands, and slowly woke up to my surroundings. Drum and bass through an open window. A motorbike off in the side streets. Pigeons warbling nervously around me.

Lots of them, I realised, on peeking through a chink in my fingers.

So many, in fact, that when I tucked my feet back up onto the bench, the birds immediately filled the space underneath. I blinked at them. They beaded me, and twitched a little closer. Which was when I saw him. The derelict. There on the bench opposite. All grizzly beard and threadbare tweed. A plastic bag at his feet. Mismeshed teeth in the grin he was quick to show me. I was just taking this in when I saw the bag twitch. The second time my stomach twitched too, and suddenly I was overwhelmed by the need to get home and away from here. Then the old boy pressed a finger to his lips, and I found myself practically lifted into the air by a storm of carving wings.

I would have preferred to ease in with a coffee. To make me feel better I prepared a whole pot while I got myself cleaned up. Then sat back with the first of many cups while I percolated a plan of action.

The woman I loved was a world away from here. Cut off from her relationship with Christine. Linked only by a modem to me. What was I going to do? How on earth was I going to tell her?

'Dearest Roxi,' I said aloud, mentally tapping out the words I planned to write. 'Hope the shoot's going well. Gascony certainly sounds like it has some good things to offer! Anyway, a few things happening at home.' I took a deep breath. 'Firstly, I'm afraid it's over between us. No easy way of saying this, really. Don't blame yourself, though. It's not you, it's me.' I got up again at this point, turned my back on her imaginary presence. 'The second thing is, when I say me, I don't mean me at all. I mean Christine. The woman you think is me. She's kind of gone a bit flaky on you. Well, on us both really. Because the second thing I have to tell you is that it's Reynard here. Always has been, actually. A double blow, I guess. Sorry about that. But if it's any consolation, I am utterly besotted by you and would be happy to take over her role, in the flesh, so to speak.'

I grimaced at the way this was going, focusing at the same time on my desk, and decided that perhaps things would flow a little easier onto my computer.

The prospect would have been easier still without Sweet William's rampant plant to distract me. It was growing more fruit by the day. Getting stronger-looking too. Mindful of those missing hours the last time I took an interest, I peeled away the tendrils that had laced around the screen and prepared to make that break.

email to: RoxiNYC
from: NuBiFem
subject: Us

Dearest Roxi,
Hope the shoot's going well. Gascony certainly sounds like it has some good things to offer! Anyway, a few things happening at home. Firstly, I'm afraid—

I knew what I had to type but my fingers just cut out on me.

'It's over between us,' I said, but they didn't even twitch. 'It is *over*.'

The cursor blinked at me. A forest animal, that's what came to mind. A forest animal facing the wrong end of a hunter's rifle. Oblivious to its fate. As the man with his finger on the trigger, however, I realised that I couldn't do it. I just could not kill off my link with Roxi. Not like this. Not by email, I reasoned. This medium which had sparked, sustained and shared so much between us. It was just too cold-hearted this way. And so I read what I had written, then cut back on a couple of words.

'Firstly,' I said, and my voice came alive as the keys followed up, 'I miss you *so* much . . .'

I knew I had done the right thing. I was sure of it, because when I logged on to send my email I found a heartfelt arrival in my inbox from Roxi herself. One which was promptly plastered over by another plague of propositions. LadiByrd. Oystagal. Str82Hell and SynDee. All of them wanting my body, on paper at least. I couldn't be bothered to start taking them down. Instead, I printed off a hard copy of Roxi's note then took it across to read by the window gallery. A message dispatched from Gascony the night before. Written on her laptop in bed, she said, because her mind had been too busy to sleep.

'I miss you madly,' I read aloud. 'More so now we're apart. Getting your email is like having one half of you here, but that just makes me want it all! Christine, I've been thinking. I love being with you, and I adore our correspondence, but wouldn't it be great if we could bring the two together?' I sucked the air between my teeth.

'Now that would be a really bad idea,' I said to myself. But as I read on, it became clear that this was one conviction Roxi planned to make happen.

'I really do appreciate what an upheaval you've been through, but I know for a fact that by talking online you've built up the confidence to express how you really feel.' I trailed off for a moment, reminded myself that Roxi was complimenting my ex and not me. 'I wish you were here so we could talk it over, Christine. So I could see you at the same time, you know? You're in my thoughts every second of the day, and night! Which is why I had to write. This place is idyllic, but it's nothing without you. I can't wait for this whole week to finish up so I can get back home. Will you meet me at the airport? It would mean so much to me. Kiss. Kiss. Kiss. Kiss. Kiss. Kiss. Roxi.'

I looked up from the file of crosses, all of them lined up for my ex, and thought back to that moment in the dressing room. Roxi's kiss for me. Barely a touch of her lips on my cheek, but enough to leave me spellbound. Even then, I knew it wasn't just the falling gown that had come between us. That stopped me seeking something more. I returned to my desk, and wondered whether Christine would even bother reading this email if I forwarded it on to her. Before I could make up my mind, however, I would first have to exhume it from under the countless Quick-Es which had arrived for me. Every one of them seeking a piece of my action. DownGrrrl. QTPyeFem. CurlySue and FurBi. Even a long shot from a chancer called RubRoy.

'Amazing,' I sighed, and began the painstaking task of deleting my way back to the only missive that mattered. '*Everyone* wants you when you're bi.'

Except nobody wanted me. Because I wasn't bisexual. I didn't go for guys. And nor was I the babe I had invented for the girls. Tallulah might have granted me a month and then some to find one, and at the time it had seemed like an age. A generous duration for a man like me. But now I could see what a safe bet she had made. I still had a couple more weeks at my disposal, but already I was thinking about making an appointment with my bank manager. Begging for an advance before the last of the money came through for the cat commercials. Not because I was short of offers. Just short of any means to follow them up. I didn't even have the heart to turn them down politely. Just kept on clicking through. Hoping to see that screen name. An email from a woman who had come to mean more to me than I cared about myself.

Birdinhand, Bushbabe and Byteme. I turned them all back. Closing one window after another. Pausing only when I came across a fox who wasn't just holding out for a response, but appeared to be answering her own questions. I clicked into her Quick-E, and scrolled down through the conversation she was busy having with herself:

Quick-E to: NuBiFem

BiSyrin2:	Online at last!
BiSyrin2:	Hope you don't mind the cold call!
BiSyrin2:	Some Vitals, I couldn't resist.
BiSyrin2:	A bi after my own heart!
BiSyrin2:	Maybe you're busy.
BiSyrin2:	I can wait.
BiSyrin2:	Get in the queue, as it were, lol.
BiSyrin2:	Am I talking too much?
BiSyrin2:	I am, aren't I?
BiSyrin2:	Before you know it, we'll be friends.
BiSyrin2:	And I'm only looking for sex!

BiSyrin2:	Oops.

BiSyrin2:	I shouldn't have said that, should I?

'Whoa!' I declared, when I finally caught up with her. I began to type, dictating to myself at a speed that forced my fingers to clatter over the keys.

NuBiFem:	Nothing like persistence to get a girl's attention.
BiSyrin2:	Hi! You are there.
NuBiFem:	In the flesh, hun. But it's not a great time for me.
BiSyrin2:	Would you like to swap pics? I'm keen to meet.

'Yeah, right,' I scoffed, my hands retracting already. 'Sure you are, mate.' It was too quick. The approach too obvious. Even I wasn't this transparent.

NuBiFem:	Sorry, nothing to swap.
BiSyrin2:	So what do you look like? What's your darkest fantasy? Fill me in!

I shook my head and typed at the same time.

NuBiFem:	When are you guys going to get real?
BiSyrin2:	What? Have I said something?
NuBiFem:	Sorry to be blunt, but my guess is you're sitting there with your monkey in hand, hoping to get me talking dirty.

A silence. I had him. Her. Whatever.

BiSyrin2:	I'll send you my pic. You can call me too, if you want. Let me know what you think ;o)

My post icon flashed up. I opened the mail. It contained the digits, as promised, and also a picture file. One tentative tap on my mouse revealed it to be the kind of homegrown snap you don't see in a men's magazine. Not on the middle shelves, at any rate. I sat back. The corners of my mouth curling tighter as I considered its authenticity. Just because the photo was suitably amateur it could still be a guy. But why bother with the phone invitation? Unless, I thought, the guy was a *breather*. Maybe even something much worse. Perhaps he was waiting for NuBiFem to call. Pants around his ankles in a figure of eight. Control and concentration mapped across his face. All I had to do was dial the number, I could have the displeasure of hearing him jostle one off in my ear. Until, of course, I introduced *myself* as a guy. Perhaps even attempt to extort five grand from him. But then, my gut feeling told me to go with it. Something about the way I had found all those thoughts spilling onto my screen, it just seemed so real. A man coming online as a woman simply wouldn't have that much to give away.

All things considered, I figured BiSyrin2 was female. And here I was, I realised with a start, contemplating this while gawping at her genuine minge.

It was only right I showed some respect. Paid some kind of compliment. She had a great smile, but in the shot on my screen that was kind of a background thing.

NuBiFem:	Wow! Shaved too! And so supple.
BiSyrin2:	(((((((Blush)))))))
NuBiFem:	You do yoga or something?
BiSyrin2:	I like to work out. Will you call me now?

A little naive for a nympho, considering the fact that she didn't know me from the next girl, as I guessed she would hope to see things. For this reason, however, I didn't have the heart or inclination to pursue it any further. A shame, because she was a fantastic looking fox. Early twenties. Languorous limbs and long platinum blonde hair. A look that was wasted on women. A man would appreciate it so much more, I thought, but what could I do? Talk her into a meeting just so I could get slapped again?

NuBiFem:	Phoning you might be a problem, actually.
BiSyrin2:	Why? Don't you like the look of me?
NuBiFem:	God, you're amazing.
BiSyrin2:	So call. I won't bite. Yet!
NuBiFem:	I just don't think you'll like the sound of me.
BiSyrin2:	Why not?

I reflected on my conversations with my dealer. About being honest from the start. About talking my own language instead of bluffing my way in another. Going by her pose in the picture, she certainly looked like a fox who understood men.

'Honey,' I said to the screen. 'I hope you're sitting down.'

NuBiFem:	There's something I haven't told you.
BiSyrin2:	What's wrong?
NuBiFem:	Only that I'm a guy.
BiSyrin2:	!!!!!!

Her virtual gasp I had anticipated. In view of the earlier accusations I had thrown her way, it occurred to me that I should clarify a few things. Quickly.

NuBiFem:	But I assure you my hands are above the desk. Where you can see them.
BiSyrin2:	!!!!!!
NuBiFem:	I swear I'm not playing with myself, all right? If I was, do you really think I could type this fast?

BiSyrin2:	!!!!!!

Great. So now I sounded like a sprint masturbator. I was getting nowhere. All I had managed to achieve was one more reason to go phone the bank.

NuBiFem:	I should have said something earlier. I apologise.
BiSyrin2:	I gave you my number!!!!
NuBiFem:	Consider it binned. I'll delete your pic, too. If it makes you feel better. Bye xx

I did as I had promised, then deleted her window as well. In fact, I went on a deleting frenzy. Taking out all the remaining Quick-E's, then wasting my Virtual Vitals.

My online life story. Eradicated with one final decisive click.

NuBiFem. New. Bisexual. Female. In screen name only now. No bi would bother me any more. Not without a searchable entry in the Vault. I just didn't want the attention. Couldn't be bothered with the hassle or the inevitable rejection. I had taken this thing far enough. All I wanted was the space and freedom to work out a way out with Roxi. An exercise in damage limitation so that when she touched down at the end of the week we didn't all crash and burn.

Feeling utterly dejected, I read Roxi's email one more time and resolved that my ex really should read it too. This plea to unite one kind of intimacy with another.

To consummate the relationship.

I just hoped she would find it in her heart to meet Roxi at the airport. Things could run on autopilot until then. I had the controls right here. But only Christine could let her down gently and brings us back to earth. As for Tallulah, it looked like she would collect come what may. Emotionally and financially, I didn't rate my chances of walking away unharmed. Sexually, it seemed, I was dead already.

33

Imagine the sound of cyberspace. Millions of people communicating at the same time. Messages streaming in different directions. Greetings. Gossip. Orders and updates. Secrets. Truths and lies. A maelstrom of binary babble, but not for each end user. People like me. People like Roxi. Both contributing to the din, but picking up on nothing except each other. A simple call and response.

It was a mating game that came to plot the remains of my week. Roxi would write in the mornings. By sundown she would have an email from me. Sometimes two. Generally about half a dozen and not one with a hint of the grief to come. I couldn't help myself. Even if it did just feed my guilty conscience. Speaking out of turn now for my ex. Using her voice, and putting my heart and soul into it. I loathed myself for giving so much. For perpetuating this sham relationship with love. *Real* love. But Roxi kept singing out for more. I couldn't just go quiet on her. Knowing she was out there. Counting down the days before we all came home.

Still, at least I didn't have to contend with any Quick-Es. Without my Virtual Vitals nobody new came into my screen. I did receive a few repeat requests from those who had already invited me into their Cyber Circles, but none of them could distract me from Roxi.

Well, maybe one.

BiSyrin2:   Hi! Remember me?

Her window appeared just as I finished my third email of the morning to Gascony. This one had proved to be the hardest of all to write, wishing Roxi a bon voyage for her journey home the next day. I was about to log off. Get some fresh air before my meeting with the bank. Hardly a thrilling prospect, especially when I pictured my manager. Doodling away there behind his desk. Waiting for me to say my piece before refusing me a loan. So even if this babe was back to belittle me, I thought, even she couldn't make me feel that insignificant.

NuBiFem:	Hello. How can I forget you!
BiSyrin2:	Not many do ;o)

'Saucy,' I said, and squared the keyboard closer to the edge of my desk.

NuBiFem:	I deleted your pic, if that's what you wanted to know.
BiSyrin2:	It was only a picture.

'Only a picture?' I declared. 'It was a work of art!'

NuBiFem:	Listen, I'm sorry if I upset you. But please don't hassle me. I'm going through a hard time at the moment.
BiSyrin2:	So does it help, pretending to be a woman?

The way her words panned out, like I couldn't afford the sex change for real.

NuBiFem:	It's not really me. Just a favour for a friend.
BiSyrin2:	Oh, come on. Why not just admit you're a man in touch with his feminine side? Don't be ashamed. I think it's cute.

NuBiFem:	Actually, I think sad is the word you're looking for.
BiSyrin2:	No I mean it. A guy being a girl. That takes courage, and I hate to say it's also quite sexy too.
NuBiFem:	You think so?
BiSyrin2:	Why don't you call me, we'll take it from there.
NuBiFem:	Take what?

She didn't reply immediately. Like she was drawing breath.

BiSyrin2:	I was wondering whether you'd still like to meet.

Now it was my turn to be shocked.

NuBiFem:	!!!!!!
BiSyrin2:	I know that feeling!
NuBiFem:	I feel bad about trying to fool you, if it's any consolation.
BiSyrin2:	Forget it. I'm over the shock, and at least you were honest early on.

I laughed, nervously.

NuBiFem:	You really want to meet? Me? A guy?
BiSyrin2:	Have you read my Virtual Vitals?

I confessed that I hadn't, and asked for a moment while I checked her out in full.

Screen Name:	BiSyrin2
Real Name:	Cathy Syrin
M/F:	Either, no preference

Age:	25
Marital Status:	Single girlie, what else?
Location:	Hotels, mostly
Occupation:	Bi-lingual translator
Interests:	Mmmm, yes!
Watch Word:	'Women welcome. Men by invitation.'

With every line I read my jaw dropped down another notch. I was tempted to print it off just to show Tallulah that women like this were out there.

NuBiFem:	I can't believe you're interested.
BiSyrin2:	Why shouldn't I bi? ;o)
NuBiFem:	Because I lied to you.
Bisyrin2:	But I forgive you, I like your candour, and here we are . . .

I didn't know what to say. I was thrilled, but hesitant, and just a little suspicious. As every wise fox should be.

NuBiFem:	Cathy, you don't even know what I look like.
BiSyrin2:	I'm only suggesting we meet, hun! Who knows what could happen after that.

I should've been elated, had I not then thought about Roxi. She meant the world to me, but I was going to have to get realistic. If not now then certainly when she returned. So was this really a betrayal? Could I be unfaithful to a woman who didn't even know she had been having a relationship with me? At the same time I was no net virgin. Until I spoke to Cathy on the telephone, my hopes stretched no further than lunch. And what was so wrong with that?

NuBiFem:	We should talk first. Just so I can be sure you're not a 14 year old schoolboy, or anything.
BiSyrin2:	Young man, I was about to suggest the very same thing ;o)

She gave me her number again. Said she was happy to do so, seeing that I hadn't misused it the first time around. I was flattered. It reminded me that I really was someone who could be trusted. After that I logged off, and set about searching my space for the phone. Reciting the digits mantra-like until I found it. In the cradle where it belonged. I punched in the number, and steeled myself. Not because I couldn't handle the school kid thing, but in case it really did turn out to be a jack off artist in his final throes. Three times it rang, then a pick-up.

'Goodness, you're keen. At least you're not a man who holds back a few days.'

Cathy Syrin was definitely female, and on my wavelength, too. The fact that she was also hugely posh was a bonus. It didn't get better than this.

'You're the first woman I've met online who'll even admit to liking a guy. I didn't want to waste time waiting to find out if you really are too good to be true.'

'Nonsense,' she said. 'You've just spent too much time in the company of computers.'

'Tell me about it,' I laughed.

She asked me my name. Just to be on the safe side I told her it was William. William Sweet.

'Nice,' she replied. 'Do you look as sweet as you sound?'

I could barely believe I was hearing her right. Why hadn't anyone like this made contact when Christine first dumped me?

'You really want to meet, don't you?'

'I'll be frank,' she said. 'My job is very stressful, but it's also very mundane. So I make up for it in my free time. With men or women. As long as they're clean and discreet, that's all I ask. But I'm not into anything heavy. No pain or relationships. Just sex.'

'How about lunch? I asked quickly, as if she might retract everything she had just told me. Specifically the last bit. 'Are you free then?'

'Sorry, I'm working.'

'This evening?'

She sighed. I heard a page flip over. 'How about tomorrow night?'

'Not great,' I said reluctantly. I knew this without having to consult my own diary. Not that I owned one. Not that I felt the need to consult my agent about it either. All I had lined up was a collection from the airport next morning, but somehow I didn't think I'd be in the right mood for some time after that. As I hadn't heard from Christine, I figured it was only right that I should be there with the bad news. Then I thought about how Roxi would feel, about the fact that she didn't deserve the misery I would soon cause her, and suddenly the immediate prospect of a meeting seemed like a bad idea.

'That's a pity,' said Cathy, after I'd suggested things might have to wait a while. I heard many pages being fanned, and bit into my lip. Thinking of Tallulah now. Reminding myself of the money. Here I was with a bi babe who wanted me. Even after I'd taken off my mask. And *I* was the one who couldn't fit into her window.

'Is there nothing you can do about tonight?' I pleaded, panicked suddenly by the prospect of missing out completely. Silence down the line. I could almost feel the phone wire pulling tight between us.

'It's my kid sister, I can't let her down so late in the day.'

'You should have said,' I replied, and suddenly I was embarrassed for having pushed the issue. 'I understand. Don't worry. Another time.' Another pause followed that didn't seem right. As if she took me for the kind of guy who'd be cross about a commitment like that.

'You know, I guess she could tag along.'

Which was my cue to follow up with nothing for a beat. Finally recovering to say, 'I'm not sure that would be a good idea *any* time, would it?'

'She wouldn't be much trouble.'

'Can't you get a babysitter?'

'Hardly necessary,' she laughed. 'She's only my kid sister by two minutes.'

'You're twins!'

'You don't mind if I bring Claire? She's identical to me in every way. So I have a hunch she'll like you.'

'How does eight o'clock sound? You know the Cafe Ragueneau?'

34

'Your new found sexuality can be a powerful force.
At times, it may take you places that threaten to
overwhelm.'
A.C. Découcher, *Bisexuality for Beginners*

'I have to see you before tonight.'

What can I say? I'm embarrassed. My conversation with Cathy had brought out the man in me. All the qualities I kept back from Roxi in connecting as NuBiFem. Lust, pride and avarice. Here they were, pouring out now. Three out of the seven seemed bad enough. Four if gloating counted as a sin.

'What's the matter?' said the voice on the other end of the line. 'First you put a bar on my screen name, now this? Anyone would think you were panicking.'

'Far from it.'

I had called Tallulah directly after finishing up with Cathy. Phoned up the first City bank in the book, described the Arctic One to the switchboard operator. She hadn't proved hard to locate. I know it was a bit rash of me, but I was still drunk on the fact that I had just scored so spectacularly. As a result I had a proposition, but it was something I had to put to her in person. Man to woman.

'Why can't you tell me now?' she asked.

'Just be at the cybercafe for seven thirty,' I said, and hung up before she could reply.

I knew she would be there. And indeed she was. Same seat, drink and smouldering stogie. For the first time, I was genuinely pleased to see her. Even kissed her without asking as I joined her at the bar. Tallulah by name. Tasty, too.

'Nice outfit,' I said, complimenting her black leather catsuit. 'Have I seen it somewhere before?'

'Present from Roxi,' she said. The material creaked as she crossed her legs. 'Some model let her have it after a photo shoot.'

'It's very you,' was all I said, and thought perhaps I should drop the subject. 'Anyway,' I pushed on, checking my watch, 'I can't chat as I've got to be some place else in half an hour.'

Tallulah tamped a shock of ash onto the floor. 'Busy boy.'

'I wanted to clarify a point in our deal.'

'Go on.'

'As it stands, I need to meet a woman online as a woman, score with her as a man.'

'That's the five-thousand-pound question,' she said, and drew deeply on her cigar.

'So what if I score with more than one woman at the same time? Do we go to ten?'

Like a backdraught, the smoke issuing from Tallulah's lips curled back and vanished. This was why I had asked to meet her. So I could see what she was really like when the chips went down. And yet despite my front, her composure held true. No choking fit or watery eyes. Just a slight tightening of her jaw muscles.

'You want to double the deal?' Not a trace of smoke as she said this. I figured it had gone for good.

'Only if you can afford it, of course.'

She reached for her gimlet. I didn't have time to order myself one. Even though I did need to calm my nerves.

'The money won't be a problem,' she said. 'Not for me.'

I looked pleased. Extended my hand. She didn't take it.

'Something tells me you won't be needing the rest of the month to get a result.'

'Who knows?' I shrugged. 'I'm happy to go the distance, if you are.'

We shook on it. Tallulah holding on until I relented.

'I'll still want evidence.'

I confess I hadn't thought too hard on this, but I wasn't going to lose out to her now.

'See you in a fortnight,' I said, and slipped from my bar stool.

I walked away victorious. Knowing she was watching. Knowing I called the shots at last, until, 'I heard from Roxi.'

Her name. Coming at me like a slingshot. Twining itself round my ankles as I tried to keep going. With my eyes still on the door, I said, 'How is she?'

'Homesick.'

'Oh.'

'Lovesick too, by all accounts.'

Warily, I turned round. 'I'm sorry to hear that.'

Tallulah swept a fleck of ash from her thigh. 'I assumed you knew that already.'

'Me?' I felt myself blanching. 'Why would I know?'

'You and Christine,' she said and crossed two long fingers. 'I thought you told each other everything.'

I shook my head. Seized the chance to back away. 'Not any more.'

'You two fall out?'

'I really have to go,' I said, and felt her eyes on me all the way out to the street.

Roxi was lovesick. So was I. Sick to my stomach just thinking about her. And yes, as I considered my imminent liaison, I felt like I was about to go behind her back. But then wasn't I there already? Somewhere she couldn't see me. A place I had occupied increasingly throughout the course of my relationship with her. I felt myself being wrenched by both roles. As an online woman. Faithful to the end. And as a real life man. Furtive from the outset.

This was supposed to be my night. A blow-out before the break-up. A stag for splitters, so to speak. But as I made my way through Soho, closer to my tryst, all I could think about was Roxi. Roxi and her influence on me. About the fool I had become since I first laid eyes on her. There in the make-up mirror. Beauty and the blockhead. As I approached the cafe, it made me realise that there was one last thing I could do for her. If only as a gesture to myself.

The act of a man trying to make himself feel better about something he hadn't yet done. I crossed the street. Closeted myself in the phone box opposite and plucked a coin from my pocket. Having held out all week for my ex to surface, I had a discourtesy call to make.

I got her answermachine. In her flat and on her mobile. I left the same message on both.

'Christine. Reynard. Listen, I'm sure you're busy with your new special friend, but a *week*! I was hoping you might have got in touch about our situation here. Roxi flies in first thing. But of course you should know that if you've been picking up my emails. All I can say is I really hope you can find it in your heart to be there. Think about it, please. Don't you feel some responsibility?'

I recited the flight details on each call, but it was only on the last one that I cut myself off without snapping a goodbye. For two *phenomenal*-looking foxes had just swept round the phone box. Crossing the street now. Moving like a pair of panthers. Turning heads as they approached the cafe. Possibly because the slits in the backs of their dresses were sharp enough to slay a whole city, but more than likely because these women were utterly identical. From their white-hot locks to their black spike heels. Collectively pushing up four glorious calves.

Cathy and Claire. The answer to my problems. Live. In the flesh. Truly a pair of bi-onic babes. I really didn't care which was which.

By the time I followed on through the door, the Syrin twins had already been seated and served. Both sipping beers from bottles. Relaxed and chatting at the centrepiece table. Right in the heart of the Ragueneau. Now I saw them for real, I suddenly felt very insecure about whether they would see anything in me. My reflection inside the window of the phone box hadn't done much for my confidence. I knew the overhead light was responsible for the ugly shadows under my eyes and nose, but the deeper flaws were all mine. It was then that I had questioned the wisdom of winding up Tallulah. Five thousand would leave me in debt. Ten thousand would force me to sell my *space*. To lose the unthinkable. That place meant more to me than my parents. In their absence, and with the exception of my florist and dealer, it was all I had.

I closed the door behind me, and willed the chimes to fall still. Straightening my shirt cuffs, I focused on the table dead ahead. Waiting for my heart to stop racing and my double date to look my way.

But neither of them seemed to notice me. Just carried on talking intimately with one another. Both leaning in on their elbows. Playing with the necks of their beers. Immediately I considered creeping round to my regular table, way back in the far corner. My own personal stronghold, from where I had observed so many women go through the same motions as I was doing now. And if any of them felt remotely like me, they must have been terrified. Not just scared of rejection. Scared of *everything*. Even the waitress startled me when she asked where I'd like to sit.

'I'm with friends,' I said, keen for her to leave me be, and realised in the same breath that I had just closed off the chance to get myself together. I would have to go for it now. Make my presence known.

Every apprehensive step I made as if the floor was about to give way underneath me. Cathy. Claire. Cathy. Claire. Despite my closing distance they were inseparable. Divine. *Devastating.* What more could I say? More importantly, what more could I offer? Surely they wouldn't be satisfied by a man like me? I hadn't even brushed my damn teeth. Another foot forward and the pair of them broke off talking. Slo-mo mirrored a smile my way.

'Hi there,' I croaked, and paused to reconsider my name. 'I'm Sweet.'

'You certainly are,' winked Cathy, or her sister.

I switched a finger between them. 'How do I tell you two apart?'

'You can't.'

'Not with clothes on.'

The other one kicked out a chair for me. 'Have a seat. What can we get you?'

I studied the laminate menu. It could have been written in Sanskrit.

'A coffee would be good. Double espresso?'

'That's some caffeine hit for the early evening.'

'Have a beer with us,' suggested the twin on my left, glancing at her opposite number. 'Or were you thinking of staying up all night?'

I shared the joke as best I could, though my grin went a little rictus-like when a hand squeezed my knee.

'Don't fret, hun. We're only teasing.'

'A beer, then. Any beer. Like yours is fine.'

My drink came quickly. Though not soon enough. I had already smoked one cigarette as if I were dependent on the tube for oxygen. Somehow, I just hadn't anticipated feeling so out of my depth here. Talking to Cathy had been a dream, online and over the phone. She had certainly been sure of her sexuality, but that was tempered by what I took to be self-consciousness. All that chatter to herself when I first found her. A chink of vulnerability that appealed to me. Here with her sister, however, things were different. The confidence overwhelmed me. Maybe it was a mutual thing. The twins combining their strength of character to produce something that was greater than the sum of their parts. Not that I had a chance to be lost for words. For these girls could talk. Jesus, could they talk. One of them would start a conversation, while the other one would finish. All I said was 'yes', 'no' and 'really?' and I had their life story. From boarding school expulsions to their shared love of everything. Skiing. Sushi. Swimming. Sex. I sat there nodding, trying to find a way in. Except I hadn't banked on the subject of sex cropping up so early. I knew my place, and it wasn't here.

'Swimming,' I said, peeling shreds off my beer bottle label. 'Wow!'

'Do you ski?'

I shook my head. Just one of those things I always plan to do, I told them, then summer comes around.

'How about sushi?' tried the other twin. 'What's your favourite? Nigiri, oshi or maki?'

I glanced at one, then the other. 'I would say the one you can eat with a fork.'

Nothing. My delivery didn't even make it to the table. Just dropped down into my lap.

'Sushi isn't for everyone.'

'It's an acquired taste.'

An awkward silence followed. I tried not to think about Roxi. Or the only remaining topic on their list.

'I should go,' I said. 'Before I say something really dumb.'

Both twins looked at me like I'd just announced my pet dog had passed away.

'Honey,' said one, pouting for me now. 'I think it's time we found somewhere for you to show us what you're good at.'

I looked between them and back again, aware of the fact that *both* my knees were now being squeezed.

'I've never done this kind of thing before,' I confessed.

They didn't look surprised.

'We understand. It's fine.'

'There's nothing like a submissive man to make us wet.'

I couldn't tell which twin shared that one with me. I was too busy gripping the edges of my chair. Hoping I wouldn't fall from this ride. For it was too late to go back. To ask them to stop and let me go home. All I could do was hang on in there as we left together. Linked to a twin on each arm, I was thrilled, chilled and petrified in equal measure. Even in the taxi I feared the door might fly open and suck me out, and later in the hotel that a cable would snap and drop the lift before it opened opposite our room.

'I should pay for this,' I reasoned, as I followed the twins inside. 'A night here must cost a fortune.'

'Don't worry,' they chimed together. 'We've taken care of everything.'

And how they had. The lights were dimmed low. The champagne on ice. Even the cork seemed primed to hit the ceiling at just the slightest touch. A charge that left them whooping while the bubbles bearded down the bottle. By accident or design, I didn't care which, it was also one of those hotel rooms where you had to lie down to get comfortable. You know the type. Frigid looking Queen Anne chair in a corner. Palatial king size bed filling up the rest of the space.

Demanding to be tested first. Already the twins had made room for me, patting the space between them.

It was *on*. There was no way out. I had come so far it wasn't an option. Even if I did have misgivings, by now all the blood in my brain had drained down to another vital organ. A place from where my confidence continued to grow. Here were two of the finest foxes. Wanting me as a man. It was a simple exchange. I didn't have to say any more. No social niceties required. All I had to do was unzip. And I was going to get paid for it.

Which was when the terms of my agreement with Tallulah came to mind. For she would be expecting evidence. She had even reminded me, back in the bar. And here I was with no way of collecting it.

'Shit,' I said to myself, a little too loudly.

'What's wrong?' asked the one lying on the left.

'We've got condoms,' said her counterpart.

All I could do was come right out with it. What other choice did I have? Rushing out to the shops was out of the question, so I just did it. Made the request direct, in the hope that somehow they could help.

The twins shifted onto their elbows, looked up at me as if they hadn't heard me right. 'You want *pictures?*'

I felt so uncouth. So ungrateful. Like I'd just been served the main meal at an all-star Michelin restaurant, and now I was asking for brown sauce.

'Can we do that sort of thing?' queried one twin, while I just stood there at the foot of the bed. Wondering if I should just leave.

'I'll go check,' said the other, and padded off into the bathroom.

I looked at her sister. The one going spare. She beckoned me to join her. Cranked me closer with her forefinger.

'We've got a whole box of tricks in there,' she disclosed, and rested her palm on my belt strap.

'Ticklers. Oils. Outfits. Maybe a camera too.'

'So you're staying here, then?'

'We *live* in hotels, hun. Sounds glam, I know, but in our line of work this is all that keeps us going.' She grinned at me wickedly, this bi-lingual translator whose body spoke so freely to me. 'I only feel at home at night.'

I stopped her fingers working my buckle. 'Can I ask you something?'

'Sure.'

'This is just sex, right?'

'The best a man can get. Or a woman.'

'Do you think it's OK for a guy to do this, just in theory, even though he's kind of involved with someone else?'

I sensed her fingers flinch under mine. An instinctive reaction to pull away. I wished I hadn't said anything, but it was still weighing heavily on my conscience. Nagging at my nerves. Conspiring to make me say stuff I really should have set aside for the night. From the bathroom, the sound of someone rummaging.

'Are you married?' inquired the twin beside me. I sensed her feeling my finger for a wedding band.

'God, no. I'm not even going out with anyone.'

'So relax.'

'But there is someone special to me,' I said. 'She just doesn't know it yet.' I heard myself say this and couldn't believe my voice was behind it. On the bed with a woman like this and I was talking like it was her *mind* I wanted to explore.

Just then her sister reappeared. Stripped to her red satin bra and suspenders. Polaroid camera swinging by a strap from her neck. Grinning like a game show hostess. Her twin flattened her hand across my abdomen.

'Why don't we worry about that tomorrow, eh?'

Tallulah would have her photo. In fact, Tallulah would be spoiled for choice. I even fantasised about giving her the set. Asking her to pick a favourite. Me with Cathy. Me with Claire. Me with Cathy *and* Claire. In this last one I could even be seen sneaking a little victory sign. Why? Because I could.

The twins had me stripped of my shirt within seconds, and I was relieved that they were happy to simply fool around at first. Just so we'd get to relax as one. Pillow fighting with me as their prize.

Shrieking when I doused them in champagne. Truly the act of a man on the winner's podium. My fizz flattening just for a moment when one of the Syrin sisters mentioned lovecuffs.

'Cuffs?' I said. 'I think I might need all hands on deck, actually.' I was lying on my back at the time. Pictures of us scattered all around. Straddled by Cathy. I knew it wasn't Claire because by then I had been shown how to tell the diference by their birthmarks.

'I know it's hard for a man to be submissive,' she said softly. 'But I swear we'll make it worth your while.'

I opened my mouth to speak but already Cathy was easing her way down my torso, marking her descent with kisses. I felt her fingers unzip me, then another pair of hands round my wrists. At this point, however, all the nerve endings in my body had turned to point towards my penis. If Claire wanted to clamp me to the bedposts, that was fine by me. So long as Cathy didn't let go of my manhood. Not that it actually needed any support.

'This won't hurt a bit,' she whispered.

'Eh?' I didn't like the sound of that. In the textbooks on fellatio, where did pain figure? There was only one wake-up call I was happy to have in a hotel room, and you had to programme the phone for it. I pulled on my restraints, and Cathy looked up with a dirty grin.

'Don't worry,' she assured me. 'You worry too much.'

'She doesn't *bite*,' said Claire mockingly who had just come back from the bathroom with a tube of chocolate body paint. She passed it to her sister. Cathy squeezed some into her hand. I let my head fall back on the pillow. Grinning stupidly. Then grinning for a different reason entirely.

'Can you believe,' I breathed at Cathy as she clad my straining member, 'that I thought you might be out to get me just then.'

'How do you mean?' asked Claire back in the bathroom again.

A rich, nutty smell of chocolate laced the air. Already I could feel the stuff hardening against the old fella. Though it had some way to catch up.

'Long story,' I replied, writhing slightly. 'Just me being para-noid.'

'Hey,' I heard Claire say. 'Want to see me in my outfit?'

'You'll like this,' Cathy murmured, and began to lick her fingers clean.

'What is it?' I asked. 'Don't tell me you've got nurses' uniforms. Even if it's only those hats I'll die and go to heaven.'

Cathy slipped her index finger into my mouth. I sucked off the chocolate, then nearly choked on it when her sister reappeared at the door.

'Ta da!' Claire, presenting herself with a hand in the air. Swinging her hips one way then the other.

'Dear God!' I declared, gripped not by Cathy any longer but by a dreadful sense of foreboding. For this babe with the blessed body had dressed herself up in a costume I had come across once before. Not a nun's habit. Not even close.

Claire was dressed in a *boiler* suit.

'Like it?' She pulled the zipper just south of her cleavage.

'Kinky, eh?' said Cathy, who retreated into the bathroom herself.

I tugged once more on the lovecuffs, but both were locked down tight. Already my erection was beginning to melt. The chocolate coating, however, really had set fast. A kind of Ice Magic, for adults.

'Let me out of these,' I begged them. 'I think I should go home.'

'But we haven't started,' said Claire. 'We've still got to do our floor show.'

'*Floor show?*'

Her sister came back from the bathroom, dressed identically now, clutching two dusty, leather-bound books. Identical as the twins themselves.

'What's going on?' I asked, my voice pitched high with panic.

Cathy handed one tome to her sister, and together they padded around to the foot of the bed.

'Relax, honey.' This time Cathy licked her finger to find her page. 'You've just been *snatched*!'

35

'Go easy when removing make-up. Harsh and abrasive
cleansers can leave skin feeling raw.'
Verity Pepper, *Make Up a Million*

It was a dick move on my part. I can't deny it. I had played right into their hands. Fabulously manicured they may have been, but that was no excuse for my complacency. The Squad had pulled it off. Lived up to their promise. My attempts to become untouchable had come to nothing. Instructing Roxi not to talk to strangers. Instructing my computer to refuse their advances by Quick-E. Instructing myself, even, to back out on dates with any woman who looked remotely left of centre. But militants this magnificent? All I can say is that they took me by surprise. Caught me with my pants down. Exposed my Achilles penis.

Which, by then, was just a shell of its former glory. A chocolate shell, to be precise. Knowing what was going on inside made it look all the more obscene. A totem of my stupidity.

'This has gone far enough,' I pleaded, as the twins consulted their books. 'Can't we talk about this?'

Cathy glanced up from her pages. 'No, but we're hoping this time you might listen.'

'To what?' I groused, still testing my restraints. She lifted the book, showed me the cover. *A Philosophical History of Women's Emancipation, from Mary Wollstonecraft to Alanis Morissette.*

I quit struggling, looked from one to the other. OK, so they had a grievance to air, but nothing about them had suggested they might be a few placards short of a protest. Until now. With the book thing.

'Excited?' asked Claire, leafing back a little.

'Ecstatic.' I sank back on the pillow. Wondering how long the lecture would take.

'Doesn't the prospect of a good story turn you on?'

I decided that the best policy would be to ignore them. Just ride out whatever they had to say until they got tired and let me go. I focused on the light fitting, but then my concentration crumpled when I felt my chocolate member moving at its foundations.

'What's going on? What are you doing?'

'Looking,' they said together.

And they did. Cracking away the base of the dark sheath to reveal a sorry sight indeed. Minutes earlier my soldier had stood proudly to attention. Now it just looked like it had been shot for desertion.

'That doesn't look too turned on to me,' said Cathy.

'Very disappointing,' added Claire.

'Well, what do you expect?' I hissed through tightly clenched teeth. 'This isn't the kind of foreplay I was expecting.'

The twins turned to one other. Looking scarily telepathic, there above my lifeless prick.

'Claire,' said Cathy after a second or so. 'It's in the bag.'

'What is?' I asked nervously, then shrank towards the headboard. 'Oh God, please no. Don't Bobbitt me. You said no pain—'

'Shhh!' said Cathy, as Claire skipped into the bathroom. 'You don't need pain to gain.'

'Gain *what?*'

'What every man desires.' Gleefully, she lifted my penis and let it flop back down again. 'The biggest hard-on of your life.'

A rattle like a shaker, and Claire came bouncing back. A fresh magnum of champagne in one hand. A tub of tablets in the other.

'*Viagra!*' It had to be. Had they styled themselves as the Tixilix Snatch Squad or something, I would have been less alarmed. But this was serious. They were proposing to mess with my manhood.

Claire flipped the lid, tipped the bottle over me, and a shower of little blue diamonds bounced off my chest. I didn't have to ask for confirmation that I was being bombarded by the miracle impotence cure.

'I don't need this,' I pleaded, as Cathy popped the cork. 'Erections aren't a problem for me. Honestly, under different circumstances, I'd be right up there with the best of them.'

'Sure you would.'

'It's true, I can't travel on a bus without my eyes glazing over. The slightest vibration through the seat, and I'm gone. Damn it, I even got wood once over a picture of Nancy Reagan. I'm *fine*. It's not necessary.'

'Oh yes it is,' said Claire, and handed her sister a pill.

'It's compulsory.'

'By rights,' Claire continued, 'we should check whether you suffer from any heart condition first. But as you don't even appear to *have* one, we can go straight into the treatment.'

'*What?*'

'Open wide.' Cathy clamped my jaw so painfully that I didn't even realise she had dropped anything into my mouth until I swallowed. 'Now drink,' she commanded, and tipped the bottle to my lips.

'Take it all the way,' advised Claire. 'If you spit, we'll be insulted.'

Champagne flooded into my throat. The twins leaving me to splutter and choke as they returned to their posts at the foot of the bed.

'Now,' said Cathy, reaching for her book once more. 'What so many men fail to understand is that Viagra won't work without some kind of sexual stimulus.' As she said this, Claire made like she was having a funny turn. Unzipping her boiler suit a little further. Tipping her head back. Moaning. Even pressing a palm to her breast. Cathy looked at me, licked her lips, then leafed back a page. 'So let's see if this text turns you on as much as it does us.'

All I could do was lie there helpless. Shackled to the bed. Physically restrained in every way but one. Forced to listen to the twins as they read in relay from page to page. The pair of them panting over every word. Enlightening me to the plight of the suffragettes like they were auditioning for a porno. After forty minutes or so, I began to feel a distinct warming around my genitals. An intensifying sensation that, to my abject horror, culminated in an outstanding erection just as poor Miss Emily Davison chucked herself under the galloping horses.

'This is outrageous,' I yelled, causing Claire to break off from the tragic tale.

Cathy looked down at my penis. 'Claire, does that look outrageous to you?'

Claire shook her head. 'Uh uh. Not yet, Cathy.'

Without further word, without even looking at one another, the twins split off around the bed and deftly administered another pill. Doubling the recommended dose.

'*Witches!*' I spat at them, champagne dribbling down my face, pooling over my collarbone while another rough diamond snaked slowly down my oesophagus. 'This can't go on.'

But it did.

One hour after another.

Page after page.

Pill after pill.

Desperately I tried to block out their torturous story. I squeezed shut my eyes, but I could still hear both twins. Quoting breathlessly from Simone de Beauvoir like she had enjoyed her clearest thinking while taking it from behind. I tried to look one way then the other, but that just made things worse. With a clock radio on each bedside table, it simply thrust the time in my flushed face. Around three o'clock I came close to blanking both Cathy and Claire from my mind, but then all I could think about was Roxi. Soon to be waiting at the airport. Gagging for a shag. Nothing mundane would replace the image. Washing up. Contemplating baked bean brands. Poking my ears with cotton buds. It was no good. Everything focused in on my enforced tumescence, and nothing I could say would stop the twins from keeping it up. From Eleanor Roosevelt to Hillary Rodham Clinton. *The Female Eunuch* to *The Beauty Myth*. I was hot for the lot. All I could do, I finally realised, was take my punishment like a man.

At twenty-four minutes past seven in the morning, somewhere between a critical overview of Andrea Dworkin and Camille Paglia, I started to cry.

'Mercy,' I sobbed 'I can't take any more.'

'Another pill?'

'*No!*'

I had lost count of how many they had fed me. Six. Maybe seven.

My body was shot through with the stuff. A nitrate nightmare. My arteries, veins and vessels so dilated you could virtually hear the blood sloshing through every time I tugged against the lovecuffs. My head throbbed like my heart, but not like my penis. Which appeared to have taken emergency measures to preserve itself in the event of my death. Hoovering up as much blood as was humanly possible, then closing the hatch behind. Could a Viagra overdose be fatal? I was terrified I might find out. That my cock would basically kill me. Even prevent me being buried on my back. Unless something could be done to get the lid on the casket.

'Please let me go,' I appealed to them once more. 'If not for me then for Roxi.'

'Roxi?' said Claire.

'Who she?' asked Cathy with rising interest. 'Is she blonde? Is she *bi*?'

And a voice answered from the bathroom, 'She's a dream.'

My attention snapped across to the open door. Shocked to learn that we weren't alone. That someone was in there, and had been so all night. A presence in the shadows. A form, yes. Stepping out now. Darkness ebbing from her face. Revealing herself to me.

'You!'

The producer.

'Rise and shine, Reynard.'

The catty madam from the commercials.

'Reynard?' questioned Cathy. 'He said his name was Willie.'

The producer ran her eyes down my body. Ticked something on that clipboard again. 'Perhaps it should be.'

Seeing her in this startling light, my memory of our past encounters rattled from the spools. Our exchanges in the dressing room. Her instant animosity towards me. The enduring warmth she displayed towards Roxi.

Quivering with rage and indignation, I raised my head from the pillow and glared right at her. 'You knew. Didn't you? All along. You must have done.'

Calmly she confirmed that she had. That she knew me better than I knew myself. But that she'd always had my best interests at heart.

'By sending me to *Purradise*!' I snapped. 'What are you, some kind of sadist?'

'Reynard,' she said dryly. 'What do you mean? Purradise.com is a website for pussy lovers. You had a problem relating to one, I thought a visit might put you in the picture.'

Frowning at her now, wondering if she even knew about my visit to the other kind of Purradise. The all-girl Heaven where I had finally broken the ice with Roxi. And suddenly I saw how it had all come together. There in her waspish smile. Of course the producer was wise to this other domain. The whole thing was a sting. I had been fitted up by a bunch of foxes. Lured into a chat room exclusively for women. I wondered how many of them knew about me. And by extension my concern turned from one kind of member to another.

'Roxi,' I said to her. 'Tell me she's not in on this.'

'Of course she's not!' A note of genuine surprise in her voice. 'But I must say, Reynard, I was disappointed by her this time. Normally, it takes no more than a minute for her to spot a man behind the screen name. And you really wouldn't want to be outed by Roxi. That girl can get mad when a guy tries to deceive her. That's why we send them her way. But this one here was good.' The producer addressing the twins now. 'He turned in a faultless performance online, and even got his girlfriend to continue his dirty work offline. Roxi fell for the whole charade he invented to keep in contact. It was inspired, girls. He really was one to watch.'

'What a guy,' said Cathy.

'A master,' her sister agreed.

'Enough!' I interrupted. Drawing breath to calm myself, I said, 'Have you any idea how degraded I feel?'

The producer grinned at the twins. 'I think we all do, yes.'

'What you've done is totally illegal,' I spat back. 'I could press charges.'

'You could indeed. Just walk into any police station and detail your complaint in full.' She circled behind the twins, faced up to the window and shot the curtains. The light took me by surprise.

'What would the duty sergeant say?' Cathy wondered.

Either we were very high up or the clouds were unnaturally low. A far flung blanket burnished copper pink by the breaking sun. At least that's how I interpreted it. Through my drugged up eyes, everything was awash with blue. Claire closed her book, and said, 'If you report this, we'd only have to give our side of the story.'

I slammed my head back into the pillow. Demeaned but not defeated. In just over an hour and a half, a plane was due to touch down. A flight from France that carried the only person I wanted to see right now. Having let myself down so dreadfully, there was no way I could allow myself to let Roxi down too. Again I appealed to the producer, as a colleague of hers, to let me go.

'If you really cared for Roxi,' I reasoned, 'you'd let her hear the truth from me. *Please*, I have to be there when her plane comes in. She's expecting to see Christine. I've promised as much in the emails I've been sending in her name, but I don't think she'll turn up. And if Roxi finds out why, and I don't get a chance to explain myself, I swear it's going to hurt her more than you could ever hurt me.'

'If I had my way,' she replied, still looking out over the city, 'I'd forbid you from seeing her ever again.'

'Then why didn't you intervene earlier?' I demanded to know. 'Why didn't you tell her about my involvement in her relationship with Christine before it got so out of hand?'

'We tried that, remember? Only you got to her before we did, in the studio reception that day. Personally, I was against approaching her at all. Roxi's an innocent in all this, and a cute one at that. If she knew that covertly we'd been using her to rid the web of blokes like you, do you think she'd even want to be in the same dressing room as me?'

'And you say I'm the one with no heart?'

'I'm just the one with no authority,' she turned to face me now. 'It wasn't my call to switch our attention to you, but I must say I was relieved when the order came through.'

'Order?' I said, surprised. 'You're not the one behind all this?'

'Reynard,' she smiled, as if I should have known better. 'I only produce the show.'

'This is insane. Who's in charge?'

'I am, hun bun.'

All eyes back to the bathroom once again. Another voice. Another sister. A solid broad in a boiler suit and a baseball cap pulled low. This one filled the frame. Just as she had once before, I realised. Only now my presence didn't persuade her to double back and disappear.

'You!'

The woman from the revolving doors. The one who had tried to reach Roxi. Pushing back her duck bill, she looked me up and down like she was scanning a meat counter.

'Good morning,' she said, and two baleful eyes returned to address me directly. 'Big boy.'

I glanced at the clock radio to my right. The minute digit flipped over.

'You have to let me go,' I implored her. 'I don't know who you are but I swear that at this moment I'm not thinking about myself.'

'It shows.'

'I need to be at that airport,' I stressed. 'If only to straighten out this mess of mine.'

She clicked her fingers, and the producer handed her the clipboard.

'According to your notes,' she said, after a moment, 'you appear to have made every effort to *avoid* straightening out.' I glared at the producer, but she was busy looking admiringly at her superior. 'You could have come clean weeks ago, Reynard. Instead you chose to go even deeper. Foiling my brunch with Roxi, even cutting off my Quick-Es to you.'

'Bad move,' tutted Cathy. 'Going cold on a woman like that.'

'Very bad move,' added Claire. 'No respect for the lady.'

'It's not the first time I've been let down by a man.' This was the ringleader speaking again. 'Some of these creeps even think they can slip away by changing their screen names. Starting afresh with a different female identity. But it makes no odds. We already know everything about them.'

'How?' I asked bitterly. 'We're talking about the Internet. How can you know so much based on a made-up screen name?'

They all had a good chuckle in response, before the producer stepped forward to enlighten me.

'Reynard, there's *no* privacy online. One of the greatest myths about cyberspace is that people think they're anonymous. Well, they're not. Far from it. Every command you make is logged on a server somewhere. Every website you've visited. Every email. Every Quick-E. Every chat room exchange. Think of a bank state-ment. Only this one lists all the transactions you really shouldn't have made.'

'You're kidding me. This can be done?'

'It's all there for anyone who chooses to hack in,' she continued. 'Not least the details you're required to register in order to get online in the first place. Even if it's just your phone number, it's enough to track you down in the real world.'

'You can be whoever you want,' said Cathy.

'But we always get our man,' her sister finished.

The duck bill smiled proudly at her girls. 'All we had to do was serve up your wildest sex fantasies and wallop, we're recon-nected again.'

'For God's sake, I'm just a *guy*!' A great sob welled up in my throat as I said this. 'We fuck up, all right? It's in our genes.'

'Indeed,' said the producer from the window. 'But someone's got to take a stand.'

'Then give me a chance to make good,' I pleaded, appealing to the whole Squad now. 'Haven't I been punished enough?'

It was then the producer turned round, took something from her pocket, and said, 'Not quite.'

'What the hell is that!' I declared, shocked by what looked like a fat marker pen. 'If you even *try* to write on my forehead so help me I'll bite out your tongue.'

Laughter all around. From everyone but me.

'It's not a pen!' The producer flipped the cap open, then slowly drew out the plunger from the bottom end. 'It's a *needle*!'

Self injection therapy. That's what I thought she said as I screamed at her to see sense. Something about a popular alternative to

Viagra. One that didn't require the impotent man to be turned on whatsoever. He could be watching paint dry, she said, he'd still have a back archer that would last for hours on end.

'But I've already got an erection,' I pleaded, as the twins wrestled to secure my flailing legs.

'Not like this you haven't,' said Cathy.

'Just don't show your friends,' winked Claire. 'They'll all be wanting one.'

The producer expelled the air from the chamber with a brief but heart-stopping squirt. 'It's in your interest to lie still,' she informed me stepping forward as I bucked against my restraint. 'Intracavernosal injection can be a relatively painless procedure.'

'It can?' I said surprised, and calmed some as I looked from the needle to her face.

'Providing you hit the right mark.'

'*Don't do this*,' I begged her, my struggle redoubled. 'Please!'

The twins increased their hold on me. Then the duck bill leaned over, pressed down hard on my shoulders, and I found myself facing her massive cleavage.

'What's the matter,' she whispered. 'Scared of a little prick?' As her hold on me increased, so her bosoms smothered me. Wrenching my head sideways, if only to keep breathing, I saw what was coming and fell still. Abandoning hope with one last show of defiance.

'Do it then,' I hissed. 'Bring it on.'

The producer closing in with the hypodermic now. Me on the sheets, unable to look any more. Screwing shut my eyes. Biting down on my lip. Snivelling in fear and trepidation. Snot like elastic from my nostrils. Then the needle, darting into my penis . . .

And it didn't hurt a bit.

'Finished!' the producer declared. 'What a brave boy you've been!'

The Viagra Snatch Squad stood easy as one. Surrounding my bed once more, looking down at me. At my genitals to be precise. Watching in silence. Like an alien might hatch from my balls at any moment.

'What's going to happen?' I asked fearfully. 'Am I going to die?'

'Nah,' said the producer, and turned away to dispose of the

needle. 'It's always this way for us. Loads of effort, disappointing end result.'

'You don't need us any more.' Cathy speaking now, closing up the zipper on her boiler suit.

Then Claire did the same, and said, 'We just didn't want to leave you feeling deflated once we've gone.'

'You mean it's over?' I gasped, sensing the end in sight. 'Thank God!'

With her hands behind her back now, the Squad leader looked to the ceiling and waited until she had my full attention.

'If it happens again, you even think about going online as a woman, Reynard, we'll sever your links. *Permanently.*'

'It won't. I promise.' I held her gaze. Kept it steady and true.

'Girls,' she said finally. 'Prepare to move out.'

A great sigh escaped my manhandled body. For a beat I just lay there, giving thanks for my safe deliverance, then slowly became aware of the fact that the Squad were leaving without first unshackling me.

'Hey,' I said, as the producer headed for the door. 'Cathy ... Claire?' But the Syrin twins filed out without saying goodbye. Leaving like I didn't even exist. Totally uninterested in the naked guy cuffed to the bed. Pills and Polaroids scattered all around him. His fiercely proud erection at odds with the fear in his face.

I looked imploringly at their leader, but she wasn't watching me. Standing in profile now. Inspecting her troops as they filed out. Her expression impassive under the beak of her cap. Tawny red curls spilling out from the back. A mercenary with a mission accomplished. Only when the last twin left did she address me. Still facing the door, with the clipboard tucked under her arm. Barking like I deserved to be demoted.

'You're a disgrace, Reynard. But we're done with you now. I'll let reception know the room's vacated. The chambermaids should be up around nine. Don't do it again, you hear me?'

'Nine! That's too late! Roxi flies in at nine.'

'Your problem,' she said. Standing square to me now, she slipped a calling card from her top pocket. Flipped it onto my chest. Like the Squad hadn't already left their mark on me. My penis had been like an iron handle for hours, and now it looked set to stay that way for longer. Honestly, if she wanted she could have picked me up by it, I would have appeared to levitate. More alarmingly, every time I mustered the courage to look down at the damage, I found my bell end staring back at me. Its single eye narrowed and scathing.

'*Please!*' I beseeched her. 'You can't leave me like this!'

'Oh, I can,' she said. 'In my experience, men need to lose something before they realise where they went wrong. It's a gender thing, I'm convinced of it.'

'Fuck gender!' I yelled, beyond control. 'I'm in love with her.'

'I thought a man once loved me, too,' she said, turning for the door. 'Until I realised he was using me to pursue his own fantasies.'

It wasn't until she turned and vanished from view that I realised who she was talking about. A man with whom I shared a common bond. I heard the door swing open. She was leaving.

'Ruth?' I called out. '*BiRuth!*'

I saw her long before she saw me. Waiting there by the railings. Laptop carrier slung over her shoulder. Travel bag at her feet. Roxi. Back from France. Waiting for her pick-up. Sighting me now as I hurried across the concourse. Surprise on her face at first. Then a smile that kept on getting wider with my arms.

It had taken me an hour to get here. Double the time I had spent attempting to persuade the vengeful force formerly known as BiRuth to see things my way. To give me the chance she had denied her husband. The fool responsible for pushing her into the virtual wilderness. The one who still held out for the kind of opportunity she finally granted me. To prove that a man could make amends. Regardless of the depths to which he had sunk.

'Right on time,' said Roxi, as I hugged her tightly. 'At least someone's pleased to see me.'

'I've missed you.'

'Reynard,' she declared. 'You really *are* pleased!' She glanced down between us. 'A shame Christine didn't feel the same way.'

I pulled away, embarrassed. My face flushing even more than it was already.

'Roxi,' I said. 'There's something you should know.'

Maybe I sounded just a little too grave. Certainly at the time I wasn't in full control of my faculties. Indeed, I had almost passed out in the taxi here. But as I prepared to level with Roxi it seemed she was braced to hear of a bereavement. Dread in her expression. Searching my face for news.

I had to tell her. Not just about Christine but the whole story. I had promised BiRuth that I would. Promised myself, too. I drew the breath that would break her heart.

But I just couldn't go through with it.

Not right now. It was too soon. I had steamed in too quick. A minute, perhaps. Maybe in the cab on the way back. Anything to savour some more of her company.

'What's happened?' asked Roxi, when I didn't follow up. 'Where's Christine?'

'Christine is . . . just feeling unwell.' I reached down for her travel bag. Felt both brain lobes squash up against the front of my skull. A moment to compose myself as best I could, let the blood run back into my body, then, 'I wasn't doing much, so I said I'd be here to meet you.'

'She knows about us then?'

'Eh?'

'You once asked me not to mention that we worked together.' Roxi paused until she had my full attention. 'You were worried Christine might react the wrong way if she found out.'

'Oh, right! So I did.' I remembered. Had I not been drugged out of my trousers, it would never have slipped from my mind.

Grinning, Roxi said, 'As if she'd think that all we did was talk about her.'

I stood up with the bag, wincing midway, and not just because her comment forced another cover up. 'I told Christine everything, and she's fine. No problems. Really.' Now I sounded weak and feeble for two reasons. I paused to find some conviction, then added, 'She's just not feeling herself, that's why she couldn't come today.'

'Poor thing,' said Roxi. I could tell she was disappointed, even though she fought to hide it. 'You know she was sick only recently. Wouldn't even let me into her flat to see her then.'

We walked across the concourse, heading for the exit. Roxi concerned for Christine. Me trying to find a way to walk that didn't look like I had contraband stashed down my pants.

'Has she seen a doctor?'

'No need, it's almost run its course,' I said. 'She's been in bed most of the week.' I grimaced. On two counts.

'She never let on in her emails,' said Roxi, to herself more than to me.

'She never lets on about a lot of things,' I muttered, sotto, then realised I was walking alone.

I stopped. Turned. Saw Roxi crouched over her laptop carrier. Unbuckling one of the pockets.

'What are you doing?'

'Duty free,' she said, and took out a small box. 'Usually I only shop for perfume but this time I thought some electrical goods might serve me better.'

'What is it?' I asked, then flung out my free hand to catch the package. A package with a picture of its contents on the side. 'A webcam!' I looked up again. Saw Roxi had an identical box in her hands. Fooling with me now, she pressed it to one eye and made out she was ninety.

'All the better to see you with, my dear.'

I thumbed my chest, aghast. 'Me?'

Roxi peeked over the box, frowning like I was testing her patience. 'Christine's the one gets weird on me face to face, not you. I figured this would be the perfect compromise. Now we can speak online, and see each other at the same time.'

'Great,' I said feebly, and tossed the box back.

It was out of my hand for a matter of seconds. I was so unprepared for Roxi to throw the webcam back that I nearly fluffed the catch. Lucky I didn't, really. For in my state I would have never made it down there to pick it up again.

'Perhaps you could give it to Christine on your way back.' Roxi hoisted the carrier back onto her shoulder. 'I was hoping to spend the day with her, but its been a long week. Seeing that she's not here I might just head home.'

I had assumed at least we would catch a cab together. As I couldn't sit down without sucking the air between my teeth, however, I decided not to insist.

'No problem,' I said, wondering whether I should tell her now. Thinking how much longer I had left with her. 'I'll send Christine your love.'

'No need,' said Roxi. 'Tell her to be online tonight. Tell her this time I'll be looking out for her too.'

I braced myself to explain why there wouldn't be a next time. That Christine wasn't sick but history. Absent from the frame. That in fact I was the one who had been filling in for her. A crime of passion for which I had now been summarily punished, but which only Roxi could forgive. All these things I would have said, had she not come across to collect her travel bag from me. A week of being too far away from her to confess, and now she was too damn close. One hand round my waist, and a peck on my lips this time.

'You're a good man, Reynard.' Roxi backing away as she said this, a fond smile and then she turned. 'What would we do without you?'

I watched her float away, but still I kept the answer back.

'Christine will be thrilled to see you again,' was what I called out instead. 'Shall I tell her eight thirty?'

36

Installing Christine's webcam was easy. It was such a basic model
it didn't even come with instructions. Just a CD-ROM with the
necessary software, a colour-coded cable and a sticky pad to fix the
camera to the top of the monitor. Once installed, it was simply a
case of switch on and smile. A two minute job for your regular net
head, but a day to set up for me.

Christine herself had vanished. Gone to earth. Disappeared, I
presumed, as had the real BiRuth before her, into another woman's
world. I didn't know where to start looking, and nor did I have
the time. All I could do was leave a pair of messages. One at the
flat. The same again on her mobile. Stressing the urgency of the
situation on both. Beg for one last favour. Just as we had started
this thing, I reminded her, so we could finish it in the same way.
This time, Christine wouldn't even have to speak on the phone for
me. All I asked was that she sit here in front of my screen. Look
a little maudlin. Type whatever I prompted her to say. Off cam,
but on message, that's how I planned it. The more I considered the
idea, the better it sounded. My alter ego wouldn't last beyond the
evening, and at the same time, Christine could properly withdraw
from the romance. Which left just my friendship with Roxi. By
keeping myself out of the picture I believed I could even be in a
position to get my shoulder damp on her tears. Maybe even turn
those consoling embraces into something else entirely. An ideal
outcome, in fact. But one which depended entirely on my ex.

I was at her mercy, it seemed, though I should say it wasn't

Christine who held me up. That was down to the drugs I had been dealt. A dose designed to remind me where I had first gone wrong. My discomfort went on the rise, in fact. Worsening with every step I was forced to take on my journey back from the airport. Even before my SOS to Christine I was reduced to walking like a duck. Pelvis rotated right back to accommodate my involuntary hard on.

At first I figured I would ride it out. My vision had improved soon after I stumbled back into my space, the blue wash fading with the effects of the Viagra. It was a reassuring sign, and I figured my penis would stand down soon after. Mind over matter, that sort of thing. But then there was the injection to consider. A cock kick start that needed no encouragement from anyone or anything. I wondered whether pleasuring myself might sate things, but in the wake of my overnight endurance I couldn't even bring myself to think sexy thoughts. Not without breaking out in a post traumatic panic.

And as my morning glory extended into lunch, so my courage and convictions dwindled.

It was the pain that sapped my spirits. A malevolent ache that spread to my testicles, then shot meteoric pains down my legs. I kept returning to the cold shower, but the bastard thing just stood there. Arrogant, almost hostile. Like it could take anything I chose to throw at it. A bag of frozen peas down my trousers. An awkward jog round the square. One after the other, then both at the same time. All to no avail.

My manhood called the shots.

Naturally, like any male in my position, I was prepared to *die* rather than seek medical treatment for something so personal. Even when the situation became so unbearable that I could only lie on my side at a right angle, all I had to do was picture how I'd feel with paramedics surrounding me and I'd be gritting my teeth just that little bit harder. Things came to a head around mid-afternoon. Desperate and half-delirious, I remembered that I had a wine cooler jacket in the freezer. All of a sudden it seemed like the most desirable thing in the world. I attempted to stand, to reclaim my posture like another elephant man before me, and passed out there in a heap.

By the time I came round, I found it wasn't just the sun which had begun to subside. Unlike the golden banded skies, however, my knob didn't look so pretty. Bruised and contused, but hanging in there nonetheless. Back under my control, at last. I still felt deeply feverish, but then I saw the clock and a rush of adrenaline kept my temperature in check. I checked my answermachine, but nobody had called. It left me no option. Belting myself into the baggiest trousers I owned, I set off on a hurried hobble to the shops.

With so little time to spare before going live with the webcam, I conceded that Christine wasn't going to roll up ready to perform for Roxi. Even so, I vowed the show would still go on. All I needed were some props.

The little eye peered out from under the foliage. In my absence Sweet William's plant had come to creep right over my monitor. Even trailed its way down the other side. Garlanding my machine in tiny flowers and forbidden fruit. It could have started up the walls to my space, for all I cared at the time. All that concerned me was the screen as I logged on ready for this final session. My swansong in cyberspace.

As her.

NuBiFem. New. Bisexual. Female. A super sensual woman with a vision. A tortured man with a plan.

I was online early. But only by a couple of minutes. Still, it was enough time to fling an email at Tony Curtis, and also to reinstate a single screen name to my Cyber Circle. Just so I could update one other man who knew what I had endured. Let him know that I had found what he was looking for. His wife, estranged for so long. The woman whose virtual monicker he had adopted as his own. Keeping his hopes alive through her. Holding out that one day the couple might connect on some level again. Physically, there wasn't much left of him. On every other level, and as I had assured his wife, BiRuth the man was a much stronger, wiser human being for the experience. A man who was ready to bridge their gender divide. Just as he had helped guide me across mine.

> **Quick-E to: BiRuth**
>
> **NuBiFem:**   **Guess who I've met . . .**

I fired off the message, and pressed my sleeve to my brow. Just then it seemed like I was facing a furnace, not the cool glow of a computer screen, and I wiped away the glaze of sweat. My head was throbbing like my groin. Indeed my whole body ached as it struggled to rid itself of toxins. I may have survived a marathon erection, but the comedown was just as hard to handle. I felt febrile and hugely hypersensitive. So much so that BiRuth made me jump as he came back at me.

> **BiRuth:**   **Talking to her now, thanks to you :o)**

I smiled weakly. Invited the Squad back into my Cyber Circle. To my surprise, however, her screen name didn't flash up next to his. And I realised that if she wasn't online in her own right then she had to be right beside her husband. Talking for real, maybe even working the same keyboard to communicate with me. Didn't these people ever log off?

> **NuBiFem:**   **Hope things work out for you.**

A cursor blink, then:

> **BiRuth:**   **You too, son. Though Ruth says you only have half an hour to do so. If you're online after that, she'll send the girls round.**

We both lol'd over that one, but I couldn't quite rustle up the real thing. Not in my condition. Although I was forced to pull focus pretty smartly just then, as the red light on my webcam switched to green and a very different window opened on my screen.

Eye-mE to: NuBiFem

RoxiNYC   Hi, Christine!! :o) xxxx

Roxi in words. Roxi in the picture. A monochrome still that refreshed every twenty seconds. Capturing her face as it captured my heart. I glanced up into the webcam. Into her own spy on my world.

NuBiFem: This is so weird, seeing you like this.

RoxiNYC: Amazing isn't it!!

NuBiFem: Unbelievable.

Unbelievable, until I say that I had done my level best to make myself look otherwise. Drawing on the memory of my real time with Roxi and my little book of make-up tips, I had mimicked her skills and turned myself into the image of my ex. Mascara. Blusher. Lippy. Liner. I applied the lot myself. Even bought all the bits from the chemist without flapping or looking flustered. None of that 'it's-not-for-me-it's-for-my-wife' nonsense. This stuff was for my own personal use, and that's what I told the assistant when she looked at me strangely. As for my costume, the long-sleeved silver top I was wearing had been rescued from the bin bag containing all trace of Christine. The one I had pledged to chuck out but which I continued to trip over every day. The padded bra, meanwhile, I had kept back from the shoot. This time, I fitted it out no problem. I looked balanced. I looked *stacked*, in fact. But my crowning glory was the hair. Purchased that afternoon from the wig makers. Long. Blonde. Platted and bowed. Christine to a tee. Damn it, I even projected myself like a woman. Assured of my abilities, having been forced to carry it off once before, under my dealer's guidance, back in the Venus Squeeze.

Of course, I wasn't fooling anyone. Not offline, at least. But over the web in a series of stuttering, grainy black and white snaps, I figured I passed muster. All I had to do was keep my head down low and type our relationship onto the rocks. That, at least, was how I saw things. Unfortunately, Roxi had a different view.

> **RoxiNYC:** Something isn't quite right.

I glanced at her picture. She seemed to be leaning in, studying her screen intently. Which was worrying.

> **NuBiFem:** What's up?
>
> **RoxiNYC:** All I'm seeing here is the top of your head.

All she could see was the top of my head because that's how I had framed myself. Dropping my seat, so the webcam couldn't capture too much of me. All too often I had trudged away from Photo Me booths clutching four sticky shots of my forehead and feeling like a dipstick. But it was an easy mistake to make, and for the purposes of this exchange it seemed like a perfectly plausible ploy. Originally, my plan had been to hit Roxi with the bad news so quickly that the words would be more important than the accompanying image. The trouble was I felt so grim that my senses were running at half speed. Slowing up to the extent that I had let her seize my lead. All I could do was raise myself into the frame and hope for the best. I depressed the lever on my chair, and with a pneumatic hiss, inched steadily towards my fate.

> **NuBiFem:** Hold on . . . How's that?
>
> **RoxiNYC:** Oh my God!!

I couldn't believe she had sussed me so quickly. I had even done my nails. Was it my top? I wondered. Christine had bought it a couple of seasons back now, but it looked good to me. For one horrible moment I thought my boobs had bust out again. I looked down, a little too swiftly in my fragile state, and promptly felt myself go into a mental somersault. I gripped the desk until the feeling passed. Wishing my temperature would come down again. I couldn't think straight. I couldn't function properly. I felt wretched. I had been well and truly snatched.

> RoxiNYC: I know you've been a bit off colour recently but you look like death warmed up! :o(

Now I was aware that I had made a bit of a bodge with the eye pencil, but couldn't help feeling slightly affronted. Whatever Roxi's reasons for being so critical, it was clear that I couldn't rely on my looks any longer. I typed on, this time with my powdered chin touching my chest. The crown of my wig now the star of the show.

> NuBiFem: Feel a bit dicky, but I'm over the worst.

> RoxiNYC: Have you seen a doctor? Should I call you one?

> NuBiFem: No need. Reynard took good care of me.

It seemed plausible, though I wished I hadn't mentioned my own name.

> RoxiNYC: Is he with you now?

Careful not to look directly into the eye of my webcam, I glanced up at Roxi's picture on my screen. Her smile had gone, and she was leaning back in her chair. As if she needed some perspective on the picture I was giving her. Like perhaps she was looking at my surroundings now and not me, I realised suddenly. For Christine's computer was at work. And nothing behind me looked much like an office. I typed fast. Wading deeper into the shit.

> NuBiFem: Ren hooked up the webcam to his PC. Said it was OK for me to speak to you from his sp . . . place

> RoxiNYC: He's a hun.

> NuBiFem: Isn't he just :o) But he's out right now.

RoxiNYC: Say hi when he comes back in, then.

I said that I would, of course, but we weren't here to talk about that side of me. I pressed my fingertips into the edge of my eyes. Exhausted from a night of no sleep, then wondered why they came away black.

'Bugger,' I cursed. I had smudged my mascara. A moment that must have been captured for Roxi. Because her concern returned to my screen.

RoxiNYC: Christine, you're crying. Do you want to lie down?

Damn right I wanted to lie down. I also wanted painkillers for my head. A blanket for my shivering body, and intensive care for my tackle. This wasn't going well. With Christine here, things would have been fine. I could have flopped back on the sofa and dictated across to her. Alone, I was in trouble. I had to get the job done. Not crank up Roxi's concern. But then somewhere in my clotted mind it dawned on me that perhaps a woman on the verge of a break-up would indeed be feeling a bit emotional. Might even let loose a sob, I decided, as I covered my face with my hands and counted to twenty. Once I was certain that the webcam had captured the moment, I began to type out what I had failed to deliver for so long. Coming as it was from Christine, supposedly, it seemed to flow much more easily then I had imagined. The picture helped, I guessed. Made it seem more real. For me, if not for the woman on the receiving end.

NuBiFem: Roxi, I can't see you any more.

Bang! There it was on my screen. Flash! There it was on hers. I waited for her picture to refresh. When it came I saw she hadn't moved a muscle. Just sat there staring at the screen. Fingers spidering the keyboard, I then realised.

RoxiNYC: Are you seeing someone else?

To be honest, I didn't really know what she was up to. I hadn't seen Christine since that moment in the Pandemonium when she told me it was over. I didn't even want to think about her current love life, however. Didn't want to think about my ex at all. She had let me down badly. Hadn't even bothered to return my last desperate call. Just left me to break my own fall. I was about to type in the assurance I believed Christine would offer, that this was about her and not Roxi, when the woman being fobbed off here hit me with a supplementary.

RoxiNYC: It's Reynard, isn't it? You two got back together.

I read her question and groaned. Partly in pain. Partly because this hadn't been the way I rehearsed it. I really didn't want to get dragged into this but Roxi was already there.

RoxiNYC: I had a bad feeling when he turned up to meet me at the airport this morning. I knew he wanted to tell me something, but not this.

NuBiFem: Ren is just a friend.

I was about to hit home what a truly great friend he could be to her too, but just then the phone started ringing. My mobile. Over on the kitchen surface. The far side of my space. Feeling as delicate as I did, however, the bastard thing sounded like it was coming through my speakers. At full volume. I broke away from my desk to get it. If only to shut off the noise.

'Reynard?' Christine's voice as I picked up.

'Where are you?' I hissed into the mouthpiece, stumbling back to my seat. Shouldering the handset, I typed Roxi a brief apology for the interruption. My grandmother again, I informed her. The gout was getting to her, so it seemed.

'I'm on my way round.' Down the line I could hear the sound of hurried footsteps. Her mobile crackled, and my ex said, 'Just picked up your message.'

'You're too late,' I said. Just speaking made me want to throw up. 'I can't even begin to tell you what I'm doing in your name right now.'

'I can imagine. As soon as I heard the engaged tone on your other line I realised you'd gone ahead.'

'You didn't leave me much choice.'

Just then the screen grab changed. Roxi with her hands in a steeple. One side pressed to her cheek. Looking at her keyboard as if she was praying for inspiration.

'Have you told her?' asked Christine.

'I'm *trying*,' I snapped. 'But neither of you is making it easy for me.'

'Hold on, I'll be there in a minute.'

The line went dead on me. I dropped the handset and looked at the still of Roxi. Her attention turned back to the screen.

> **RoxiNYC:** You know, one thing bugs me.

As I read her words it seemed as if the whole monitor was rocking gently to and fro. Like it was swinging from some invisible cord. The spins were coming back, this time with a vengeance. I exhaled, long and slow. Steeling myself for one more round. If I could just keep going until Christine arrived, then maybe she could take over and I could clean up from the floor.

> **NuBiFem:** I understand if you're angry.

It was a line I had to retype before it was in a fit state to send. The damn keys just wouldn't stay still. Kept dodging my only two fingers that functioned. I wasn't going to make it, I realised. My body was begging to go horizontal. It was that or vomit, right here in front of the camera. As a last resort, I went for some sobbing again. An excuse to hold my skull together. Stop the sickness rising.

> **RoxiNYC:** What bugs me is that you never let me get to know you as a whole. I gave you everything. You always kept one side back.

NuBiFem: ?????????????

I was sinking fast. Reduced to pressing one key. Desperate for Christine to get here.

RoxiNCY: You know what I'm talking about here!

NuBiFem: ?????????

RoxiNYC: Do I need to spell it out?

NuBiFem: ????????

RoxiNYC: Fine! Online we talk. Offline we fuck.

I had to get a grip. Just for a second or so. If only to calm her down. I swayed back in my seat. Steadied the keyboard, ready to type. When I glanced up at the screen, however, I saw in the freeze frame that Roxi was getting up from her station. The shot refreshed, and suddenly there she was leaving the room. Like there was something more important to attend to than *this*. I frowned. Wished she had invested in a webcam that worked a bit faster. Drawing on this moment of respite nonetheless. Wondering all the time what had become of my ex. Which is when I saw her for myself. There in the next still. Trailing Roxi back into the room. The guest I had been expecting. *Christine.*

Suddenly I didn't feel sick any more. I just felt numb. Freezing myself at the sight of the two girls together. Facing one another now. Their expressions jumping wildly every twenty seconds for what seemed like an age before Christine pointed at the webcam and the love of my online life turned my way.

I looked at Roxi.

She looked at me.

Our connection finally severed.

My mobile started ringing again. It was Roxi on the other end. I knew it was her. I knew because in the next screen shot she had Christine's mobile pressed to her ear. I couldn't pick up, however.

Not as me. Reynard.

For once, I was lost for words. Then lost for pictures, too, as the light on my web cam flicked from green to red and the window turned to static. In a daze, I logged off myself. Reeling in the cut cord, that's how it felt as I shut down. Feeling sick for a different reason. More so when my mobile stopped bleating and my land line took over. The one I had just freed up. It had to be Roxi. Christine had all my numbers. All the means of hunting me down. This time, however, my answermachine spoke for me. Played out a message I had forgotten about myself. One I had prepared for her many weeks ago. Long before our relationship ran away with me.

'Don't hang up, Roxi. I'm afraid you have got the right number. Obviously this isn't the voice you wanted to hear, and for what it's worth I feel like a shitweasel. I know you've been hit on by men like me before, but I didn't do this to hurt you. I swear. If anything, I'm the one who's lost out. That's all I wanted to say.'

She didn't leave a message. Just hung up and left me with a dead tone. A sound that consumed my space. Inside and out. Deafening me as I faced my screen. Switched off from both worlds. Blinking back tears. My lashes sticky with mascara.

forgiveness?

37

My space was never designed for books. There are no shelves built into the walls. No surfaces for them to stack up. If I read a book I tend to pass it on afterwards. Recommend it to a friend. That sort of thing. It doesn't mean I'll forget it, however. A book that speaks to you can stay in your life for ever. Striking chords when you least expect it. Always there to help make sense of your world.

'So, you're alive.'

This was the first thing my dealer said. The first thing anyone had said to me for two weeks, in fact. It was the last day of the month. I was back on my feet physically, but the rest of me had a long way to go. Sweet William only had to look into my eyes to see that I wanted to shuffle back up the stairs. Ball up in the corner of my space again. He peered over my shoulder, his forehead rippling into a frown, then gently shouldered me to one side.

'Come right in,' I muttered, wincing as he found the lobby lights.

'Bitch, what kind of welcome is this for a guest?'

I turned to face the mess. The tangled wreck of wires and vine, circuit boards, paper sheets and fractured plastic housing. Willie, standing on the second step. Looking down like he expected something to jump out and bite.

'You wouldn't understand,' I said. 'But it made me feel better.'

I admit, things had conspired to look a little bit like I might have lost it. My computer was probably the most satisfying of all the things I had hurled from the top of my space. The monitor, too, had made a good noise. Imploding on impact. Taking with it Sweet's ever creeping plant. Surprisingly, Christine's bin bag had survived intact. Just bounced down the stairs and into the far corner. Unlike *Bisexuality For Beginners*. The battered covers splayed on top of the heap. A bird with broken wings. Pages for feathers. Scattered all around. More pages than it had originally contained, I should say, as I had also ripped up the little book of make-up before flinging it onto the pyre. I was embarrassed about the flowers most of all. At least a dozen bouquets. Lavender. Honeysuckle. Peony and lupin. Poppy. Crocus. Cornflower and magnolia. Each bunch beyond their best. Curled up and shrivelled. Still in their wrapping. Discarded by a man beyond caring.

'So whatever happened to grateful?' asked Willie, venturing a boot tip into the heap. 'Boy, you got it bad.'

Every day Sweet William had stopped by. Every day he had rung the bell. And every day I had opened the door to find cut flowers on the step. Until today, when my florist and dealer presented himself. Nothing else. Had I known I would find him there, I would have cleared up a little. Hidden the fact that I had dumped his every offering. Adding to the ruins of my life.

The smell of rotting flowers hung in the air. Willie sighed. Pushed his fists into his puffa.

'Sweet, I'm sorry. It was a beautiful gesture.'

He just stood there shaking his head. 'A waste of good gear more like.'

I hadn't even considered that any of them might be a cover for drugs. Then again, I had once heard Willie rate a consignment of Dutch tulips as a 'Class A delivery', so what did I know? I shut the door, unconcerned by the dragging sound that went with it. Willie looked down at my feet.

'You got post.'

I didn't need to look to know. I just hadn't bothered to pick up any of it.

'Reynard,' he said, like mine was the first name on a register. He jabbed a thumb over his shoulder. 'Go shower. Get cleaned up. You got eggs?'

My dealer insisted on cooking them sunny side up. Before I stepped into the bathroom he had asked me how I liked them. I said hard-boiled. Not only did I step out to find them sunny side up, I also found he had opened my mail.

'Willie!' I protested, leafing through the pile of ragged-edged envelopes on the breakfast bar. 'This stuff is private.'

'Not any more,' he said, still cooking with his back to me.

'Yeah, but all the same—'

'All the same, someone's got to get your life up to speed again. Man, you have bills there need paying. A letter from your bank manager. Some shit about a loan you could've seen me about and probably for less vig, too.' He broke off to motion across the kitchen. 'There's also that bundle from your agent. Fan mail, apparently. Though you wouldn't know it 'cos it's all written in wop.'

I picked up the Jiffy bag in question. It was stuffed with airmail envelopes. Willie had opened two of them, and then evidently given up on the rest.

'Korean,' I said, smiling to myself. 'The commercials were expected to go down well. Though I must admit I was sceptical.'

My dealer turned round. Frying pan in one hand. Spatula in the other. It was then I noticed that he had taken off his puffa. I couldn't think of a time I had seen him without it. And I certainly hadn't seen him in a pinny before. I didn't realise I even owned one.

'Get some plates,' he ordered. 'I'll show you something goes down well. Even a White House intern never slipped down this easy.'

I laughed. For the first time in weeks. My dealer was as cracked as his eggs, but I loved him for it.

We talked as we ate. Chewing over Sweet's plans to diversify. Invest in a hothouse, he was thinking. Maybe next year. Maybe the one after. Start growing his own. Cut out the middlemen. That sort of thing. We talked about my career, too. Mainly my direction. Like whether I should submit to pressure from my agent and look east instead of west. Go against the flow of all the other young pretenders in town. In Korea, Willie thought I probably wouldn't be able to step off the plane without being mobbed. They do that shit over there, he said. Go crazy for one-hit wonders. Make sure their stars burn

351

bright before they fade away. I told him I was giving it serious consideration. Sweet said he would worry about me if I went. It was one of those occasions where we talked openly about a lot of stuff except for the one thing on my mind. The reason I had cut myself off from the world around me. We didn't discuss it because basically I didn't bring up her name. I knew my dealer would listen whenever I was ready. I just wasn't sure the time had come. Then Sweet happened to mention that someone we both knew had passed away. After that, there was only one person I wanted to talk about.

'Seriously?' I said when he told me the news. 'The tramp with a penchant for pigeons? *Dead?*'

'Supplied the flowers for the funeral myself.'

'What did he die from?'

'Something he ate, I imagine.' Sweet, speaking and chewing at the same time. Dimple on his chin squashing in, flattening out.

'The square won't be the same without him.'

'More pigeons, maybe.'

'God,' I said, and pushed my plate to one side. 'You see someone every day, you never think you'll miss them until they're gone.'

My dealer sat back. Swallowed his final mouthful. I thought he was going to speak then. But he didn't. Just sat there looking at me. Picking his teeth. Waiting for me to begin.

Roxi.

Everywhere I looked. In every thought. In every sound. Throughout the last two weeks I had only left my space for milk and cigarettes. Any further, I feared I might never come back. Because every time I saw her, in a crowd, in a cloud, in a passing car, I thought I would fall apart again. As I had on the night she learned the truth about me. As I began to feel once more, sitting opposite Sweet.

'Things never seemed this bleak after Christine finished with me.'

'You weren't in love with her. It happens.'

I cleared my throat. Said I had him down as a told-you-so.

My dealer reached for his coffee. 'You're in love with someone, it doesn't matter what advice you get. You only listen to your heart.'

Just talking about her again was enough to make my lips go twitchy. I squeezed my eyes shut for a beat. Pinching out any tears before they started. Feeling like I shouldn't be in this state, two guys together.

'How did I let this happen, Sweet? I fall for a woman who's out of my league and bisexual with it. Why didn't I just stop at the start, you know? Write her off as wishful thinking.'

'Since when did being classy make her unavailable? Or being bi, for that matter. OK, she gets jiggy with chicks sometimes. But not exclusively, and she made that clear to you.'

'The closer I got to Roxi,' I reasoned, 'the harder it was to work her out.'

'That's because you kept trying to give her what you thought she wanted.'

'So what did she want then?'

'You.'

I scoffed at the very idea. Swiped the palm of my hand across the table. Running the crumbs underneath. Willie talked a good fight. The problem was the fight was over. Even the commentary had run its course. Which made me think of someone other than Roxi.

'Did I tell you I've been emailing Tony Curtis?'

Sweet William looked blank at me. 'He a counsellor or something?'

'Willie, *Tony Curtis*.'

Now he woke up to the name. 'No shit. The *man* Tony Curtis?'

'That's what I said.'

Either my dealer was another big fan, or he could see it was a way for me to try and move on. Away from what could have been.

'Wrote to him practically every day,' I revealed. 'Ever since I broke up with Christine. I've never met him, obviously. I don't even know him. Just chanced upon his screen name and went for it. Told him everything, too. All about Roxi. NuBiFem. The lot. I guess it helped me get a lot of stuff out of my head, but looking back it was a crazy thing to do. As if a big Hollywood legend like him is really going to want to hear about my love life.'

'Why? What did he say?'

'Nothing,' I said. 'I don't know what possessed me to think that he'd ever reply. I mean, why would he? Just because I found a way to connect with him, it doesn't mean he wants to connect with me. Same with Roxi. It all boils down to the same thing. I got connection problems.'

Sweet lifted the dishes from the table. Then stood there, considering me.

'These emails,' he asked finally. 'Did Mr Curtis cut them off? Put a bar on your screen name?'

I shook my head. 'Nothing ever came back, as I recall.'

'No return to sender? Whatever tricky shit it is you can do with computers nowadays.'

I shrugged. They had all got through.

'So will you shut up, Reynard. You connected! You and *Tony*. Jesus, wait until I tell my suppliers! Of course, I'll have to say it was me, not you. If it gets me discount, I'll pass it on.'

I smiled, feeling melancholy still but brighter nonetheless. 'Why can't I see things like you?'

'You're doing it again,' my dealer complained. 'Always thinking you got to be someone else to get somewhere.' He carried the dishes to the sink. 'Anyway, you wouldn't want to be me.'

I looked across my space at him, unsure if I was supposed to have heard that.

'Can I ask you something?' I said after a moment, addressing the man with his back to me. 'Something personal?'

My dealer began filling the sink, but didn't acknowledge my question. Like he knew I was going to ask him regardless.

'Are you gay?'

Sweet waited for the suds to froth up, then spun the taps. Shut them both off. Looked over his shoulder. 'You keep any Marigolds?'

Was that an answer? I wondered. I shook my head, said I didn't use that sort of thing.

My dealer shrugged. Started with the pan. Then he said, 'You've asked me this question once before. Only less direct, and not as nicely.'

I felt myself redden. Thought back to the day I had taken him into my confidence about my screen name switch, then lost it when I didn't get his approval.

'I still feel bad about that,' I said. 'I was just angry with you because I knew you were right and I was wrong.'

'I always am.'

'But that's why I'm asking you, Willie. You understand women like you *invented* them. You know what makes them tick better than any man I know, but it's an objective view. From a distance. And I'm thinking maybe that's because the desire isn't there to get closer.'

'I'm not gay,' he said abruptly.

'Then what?'

This time he turned to face me. Grabbing the dishcloth as he came round. Balling it in his hands.

'Remember I told you once about that friend of mine? The one who took the buckling test?'

'For impotence?' I said uncomfortably.

'It was me.'

'You *tested* the test?' I wondered why my dealer hadn't boasted of this before. 'That's incredible news.'

'Reynard,' he said gruffly. 'You think if I tested the test I'd be all shy about telling anyone? Man, I'd be out there with it. Minting my own trophies. Selling myself as a legend.'

Then he asked me to think again, and I realised what he had meant. Sweet William must have *taken* the test as someone hoping to find a cure.

'But it's treatable,' I said to him. 'Isn't it?'

Sweet William shrugged. 'It's what I am, Reynard. I do drugs to make the most of what I've got. I'm not interested in medicating myself to make up for the stuff that's missing. Not any more. One time I trialed some shit for a pharmaceutical company, I got the boner I always wanted. But it didn't come from the heart, so to speak. Left me even more turned off.' He leaned back, then grinned at me. 'I guess that makes me some kind of dyke.'

'How so?'

'I reject dick entirely, for the greater pleasures to be had elsewhere.'

'Whatever turns you on.'

'Flowers,' he replied, coming right back at me as I realised what I had said. Laughing with me at my choice of words. 'Flowers are what make my world go round.'

I was glad for Willie's company, though I understood when he said he had to go. Get back to the stall and water the merchandise. We all had lives to lead, and though I was still hurting, at least I was smiling again. Ready to rejoin the world.

'I know a bit about impotence,' I revealed, as my dealer retrieved his puffa from the sofa. 'I had a friend once tried Viagra.'

'Yeah? What happened?'

'I don't think he'll do it again.'

'Maybe he just had a bad experience.' Sweet made for the door. 'If he really wants an end result, tell him he should try it again. Gear like that always works if you follow the instructions.'

'Tell me about it,' I reflected, and suddenly I was back at Roxi. Wishing I had read her right. Looking into the middle distance like there was nothing else worth looking at. Even Willie as he walked back to his chair. Flipped it round and straddled the seat. He glanced at his watch.

'Man, you gotta stop bringing everything back to this fox. It's going to hurt for a long time, but you need to move on while you deal with it.'

Move on from what, Sweet? A broken relationship? Roxi didn't even know about me until the last minute. I'm trying to get over something that never happened. That I didn't actually experience. I might have been unsure about my chances when I met her, but the closer I got as Christine, the more convinced I was that in fact we were absolutely right for each other.'

My dealer smiled sympathetically, then slipped another glance at his watch. 'I have to go, Ren. Maybe you should be telling Roxi this. Not me.'

'Oh right, yeah. Like she wouldn't sock me in the mouth before I could open it. I'm only telling you because I can't tell her.'

'OK, so if I was Roxi, what would you say?' He raised his hands. 'I promise anything you say won't result in a bitch slap. Unless, of course, you get fresh and try to score on me.'

I looked out of the window gallery. Across to the square and a scattering of pigeons. A young mother with a pram was sitting out there, in the shade under the trees. Oblivious to the birds. To the vacant bench opposite.

'I guess, if you were Roxi, I would tell you that I loved you. Something I never got a chance to say as me. I only ever said it for Christine, and look what happened there. Even we're not speaking any more.'

'What am I supposed to say to that, you think?'

'I dread to think. Don't hit me.'

'You know what I would say?' he decided. 'That I admire your honesty. That we should eat.'

'Sure,' I said. 'Maybe.'

'No, I mean it. We should go out, Ren. How about tonight? Tonight is a *great* idea.' My dealer. Standing now. Answering his own question before I even realised it was meant to have come from him. Changing the subject, as if to say he was done. Like what I did from here on out was up to me.

'I'm not sure I'll be much company, Willie.'

'You got to eat,' he reasoned. 'If you want to be a big strong winner, Reynard, you can't just live off milk and nicotine. A fortnight, maybe. Providing you're on full fat and no filters. After that, food is the only way forward.'

I watched Sweet climb out of the chair. His eggs really had gone down well.

'I'm only going to eat with you if I get to choose the drinks.'

'You always get to choose,' he said, looking back as he opened the door. 'Don't you?'

'Never,' I informed him. 'This would be a first.'

'So long as it's nothing poncey.'

'Damn right,' I said. 'I long for a drink with no umbrella in it.'

'You wouldn't say that if it was raining,' he cautioned, stepping out now. 'I'll book something up. We'll talk more later.'

'Sure,' I said. 'And thanks.'

No problem.' The door closed, and I listened for his boots on the stairs. Nothing, for a beat, then the door swung wide open and there was my dealer, his whole face twinkling at me. 'What do you fancy, by the way? Indian? Chinese? *Korean?*'

38

French. After having given me the option, Sweet William decreed that we would be eating French. I didn't eat French, I told him when he phoned. Not outside France. Bad meal in Bow some years ago. Undercooked snails in an overcooked sauce. Willie strongly advised me to stop being a mince. How could I write off the world's finest cuisine simply because one dinner didn't sit well? Just dress nice and be there, he advised me. Be where? I asked. He gave me the time. He gave me the place. Spelling out the name because he couldn't pronounce it. My dealer, the Francophile.

The table was booked under the name William. I only knew this because the waiter wasn't going to let me into the dining room until I confirmed the reservation. Which I did on the third attempt. I was also ten minutes late. Sweet would understand, but it was no surprise to me that the staff might be offhand and snotty. Not because I was late, however. Not because this was a French restaurant either. But for the simple reason that I smelled of cheap whisky.

'Your companion has ordered already,' he said, and reluctantly opened the door for me. 'Perhaps Monsieur would like some water with the menu.'

I had felt good after Sweet left me that afternoon. Good enough to clear up my space. Put out the rubbish. Put on some music. Miles through my open windows. Trumpeting my return to the world. I even got out myself. The butcher's. The baker's. The bookmaker's, too. Like I said, I was feeling good. Eager to cash in on my new-found optimism. Then I came back to my space. Switched on the TV to wait for the race. Found myself faced with *Cagney and Lacey*. An old favourite of mine. An old favourite of Roxi's, I also recalled. And there I was again. Feeling bad. A face like Harvey. Mournful and morose. The mark of his redundancy, and mine. Watching him made me feel just as housebound. Except nobody special would be walking back through my door before the credits rolled. Someone to make the drag of my day more bearable.

The race followed afterwards. My horse might have won. More likely it fell at the first. Either way, I couldn't face what seemed inevitable to me. I had to watch something else.

Something three floors up.

Which was why I arrived at the restaurant late, with whisky on my breath. I hadn't returned to the rose garden in weeks. As soon as I drifted back, however, it felt like I had never left. Christine's curtains were drawn, but it made no difference to me whether she was in or out. Even when I saw her leaving I didn't trouble myself to think where. For I hadn't gone there to see my ex. I wasn't hoping to see anyone special at all, in fact. I was there for me, and I didn't plan to leave until I had made some kind of peace with myself. Found a way to stop feeling so alone. Even when the sun went down and the dispossessed came out. Gathering to pool their resources.

The bottle was half full when it finally came round. I passed it on half empty. Glassy-eyed from the searing hit, but fired up to move on at last. Meet up with Sweet William. Get some food down me. Carry on with the rest of my life. I hadn't found what I was looking for, but it was like the man said. I had to eat if I wanted to be a big strong winner. Even if it did mean eating French outside France.

'Reynard!' A hand in the air and I found my bearings. That is, I saw where I was supposed to be sitting. I just couldn't see Sweet anywhere.

'Christine?'

'What are *you* doing here?' As she said this, her eyebrows sloped into those two little Gallic accents.

'Sweet William asked me.'

'Me too. But I assumed it was just him and me.'

'You and Willie, huh? Does this mean you're dating men again?'

Christine tensed in her seat, but softened up when I apologised. What I had said, it was uncalled for. I was cross with my dealer, I explained. Not her. For a beat I considered leaving, then I figured I should still eat. Be a man about it. Moan at Willie later.

'So where is he?' I asked, and chose to sit opposite my ex. Sweet could take the place laid out between us. Mediate, if necessary.

'Just phoned through,' she said. 'He's running late. Trouble with the police.'

'Shit! He's been *busted*?'

'Far from it. He's the one pressing charges, by all accounts.' I looked at Christine quizzically. She added, 'Some mad biddy slashed up his stall.'

This time it was her turn to give me a look.

'Why are you smiling?' she asked. 'It's not funny.'

'You're right,' I said, chuckling now. 'But having invited me here under false pretences it's probably better he has to deal with her than me.'

Christine made it clear she wasn't going to speak until I looked as gravely serious as she did. It took a couple of false starts, but I got there.

'Willie's a good man,' she said, finally. 'And a good friend to us both.'

The waiter followed up with a carafe of mineral water. I sent him back for a bottle of red wine to wash it down. Any red wine, I added, just in case he was planning on coming over all complicated with a list. I poured myself some water. Cleansed my palate, then offered up my glass to Christine. Why not? I was here.

'To friends?'

My ex wore a black camisole and lace cardigan. I could have gone on, but just then I was more interested in the way she held my gaze. Like all I had to do was think and find my answer. I set my glass back on the table. No toast necessary. We would be OK.

'I thought about calling,' she said next. 'But I assumed you'd be mad at me.'

'I was mad at myself, Christine.' I studied the menu. It was written in French. All of it. No translation at the back. Nothing.

'I went to see Roxi because I cared about you, Reynard. I heard your message and I knew you couldn't stop what we had started. Do you understand?'

I said I understood. Unlike my interpretation of the menu.

'What are you having?' I asked.

Christine consulted her menu briefly and, quick as a sneeze, said, '*Caillesauxfeuillesdevigne.*'

I looked up at her as if she'd just spoken in tongues. Which, in a way, she had.

'Since when did you speak French?'

'Evening classes,' she beamed. 'Started a couple of weeks ago. Zoë and I, it didn't work out, and I found I had time on my hands. You mentioned it to me once, and it got me thinking maybe I'd expand my horizons.'

'Well, I'm amazed,' I said, sitting back now. 'I never realised you had it in you.'

'No,' she replied, and took her smile behind her menu. 'You never did.'

'So what is that thing you just said?' I consulted my menu again. 'Is it good? It's not pigeon, is it?'

She shook her head. 'Quail wrapped in vine leaves.'

The waiter appeared as she said this, and it was directed at him as much as me.

'Monsieur?'

I contemplated the menu once more, then snapped it shut and said, 'The same, I think.'

'*Bon.* Your wine is on its way.'

'*Merci,*' I said, confidently, but Christine didn't appear to hear me. Her attention drifting away from the table like the waiter.

'Where's that wine?' I muttered, aware of how generous but empty my glass was. 'At least from France you can guarantee a decent body.'

'For sure,' said Christine, her eyes tracking something behind me. 'Unforgettable.'

'You haven't even tried it yet,' I reminded her, twisting round to see what the waiter had brought us. Only it wasn't the waiter, and I was wrong about my ex. She had definitely tried this one. Berry-red dress. Evocative bouquet. A vintage year too. Twenty-one in net years. Twenty-four in real life. Like any complex structure, however, all I could do was wait and see what she had to deliver.

'Your friend had to cancel.' Roxi, taking her place at the table as she said this. Calm. Composed. Collected. Sweeping her hair from her shoulders. Flaring her napkin and settling in. Unaware or unconcerned that her dining companions were regarding her in stunned silence.

Then, having clicked what my dealer had done, I said, 'His loss, our gain.'

Roxi wiped a mark from her knife before addressing us both. The cutlery had seemed immaculate to me, which was a little alarming. 'He asked if I'd like to join you instead,' she said next. 'Why not, I thought to myself. I'd only be staying in otherwise. Been doing a lot of that lately.'

The waiter handed Roxi the menu. I was braced for her to swat me with it.

'Have you guys ordered?'

Christine and I looked at one another. Nodded as if to confirm this was really happening.

'Then I'll have whatever they're having,' she said, and just handed it back without even looking. 'I know they got good taste.'

My dealer was a bitch, but I loved him. Christine and Roxi? What can I say about them? I was in the company of women, and we had a thorny relationship to discuss. Unlike my morning with Sweet William, it seemed there was only one way to broach the subject here, and that was to come right out with it. Honestly, women have some balls. Roxi, having passed back the menu she said, 'Haven't seen you online, Reynard. Given up being a girl?'

'My computer,' I replied after a moment. 'It broke.'

Roxi unfolded her napkin, smoothed it over her lap. 'Seems like a lotta things got broken recently.'

She didn't need to say any more. I knew what she meant. My ex, however, looked at me like she was waiting for an autocue. As if she was unable to function under the pressure of this meeting without some prompting from me.

'Her *heart*, Christine. Mine too.'

She pulled back from me surprised. Affronted almost. 'I knew *that*, Reynard. I just wondered when you were going to apologise for being the one who broke it.'

'How can you say that?' I exclaimed. 'You walked out on me without the slightest consideration for how I'd feel.'

'Because I knew you'd feel nothing is why.'

'Enough!' commanded Roxi, and held a palm out to each of us. 'Yeah, you broke my heart. You both did. But actually I was talking about my webcam. Cheap piece of crap died on me seconds after I learned about you both. Like it couldn't believe what it was witnessing and refused to function for another second.'

A silence descended over the table. Like a big bell jar had just cut us off from the other diners. All three of us glowering at one another over the candles. Then grinning in spite of ourselves.

'What can I say?' relented Roxi first. 'I'm through with technology.'

'I'm through with *men*,' said Christine, smiling. 'Present company excluded.'

The two girls looked my way. I shrugged. Sat back as dinner was served. 'Hey, my hardware was obsolete from the start.'

Our dealer was a bitch, but we loved him. Me. Christine. Roxi. He had brought us together in a way that we had never been before. It was good. Not just for me. We *all* felt good. Out in the open, at last. Better for talking things through. I even overcame my apprehension and admitted something to Roxi that I had only ever practised on Sweet. That I really had loved her, and not just online.

'You don't need to tell me that,' she said, smiling fondly.

'You knew?'

'Only that a guy who talks to me about girls and cars must have romance on his mind.'

I sat back for a moment, picking back through our time in the dressing room. 'Of course, I could've stayed silent,' I said. 'But that would've lowered the tone.'

'Either way, Ren, I was involved with Christine at the time. At least I thought I was.' The way she said this, my comment falling under something heavier than I could handle. I looked at my hands, listened to her from there. 'For what it's worth, I miss our conversations. I miss talking to you. In every way.'

'I miss it too,' I added quietly, thinking all of this was such a waste.

'You know what I miss?' chimed Christine. We both turned our attention to our ex, and suddenly the words deserted her. 'It's not important,' she said hurriedly, waving us away.

But it was. I knew what she missed. Her part in the deal. The physical side of things. I wondered whether Roxi missed it too. I know I did. With one of them for sure. The one who had just spoken without thinking. Who was blushing now from her neckline up.

'You know what I *don't* miss?' I ventured in a bid to spare Christine. 'That bastard cat. I never liked cats. I see a cat now, straightaway I wonder whether it's got more people working for it than I do.'

We relaxed. Laughed a little more too. Mainly at my expense, but I was a joke that was happy to laugh at himself. And though we continued to be open about what we had been through, nobody mentioned where we could take things from here.

Christine's little indiscretion? That was what had hatched the thought for me, but that was all it was. A notion. A fancy. All the way through our main course, however, and into a second bottle of wine, it continued to set down roots. An arrangement that might satisfy us all. I even wondered whether Sweet William had designed and directed the notion as he had the dinner. I was sure my companions must have been considering the very same thing. A way we could all get on. Wasn't it obvious in the way we had warmed to each other? The sentences Roxi would pick up from me like a baton. The glances Christine continued to steal from her. Talking to us both with her body. I could see what she was trying to say. I just didn't know how to say it in my own words. And the longer it went unmentioned, the more unmentionable it became.

Realistically, just how *do* you orchestrate a threesome? You always hear about the problems it can throw up once you're in the sack. The potential for jealousy and insecurity. Who gets to start and with whom. I knew of two one-off problems from experience, namely

Cathy and Claire. But with a more meaningful proposition, like the one I had in mind, it seemed to me the problems kicked in before anyone even got to see any sheet action. I mean, what was the etiquette here? How did you hit on two people at the same time without either of them feeling slighted?

I couldn't fathom it socially, let alone sexually.

Every time I shared a moment with Roxi, anything from a glance to a comment about the food, I wondered whether I ought to duplicate it for Christine, tailor it for her, or just keep dropping it altogether. Which was why I came to the conclusion there was no way you could get off with two other people at the same time without discussing it first. The only problem was how.

'Anyone come to a decision?' I asked. At the time we were all quietly contemplating the dessert menu. 'I know I'm still hungry.' Surreptitiously I peered over the top of my menu. Christine knew what I meant. She was with me. Indeed, she looked *ravenous.* I could tell by the way she kept undressing Roxi with her eyes.

Roxi, however, seemed to have misread me. Still looking at her menu, she said, 'I think I might just settle for coffee.'

The waiter noted it down in his pad.

'I recommend the gâteau,' Christine suggested brightly. 'We could split it.'

'*Three* ways,' I finished for her.

We both looked at Roxi. So did the waiter. It was her decision. For a moment she returned to the menu, but I still couldn't work out what option she was considering. Then a blink, and her menu was closed.

'You two go for it,' she said. 'I'll watch.'

I switched my attention back to Christine now. Masks of confusion on our faces. What did she mean, 'go for it'? Could I make love with an audience? Or was Roxi some kind of cake voyeur?

'Why don't you try my share,' Christine suggested, a note of desperation in her voice now. 'Couldn't you manage just a finger?'

A finger. I leaned into the palm of one hand. Groaned ever so slightly. This had gone too far. I was embarrassed for us all. Roxi declined politely, but I could see she was wise to the situation. She knew. And in that same moment I also understood why she hadn't responded directly. Whatever it was we were trying to say, I realised, all we had to do was come right out with it. That's how she saw things. That's how it always was with her. Be honest. From the start.

'Christine,' I said, motioning at the gâteaux. 'She's had enough.'

A private smile from Roxi, and I knew that I was right. What's more, I saw that it was the first time I had really spoken for a woman. Used her language to the letter. Even interpreted it for another woman. Roxi had finished. She didn't want any more. Not cake. Not either of us, I could see that now. Indeed, I realised it was something she must have considered and dismissed before she even sat down. Otherwise, I accepted with absolute conviction, she would have suggested the idea herself.

Roxi. Bisexual Roxi. In the company of a man. In the company of a woman. Sitting midway between us both. A place that made her comfortable. As it should with me. As it would with Christine. Around a table with friends. She caught me looking at her. I didn't look away.

'I'm glad I saw you again,' I said. 'I'm going to hold it against Sweet William for a week, but he did the right thing.'

The coffee arrived just then, along with a generous slice of gâteau. I wasn't sure whether the waiter had witnessed this kind of charade going on before but he positioned the plate directly in the middle of the table. Even moved the candles for easy access.

It was getting late.

A couple at the table next to us were just leaving. Exchanging glances and private smiles as they wove between the tables. Probably heading home to jump on each other's bones, I thought perversely. But that was their affair. We had our own special arrangement. I checked my watch, then quickly clipped a hand across my cup before the waiter could fill it with coffee.

'I'm fine as I am,' I said. Then, to Roxi and Christine, I announced that I should be going.

'What about the gâteau?' protested Christine, midway through her first bite. 'I can't manage this on my own.'

'I'm sure you'll do a good job,' I assured her. 'There's someone I have to see.'

Roxi stood as I did. 'I'm glad I saw you too,' she said, as if it was something she'd been storing up. 'I'd like to do it again some time. With both of you.'

I glanced at Christine. Her hand hid a mouthful of cake but her eyes were shining brightly.

'We should do that,' I replied, smiling back at Roxi now, and for a beat I saw her as she first appeared to me. Astounding. Inspiriting. *Untouchable.* Then her gaze fell away, and I wondered whether she had read my mind for real. That now she knew for sure how much she would always mean to me. I felt awkward as she returned to her coffee, but I also felt that finally she had let me go.

'Listen,' I said, and patted down my pockets. 'I'd like to pay for this evening.'

'No way,' Christine declared and reached for her bag. 'This one's on me.'

'It's my treat,' insisted Roxi. 'You guys can buy the next one.'

I wasn't going to back down. But nor was Roxi. Or Christine. There was only one option, we could all see that. Christine rummaged in her bag. Roxi unclasped her purse. My wallet sprung open easily. For I had been to the bank earlier. Sorted out my finances. I looked awkwardly at the other two. Painfully aware that having settled on a three-way we could all agree upon, I was the one with the potential to cause problems. I pulled out the smallest note I possessed, and suddenly felt extremely sheepish.

'Can either of you break a fifty?'

39

So, I didn't get the girls. Not one. Not the other. But then, it was never really going to happen was it? Not beyond my imagination, at least. How could it, realistically, when I was so incapable of being straight with either of them? I guess maybe that's just how I am. People are sly just as people are bi. It's in my nature. Part of my make up. Even as I kissed Roxi and Christine good night, I held something back. For I really did have to attend to a little business, but I planned to mix it with some pleasure.

I logged into the cybercafe with just five minutes to spare. Five minutes before the proprietor flicked the big switch for the night. Cut off all connections to the outside world. Despite the fact that it was approaching midnight, the place was packed. Ranks of browsers at their stations. Faces bathed in the glow from their screens. And up at the bar, an empty stool. An empty glass. An ashtray supporting the last inch of a smouldering stogie.

I looked around. She wasn't online, she wasn't *anywhere*, but I figured I'd get myself a nightcap anyway. Midway down the central aisle, however, I saw that one of the stations was about to become vacant. Some spry silver surfer with a face whipped up like an ice cream had just stood up to leave. I hovered while he gathered himself together. Waited politely for him to wrap his shawl round his shoulders, and smiled gratefully as he made way for me. Freeing me a space to finish my business. For I may have crashed my own computer, but I hadn't forgotten that I still had a screen name out there. One that needed reassigning.

NuBiFem. New. Bisexual. Female. Her reign was over. The Queen would soon be dead. And in a bloodless coup, I would return. As me. Ren 125733.

The welcome screen began to build. As it neared completion I closed my hand over the mouse. Preparing to pounce. To seize her crown. I didn't expect to be foiled in this bid. Ambushed, as it turned out, by the fact that post was waiting.

But not just any email, I realised, on reading the sender's name. This, to me, was like a royal telegram. A once in a lifetime connection.

'I don't believe it,' I said, staring wide-eyed at the screen. 'He wrote.'

I had post from Tony Curtis. The man himself had got back to me.

I read the contents once, twice, three times, and I *knew* that he had been listening. So maybe he had just strung me a line from an old movie of his, but it meant the world to me. I read it a final time. I even went beyond his best wishes for the future, and studied the string of coding underneath. The path header that described its journey here through cyberspace. Listing out the servers it had leapfrogged on the way. Dispatched from one terminal. Delivered to another. An email, I realised, that had orbited the virtual globe and come full circle. Starting out from the same place it finished. Right here in this cybercafe.

And from this very same work station.

I jumped up. Circled around. But he was gone. I couldn't see him anywhere. The only person I recognised was Tallulah. Back there on her stool like she had never left it. I figured she had been in the washroom when I came in. Even the best of us have to fix our faces some time.

'You'll never guess who's been in here,' I said, hurrying over to her. 'Tony Curtis.' I stood back to let her digest this. Waited for a reaction as if I had just delivered a punch line.

'Who?'

'Tony Curtis,' I stated again. '*The Persuaders*? *The Great Race*? *Spartacus*?'

She looked at me without registering, but I gave up there. One relationship that was perhaps best kept to myself, I decided. And even if Tallulah did make the connection, I doubted she would even believe me.

'Here we are then,' she said as I climbed onto the stool beside her. 'The Day of Reckoning at last. What have you got for me, baby?'

For a moment I just looked at my knees. Considering how to handle this, her ten-thousand-pound question. My space, after all, was at stake. I glanced up at Tallulah, but I didn't shrink away.

'I've got a picture,' I said, and reached for my back pocket. 'Actually,' I added, looking round before handing her the Polaroids, 'I've brought two.'

A silence as she considered them. First one. Then the other. Me with Cathy. Me with Claire. I didn't think she needed more details. And then the moment I had been waiting for. A change in her glacial expression. The drop in her guard I had held out to see for so long. For me, the moment was pure pleasure. But it wasn't shock or dismay that I saw in her, but a wolfish grin just like my own.

'I could argue that you rigged this for the camera.' She looked up from the shots. 'But you would've had to pay a *fortune* to get a double act as fine as that.'

'Exactly,' I agreed. 'It just wouldn't have been worth my while.'

She handed the evidence back, and I knew where her hand would go next.

'You win,' she said, turning to face the bar now with her money clip in hand. 'Do you want to count or shall I?'

I took the entire clip from her. Then restored it to her inside pocket.

'Keep your money.' I patted her jacket for good measure. 'I've got my pride.'

She looked at me in disbelief. But I had meant what I said. Just being here, feeling like I did, was worth far more than she could ever afford.

'Then at least let me buy you a drink.' She showed the barmaid her empty glass. 'You must be thirsty after something like that.'

I studied the wall of optics at the back. Wondered whether

Tallulah would actually get me what I wanted. Then decided to pass on the offer.

'To be honest I've had enough,' I said. 'I might just go home.'

The barmaid glanced at Tallulah. Tallulah shrugged and handed over her glass. I slipped off my stool, preparing to leave, but found my feet weren't the first to reach the ground. I looked at Tallulah, standing just inches from me. A couple above me too.

'I'm walking you back,' she said, turning to crush her cigar in the ashtray. 'It's dark out there.'

Tallulah by name. A gent by nature, in some ways too.

A gent in some ways, but a woman at heart, I discovered as we headed east. Talking in the cab on the way back to my space. Sharing things I never shared with a woman before. Not as me, at any rate. Together we went through the trinity. Life. Love. Everything. An exchange that continued from the cab to the pavement and our amble through the square. For Tallulah insisted on escorting me to my door. Up ahead, I saw that I had left a light on in my space. Shining out in league with the stars in the night sky. A huge half moon hung above the city, too. Floating with us, it seemed, as we passed under the boughs. Pausing only while Tallulah lit up a fresh cigar.

'You know something,' I said. 'You never offered me one of those.'

'You never asked,' she replied, and struck up a match with her thumb. 'Besides, you don't look the type.'

'Maybe I'm not. But you never know until you try these things.' I watched the ember flare. Tallulah stoking up the stogie. A firefly in the dark.

'So what do you think of me now?' I asked, then reached out and plucked it from her mouth. Didn't even think what I was doing. Just did it. Like this demanded her full attention. What did she think of me? She looked a little surprised, of course. A little piqued. A little lost without it. Still, I had found a way in with her.

'You really want to know?'

I held the cigar like she did. Fingers on top. Thumb underneath. Determined to show her it was in good hands.

'The honest truth,' I said. 'Now you know the whole story.'

I took my first tentative puff. Tried not to cough. Then spluttered out smoke like a dodgy exhaust.

'I think you did what no other man would dare.'

'But I didn't do it,' I reminded her, recovering my poise. 'I fucked up.'

'You did what you had to do. It doesn't matter that you were never going to get what you really wanted. What counts is that you put your heart and soul into it.'

Another attempt with her stogie. This one with more confidence.

'I did give it everything, didn't I?'

'The works,' she confirmed, and linked her arm through mine. We drifted on. 'I've never seen anyone foul up quite so spectacularly.'

'Now you're just trying to flatter me,' I said, relishing the moment.

'I mean every word,' Tallulah insisted, and I believed her. Really I did. Swaggering now like a big strong winner. Blowing cigar smoke at the bright side of the moon. Wondering too how far she planned to go. 'I've never seen a guy so committed to a lost cause. You made a balls of everything, baby. Really screwed up badly. But boy, you did it with style. You did it with class, Reynard. You did it with *panache.*'